PRAISE FOR  N

"Karla Sorensen's books are pure magic!"

—Penny Reid, *New York Times* bestselling author

"An expert at her craft, no one writes heartwarming characters with emotional depth like Karla Sorensen. She's a perfect fit for readers who love to laugh, build a found family, and fall in love."

—Kandi Steiner, Amazon #1 bestselling author

"If Karla writes it . . . I'm reading it."

—Devney Perry, *Wall Street Journal* bestselling author

"It was beautiful, heartbreaking (yet it put me back together, too), and the perfect mixture of spicy and sweet."

—Megan Reads Romance on *The Best Laid Plans*

"Sparkling tension between our main characters, a slow burn that doesn't leave you unsatisfied for too long, witty and smart banter, all blended together with romance that feels right and natural."

—Helpless Reads on *The Best Laid Plans*

"*This book*, you guys. *The swoon*. I cannot even tell you. It's a delicious, heartfelt, sexy slow burn that gets you in the feels. I couldn't put it down."

—Angie's Dreamy Reads on *Focused*

"*Baking Me Crazy* is . . . well, what is it not? It's beautiful. It's thoughtful. It's so well written that I'm jealous of Sorensen's pen . . . I loved it."

—Adriana Locke, *USA Today* bestselling author, on *Baking Me Crazy*

The BEST OF All

The Washington Wolves

The Bombshell Effect

The Ex Effect

The Marriage Effect

The Bachelors of the Ridge

Dylan

Garrett

Cole

Michael

Tristan

Three Little Words

By Your Side

Light Me Up

Tell Them Lies

Love at First Sight

Baking Me Crazy

Batter of Wits

Steal My Magnolia

Worth the Wait

The Best Men

The Best Laid Plans

The BEST OF All

The Best Men, Book 2

KARLA SORENSEN

Montlake

Text copyright © 2024 by Dutch Girl Publishing, LLC
All rights reserved.

Published by Montlake, Seattle

www.apub.com

Amazon, the Amazon logo, and Montlake are trademarks of Amazon.com, Inc., or its affiliates.

ISBN-13: 9781662514418 (paperback)
ISBN-13: 9781662514432 (digital)

Cover design by Letitia Hasser
Cover photography by Michelle Lancaster

Printed in the United States of America

To the readers salivating for Liam's story.
He lived in my head for months,
and now you have to deal with his grumpy ass.
You're welcome. (Mom, I'm sorry in advance for how
much he swears. It couldn't be helped.)

Prologue

Zoe

Two and a half years ago

There was something bittersweet about walking alone through the labor and delivery wing when all you'd ever wanted was to start your own perfect, happy family.

It was even more bittersweet when you were still trying to get used to an empty ring finger and a wide-open stretch of future as a newly single woman.

The divorce was probably the best decision I'd ever made. Marrying him in the first place? Not so much. Sometimes the yearning for something leads to *really* shitty decisions, as I'd learned. Like picking a husband who, in the end, was a grade A douchebag with great acting skills and the emotional bandwidth of a teaspoon. The only things that man truly loved were his bank account and his healthy hairline.

There was a reason why I fell in love with him. Plenty of them, actually. Not even my best friend questioned him at first.

He was so handsome. Successful. Loved his mom. Brought flowers on our first date. Held open the door and didn't even attempt more than a sweetly lingering kiss when he dropped me off.

He did all the right things for someone like me in the beginning. When I say *someone like me*, I'm referencing the little girl who devoured books with happily-ever-afters as soon as she was able to snatch them off the library shelf.

When you've gone your whole childhood with your nose in a book, inhaling fairy tales where the knight slays the dragon, saves the princess, and rides off into the sunset with her, it gives you a great imagination.

Too great, actually.

Because I'd done a bang-up job of imagining that Charles would be the perfect husband. Instead, I'd ended up right where I started—single, and still living with the ache buried deep under my ribs.

That ache had a name, of course. It was a tangible yearning for something.

Something that I'd willingly sacrificed because I couldn't handle sticking with a marriage like that any longer. Leaving him, right though it was, meant hitting the pause button on the things I really wanted: growing old with a partner who loved me and raising a houseful of children together.

We had tried for kids for a few years. But it never happened.

That was the bittersweet part of starting over. I could truly walk away from Charles without looking back. But as I stood outside my best friend's hospital room, the slight tang of bitterness faded into a wispy puff of air the first time I heard Mira Grace Spencer cry.

All that was left was the sweetness.

With an obnoxiously large stuffed duck tucked under my arm, I knocked gently on the door.

"Come on in," a deep male voice called.

"It's me," I said. As I turned the corner, the sight of my best friend's husband cradling a tiny bundle in his muscled arms had my heart absolutely melting into a puddle.

He barely took his eyes off the loud, squawking baby in his arms to greet me, but I did get an exhausted smile. "Hey, Zo. Amie's in the bathroom with the nurse."

Only a few hours old, Mira's scrunched pink face was probably the best thing I'd ever seen.

"Oh, Chris," I breathed. "Look at her." I pushed up on my tiptoes to press a kiss to his cheek. "She's perfect."

"She is." He glanced over at me, grinning when he saw the duck. "Holy shit, Zoe, that thing's five times bigger than she is."

I laughed, settling the duck into the chair in the corner of the room. "If I'm gonna be the favorite aunt, then my bribing begins now."

The bathroom door opened, and Amie's groan had me turning around.

"There's the hottest mama I know," I said.

She shuffled closer, exhaustion stamped all over her face. "You're here," she said, accepting my hug with a happy sigh. "How frickin' gorgeous is my kid? I'm not imagining it, right?"

"No," Chris said firmly.

I laughed. "Not even a little. She's incredible."

The nurse came out of the bathroom just as there was another firm knock on the door.

"That's probably Liam," Chris said. "He said he'd stop by on his way out for the team flight."

My smile dropped immediately.

Amie caught the instant change on my face. "What is it?"

I shook my head. "Just . . . haven't seen him since . . ." I paused, wiggling my empty ring finger.

"Come in," Chris said.

When the door pushed open and *he* walked in, I just knew my cheeks flushed pink. "He's going to be obnoxious about it," I whispered to Amie.

"I will punch him in the balls if he is," she whispered back. "And no one will mess with me today, because I just pushed an eight-and-a-half-pound human out of my hoo-ha."

Liam's eyes tracked the room quickly, stopping first on Chris holding Mira. His face softened, maybe as much as I'd ever seen it soften. But in the next heartbeat, his gaze landed on mine.

And it held for a long beat—until those eyes of his darted down to my frickin' ring finger.

My chin lifted.

I dare you, I thought. As I did, my heart hammered away in my chest. It had a horrible tendency to do that whenever I interacted with Liam Davies for too long.

Maybe he had a stronger sense of self-preservation than I'd originally thought, because he didn't say a word about my freshly finalized divorce, my newly single status, or the horrible, horrible truth that he had every right to gloat.

While I waited for him to say something, the nurse broke through the growing cloud of antagonism in the air.

"Amie, just let me know the next time you need to use the bathroom. I want to watch for more blood clots, okay? That last one was about the size of a baseball."

Liam's eyes closed. "Fucking hell, I do not want to hear this."

At the sound of his voice, I had to fight a small shiver. He'd always had the most delicious accent I'd ever heard in my life. Ruined, of course, by the fact that he was an absolute prick who couldn't be nice if his life depended on it. I wasn't entirely convinced that the man hadn't come straight from Ebenezer Scrooge's direct lineage.

Amie laughed, smacking him in the stomach when he leaned in to give her a light peck on the cheek.

"Well done, Mum," he said gently. "You popped out a human."

She eased herself into the bed, and I didn't miss the way Liam stared pointedly at the ceiling.

"What are you looking at?" I asked.

His eyes never wavered. "There's not a chance in hell that I want to see her bits right now if there's talk of blood the size of baseballs. I'll wait until she's properly covered, thank you."

I rolled my eyes. "She's wearing a robe."

"Those robes don't cover shit."

Amie laughed again. "I've also got some serious granny panties going on under here. They're awesome. I'm gonna steal, like, five pairs and take them home with me if I can."

The baby was quiet now, and Chris approached with a gentle smile on his face. "Who's next?" he asked.

I didn't even wait to hear what Liam had to say; I elbowed him out of my way. Hard too. Right in the stomach. He let out a small *umph*.

Chris and Amie laughed.

So very carefully, Chris eased the tightly swaddled bundle from his arms into mine. When she was settled against my chest, I sighed contentedly, heart bursting into a million little pieces.

"Hello, sweet girl," I whispered, leaning down to kiss her forehead. "Happy birthday."

It was amazing how instantly you could love someone, I thought. She wasn't any part of me physically. Wasn't even my child. But her button nose, rosy face, tiny wisps of dark hair, and small, spiky eyelashes—every single bit of her—made me feel overwhelming, heart-churning love.

And, yeah, my ovaries were wailing a little, but they'd get over it. Eventually.

This certainly helped, because now I had someone to love and spoil.

My eyes burned, and I blinked back tears when I realized everyone was watching me. Amie sniffled in her bed.

"I've already cried so much," she said. "Don't make me start again."

I exhaled a watery laugh. "I can't help it. You have a *baby*."

Chris grinned, nudging a stoic Liam with his shoulder. "Want to hold her next?"

"Absolutely not."

My jaw dropped open, even though Amie laughed delightedly. "Oh, come on, Liam! You can do it."

He tucked his hands inside his pockets and shook his head, eyes darting over to me and Mira. "She's too little. I'll break her or something."

Chris laughed. "You're not gonna break her. You can sit in the chair, and Zoe will hand her off."

"I'd rethink this if I were you, Chris. His attitude might be contagious, and Mira's first words will be *bloody fucking hell*," I said, mimicking his British accent.

Amie laughed so hard that she clutched her stomach and groaned. "Oh, that hurts."

Chris swiped a hand over his smiling mouth as Liam glared daggers in my direction.

I smiled sweetly. His eyes narrowed ominously.

"How's life treating you, Valentine?" he asked, voice smooth and dangerous.

My smile fell.

"Liam," Amie said in a warning tone.

He gave her an innocent look. "Just making polite conversation."

Innocent, my ass.

"You look . . . different." His eyes—vivid, mossy green, and completely unreadable—passed quickly over my face and down my neck until they landed on my hands, where I held Mira against my heart. "Like you're missing something."

Asshole.

My chin notched up. "You cannot bait me, Davies. If you've got something to say, just say it. Politeness has *literally* never stopped you before."

His dark eyebrows arched slowly. "You'd be shocked at how many thoughts I keep bottled up in my head."

"A truly terrifying prospect indeed."

Chris and Amie traded a loaded look.

Liam's gaze dropped momentarily to my favorite shirt—the one I usually wore just to piss him off. Today, of course, was just a happy coincidence.

"You did that on purpose, didn't you?" he asked quietly.

I smiled again, shifting the warm bundle that was Mira so he could see the red-and-black Wolves logo. I'd had the shirt since high school, and even though I'd lived in Denver since college, I took particular delight in wearing my home team gear whenever I was around Liam.

"Want me to get you one? I'm heading back to Seattle to visit my parents next week. I'm sure it comes in a size big enough for your ego."

His eyes flashed.

The moment was broken when Mira started squirming, her face furrowing ominously.

"Uh-oh," I muttered.

"Batten down the hatches," Chris said.

And then she let out a mighty wail. I tried shushing and rocking, but she wasn't having any of my soothing techniques. Chris took pity on me, walking over with a smile. I transferred her into his waiting arms and let out a slow breath.

Liam watched the crying baby with a slightly pinched expression.

Chris stopped next to him. "Care to see if you've got the touch?"

"Are you mad?" he asked. Then he glanced down at Mira. "What do you want *me* to do about it?"

Amie covered her smile with one hand and watched.

Liam studied the baby, then reached out to pat the top of her head. "There, there. You can stop now."

Chris, somehow, swallowed his snort of laughter. Amie didn't.

I rolled my eyes. "No wonder you're single," I muttered.

His eyes sharpened. "What was that?" he asked.

"Nothing."

There was no chance in hell I'd repeat it. It was like dangling a chunk of bloody chum over top of a shark. He'd snatch it down faster than I could blink, and I'd be the one left in the cross fire.

And more than anything, I hated the lingering feeling under my skin when he studied me just a little too closely. Because he was all quiet and broody and never actually used adult human words to explain why

7

he was doing it. He'd just grunt or make this annoying low humming sound that could mean a million different things.

Years of dealing with Liam had never left me feeling any more comfortable in his presence.

Especially when he'd turned out to be so aggravatingly right.

We locked eyes as Chris handed the baby to Amie. She'd untied the front of her robe, smiling up at Chris when he draped a muslin blanket over Mira and tucked it behind Amie's shoulder.

As soon as Mira latched on to Amie, the room fell quiet.

"Want us to go?" I asked.

Liam tucked his chin down toward his chest and rocked slightly on his heels.

Amie winced slightly at whatever Mira was doing under the blanket, then shook her head. "No, you can stay."

"I need to be heading out," Liam said. "Flight leaves for the game in about an hour." Chris and Liam were teammates in Denver, had been for more than a decade.

Chris nodded. "Give 'em hell for me."

"Fucking Kansas City," Liam said. "I'm sick of them winning."

Chris laughed.

The two men were so different. I'd thought it a million times. They both played defensive end, a position meant to intimidate and terrify quarterbacks everywhere. That meant their builds were almost identical— long legs, strong arms, big hands, a broad chest, and slim hips.

But that's where the similarities ended.

For as big and intimidating as he was on the football field, Chris was warm and funny and kind. One of the most welcoming people I'd ever met. He had this tendency to adopt people into his life, maybe because he and Amie had been only children, both without parents now, and it was his way of building a family.

No matter where it came from, they'd embraced me without question. The same with Liam, much to my chagrin.

Chris and Amie were Liam's family just as much as they were mine. Which was why I had very little choice but to cross paths with him, no matter how much of a dick I thought he was.

"Before you go," Amie said, shooting Chris a quick look, "Chris and I wanted to ask you both something."

Liam glanced over at me, and I fought the flush in my cheeks when he, yet again, looked down at my empty ring finger. But his expression never changed.

"What is it?" I asked.

Chris set one of his big hands on Amie's shoulder and smiled. "We'd love it if the two of you would be Mira's godparents."

I laid a hand on my chest and let out a soft exhale. "Really?"

Liam's jaw clenched. "What does that mean?"

Amie adjusted Mira slightly under the blanket and winced again. "It means you'll look out for her. Be there for her when she needs it. Chris and I don't have family; she won't have aunts and uncles and cousins running around as she grows up. But we'd like her to have you guys."

My eyes welled instantly, and this time I didn't fight it. "Of course. I'm honored; thank you."

Chris and Liam were locked in some wordless conversation, and I couldn't help but note the tension held in Liam's big frame. His shoulders, already so broad and heavily muscled, were rigid.

Chris held out his hand, refusing to concede to whatever little battle was happening in Liam's head. "Stubborn asshole that you are, you're the closest thing I have to a brother," he said, his deep voice even and steady and sure.

"Fuck," Liam muttered quietly. Then he clasped Chris's hand. "You'll probably regret asking me this when I give her completely bollocks advice."

"I don't doubt it for a second," Chris said.

Amie laughed from the bed, a contented, happy laugh too. I tore my gaze away from Liam's serious face, his undeniably handsome features.

My ring finger had never felt more naked than when I was around him.

And somehow I knew that this one hospital room visit . . . it shifted something big between the four of us.

Of course, I never could have guessed how much. That wouldn't come until a long time later.

Chapter One

LIAM

Present day

For a guy who didn't want a family, it was nothing short of laugh-your-balls-off irony that I ended up as the father figure to an entire fucking team of idiot football players.

"You can't spend all your money on betting and women, Richards," I told him.

He gave me a look, one of those stupid puppy-eyed looks that made me want to punch him in the throat. "Why not?"

"Because it's stupid," I barked. "You won't play forever, and trust me when I tell you that the money dries up faster than you can imagine when you're tossing it at every set of long legs that opens in your general direction. And there will be lots of those if you keep this up."

One of the veterans, also just out of the shower in the locker room, sent a smirk in our general direction. "Might as well listen to him, Richards. He doesn't spend his money on jack shit, so he's probably got more in the bank than the rest of us combined."

Richards eyed me, and for a brief moment, I saw just how much he didn't care that my bank accounts were full, considering they all knew my bed was empty of female company.

Football was my mistress—had been since the age of eighteen. She was demanding and harsh, beat the shit out of me on the regular, and I kept coming back for more. There was nothing left in the tank for anything outside that.

I leaned in. "Listen, rookie, you've got one career. If you're lucky, it's a long one. But that's no guarantee. You'll have plenty of assholes who want to take every single pretty penny out of your pocket, and it's up to you to make sure that your future—whatever it looks like—is taken care of when your body decides you're done."

"I just don't think it's that serious. I'm having fun." Richards shrugged. "You should try it sometime."

Someone whistled. A couple of other players in the locker room laughed quietly. But they sure as fuck weren't laughing at *me*.

They knew better.

Richards was new to the team, a postseason transfer from Las Vegas, and it was clear he thought I was being a stodgy old fart who only wanted to ruin his *fun*. But in the past week, the flashy player had already made tabloid headlines for his over-the-top goodbye party in Vegas, where he was photographed leaving with *three* women, who departed his hotel room the following morning with smudged makeup, tangled hair, and shit-eating grins on their faces.

Those same women shouted from the social media rooftops about the shopping sprees and cars he'd promised them.

In making conversation with his new teammates, he'd mentioned that, despite how much he got paid, he always felt like he was broke.

Richards, as it turned out, was a dumbass.

And anyone who'd played with me knew I didn't tolerate dumbasses on my team.

When I leaned against the wall, crossed my arms over my chest, and leveled him with my infamous glare, he let out an uncomfortable laugh.

But I wasn't done.

"You don't believe me," I said. "That's fine. Spend all that money on stupid shit and stupid parties and people who don't care about you, and see how many people respect you for it. Maybe you have more fun than I do, Richards." Slowly, I cocked an eyebrow. "Do I look like I'm jealous?"

He swallowed, pink slowly climbing up his cheeks. "No."

"Fucking right, I'm not jealous. Wanna know why? Because everyone in this locker room respects me. They'll fight for me, because they know I've always, *always* fought for them. You walk out onto that field your first game here, when the lights are blinding and the fans are screaming and the fireworks are filling the sky, and the men lining up next to you are the only thing that matters. It's just us in that uniform; we put our bodies through hell every week to play a game, because it's the life we want more than anything. But all the glitz and the money and the sex . . . it's meaningless at the end of your life, I promise."

My chest started tightening at the end of my little speech, and the locker room went quiet around us. Richards looked down at the floor, suitably chastened.

Once I was able to swallow past the lump in my throat, I continued. "I know you don't know me well, but that'll change. Every week, every day, we'll be right here, and you'll find your place on this team. In this family. And we'll always want our family taken care of, even if that means you say the hard shit, yeah?"

And fucking hell, my voice almost cracked at the end.

Richards looked up. "Yeah."

I exhaled slowly. "Good. I'm not saying you can't have fun. We've all blown off steam from time to time. But don't be an idiot about it."

He gave me a slow nod. The locker room filled with noise again, with low conversation and occasional laughter. Even though it was the offseason, with a couple of months to go before training camp started, we were all at the facilities just about every day, putting in our time in the weight room. On the field for conditioning. Meeting with our coaches.

But more than that—as the hushed sounds in the room reminded me—we'd been there grieving together.

Richards cleared his throat before he walked away. "I'm sorry about your friend," he said. "I know I came to the team . . . after. But I saw it on the news."

After.

My chest went tight again, like someone had jammed a great bloody fist underneath my ribs and pulled on a crank that I didn't know existed. My bones creaked with the force of it, and I had to take a long, deep breath before I could speak.

"Chris was a damn good football player," I managed. "But he was an even better friend. The best husband and father. And every guy you see in here," I said, gesturing to the players in the room, "they lost someone, same as me. And we didn't just lose Chris. We lost his wife too. Their daughter lost both her parents." I held his gaze unflinchingly. "One stupid mistake—someone having a bit too much *fun* before they got in their car—and we lost part of our family here. Remember that when you go around bragging about the fun you think we should have. We've all lost a bit of our taste for it the last couple weeks."

Luckily for Richards, he was intelligent enough not to take what I said personally.

"Got it," he said quietly. He nodded again, this time with a touch more deference, and moved over to his locker. I turned to mine, staring at the one to its right.

Chris's locker.

His bag was still in it. His practice jersey. A picture taped at the back of him and Amie and Mira.

I'd looked for her at the wake, but it seemed they'd kept her away, because she hadn't been at the funeral either. Probably for the best, given that she was less than three years old. I didn't even know how aware she was of the way her world had been rocked.

It had been hard enough for *me* to sit there, shoulder to shoulder with my teammates, and we were fucking adults.

As my eyes burned a hole in the belongings none of us could bring ourselves to remove, a heavy hand settled on my shoulder.

"Got a minute?" Coach asked.

I nodded. Suddenly, I wanted out of that locker room. I wanted away from that locker full of my friend's things. My hands itched to get a box, throw it all in there, and tuck it away.

When I joined Coach Freedman in the hallway, he had a serious look on his face. But then again, he always did. It was why he and I got along so well. His seriousness was rooted in age and a life spent dedicated to the sport we both loved. Mine was simply because I was an asshole, and somehow people seemed to like me for it.

"How's everyone doing?" he asked.

I crossed my arms and sighed. "Okay, I think. Might be time to clean out his locker."

Slowly, his gray eyebrows rose. "You sure about that? There's no rush, if the guys aren't ready."

But what he really meant was if *I* wasn't ready.

"They'll be ready soon," I said, voice a touch harsher than I intended. "Last thing we need is to keep staring at his goofy-ass smile all the time and thinking about his horrible fucking jokes."

Coach smiled, sad and understanding. "I miss him too."

I cleared my throat. "Is that all you needed?"

"No." He scratched the side of his face, looking uncharacteristically nervous. "I got a phone call patched through the front office. They were looking for you."

"Who?"

"Chris and Amie's lawyer," Coach said quietly. "He needs you at his office as soon as you can get there."

My stomach hollowed out, but I didn't drop his gaze. "What for?"

"He didn't say. But it sounds important. He found some documents relating to Chris and Amie's will. He said he tried the number on file but couldn't leave a message." Coach gave me a knowing look. "I didn't tell him what happened to your last phone and that your voicemail box has been full for months."

Finally, I broke his gaze and stared down at the floor.

Kind of him, really. Considering I'd smashed my cell phone against the wall of the conference room where they'd told us about the car accident. Followed by a chair that I'd hurled at a TV screen.

But none of that destruction had helped much. That's the thing about helpless rage. There's no place you can put it where it lessens the toll on your body. I still felt it churning in my bones and my blood, with nowhere to go. It was stuck under my skin, day in and day out.

Wordlessly, Coach handed me a slip of paper. On it were the name of the lawyer and an address.

"He said if you can be there at three, he'd appreciate it. Apparently, this can't wait."

The longer I stared at the paper, the more the words blurred, and I refused to look into Coach's face until I'd willed back any hint of moisture in my eyes.

"You sure you don't know why he wants to see me?" I asked. "Because if you know, tell me now so I don't feel fucking ambushed in some stuffy office with some stuffy lawyer."

The side of his mouth hooked up in a smile. "Trust me, if I knew, I'd tell you. I make it a point not to send you into situations where you feel backed into a corner." He smacked my shoulder. "Call me later if you need to talk about it. Whatever it is."

I glared at the piece of paper, then shoved it into my pocket.

Fifteen minutes later, I was driving into downtown Denver with a sinking feeling in my gut that whatever the lawyer had to tell me . . . I wouldn't like it.

Chapter Two

Zoe

One of the weirdest things about life is how you change without even realizing it's happening. Change comes in such tiny increments, water dripping slowly into a bowl, and before you know it, everything is overflowing. The mess materializes before you realize you've got something to clean up.

It's not always like that, of course. Sometimes you're stuck in a situation where some cosmic asshole cranks the hose on full blast, and you have no choice but to try not to drown in the wake of what's been unleashed in your face.

I'd experienced the first kind of change throughout my failed marriage and the years that followed, where I had to figure out who I really was.

I was Zoe Valentine—party of one, expert third wheel to my best friend and her husband, with all the time in the world to do whatever I damn well felt like.

But the second kind of change—the asshole hose to the face—was the only way I could describe the last two weeks of my life.

It would've been hard enough if it were just me.

But it wasn't just me anymore.

Hell, I hardly recognized myself in the mirror most days. Speaking of mirrors, there was one across the lushly decorated room, so perfectly clean that I was doing my absolute best to avoid looking in that direction, because it showed everything.

The lawyer's office—home to the spotless mirror and the nice decor—was shiny and immaculate.

I was not.

Sure, I'd swiped on a coat of mascara and some passably clean clothes for this last-minute meeting, but my already wild hair was pushing the limit of what dry shampoo could do for it, and from the corner of my eye, I caught sight of a macaroni noodle buried in some messy waves.

I batted at it, sighing in defeat when my fingers got tangled.

When I finally plucked the noodle out and didn't immediately spy a trash can, I had no choice but to tuck that sucker into the pocket of my jeans.

Apparently, this was something I'd have to get used to. And I'd gotten used to having a *lot* thrown at me the last couple of weeks.

When a rotating list of those things started spinning on a carousel in my head, I rubbed at my chest, which had begun to feel tight and heavy with worry. That drowning, sputtering sensation came back with a screaming vengeance.

No. No one was going to take her away from me.

There was no stifling the loaded sigh that came in the wake of that singular thought. I needed a nap. And a shower. And something signed in blood that would allow me to keep her.

This time, my sigh was heavier, slower, and weighted down with all the worries that crept into my brain when I tried to get to sleep.

Those two sighs were deafening in the hushed space.

It was different from the pockets of quiet I'd gotten at my house the last two weeks, and those had been strictly confined to the spotty naptimes she'd allowed, and the very limited window of time in which I managed to stay awake after I got her into bed.

Most nights, I face-planted onto my pillow less than twenty minutes after she was lights out, which was hardly enough time to fully appreciate the lack of noise.

Mira Grace Spencer was particularly talented at decimating any quiet that existed.

And, really, I was thankful for that, because if I'd had to sit in my house alone, next door to Chris and Amie's empty, quiet one, I'd probably lose my frickin' mind.

Mira was the best distraction in the entire world, even with the lack of sleep and the mountain of worry that now came with every single decision I made.

Wasn't that funny?

You could want something for *decades*, think about what it would be like, think that you'd fully prepared, but when someone actually plops a child into your lap and says, *Here you go—she's your responsibility now*, all that want and thinking and preparation is absolutely fucking worthless.

And on that desolate thought, the missing office manager entered the room through a door disguised as a bookshelf.

She didn't notice me at first. I studied her tailored suit, a pretty shade of purple, and vaguely remembered the days when I also looked like a functioning human being when I walked out the door.

When I didn't have bags the size of Samsonites under my eyes.

When I had clean hair, free of orange-coated pasta.

When I didn't occasionally eat ice cream for dinner because it was easier that way.

Oh yes, the Zoe of old was a bit more on top of things when she faced the world. Not that I'd left my house in the last two weeks, but still . . .

The office manager's eyes lit up. "You're a bit early. I'm so sorry to have kept you waiting."

I waved the apology away. "It's fine. I was just . . . enjoying the quiet."

As she took her seat behind the desk, she smiled. "Just to clarify, you're Mrs. Valentine, correct? What a sweet name. You must love Valentine's Day."

"Zoe," I told her. "Please call me Zoe."

It was much easier to leave the Valentine's Day comment untouched. For years, my dick of a (then) husband had ignored it because he thought it was too commercialized, and this last one had been spent with a sweet, thoughtful date who'd brought me my favorite flowers and cooked a delicious dinner at his house before cuing up my favorite movie.

Two weeks later, he had unceremoniously bolted after the surprise arrival of my best friend's child.

Too much pressure, and nothing he was ready to deal with. So, no, Valentine's Day didn't have a great track record in my book.

As quiet covered the office again, I started picking at my nails, a habit I'd successfully curbed in college but taken up again in the last couple of weeks.

It was either that or drinking, and drinking didn't seem like the wisest life choice, so ugly nails was the winner.

"You didn't bring the little girl with you?" she asked.

Now my smile was easy, no internal sighing or repressed urge to bolt from the room. Mira made it easy to smile, which was about my only solace in this giant clusterfuck.

"No, she's at home with a neighbor. I wasn't sure what the lawyer wanted to discuss, so I thought it would be better to come alone."

Her eyes widened, big and brown, just like the wood paneling covering the wall behind her. "I've been hearing so much about her since we started sorting through your friends' paperwork. What a tragedy," she added quietly. "I'm so sorry for your loss."

"Thank you." As I managed a weak smile, I picked off an edge of my nail, and it fell soundlessly into the plush carpet. Even if she meant well, even if the words were delivered with the very best of intentions,

I kinda wanted to scream when someone told me they were sorry for my loss.

Which was unfair, of course. But the thought bloomed every single time I heard it.

And I'd heard it a lot lately.

What were they sorry about? They hadn't done it. They hadn't been drunk out of their minds and driving into oncoming traffic.

I'd rather have someone look me in the eye and say, *This sucks, and there's nothing I can say to make it better.*

It was hard to swallow around the lump in my throat. It had been hard for *me* to know what to say those first few nights I'd rocked Mira to sleep because she was crying for Mommy and Daddy.

She missed them. A different way than I did, because she didn't—couldn't—understand. It took enough out of me just to keep my own tears quiet while I wiped away hers.

All of this—the slow changes and the big, furious changes—had me feeling horribly on edge and ready to burst. Into tears or screams or I didn't even know what anymore. All day long, I tiptoed that fine line between wanting to bawl my eyes out and wanting to punch someone. I wasn't sure which would make me feel better.

The receptionist must have read the tension in my face. She gave me a small, polite smile. "Byron will be out in just a minute. We're waiting for one other person, and then you'll get started."

My stomach went cold, like someone had shoved a giant block of ice in there. "Who are we waiting for?"

She glanced down at the computer screen. "Liam Davies."

The ice in my stomach bottomed out, settling somewhere in my feet.

"What?" I whispered.

Thinking I hadn't heard her, she repeated the name with a courteous smile on her face.

I did not smile back, which was a really big deal because I was nice. I was friendly. I *always* smiled back. But not when someone casually dropped his name like everything was going to be fine and dandy.

As I conjured an image of him in my head, he walked through the door, looking like a human embodiment of the grumpy emoji. Dark hair, green eyes, scruff-covered jaw, and a furrowed brow that never quite seemed to go away. If he was capable of smiling, I wasn't sure I'd ever seen it. Definitely not aimed at me.

He sure as hell wasn't smiling at the receptionist, and when he caught a glimpse of me, his brow furrow somehow deepened.

His eyes dropped to the Washington Wolves shirt I was wearing, and something in his gaze flickered.

Once upon a time, wearing a Washington shirt or sweatshirt or hat was a lighthearted joke. Something Chris teased me about endlessly. Something that always garnered a reaction out of Liam.

But it didn't feel so funny today.

I crossed my arms tight across my chest. It wasn't much of a barrier, but it was better than nothing.

The receptionist smiled, undeterred by the cloud of foreboding that wafted in after Liam. "Mr. Davies, if you'd like to take a seat, Byron will be out in a moment to meet with you and Mrs. Valentine."

"Miss," I corrected. They both looked down at my bare ring finger. "It's Miss Valentine," I said. "Or Zoe. No Mrs. . . ." My voice trailed off, and they were both staring at me. I cleared my throat as I tucked a stray piece of hair behind my ear.

Liam's eyes narrowed, and after a brief hesitation, he took a seat, leaving one open in between us. His legs, covered in black athletic joggers, were about a million miles long when he stretched them out in front of him. He settled his hands over his trim waist, and I studied him openly. His Denver shirt stretched over his chest, the sleeves snug around his thick arms, where the ink-covered skin never failed to do annoyingly fluttery things to my stomach. Even now, even with everything, I saw the tattoos and felt that flutter. The last time I'd seen him

22

was at the funeral; I'd caught a brief glimpse of him standing in the back by his teammates, a row of dark suits and somber expressions.

The difference for Liam was that his expression always looked funereal.

Silence stretched between us, so tense that I could practically feel it snapping at the edges. I rolled my lips between my teeth and fought the urge to pick at my nails again. My mind was clogged with racing thoughts, and I could hardly make sense of a single one.

Why would he be here too?

I tried to recall my conversation with Amie, when she'd told me about the plans they were making . . . in case.

There aren't very many people I'd trust to raise my daughter, Zoe. You're one of them.

The remembered statement, accompanied by a very inconvenient flashback of the day Mira was born, had my stomach churning.

But that couldn't mean . . .

Oh gawd, it could.

It *could.*

Behind my ribs, my heart clanged awkwardly, unable to settle into a normal rhythm.

Liam closed his eyes, tipping his head back to exhale audibly. "If you don't stop staring at me, I'm going to lose it," he muttered under his breath.

Now it was my turn to narrow my eyes. "Hi, Liam. It's nice to see you too. I've been okay the last couple weeks," I said smoothly.

His eyes opened, snapping over to mine. It was almost impossible not to want to shrink back from the force of that gaze. But I refused to give in. For so many years, we'd existed in a space of snarky back-and-forth, something that straddled an indefinable line. It wasn't flirting, but it wasn't outright disdain either.

"Mira is fine," I continued. "I'm so glad you asked. Your concern for your goddaughter is overwhelming."

It wasn't my most gracious opening. Even if it came from a never-ending pool of grief, a place of little sleep and lots of stress, I fought the urge to apologize, barely managing to swallow it down.

Liam leaned in, the roped muscles of his arms popping underneath his white Denver T-shirt as he did. "Zoe," he said, voice low and smooth, "I know you well enough that I'm not going to sit here and spew bullshit niceties when I don't want to be here. I don't know what this is about, but your presence makes it seem about a hundred times more complicated than I'd like it to be."

My pulse thundered in my ears because . . . I wasn't even sure *why* I was having such a visceral reaction. It was almost like his brutal honesty made the air around us vibrate with a higher frequency, something that couldn't be comfortably sustained.

The waiting room had seemed dark before, with no windows letting in any of the Colorado sun. But with the addition of Liam, it was like someone dimmed the lights even further.

I sat back in my seat, mimicking his posture by crossing my arms over my waist. My legs weren't nearly as long as his, so I kept one crossed over the other.

As I usually did when I had nothing to distract me, I thought about Mira. The responsibility of raising her.

And this meeting would likely change every single thing I'd planned. There was no other reason he'd have us both here.

My hands trembled, and I clenched them together tightly to keep it from being obvious.

The door to the office opened, and a tall, thin man wearing wire-rimmed glasses greeted us with a reserved smile. We stood as he approached, and he shook Liam's hand, then mine. "I'm Byron Cogswell. Our firm took over Chris and Amie's trust after their last lawyer retired. I apologize that it took us a couple weeks to get everything sorted out. It's been . . . hectic," he said with a sad look in his eyes. "Please join me in my office, and we'll get started right away."

For a brief moment, I locked eyes with Liam. He towered over me, and the thoughtful look on his face was just about my undoing. It didn't take much to make me cry these days.

Mira smiling, reminding me so much of Amie that it knocked the breath from my lungs.

A song or a smell that stirred up memories of weekend hangouts at their house.

If he looked at me much longer, trying to untangle all the same things I was, I'd start crying in earnest.

As Byron showed us to a small table in the corner of his office, I graciously accepted his offer of coffee, which Liam waved away.

"Ahh," Byron said. "You'd probably prefer tea."

"Because Brits don't drink coffee?" he asked, sarcasm thick in his accent.

Byron coughed. "Of course they do. My apologies."

Liam shook his head. "It's all right. I'm a bit on edge."

I snorted, but it wasn't quiet enough, because Liam pinned me with that glare again.

Instead of doing something really mature, like sticking my tongue out, I pinched my eyes shut and clasped my hands in my lap. When I opened them again, I studied what was in front of us. On the glossy table were two thick binders with Chris's and Amie's names printed on the spines in black ink, as well as two manila folders, each holding a handful of papers. There were also two pens. Expensive pens.

One tab had my name on it.

One tab had Liam's.

My heart kick-started with a jerk. For a brief moment, I wondered if I'd pass the hell out right there at the fancy table, with the fancy lawyer and the asshole football player as my witnesses.

"This about the house they bought?" Liam asked. His eyes held a strangely hopeful gleam.

I had to blink at his sudden question. I'd almost forgotten about it, with all my focus on Mira.

The lawyer smiled. "No. The Michigan property was left to someone else," he said. "One of Chris's friends from college—Burke Barrett. I was just on the phone with him before our meeting."

Liam's jaw tightened, but he managed a short nod.

That hopeful gleam was gone. My gut screamed at me that this meeting was going to end up in a massive shitstorm, but there was no way to swerve out of the way.

Byron handed me the coffee as he took his seat, and I let the heat of the cup warm my frigid hands. Liam's face was inscrutable, but he tracked Byron's every move with interest.

I tore my gaze away from Liam's rugged features, because even if I had a *really* good guess as to what the lawyer was going to say, I wanted to watch him too.

Byron settled his hands on the table and let out a deep breath. "There's no easy way to go about this, given the tragic loss of your friends." He gave us both a sympathetic look, and I could see the kindness in his eyes. Already, my ribs squeezed uncomfortably tight. So did my throat. "But I think it's best if we get straight to the point, and then I'll answer any of the questions you might have."

Liam shifted in the chair, clearing his throat in a show of nerves.

I set the coffee down, afraid to spill it on my lap, and then ran my hands through my hair.

Byron nodded. "Okay, then." With crisp movements, he opened up the first manila folder and then the second, sliding one in front of each of us. "Even though their trust was extensive and it took us a couple weeks to get everything sorted, these few pages are what matter when it comes to both of you."

I didn't look. I didn't need to.

Liam snatched up the folder before him, his mouth moving slightly as he read through the words. "*What* the bloody hell?" he breathed.

I pinched the bridge of my nose. I knew. Without Byron saying a word, *I knew.*

The lawyer gently cleared his throat. "The two of you were chosen by Chris and Amie to share guardianship of their daughter, Mira."

I exhaled in a hard puff, then felt my ribs quaking as I tried to suck in a quick breath to fill my frozen lungs.

Liam snapped the folder shut and tossed it down on the table. "Absolutely fucking not," he yelled.

My eyes slammed shut, and I leaned forward, dropping my head into my hands.

Chapter Three

LIAM

I was out of my seat before I had the coherent thought to move. My hands fisted at my sides, and my blood roared through my veins like a tidal wave. Everything crashed and clanged around in my head—nothing clear enough to process.

It was just . . . loud.

So loud.

No. That was the only thought I could pluck out of the entire mess.

When I was younger, my mum used to let me watch *The Charlie Brown and Snoopy Show*. She hated setting me in front of the telly, but sometimes she needed the break. And I always loved the parts where Charlie was at school, his teacher's voice some distorted, strange sound that didn't make any sense.

When I speared my hands into my hair and tried to take in a deep breath, tried to make sure I was still breathing at all, the lawyer's voice likewise pierced the chaos in my head.

I stared at him for a beat and noticed his mouth was very much moving, but I could not understand one fucking word he was saying.

Right. There were other people in the room.

Zoe was in the room.

Amie's best friend, whom I didn't actually dislike. I just didn't know how to fucking talk to her. Every time we were in the same room, she'd look at me with those bright golden-green eyes, and because I'd never seen eyes like that, I always felt the urge to growl at her until she went somewhere else.

Zoe, who at the moment had her head in her hands, her mass of wavy hair falling over the sides of her face so that I couldn't see those eyes and definitely couldn't tell one way or the other what she thought of this bleeding idiocy.

Her shoulders trembled slightly, and a cold slice of panic knifed through my ribs at the thought of this making her cry.

"No."

The word came out in much the same way that I'd pushed out of my chair. Zoe stilled at the sound of my voice. The lawyer stopped his yammering and tilted his head to the side.

He cleared his throat. A delicate little sound. Like he was about to cross a minefield covered with shards of glass and wasn't sure how to navigate it without losing a fucking limb.

"I know this is a shock," he said slowly. "We can talk through all of your reservations."

"Don't need to." I set my hands on my hips. "I said no. Don't want kids. Never have, and Chris fucking knew that." My voice got louder. The panic churning restlessly under my ribs did too. It felt like a bomb was going to explode through my skin.

Apparently, the news was enough to make Zoe, the sweet friend with the sweet face and the golden eyes, explode too.

"But they *chose* you," she yelled, turning in her chair.

I wished she hadn't.

No one could be quite prepared for a look to gut them clean through. But she managed it effectively. She wasn't any happier about this than I was, but buried in her face, pushing through all the other things she was likely feeling, was the kind of naked grief that was uncomfortable to meet head-on.

Her eyes, as bright and glossy as the surface of that stupid table, shone with it, and despite how much I wanted to, I couldn't look away.

"They chose you," she said again, more quietly this time. "Because they thought it was best for Mira to have both of us."

"I didn't ask them to." I kept my voice low. Kept it even and steady.

A fucking miracle, really. And maybe she recognized the dangerous quality of that low, even, and steady tone. But she tilted her chin all the same.

"They didn't have *time* to ask."

Fucking. Hell.

Was I bleeding?

If she'd swung a steel beam into my balls, it would've had less of an impact. I held her relentless gaze for only a moment before conceding to the winning blow.

Her phone screen lit up on the table, and the picture saved as her background image snagged my attention.

It was Mira—cheesy smile, messy face, and her mum's eyes.

I rubbed at my chest, surprised that I could still feel my heart working.

Zoe noticed me staring and took a quick glance at the phone. "Forgive me for being rude; I need to answer a question for the babysitter."

A hundred questions sprang to the tip of my tongue, and no matter how hard I tried, I couldn't hold the first one back. "Who'd you leave her with?"

I felt her eye roll more than I saw it, because her fingers were flying across the screen. "Rosa lives across the street from me, so she was Chris and Amie's neighbor too. She raised four kids and has twelve grandkids, so she's perfectly capable, I promise." Zoe set the phone down, then settled back in her chair with a dejected slump. "She's been . . . helping."

Byron took the silent moment after her statement to raise his hands. "I think maybe we should take a five-minute break and get a drink, maybe cool our heads a little bit now that the shock has worn off."

Slowly, I arched my eyebrows. "Has it now?"

Most of the rookies hated it when I talked to them like that. They'd shrink back into their lockers when I used that tone. Because they knew it meant they should proceed with caution, if they'd done something to piss me off.

"I can't imagine how hard this must be for both of you," he continued, undeterred. "Zoe, you've done a wonderful job with Mira, from what I'm told."

She sighed. "Thank you. She's . . . she makes it easy." Her voice gentled. "Mira is a great kid."

Fuck.

Fuck.

Fuck.

My skin was too tight and my temper too fragile, fraying at the edges like a rope about to snap. I pinched my eyes closed, conjuring her smiling little face. I hadn't seen her for at least a month, during one of my last visits to Chris and Amie's.

It hurt to remember them. Remember how things used to be.

But sometimes I did exactly that—drowned myself in the past because the pain was so much better than the sadness.

With my eyes closed to the people watching me, I clawed up the memory.

Mira was tugging at the hem of my shorts, grabbing for whatever food Amie had prepared for us. "This is my dinner, kid," I told her. "Don't you get your own?"

Amie laughed, scooping Mira up into her arms to blow a raspberry into the little girl's neck. Her giggle pulled a reluctant smile to my face.

"You talk to her like you talk to the team," Amie teased. "Here."

Then she deposited Mira in my arms and laughed at the shock on my face. "I don't know how to hold kids," I told Amie. Mira squeezed my nose, and I made a low growling noise that made her laugh.

She pinched my nose a second time, then smiled that little smile, with bright-white teeth and eyes that shone expectantly.

So I made the noise again.

Amie grinned at us, patting me on the arm. "See . . . you do just fine, Liam. You just need a little push every once in a while."

I swiped a hand over my mouth now, pulling out of the memory before it could make things worse.

"Mr. Davies," the lawyer said, "if you don't think you need a break, please take a seat, and we'll start going through all of this."

I didn't move. "Don't need to take a seat."

The fucker smiled.

A soft smile. A gentle smile. Like he *understood.*

He didn't understand shit.

"Please." He gestured to the chair.

For a split second, I thought about picking it up and heaving it across the room.

But I wasn't with my team. I wasn't surrounded by people who knew me, who knew the man I was underneath the horrible urge to lob objects when shit knocked me sideways.

So I closed my eyes again and thought about that cute little shit who pinched my nose to make me growl, and then I yanked the chair backward so I could sit down. Beside me, Zoe took a slow, deep breath.

I bet she wasn't thinking about breaking chairs.

When I pulled mine closer to the table and calmly rested my folded hands on the surface, her shoulders relaxed incrementally.

I'd done that. I'd made her tense.

The realization tasted like acid in my throat, burning all the way down.

Byron nodded again. "Good. Keep in mind that figuring out the best way to do this will take time and honesty on both your parts." He gave me a steady look. "It will require *patience.*"

I cocked an eyebrow and clenched my jaw.

Byron didn't so much as blink. Somehow, the skinny lawyer with wire-rimmed glasses had bigger balls than half the guys on my team.

He continued. "And if you're willing, I'd highly suggest meeting with a counselor—together and separately—to help you navigate the inevitable stresses that will come with the two of you sharing guardianship of Mira."

"No."

They both looked at me.

Byron was unsurprised. Zoe was annoyed.

Good, because I was annoyed too.

"That's it?" she asked. "You're just gonna say no to whatever you don't feel like doing?"

I crossed my arms and studied the table. "I don't need a counselor, because I'm not fit to be anyone's guardian."

"On that we agree," Zoe said sweetly. Then she smiled.

It was not a nice smile. The sweet friend might not have been into throwing chairs, but she sure as fuck was thinking about punching me in the nuts.

"Regardless," Byron said, "your best friend and his wife felt that you *were* fit. Both of you."

Briefly, I flicked my gaze over to Zoe. Then I narrowed my eyes. "You don't seem terribly surprised by any of this."

She swallowed. "Amie and I . . ." Her voice trailed off. "We had a conversation about it when they were making their trust decisions. She told me there were only a couple people she could imagine trusting with Mira, and I was one of them."

I tilted my chin up and stared at the ceiling for a beat. But I could feel her golden bloody eyes fixed heavily on my face.

I turned back to her and met those eyes unflinchingly, a zing sliding down my spine when she didn't look away.

"Me being the other," I finished.

"Apparently."

Byron cleared his throat, then slid the folders closer to us again. Mine had traveled a bit farther than Zoe's when I'd slammed it back down onto the table.

"I know it doesn't help right now," Byron said, "but there were a few loose ends in Chris and Amie's trust. Naturally, they felt like they had plenty of time to have conversations with everyone involved."

I clenched my fists.

"Where do we start?" Zoe asked. "Mira is with me at my house right now, but . . ." Her voice trailed off, and she glanced in my direction. "I don't even know where you live."

"Doesn't matter," I managed.

"Here we go," she said on a sigh. "You are impossible."

"On the contrary. I'm going to make this very, very easy for you." I spread my hands out wide. "I'll send you a check every month to help out with Mira, and you'll never have to deal with me."

Her eyes narrowed. "Are you being serious?"

"I am." I shot her a smile, then aimed one at Byron, who was sitting back in his chair and eyeing me with interest. "Tell me where to sign and I'll be on my way."

He blinked a couple of times. "Ah, nothing for you to sign at the moment. This was . . . informational in nature. We'll deal with finances at a later meeting; that's when I'll have bank paperwork for you."

"Excellent." I pushed my chair back and notched my fingers at my temple in a salute. "Byron, have a lovely day." I glanced down at Zoe, who gaped at me, eyes wide. "Valentine, I'll drop a check in the mail."

And I walked out before I could do any further damage.

Chapter Four

ZOE

In the moment after Liam stormed out of the office, the lawyer and I did nothing except exchange stunned looks.

I blinked, a shocked exhale escaping my lips in a puff.

Byron blinked too, then blinked again.

"Well, shall we continue reviewing the paperwork?" he asked. I'd have given him an A for infusing the fakest of all confidence into his voice.

The shock faded at the idea that we'd just continue. That Liam "I'm a Big Grumpy Brit" Davies was just allowed to act like a big grumpy child whenever he felt so moved.

And in place of the shock was a blinding, white-hot anger.

"What a dick," I breathed.

Byron cleared his throat. "He certainly"—he paused, choosing his words carefully—"doesn't handle surprises very well."

He'd send me a *check*.

His friends had died. They'd loved and respected him enough to ask him to help raise their child, and he'd . . .

I couldn't even think it again.

Remember when I said I was constantly walking a tightrope between wanting to bawl my eyes out and wanting to punch someone? I was out of my chair before I could register another thought.

It looked like I was stepping firmly into the camp of violence.

"Miss Valentine?" Byron asked.

"I'll be right back," I called over my shoulder.

Sure, his legs were, like, a foot longer than mine, and I needed to sprint to catch up with him in the parking lot, but I was fueled by some pretty righteous anger, and that made up for a lot.

By the time I yanked open the door of the lobby, Liam was just easing into his dark SUV.

"Hey," I yelled.

He froze.

"Don't you dare get in that car," I warned.

He tipped his head back and swiveled in my direction. Annoyance was stamped all over his face, and the hard line of his jaw was so tight that it seemed a miracle the bone hadn't cracked.

Liam slammed his car door shut, settling his big hands on his hips while I crossed the parking lot.

Why did he have to be so big? My righteous anger ebbed a little when I had to tilt my chin up just to make proper eye contact and level a glare at him.

"You can't just leave," I said.

"Watch me."

I blew out a hard breath. "I get it. It's a shock, and you weren't ready for it."

His jaw clenched, and for a moment, he averted his eyes.

"I know it's easier for me because I've had her since . . ." I paused. "I've had her with me, and Amie told me about their trust. But you can't just ignore what they're asking of you."

His eyes narrowed the slightest amount, and I thought maybe he'd listen. Consider doing the right thing.

"I told you I'd send you a check every month." He spoke slowly, like I couldn't understand him. "If I was ignoring it, I would've walked out, and you'd never see me again."

It would have been *so* easy to knee him between the legs, given the height difference. I could have just snapped my knee up and caught him *right there*.

He whistled. "Someone is thinking violent thoughts."

I smiled. "Just imagining the sound you'd make if I kneed you in the balls right now. I'd play it on a loop whenever I needed a pick-me-up."

Liam leaned in, a decided gleam in his stupid dark-green eyes. "This the stuff you used to say when you worked at the hospital? I'm having a hard time believing they didn't sack you, Goldilocks."

"Don't call me that, and don't change the subject."

He leaned back against his car and eyed my hair, which—on a good day—was unmanageable. Today had not been a good day, and standing outside while the breeze tossed it all around certainly wasn't helping. I yanked a hair tie off my wrist and wrangled my mane into a low bun.

He smirked.

At the sight of that twist of his lips, I contemplated the possible ramifications of punching him while standing in a lawyer's parking lot.

Instead, I pulled in a long, steadying breath. And I thought about Mira. Just like it always did, my chest went warm and tight and heavy. The pressure of raising someone else's child was unmatched, especially when you hadn't been expecting it to happen.

Maybe I'd been thrown into the crucible of this situation a couple of weeks before Liam, dealing alone with the little girl crying for her parents when they didn't come back after a few days, but I could not ignore the fact that they'd wanted him in it with me.

If nothing else, there was someone else to bear the load of the pressure.

"They asked you for a reason," I reminded him.

"Bet you're racking your brain trying to figure out what that is, aren't you?"

I held his gaze unflinchingly. "Yes."

His head reared back at my honest answer, but it brought some of his hostility down . . . just a touch.

I rubbed my forehead, where the beginnings of a headache had started to bloom. "I know we've never been friendly, Liam."

"You don't say," he drawled.

It wasn't even hard to contain the eye roll because now this was about something so much bigger than how he'd gotten under my skin over the years.

"But we don't need to be friends right now." I folded my arms around my waist and looked into the distance for a momentary reprieve from those eyes of his. Even the far-off mountains didn't offer as much comfort as they normally did. I met his gaze again. "This is about Mira."

Everything about Liam was hard. The way he held his tall, muscular frame, the set of his jaw, the look in his eyes.

"You might take issue with what I'm saying, Zoe," he said. "But that won't change it. Stop and think that maybe Mira's the reason I'm keeping my distance. I won't be any help to her, trust me."

I opened my mouth to argue, but he pivoted, yanking open his car door and sliding in before I could say another word.

My stunned silence continued as I walked numbly back into the office. Byron was on his laptop, and he closed the screen as I took my seat.

"Will Mr. Davies be joining us again?" he asked quietly.

I shook my head, fighting an ache as it crawled up my throat and threatened to come out in the form of an exhausted sob.

Byron pushed a box of Kleenex in my direction, and I gave him a tiny smile.

"Ready to continue, or would you like to reschedule?"

I blew out a slow breath. "Do we have to do anything legally if he's not involved?"

"Not unless you want to. We can take steps to petition the court to remove Liam as a guardian, and if he agrees to take part in that process, it would be fairly painless. Just some time and paperwork." He shrugged. "Or we can leave it as is and see if he has a change of heart."

I laughed under my breath. "I don't see that happening."

He tilted his head. "You're sure?"

I thought of what I had come to know about Liam over the years. Stubborn. Willful. Argumentative.

But in moments where he hadn't known I was watching, moments with Chris and Amie and Mira, I'd gotten glimpses of someone else entirely.

"No," I admitted. "I'm not sure. Of anything."

He studied my face. "Let's just keep the rest of the appointment simple, okay? Sign a few papers while you're here. We can get you on the trust account they set up for Mira's care. We'll revisit some of the less pressing matters another time."

Byron slid the folder back in my direction.

With my heart hammering in my chest, I picked up the heavy pen and started signing papers.

Taking a deep breath as Byron swapped out one finished page for the next, I thought back to something he'd said earlier.

"The house in Michigan," I said. "You mentioned a friend they'd left it to."

Byron nodded. "He played at U of M with Chris. If it helps, he was just as shocked as the two of you."

What I knew of the house was little. It had belonged to Chris's grandparents when he was young, then fallen into massive disrepair. Chris and Amie had intended it to be someplace special for their family as they raised Mira, and for whoever else came along after her.

"So that's not something I have to worry about?" I asked.

He shook his head, a slight smile hovering over his lips. "No. Just Mira."

Just Mira, I thought. *Just raise their child. By myself, apparently.*

By the time I drove home, my whole body ached from the twists and turns of the day's emotional roller coaster. I needed a bath, some wine, a gallon of ice cream, and a good, solid cry in the closet, where no one could hear me.

As I wound through the streets of our neighborhood, I wondered what might have happened to Mira if I'd never met Chris and Amie.

If I'd decided to go elsewhere for college.

If I'd ended up in a different job instead of working in accounting at the hospital nearest to their neighborhood.

If I'd never met Charles at that hospital—in his perfectly tailored three-piece suits.

If I'd never moved next door to them.

If I'd never kept the house when I kicked my ex out two and a half years earlier.

I'd never grown up dreaming of a fancy house in one of the wealthiest suburbs of Denver, but the moment I laid eyes on that brick Tudor, with its beautiful garden and wrought-iron gates around the front yard, I knew it was where I was supposed to be.

Cherry Creek was a mix of elaborate mansions and older homes like mine, with established trees and a community hum that I loved.

When I pulled my car into the garage stall, I took a moment to lay my head back on the seat rest and try to make sense of what had just happened. But the moment of unsteady peace was interrupted by the door from the house opening.

Rosa had Mira perched on her hip, and the moment Mira saw me, she scrambled to get down. I opened the car door with a laugh and had hardly pulled my legs out of the vehicle before she was climbing up into my lap.

"Hey, bugaboo," I said, kissing the side of her face. "Mmm. Someone had peanut butter and jelly for lunch."

She nodded. "Rosa make it."

"Oh man, I bet her sandwiches are so yummy." I kissed Mira's cheek again and sighed when her skinny little arms tightened around my neck.

Since the accident, I'd hardly left Mira's side. We survived on take-out and grocery deliveries and Amazon Prime, like God and the introverts intended.

But since I'd been gone for a couple of hours, she'd likely cling to me for the rest of the day.

Or maybe I'd cling to her. It was a toss-up.

Rosa held the door open for us with a smile while I tried to navigate exiting the vehicle with my purse, the manila folder, and Mira clinging to my neck. Rosa took the folders when I held them out, and I smiled gratefully.

"How'd it go?" she asked.

I gave her a look. "I think we need privacy for this one."

"What's privacy?" Mira asked, playing with some wisps of hair that had escaped from my haphazard bun.

"Privacy is when someone needs to be alone, but if you want to go turn the TV on in the family room, that's enough for me and Miss Rosa to have a very adult conversation." I set her on the kitchen island, and she kicked her legs against the cabinets. "Is that okay?"

She nodded. "*Moana*?"

I gave Rosa a questioning look, but she shook her head.

I tweaked the tip of Mira's nose. "Yes, you can watch *Moana* again."

Hooking my hands under her arms, I set her down on the floor, and she took off running into the family room, jumping excitedly when I cued up her favorite movie.

When I got back to the kitchen, Rosa was pouring a glass of chardonnay. I smiled. "How did you know?"

"Because you look like shit."

"Thank you, Rosa."

She slid the wineglass across the island. Every single day, she wore her pure-silver hair back in an elegant chignon, never so much as a strand out of place. Around her neck was a ruby cross that her husband had bought her for her sixtieth birthday. Red rubies for his Rosa. I didn't know anyone else who could pull off a ruby cross. Somehow, she did. Together, she and her husband had raised a boatload of kids and balanced successful careers. Before his death a few years earlier, her husband had been a successful ob-gyn, and Rosa had been a pediatrician until she retired.

When Chris and Amie died, she immediately stepped in to help me with Mira.

"Tell me."

"I have shared guardianship of Mira with Chris's best friend." When a quick glance at her face told me she was going to listen before reacting, I took a slow sip of chardonnay and then set my glass aside, knowing the wine would only make my headache worse. "You remember Liam Davies?" I asked.

Her eyes gleamed. "How could I forget? He's delicious. I wonder if he'd go for an older woman."

I gave her a look, and she chuckled.

"Kidding," she said.

"He is an unmitigated asshole."

Rosa laughed. "I don't think he actually is, though. Do you really believe that?"

I didn't know what I believed. Which made everything so much more complicated.

"Have I ever told you what he said to me the first time we met?"

She shook her head, taking a seat at the island and picking up the discarded glass of wine for herself.

I tugged at the ponytail holder until my waves were free and I could dig my fingers into my scalp. Thank goodness no more noodles came out. A girl could take only so much in one day.

I sat like that for a moment, hands speared into my hair, staring down at the counter, mind churning back to the first time I'd laid eyes on Liam.

"It was probably ten years ago," I told her. "I was in the middle of planning my wedding to Charles, and I was so stressed. All week, I'd been buried in spreadsheets and budgets and invite lists. All I wanted to do was relax and read and not think." My eyes closed unwittingly. "I didn't even hear him come in at first, but when I looked up from my book, he was there. Just . . . *staring* at me."

She listened quietly, sipping on the wine while I got lost in the memory.

"I mean, objectively, he's just . . . stupidly hot, right?"

Rosa hummed.

"He wasn't a dick right off the bat, but he did stare at my ring for a few seconds before he introduced himself. When he shook my hand, we kinda just . . . stood like that for longer than was polite." My brow wrinkled. "Then Charles came into the kitchen, and Liam let go of my hand."

"I can only imagine how well those two got along."

I laughed. Then laughed even harder.

I didn't stop until my eyes actually welled up with tears, because that entire evening had been such an unbelievable disaster. Charles showed his pretentious asshole side for the first time in our entire relationship, and Liam . . .

When my laughter ebbed, I swiped a thumb under my eyes and exhaled slowly. "By the time dinner was done, Liam had called Charles a bottom-feeding dick whose head was shoved so far up his own ass that it was a miracle he could see where he was walking."

Rosa choked on her sip of wine.

"And then"—I paused, sucking in a sharp breath as I remembered the words as clearly as if he'd said them yesterday—"he wished me luck with husband number two and said he hoped I had better decision-making skills after I was done with husband number one."

"No," she breathed.

Somewhere in the middle of the story, I'd started picking at the edge of my thumbnail. "Yup."

Even a decade later, I felt the sting of that comment just as clearly as the moment he'd said it.

"Charles really did have his head up his ass," Rosa said.

I gave her a look. "Not the point."

"And you did get divorced from him." She set her hand on mine. "Which was an excellent life choice, as you know."

"Whose side are you on?"

She grinned. "Always yours, my dear."

I laid my arm on the counter and dropped my head down. "He wants nothing to do with Mira. Said he'd send a check every month."

Rosa ran her hands through my hair. "Maybe that's a good thing, if you two really don't get along."

I turned my head until I could see her face. "But I'm not the one who made all these decisions. Chris and Amie did. They worked on this trust for weeks, maybe more. And isn't it my job to respect their wishes? They're entrusting me with their daughter. I can't ignore the fact that they wanted this other person to be part of the picture as Mira gets older."

"Give him time," she said. "Maybe he'll change his mind."

"You know what bugs me the most?"

She arched an eyebrow. "That he was right about Charles?"

"No." I stopped. "Well, yes. But besides that." I sat up and stared across my kitchen at the photo of me and Amie stuck to the fridge with a Denver magnet. "That she didn't tell me. She knows he drives me crazy."

Rosa's hand squeezed mine.

"*Knew,*" I corrected. My throat was stiff and swollen, ratcheted tight with tears that desperately wanted to escape and emotions that I'd done my best to keep in check. "She knew. And I can't understand why they chose him. What kind of selfish person just tosses a check at a situation like this and walks away?"

"I wish she'd told you too, honey. I think she would have."

Eventually.

If she'd had time.

In the family room, Mira giggled at the chicken, and my heart clenched in my chest.

A tear spilled over my cheek. "I miss my friend," I whispered.

"I know you do." Rosa turned on her stool. "Hug or no hug?"

A watery laugh escaped my lips. "Hug."

The tears came faster once Rosa folded me into her strong embrace.

Chapter Five

LIAM

"Let's get a fucking move on, shall we?" I yelled. "The defensive line won't fix itself, assholes."

There were a few grumbles on the field, and our defensive line coach gave me a nod when the O-line started moving a bit quicker on the next play.

"Oy! Watch for the blitz," I called to the center. "Don't act like you can't see him back there, McCaffrey."

The player in question straightened, his hands going to his hips. "You our coach now, Davies? Because last I checked, you're supposed to be lining up against us, old man."

I fought a smile when the guys around him hooted and yelled. "I'll line up when you prove you can block worth a shit. My mum can do a better job at stopping the run."

He flipped me his middle finger. "Your *mum* didn't have many complaints last night."

If I'd thought he was being remotely serious, I would've tackled his ass right there, even if he outweighed me by fifty pounds, but I rolled my eyes and whistled for them to start the play from the top.

My defensive coordinator came over and stood shoulder to shoulder with me while we watched it unfold.

"Better," he said. The defense managed to interrupt the run, keeping him to only a couple of yards before they brought him down. "But we still need someone stronger on the left side."

Where Chris used to play.

I grunted.

He gave me a sideways look. "Not that I'm complaining about the extra coaching help, but out of curiosity, how come you're not lining up with them?"

"Don't feel like it."

"Well, good thing you're not, like, contractually obligated to play or anything."

I glanced at him. "Did we start training camp a few months earlier than I was aware of?"

He sighed. "You're touchier than usual."

Yeah. Because I was in a pissy fucking mood. I felt like there was a churning black cloud hovering over my head at all times, trailing behind me no matter how fast I tried to outrun it.

I'd worked myself to the bone in the weight room the last three days, and nothing had ripped Zoe's gutted facial expression out of my mind when I tore out of that parking lot.

I was afraid to line up against anyone on my team. The last thing I wanted was to injure someone because my temper got unleashed at the wrong time.

And the unleashing was why I played this sport.

Nothing heated my blood like a good tackle. The pounding of my cleats in the grass when I chased someone down. The sound made when I leveled the person trying to get past me with the ball. The rush of adrenaline that came after.

It was the cleanest, neatest way for me to give all that rage bubbling beneath the surface a safe outlet.

Just one of the reasons why football—the football back at home in Great Britain—didn't hold much appeal for me. In that sport, knocking an opponent on his ass with as much force as humanly possible was generally frowned upon.

That, and the fact that every time I had played as a lad, I was constantly reminded of how much I looked like my dad. Ran like my dad. Kicked like my dad.

Every coach who asked me if I could defend like he did? Salt in an open fucking wound.

Didn't take long to realize just how much I didn't want to play any sport that would have me stepping over his shadow.

My friends thought I'd gone off my bloody rocker when I told them I wanted to play American football. My mum understood, but she was the only one.

Moving here, going to college here—it was the only thing that had made sense to me.

Until this week. The last month, really. I wondered all sorts of things in the middle of the night, when I sleeplessly stared up at my ceiling.

If I'd gone to another team, I never would've met Chris. If he hadn't been such a persistent ass about befriending me, then I wouldn't feel like I did right now.

Helpless.

Angry.

Like the biggest selfish prick in existence.

Yet none of those things made me feel like I was wrong. Mira—and Miss Zoe Valentine, with her big, expressive eyes—was much better off without me hanging around. The pretty, golden-haired friend with the pretty smile would raise Mira exactly the way Chris and Amie had wanted.

All I'd do was fuck it up. Or worse.

And reminding myself of this in the wake of that stupid, stupid meeting was what had me stomping around the facilities with a permanent frown on my face, and my teammates wondering what the hell had happened.

"What's the new guy's name again?" my coach asked.

"Richards."

"Richards," he yelled, "come over here a second."

Richards hopped up from the field, spitting out his mouth guard as he did.

"Yeah, Coach?" He eyed me nervously as he approached. Couldn't blame him, I guess. Everyone was eyeing me nervously this week. "Did I do something wrong?"

"No. That was good. Just make sure you plant that back foot with more weight on it, okay?"

Richards's brow furrowed underneath his helmet, and I sighed audibly. "Do you understand why he's saying that?"

Richards shook his head.

I jerked my chin up. "Stand like you're lining up."

He did, spreading his legs one in front of the other and bracing his body to push forward.

Coach motioned for the imaginary play to start, and in one surge, I had Richards flat on his back.

I stood over him, gripping his jersey before I hauled him up to a standing position. Then I got right in his face.

"You're thinking about going forward, yeah? You've got all your weight on your front foot, and when you go up against someone bigger and meaner and angrier than you, it doesn't take much for me to knock you on your ass."

He was breathing hard, hands on his hips as he listened.

"You plant that back foot. Like this." I stopped and showed him, digging my toe into the turf. Then I grabbed the bottom of his helmet and tugged him even closer. "You be immovable, do you hear me? There is no one out there who can push you around, or take you down, or put you on the ground unless you let them. How often do you see me down after we line up?"

He swallowed. "Not very often."

49

"That's right. Because in my head"—I tapped my temple—"I am a stone fucking wall, and no one is strong enough to push through it. You remember that."

I shoved him backward, and he nodded resolutely before heading back with the rest of the team.

When I turned around, our head coach—a grizzled, no-nonsense guy by the name of Freedman—had joined, and he was watching me curiously.

"What?" I asked.

"Walk with me, Davies."

"I was just about to line up for the next play."

The defensive coach cleared his throat.

Coach Freedman held my gaze. "Now, Liam. Let's go." It wasn't a request.

When we were about twenty yards away from the team, he stopped and turned, his playbook tucked underneath his arm and a wad of chewing tobacco bulging inside his cheek. "You've been a giant prick all week."

All right, then. No fucking around today. I blew out a slow breath. "Yes, sir."

"What was that meeting with the lawyer about?"

"Am I obligated to tell you?" I asked.

His interest sharpened even further. "Of course not. But there's been a marked difference in you since that afternoon. Normally, every guy on the field views you as an extension of the coaching staff. You could step into my shoes tomorrow and no one would blink, because you've always been one of the most natural leaders on this team. Since day one, it's been that way."

I held my breath, waiting for the *but*.

"But," he continued, "it's been different the last few days. You're unapproachable. Snapping at everyone. And I have to worry just a bit about how hard you've been working yourself in the weight room. What

I don't need is one of my captains injuring himself in the offseason because he's not willing to talk about what's going on."

I slicked my tongue over my teeth, dropping my gaze to the field for a moment.

"Chris did something stupid," I said, voice raw and low. "And I can't make peace with it."

Coach took a deep breath. "What'd he do?"

I clenched my jaw so tight that I felt the ominous creak of my molars grinding together. The words didn't even want to pass my lips because they were so ridiculous. "He . . . he made me guardian of his kid. The daughter." I blinked a few times, studying Coach's reaction so hard that my eyes started to burn. "Me and Amie's best friend."

Coach rocked back slightly on his heels, eyes widening. "So you're moving into their house or something? Or you'll do shared custody?"

I scoffed. "I'm not father material, Coach. I have never wanted a family, and Chris knew that." My voice got louder. Angrier. "He's the only person who's *ever* known that, and he did something stupid like this. I can't fucking figure out why, and I can't ask him, because he's fucking dead!"

My chest heaved, and I could hardly suck in oxygen fast enough. Like I'd just run a bloody marathon.

How ridiculous.

Coach narrowed his gaze and watched me. He didn't say a word while I caught my breath, reined my temper back in. The roar in my ears dulled, and my pulse slowed to a manageable rhythm.

Still, he didn't speak.

He just watched me. Studied me. I felt as if he'd pinned me to a corkboard like an insect specimen, trying to figure out what made me tick.

"I'm not doing it," I said. "Told the friend I'd send her a check every month. She can use it for whatever Mira needs, but I'm not playing daddy to some little girl who deserves someone a helluva lot better than me for the job."

His eyes sharpened. And still, he stayed silent.

I pointed a finger at him. "Stop it."

His eyebrows rose slowly.

"Stop it right now," I barked. "Quit fucking looking at me like that."

"Like what?" he asked. So fucking patient.

The words could hardly come up my throat. They were dragged kicking and screaming the whole way, because it was the last thing I wanted to admit out loud.

But no matter how hard I tried to suppress them, they came up all the same.

"Like you're disappointed in me," I managed. The words tumbled out like I'd ground them to a bloody pulp.

There. I'd nailed it in one. Understanding filled his eyes, and I wanted to punch something. Not him, though, because he'd probably punch me right back, and I'd end up with a broken nose.

"You're better than this, Liam," he said. "You're a better man than ignoring your friends' wishes."

I took a step forward. "I'm a better man by knowing what I'm not capable of, and filling some mythical father role is not in the cards for me." My skin was crawling at the thought of it. Shrinking too tight around my frame, like the slightest jolt of energy would have me exploding in a messy burst.

The thought of trying to be Chris, of trying to do the things he did so effortlessly—playing dolls with her, drinking her imaginary tea, and showing her how to swing that big plastic bat in their backyard, even when she couldn't aim for shit.

Damn it all to hell. My eyes were burning, and I couldn't fucking make it go away.

"He was the best dad I've ever seen," I told Coach. "He was patient and sweet and kind. He made her laugh all the fucking time, and I cannot be like that." I hit my chest with a fist. "I do not have that inside me."

"Don't you?" he asked. "I'd argue differently."

"Don't turn this around and try to coach me through this. It has nothing to do with the team or me as a football player."

Now it was his turn to lean in, and I fought the urge to back away from the intensity in his face. "Everything you do is a reflection of this team and the family we've built. You preach that more than anyone I know. It's why they respect you so damn much in that locker room, Davies. Why Chris respected you so much."

I swallowed, unable to hold his stare any longer.

"You're better than this," he repeated.

I took a deep breath and let it go. "No, Coach, I'm not."

And I walked away before he could say another word.

No matter who was staring at me, I didn't stop until I shoved open the doors of the locker room. My heart rammed against my ribs at the sight of the nearly empty space. A few of the guys were lounging on the benches near their lockers, and they glanced up when I strode over to Chris's locker.

I set my hands on my hips and stared at the contents.

Rashad and Micah walked over, concern heavy in the air.

"You okay, Davies?" Rashad asked.

My jaw clenched before I answered. "No. I want this shit gone. We've been staring at it for too long."

They traded a look, though neither of them dared push me.

My voice was raw as I spoke again. "I need a fucking box."

But neither of them moved. Rashad simply settled his massive hand on my shoulder. "I know, man. We got you."

Something rattled deep in my chest, and I fought a snarl at the moment of kindness he was showing me. It wasn't just kindness, though.

The *grace* of his reaction.

I didn't want it.

I didn't want any of this.

A box appeared next to me, and it was attached to Coach Freedman's hand.

Looking him in the eye felt like a herculean task, something I wasn't nearly strong enough to do. But I took the box with a slow nod and set it on the bench.

I tossed Chris's bag in there without a single glance at what was inside.

Then I picked up the box and swept in all the loose shit from the top shelf. Deodorant and mouth guards. Eye black and a spare shirt with the sleeves ripped off. A few receipts and some ChapStick.

"Messy fucker," I muttered.

Rashad exhaled a laugh. "Yeah, he was. Amie's the only reason that house was clean. He was always leaving his shit around, wasn't he?"

It should've taken longer to clean all his things out. An amount of time that represented exactly how important he was. To me and to everyone else.

But less than two minutes later, everything was gone.

Everything except the picture taped to the back.

My throat burned. My eyes filled with sand that I couldn't blink back. And like a coward, I refused to look at their faces while I carefully pulled up the edges.

Once the photo was tucked inside the safe confines of the box, I let out a slow breath and closed the top, folding the edges so that it wouldn't open up. "It's done," I managed.

Coach clapped a hand on my back. "We'll leave it empty for now, okay?"

It was tempting to let my teammates offer comfort. To allow our shared grief to lessen the ache gnawing at my insides.

But I didn't. Because I wasn't entirely sure I deserved their support right now.

"Do whatever you want with it," I told him.

I gave the locker one last long look, then picked up the box and left.

Chapter Six

ZOE

"One more, pleeeease."

"I can't," I said. "I think you broke me."

Mira giggled, and her warm, soft hands gripped my face until I had no choice but to open my eyes. She pressed her forehead against mine, her features going blurry because of how close she was.

"You not broken; you need a nap."

We'd been playing a modified game of tag in which Mira instructed me to act like various animals while I chased her around my fenced-in backyard. During the last round, I was deemed a crab, and it became clear that my crab walk needed some work. My glutes were going to be sore for a week after that one.

"I do need a nap," I told her. Then I tapped her nose. "So do you, young lady."

Mira took off running, her curly hair streaming out behind her. "No nap! I not tired."

I snorted. She could be falling asleep at the dinner table and would still say she wasn't tired.

Because I was allowed to chase after her in my human form, I caught her quickly and swung her up into my arms. She arched her back when I tickled her side.

"Come on, Mirabelle, you need some quiet time, okay?"

"Das not my name," she said through her giggles.

I blew a raspberry into the side of her neck. "No, but that's what I call you, pretty little girl."

Most days during her quiet time, she ended up fast asleep in the upstairs bedroom that we'd turned into hers. But given her current energy level, I wasn't sure as I wrangled her into the house that we'd get any actual rest.

Which was problematic, because she had a penchant for waking up in the middle of the night to throw a two-hour party, and I was ready for the phase to be over.

We walked into the bathroom, her arms still tight around my neck, and she refused to let go when I tried to set her down.

"One tinkle and we'll get a sticker for your book."

"Two stickers?" she asked, immediately setting her feet down on the ground.

"One sticker." I gave her a look when she pushed her lip out in a pout. "You know the deal, kiddo. One sticker for number one, two stickers for number two."

She set her jaw mulishly. "No number two. I hate stickers."

Good.

Awesome.

I tapped the edge of her chin with my finger. "You can try, though."

While she did her business, I washed my hands and sighed internally. Potty-training regression wasn't uncommon at all when a child had experienced a major loss, and I reminded myself that we'd already made progress the last couple of weeks.

Four weeks of the single-mom club already under my belt, and I'd come to understand that in situations like this, time moved in strange, immeasurable ways.

The meeting at the lawyer's office felt like it had just happened.

Sometimes.

Other days, it felt like it had been a year ago.

Most days, I managed not to think about Liam.

Sort of.

My days were spent in a loop; each one felt long and exhausting. But at the end of each week, I could hardly believe how quickly they had passed.

I remembered feeling the same way when I worked full-time at the hospital. But it was nothing compared with raising a toddler—on my own—day in and day out. No one handed me an instruction manual. There was no easing into it. I just had to deal with it. Answer questions on my own. Figure out what she wanted the hard way.

Like when I'd tried to give her broccoli at dinner and it had ended with so much screaming and crying that I was sure someone was going to call the cops on me.

Mira did not like broccoli.

Noted.

When she finished in the bathroom and did a passable job of washing her hands, I followed her into the bedroom.

Because I had been advised not to give her too much change at once (the beauty of my mom being a therapist), Mira was still sleeping in a crib. Without fail, she tucked herself into the top right corner, pulled her stuffed duck under her arm, and then rubbed the edge of her soft yellow blanket against her face.

Her eyes were still bright and awake, but she didn't fight me on lying down.

"Just a little quiet time," I told her.

"Five minutes?"

I smiled, leaning down to tap the edge of her nose. "Maybe a few more than that. I'll check on you in a little bit."

"I have my froggy?" she asked. "Duck needs a friend."

I glanced back at the pile of stuffed animals. No frog in sight. It was likely still in her bedroom next door. "I'll look for it, okay? You close your eyes, and I'll bring it in if I find it."

Mira nodded.

"I kiss you?" she asked.

Despite how precocious she was, Mira hadn't quite learned the proper way to phrase things when she was asking for something specific, and when my heart melted in my chest, I kinda hoped she never did. I leaned down to kiss her forehead, and she patted my cheek as I did.

"Have a good rest, kiddo," I whispered.

She smiled, and already her eyes looked just a little bit heavier.

When I left her bedroom, I sagged against the wall.

From where I was standing, I could see Chris and Amie's house through the window at the end of the hallway.

Once, Amie and I had joked that we should put in a walkway connecting our houses. It was shortly after my divorce, when I was still adjusting to living in the big house by myself. So many nights I'd found myself in their kitchen, eating ice cream with Amie, because sometimes that was the healthiest way to deal with life's shitstorms.

I pulled out my phone and sent a text to Rosa.

Me: Can you sit here for a few minutes? She's having her quiet time, but I need to look for something at the house.

Rosa: Be right there.

While I waited for Rosa to arrive, I didn't even hesitate to grab a carton of mint chocolate chip out of the freezer, pull a spoon from the silverware drawer, and dig in unceremoniously. She let herself in through the front door, eyeing my eating habits with unconcealed judgment.

"Bit early in the day for that, don't you think?"

"Not everyone eats apples when they're stressed, okay?"

She raised a haughty eyebrow. "I never should've told you that."

I laughed around my bite of ice cream, then put the carton back into the freezer. "This shouldn't take me long," I told her.

But Rosa waved me off. "Take your time if there's anything else you need to do over there. Any idea when you'll sell the house?"

I shook my head. "Technically, that's the lawyer's decision. He's the executor of their estate. I think he's waiting on guidance from me."

I made a vague gesture with my hand in the direction of where Liam lived, wherever the hell that was. "In case what's-his-name ever pulls his head out of his ass."

"Fuck that guy."

I barked out a laugh. "Rosa, I've never heard you say an ill word about him before. What a delightful change of pace."

She took a seat on the couch and sighed, pulling her Kindle from her purse. "Yeah, well, that was a couple weeks ago. I thought he'd change his mind by now. Clearly, having a great ass and perfect arms and the sexiest accent known to man doesn't actually make you a good person."

"A shocking realization, I know."

Rosa grinned, then shooed me out the door. I snagged the key to Chris and Amie's from the hook in my laundry room, then walked down the cobblestone path that led to their backyard gate.

Their house was bigger than mine, with the arched architecture and big windows of an Italian villa. Their yard was bigger too, with a pool and mature trees giving much-desired privacy to their property. The pool was still covered, and I couldn't decide if it was worth hiring someone to come open it so that Mira and I could use it during the summer.

It was somewhere on a mile-long list of decisions that weren't pressing (they didn't really matter), but good Lord did those decisions weigh heavily on my shoulders.

The house was quiet and dim when I let myself in through the back door from the patio. For the first time since the accident, it smelled musty and stale. That alone had my heart hammering just a little bit harder.

It would only get worse as time went on.

Rosa had hired a crew to come in and clean the house the week after they died. It was too hard to walk in and see Amie's coffee mug still sitting in the sink. Her book tossed onto the end table by the couch. Chris's Denver hoodie slung over the back of a dining-room chair.

Those things were gone now, so even with the slightly stale scent, it felt a bit less like walking through a graveyard.

I kissed the tip of my finger and pressed it against the family photo that hung on the wall, then slowly made my way upstairs to Mira's bedroom.

The walls were still painted a gorgeous soft blue—the shade Amie had chosen when she was pregnant. She'd said it made her feel like she was looking at the sky.

When I peeked into the crib, I saw that it was empty of stuffed animals. I pulled open a few drawers and riffled through them but still couldn't find the frog Mira wanted. While I was there, I grabbed a few items of clothing and tucked them under my arm.

As I tugged open a bin at the back of the closet, a sound from downstairs had me freezing in place.

I paused, listening closer.

It was the unmistakable sound of a door opening.

Heavy footsteps on the floor.

My heart pounded wildly behind my ribs, and I realized I'd left my phone behind after texting Rosa.

"Shit," I whispered.

Not that I thought a burglar would politely come through the door, but there was no way for me to get out of the house without going back down to the main floor. I tiptoed out of the bedroom and held my breath as I eased into Chris and Amie's room.

"Please, please, please," I mouthed while pulling up the bed skirt.

Jackpot. Amie had always kept a metal baseball bat underneath her side of the bed for protection when Chris was at away games.

Chris had teased her relentlessly about it.

"What's your plan?" he'd asked with a grin. "Close-quarters combat so you can whack him in the head?"

But the bat had remained in place.

I gripped it tight in my hands and took a deep breath before starting down the stairs. The top step creaked when weight was put on it, so I skipped that one, almost pitching forward when the bat just about swung into the wall.

I winced, but nothing happened. I took a few more steps.

Whoever was in the house was rummaging through some drawers in the kitchen, and my fingers held that bat with a death grip.

Now I was just pissed. Who the *hell* thought they could break in here and take my friends' stuff?

In my head, I was Lara Croft. I was Buffy. I was Wonder Woman. And I'd absolutely fuck someone up if they tried to take a single thing from this house.

The last few steps had an open railing, so there was no hiding my presence once I cleared those.

I'd jump down.

Yell.

Swing.

Then *keep* swinging.

The bottom steps came closer, and I pinched my eyes shut.

Go, I yelled in my head.

With a roar fit for an Amazon queen, I charged down the steps.

"What the bloody fuck?" I heard him yell.

Bloody.

British.

British accent.

It was the accent that messed up my glorious warrior queen entrance, because I'd already started to swing the bat when my toe caught on the edge of the stairs, and I pitched forward.

The bat lodged itself in the drywall, and I tumbled forward, landing on my ass on the floor, where I found myself staring up into the face of one Liam Davies.

And the asshole was smiling.

"My goodness, that was entertaining." He clucked his tongue. "What were you gonna do? Bash my head in? I'm glad your aim is as bad as your entry."

"Fuck off," I snapped, groaning when I tried to roll to my feet. "*Ouch.*"

The smile melted off his face. "You all right?"

"No." My ass would be sore for a week, and that was *nothing* compared with the bruising my ego had just taken. "What are you doing here?"

"I've always had a key to their house. No one told me I had to give it back."

"Maybe because you stormed out of the office before we could tell you *anything.*"

I raked a hand through my hair and grimaced when I realized the bat was still stuck in the wall. Liam sighed, holding his hand out to help me up. I smacked it away and got up without his help, thank you very much. My entire body screamed in protest.

"Why are you using the key now? Have you come here before?"

He glanced around, eyes darkening. "No."

I rubbed my tailbone and winced. No crab walking for me for a few days.

"Cleaner in here than I thought it would be," he said.

"Rosa hired a cleaning crew to come in and pick up everything so that I didn't have to do it."

He grunted. "Lady from across the street? With the white hair and the scary eyebrows?"

I rolled my eyes. "They're not scary, but yes."

"She watches the girl for you."

With a tilt of my head, I studied him before answering. "You can't even say her name."

"What a load of bollocks! Yes, I can."

"Then do it." I crossed my arms and faced him fully. "Look me in the eye and say her name."

Liam sighed and did that thing with his face where he pretended to glare but was really just stalling. "This is ridiculous."

"It's quite easy, actually. If you feel so guilty about betraying your friends' final wishes that you can't even say her name, then I'm glad you're walking away." My face was hot, my tone loud and harsh. "Go. Whatever you're doing here, be done with it."

His jaw clenched. "You used to be nicer to me, Valentine."

"Yeah, well, I've changed the last month. I no longer care if you like me or not." I held his gaze unflinchingly. "What are you doing here?"

"Dropping off the shit from his locker. Couldn't handle looking at it, and it's been in my trunk for a few days. Got sick of hearing it rattle around back there."

My attention darted to the box on the island. "What's in there?"

"Fuck if I know. I shoved it in there and taped it up. Last thing I want to do is go through someone's private shit."

I walked over to the box and started peeling back the folded edges.

"Oy!" he barked. "I want no part of this. You have some morbid curiosity, indulge it when I'm gone, yeah?"

There was a Post-it on the counter, and a pen. That's what he'd been looking for in the drawers. On the note, he'd messily scrawled a message: *Chris's locker shit. Do whatever you want with it.*

I shook my head slowly.

Liam was no different from the kids my mom saw in her office every single day. When I took a pause and pushed past my anger toward him, it was easier to filter through the way he was acting and see the messy, tangled roots.

He was a big man with big feelings that he wanted nothing to do with.

It wasn't my job to usher him through that. But I felt guilt all the same. I peeked up at him through my lashes, and he was still studying the house with a tired look on his face.

That was the second thing I noticed, now that I wasn't trying to decapitate him or accidentally give myself a concussion.

Liam looked like absolute hell. Like he'd barely slept in days.

I took my hands away from the box, and when he noticed the movement, his big frame relaxed.

My chest ached as I fought with my warring instincts about how to handle this man. It was the bags under his eyes. The complete exhaustion stamped across his rugged features.

"Mira would love to see you," I said quietly. "I know she liked you."

"Yeah, well, kids have shit taste sometimes."

I simply stared at him for a moment, until he broke eye contact and looked at the floor.

"I am trying, Liam." I raised my shoulders and let them fall helplessly. "I am *trying*, because that's what they wanted. It matters that this is what they wanted. Just . . . come and see her sometimes. Hang out with her. Talk to her about her dad. I'm not asking you to split custody or move into the house. I'm asking you to just try."

His jaw was so tight, his eyes unrelenting.

"It's not that simple," he said quietly. "You can't do something like this by halves, and I have nothing to give her. Not any of the things she needs."

"It *is* simple," I told him. "You're the one complicating it. And if you're too chickenshit to come hang out with a little girl who misses her dad, then I don't know what to tell you." I left the box where it was and stepped around the island. He braced for impact, even though I had no weapon this time. "I'll tell you this, though. Don't send me a penny. I don't want your money."

"Don't be stubborn. I can help."

I laughed. "'Don't be stubborn,' he says." I shook my head. He could hardly look me in the eye. "Go home, Liam."

I'd be damned if I stood there again and watched him storm out.

I brushed past him, and when my shoulder bumped against his, he rocked back on his heels, emitting a harsh puff of air.

"Lock up before you leave," I told him. "And leave the key on the counter. This house is for family."

Chapter Seven

LIAM

To be perfectly clear, I did not believe in ghosts.

Even when I was young, I thought Casper was a wanker who needed to get a life. Haunted houses were a giant racket. And the idea that no one else figured out that the little kid in that stupid movie could see dead people was completely idiotic.

However . . . none of that explained the dream. The one that left me staring at my ceiling for hours, my hand over my wildly racing heart.

The night I came home from Chris's house—where I'd left that bloody box sitting in the middle of the island, and a hole in the wall from the bat Zoe had swung at my head—he appeared in a dream.

Wasn't really a dream, I suppose. More like a cloudy memory that came to me in my sleep. Something I'd forgotten.

Early in our Denver years—Chris already settled with Amie and me happily not settled with anyone—we'd talked about what the rest of our careers might look like.

"I'll play 'til they drag me off the field," I told him.

We were sitting in the front row on the fifty-yard line, drinking beers in the dark stadium.

"No, you won't," he said.

He was so fucking smug, always thinking he knew me best.

I gave him a look. "What makes you say that?"

"Because I know you."

"Fuck off."

He laughed. The absolute git. He had a big smile, wide and happy, that showed all his straight, white, perfectly American teeth. "Mark my words, Liam. You play because it's your favorite outlet, and I get that. I get all the reasons you chose this game over that other one," he drawled.

I rolled my eyes and took a drag of my beer.

"You play because of the brotherhood," he continued. "You take care of your teammates like they're your family."

My only response was to shift in my seat. I didn't remember doing that in real life, but in my dream, his words were starting to make me uncomfortable.

"You say you don't want a family—"

"I *don't*," I interrupted.

Chris ignored me. "You'll want to take care of them too. Once you find the right one."

This, unfortunately, is where the memory changed into something else.

I tried to get out of the seat, tried to walk away. But my legs were useless. I couldn't move, no matter how hard I tried.

"You'll take care of mine, won't you?" he asked.

Then his hand, big and strong and relentless, gripped my arm. His eyes seared straight into my bleeding soul.

"Won't you?" he asked again.

That's when I woke with a startled gasp, which dragged my mind into the here and now. The dark room where I lay in my bed. The sheets were twisted around my legs, like I'd thrashed myself awake. My hands shook a little bit as I swiped them over my face, and the skin on my back was damp with sweat when I sat up in bed and took a few deep breaths.

"Fuck," I sighed.

I never did get back to sleep.

Instead, I laced up my trainers, tugged on some athletic shorts and a sweatshirt, and went for a predawn run in my neighborhood, needing the relentless pounding of my feet against the pavement over a sterile gym.

April in Colorado was always a gamble when it came to the weather. We'd gotten snow the week before, one last grasping attempt from winter as it ushered itself out. But it had melted almost immediately. This morning, the skies were still, but it smelled like rain as I punished my body for that stupid dream I couldn't shake.

My lungs heaved the farther I ran, and instead of seeing Chris's face, I saw Mira's.

I saw Zoe's when she'd chased me down in that parking lot.

When she'd charged down the steps, ready to decapitate me because she thought I was a burglar pilfering from her friends' house.

And again when she'd told me to leave the key behind.

It's for family, she'd said. Like she hadn't just twisted the proverbial knife straight in between my shoulder blades. It was a wound that I'd earned. I couldn't be mad at her for doing it, no matter how badly I wanted to be.

On the final stretch of my run, with my house in view, I sprinted. My muscles screamed in protest. My lungs bellowed from the effort to breathe.

You'll take care of mine, won't you?

The sound of my feet as I slowed to a stop, the slap, slap, slap against the pavement, wasn't enough to drown out the memory of his voice.

He'd never said that to me in real life. Not once.

I bent over, hands on my knees, as I tried to catch my breath.

I couldn't. It simply wasn't there.

Because either my brain had planted that guilty message after I'd drifted off to sleep, or my asshole best friend had just hijacked my dreams to remind me what a selfish git I was.

I stood, hands on my hips, and stared up at the house where I'd lived for twelve years. I'd bought it with money from my rookie contract. It wasn't big; it wasn't flashy. It was fine for me.

The bigger house I'd purchased was for Mum, her husband, and my two half sisters, who at the time were still young enough to live at home.

That was a home for a family.

Mine was just a house. It had walls. Nice-size rooms and a pool in a private backyard where no one could watch me do my laps.

Chris and Amie's house had been a home too. I liked being there. Always felt at ease when I walked through the door.

Pinching the bridge of my nose, I had to clarify that statement.

Had felt at ease.

"Fuck," I muttered under my breath.

I thought about calling my mum for advice, but I bloody well knew what she'd tell me. With an ocean between us, I could practically hear her voice.

Liam Andrew Davies, you apologize to that young lady. You apologize, and then you fix it, because the only apology that matters is the one that comes with changed behavior.

"Fuck," I said, just a bit louder.

"Morning, Liam," my neighbor Bill called out as he wheeled his trash bin to the street.

"Sorry, Bill."

He smiled. "Used to it by now, buddy."

I nodded, then sighed as I went to get my own bin.

Two hours later, freshly showered and so uncomfortable I wanted to tear my skin off, I pulled into Zoe fucking Valentine's driveway.

I stared at the house for ten long minutes before I could get out of the car.

Her house looked like something I'd find outside London. The iron fence, the Tudor styling, the well-tended plants and flowers she'd cultivated to make it look sweet and friendly.

All in all, it was like its owner.

Except when she was facing me, of course.

I'd been uniquely talented in bringing out Zoe's hidden feisty side. Amie had constantly told me how strange it was that Zoe was nice to everyone. Except me.

I shoved open my door with a grimace, because ever since the moment I'd met her and couldn't keep my stupid mouth shut about the utter arse she was marrying, she hadn't been sweet and friendly with me.

There was something about her. I'd never done a good job of defining it in my head. Likely because she defied any sort of label my feeble brain was able to give her.

I wanted to be close to her. Wanted to see her smile.

And I wanted to push her as far away from me as humanly possible, because proximity to Zoe Valentine was dangerous.

It had felt like a mockery, the ring on her finger that first night, because for the first time in my life, I'd met a woman who knocked the breath from my lungs when she smiled.

I hated that she was taken. I hated that she made me feel that way. And I hated even more that she was marrying some idiot who needed to be punched about as badly as anyone I'd ever met.

Naturally, that meant I was a dick to her every single time I saw her. Just to make sure the lines between us were clear.

And now?

Now I was strolling up to her door before it was polite to drop by someone's house, and there was every fucking chance she'd slap me across the face before accepting an apology.

I didn't even know what my plan was. Didn't know what I was going to say. But somehow I knew that if I didn't say something, Chris and his big smile and his annoying ghost ass would keep showing up in my dreams.

He'd haunt me, the fucker, and be bloody cheerful about it, if I had to guess.

I let out a slow breath and walked up to the front door.

Before I even knocked, I heard Mira crying.

Loudly.

I pinched my eyes shut and started to turn around.

"Good morning."

At the dry tone, I looked over my shoulder.

The neighbor with the scary eyebrows was walking her tiny little dog. And while he took a shit on the grass, she watched me with one of those brows quirked up and a poo bag waiting in her hand.

"Going somewhere?" she asked.

"What business is it of yours?"

She barked out an amused laugh. "Despite all evidence as to why I shouldn't, I like you, Liam."

"You really shouldn't."

"Believe me, I know." She bent over and picked up her dog's waste, then tied a knot in the bag. Her animal stared me down, scratching the grass behind him. I stared him down right back and made a growling noise in the back of my throat, baring my teeth while I did. Rosa laughed outright when her dog pricked up his ears, like he was readying to charge me. "Oh, calm down, Peanut. He's harmless."

"Am I?" I drawled.

Her eyes were shrewd. "No, I suppose you're not. But that's why you're here, isn't it?"

Bloody know-it-all neighbors.

She started down the sidewalk. "I'll make sure to tell Zoe I saw you, if you're about to leave."

I set my hands on my hips, but she'd already given me her back.

"Fuck," I whispered.

The screaming had intensified, but I turned back toward the door, pressed the doorbell, and tucked my hands behind my back. Inside the house, I heard Zoe's attempt to soothe Mira.

Unsuccessfully.

And the screaming came closer.

I rubbed at the bridge of my nose, dropping my hand just as she opened the door.

Zoe had not been awake as long as I had, given she was still in her pajamas, her hair wild and untamed around her face.

Her legs were bare and tan, covered only by small black sleep shorts. And her face was slack with shock at the sight of me.

Behind her in the family room, Mira continued to scream. I couldn't see her, but I'd bet the entire neighborhood could hear the sounds coming from that child's mouth.

"I'll be right here on the porch, Mirabelle," she said. There was a slight pause in the crying, even though Mira didn't fully stop. "And I promise you we'll find Froggy today, okay?"

The wailing intensified, and Zoe stepped out onto the front porch so she could close the door behind her. She crossed her arms tightly over her chest, which I did *not* stare at, because it didn't matter if she was wearing a bra behind the black sleep shirt, and I wasn't a fucking pervert.

"What are you doing here?" she asked.

It wasn't said harshly. She wasn't glaring. And somehow that made it all so much worse.

No, Zoe was exhausted. That much was obvious.

"You look tired."

The words tumbled out before I could stop them, and when her eyes narrowed in annoyance, I knew I'd fucking stepped in it.

"Do I? Maybe it's because we were up half the night, and I don't sleep much anyway these days, because I suddenly found myself a single mom to a child who didn't come with an instruction manual, you pompous prick." She tilted her head, and that gaze she aimed in my direction was like a fucking weapon. She could level cities with those eyes, and I fought the instinct to cover my balls. "Is that why *you* look so well rested, Liam?"

I held up my hands. "I'm sorry."

She tightened her arms and gazed down at the ground. I could breathe a bit easier when she did. I'd never liked the way my chest felt when Zoe Valentine looked at me.

71

"For what I said just now," I continued. "And for not stepping up to help you."

Her face snapped up, her gaze snagging on mine. But she didn't speak.

The words were hard to force out, but I kept Chris's face in the forefront of my mind while I did. "I don't want to fight with you. I don't want to make this worse than it is, and it's already fucking awful."

She licked her lips, and I also tried not to stare when she did that.

Zoe had pretty lips. Soft and pink and the perfect frame for her smile. Not that she ever smiled at me anymore.

Not that I'd given her a reason to.

"Liam," she said with a sigh, "what do you want?"

My brow furrowed. "To apologize."

She searched my face before she spoke again. "Right, but beyond that. Do you need anything from me?"

"No."

"Okay. Because I have nothing in my emotional tank for you right now." She gestured to the house, where the sound of Mira crying had only slightly abated. "She gets everything I have. I can't coddle you. I can't make you feel better about . . . whatever this is." Then she lifted her shoulders in a helpless shrug. "So you're forgiven. For telling me I look like shit—"

"That's not what I said."

She gave me a warning look.

Again, I held up my hands. "Fine."

"I don't know if I can forgive you yet for not helping, though," she said. "Maybe in time, I will."

My jaw clenched, and I stared down at the concrete of her front porch. "Fair enough," I ground out.

The screaming intensified until it reached a sharp crescendo, and Zoe let out a ragged sigh. When I glanced up, she had her eyes squeezed shut and a hand covering her mouth. As she dropped it, I saw a warning tremble of her chin.

Oh no.

No.

A tear slipped down her cheek.

"Shit," I mumbled. "Please don't cry," I begged.

She sucked in a breath. "I can't help it," she said, her voice thick with tears. "I'm so, so tired." Another tear slipped out.

Briefly, I raised a hand to . . . I wasn't sure. So I scratched the back of my neck.

She covered her face with both hands, and her shoulders shook. "You are the last person I want to cry in front of, trust me."

My hand reached out again, and I patted her shoulder. Awkwardly. Just a few short taps.

"There, there. It'll be . . . it'll be fine."

She dropped her hands to stare incredulously. "Seriously?"

"Well, I'm assuming you don't want me to hug you," I said, feeling slightly affronted.

"No." She scrubbed her face again. "I'd cry more if you did."

"Then I definitely won't."

Zoe exhaled a sound that might have been a laugh under any other circumstance. Her eyes were slightly red and her cheeks pink. Her hair was a mess. There really were dark circles under her eyes, the exhaustion stamped all over her face. And somehow, quite impossibly, she was still so beautiful that I could hardly look at her.

I hated it.

"I don't know how people do this alone," she said. "It's so hard."

The words came out so quietly, almost like she'd never meant to admit them aloud.

And the second I heard them, I remembered my mum crying over a pot of mashed potatoes shortly after we left my dad. We'd eaten potatoes cooked a dozen different ways in those first couple of months. Because they were cheap, and they were all she could afford.

I don't know how to do this, she'd said.

She'd done it, of course. Because my mum was the strongest woman I'd ever met. And she'd done it because she had to.

My chest caved in, and I couldn't stop it. It wasn't even bricks tumbling out of place or a crack in the foundation.

Something, a guard or a wall or a barrier, just . . . poof! Disappeared. I knew it would build itself back up again eventually, because it always did. But in that moment, I couldn't feel anything holding me back from wanting to be whatever she needed me to be.

"I'll help," I heard myself say.

"What?" she whispered.

Fuck. *Fuck*. What had I done?

Panic had me talking fast, my voice hard and harsh.

"I'm terrible when kids cry, and I'll be rubbish at it, and I guarantee you'll regret ever putting me in charge of her."

Hope filled Zoe's eyes, and fucking hell, it tore my heart into a million pieces.

"Really?"

"I'm not joking—you'll regret it. Probably tomorrow. I already do."

She let out a shaky exhale, almost like a laugh. "You'll help? Like, really, physically help?"

I shifted uncomfortably. "Can't right now. I have to go meet with Coach and then run some drills with the rookies because they're awful. But . . . yeah, I'll help."

Zoe's lips curved into a tentative smile. My chest cranked tight at the sight of it.

"Okay. Maybe . . . call me later, and we'll figure something out?"

Fuck. Ing. Hell.

What had I done?

There was no taking it back. Not when it had transformed her in an instant.

Even as rampant anxiety dug its icy claws into my stomach and yanked, I knew I wouldn't take it back.

I managed a jerky nod and quickly strode to my vehicle. Zoe's eyes burned into my back the entire way. In the background, there was no escaping the sound of my friends' daughter, bawling her bloody eyes out over a stuffed frog.

You'll take care of my family, won't you?

"You better not show up in my dreams tonight, you asshole," I said as I punched the ignition button. "I'll never forgive you if you do."

Chapter Eight

ZOE

For the first time since all this had started, I was mentally prepared to see Liam.

What a *nice* change of pace.

No ambush in the lawyer's office, no burglary scare or swinging bat, and no early-morning surprise visit on my doorstep when I wasn't wearing a bra.

This time, I was ready.

Rosa was with Mira, and I was waiting in the kitchen next door with a solid plan and an impressive stack of binders.

They were color-coded and had matching tabs.

I stood up to pace the room, sliding a nervous hand down the front of my shirt. It was one of my favorites, a V-neck with flowy sleeves and a pattern of tiny purple and blue flowers. I'd also smoothed my hair . . . sort of.

When I heard his vehicle pull into the driveway, I felt a flurry of nerves take flight in the pit of my stomach. I didn't need to usher him in like a guest, but when there was a soft knock on the front door, I winced.

I had told him the house was only for family. And, apparently, Liam's new thing was listening to me.

I'd never get over the shock.

Determined to start this off on the right foot, I managed a polite smile when I pulled the door open. "Hey," I said softly. "Thanks for coming."

Instead of answering, he simply gave me a thorough once-over—his eyes trailing from the top of my head to the tips of my toes—and then walked into the house with a curt nod.

Something about the way Liam studied me was unnerving. It always had been. And because this time would be different, I decided to tell him.

"I never know what you're thinking when you look at me like that."

Because I was walking behind him, the only noticeable sign that he'd heard me was the slight stiffening of his broad back.

"I'm not sure you want to know, Valentine."

I sighed. "I do have a name."

"Isn't Valentine one of them?" He took a seat at one of the stools next to the island, folded his hands on the counter, and gave me an expectant look. "Everyone uses last names on the team."

"If we start off with that kind of dynamic here, we're in big trouble."

Liam quirked an eyebrow. "How so? I quite like the team atmosphere. I'd trust all of them with my life. Except the stupid rookies. Don't know them well enough yet."

There were always a few kids in every class who thought they knew better than the teacher. It was so easy to imagine Liam as one of those smart alecks. Someone who argued. Someone who tiptoed over the line whenever he could manage it.

Instead of taking a seat, I leaned up against the edge of the counter and studied his face, trying to undo him in the same way he always undid me.

But he met my stare unflinchingly.

And that was unnerving too.

"Trust them with your life?" I asked. "That's a bold statement."

"Accurate, though." He glanced around the house. "I wouldn't be here if Chris hadn't felt the same, yeah?"

Ten points to the grouch.

I lifted my brows in brief concession. "Fair enough. But no ass slapping and no yelling, because I know you guys do that too."

His lips twitched, and oh, I swear he almost smiled. "I'm trying very hard not to make an inappropriate comment about ass slaps, Valentine."

"I appreciate your restraint."

"Figured you would. That's what I'm known for. My epic restraint."

My lips fought a smile. "What changed your mind?" I asked. "I was not expecting you yesterday."

"That freckle-faced asshole showed up in my dream," he said.

"Chris?"

Liam's chin lifted in a sharp jerk. "Remembering something we talked about a long time ago. Before I'd met you, even." He swallowed. "When I came to your place to apologize, I didn't . . . I wasn't planning on helping, if I'm being honest."

"I think we *have* to be honest, if we're going to do this," I told him.

"No bullshit. There's no place for it."

I picked at one of my nails and nodded in agreement. "No bullshit."

Liam glanced back into the family room. "Where's the kid?"

"At my place with Rosa. I wasn't sure how this first meeting would go, and she's already been through enough. I don't want her witnessing any arguments about who's going to take care of her."

With fascination, I watched the tips of his cheekbones turn the slightest shade of pink.

Was he embarrassed?

"How's she doing?" he asked, voice a low, rough rumble. "Does she, you know, ask for them?"

"Sometimes." I rolled my neck but couldn't stretch it far enough to feel it pop. Too much tension in my entire body for that. "Less the last couple weeks."

His face was unreadable. "Suppose that's good."

Was it? I rubbed the side of my neck; the muscles underneath my skin were hard as rocks.

"Neck problems?" he asked, his eyes trained on my hand.

"Just a little tense."

He made a grunting noise. "You should get someone to work on that."

"That also a team bonding thing?" I asked.

Liam rolled his eyes. "Yes. I give all my teammates massages."

I laughed.

When I did, his eyes warmed. Just a little. Then he looked away.

"Right," he said before clearing his throat. "I'll move in here if you're okay with it. I'm assuming we need to talk to the lawyer about all this."

"You'll sell your house?" I asked.

"It's just a house. The kid should be able to be here if she wants. This was her home."

We'd been here only a few times. I took a deep breath. "No bullshit, right?"

"That's my preference, yeah."

"She'll go into their room and look for them," I told him unflinchingly. "That's what she does when we come here. She didn't cry last time, but you should prepare yourself for when it happens."

His jaw clenched. "Noted."

"I'm supposed to be gone next weekend. Just for two nights. Rosa was going to watch her for me."

Liam's eyebrow arched slowly. "Getaway with the boyfriend?"

My cheeks flushed hot. "My mom is having an outpatient procedure, and I promised I'd be there to drive her home and make sure she's okay afterward. And . . . there's no more boyfriend, not that it's any of your business."

He made a low humming sound that lifted the little hairs on the back of my neck. "He wasn't around long."

"Tyler was a nice guy," I told him. "But then the accident happened. And then we found out about Mira . . ." My voice trailed off. "It was a bit too much to put on a new relationship."

"He bailed?" Liam asked.

It took everything in me not to drop his shocked gaze. Slowly, I nodded. "It was a pretty mutual decision, but yeah. And I can't blame him."

"What an absolute git."

For a moment, I couldn't do anything but stare.

Then I burst out laughing.

Liam's face was full of confusion at first.

Then I laughed even harder.

"You're serious," I managed through my helpless laughter. Tears sprang to the edges of my eyes, and I wiped them away. "Oh gawd, you are actually serious right now. You giant, raging *hypocrite*."

He scoffed, crossing his big arms over his big chest. "It's not funny. I had perfectly valid reasons for what I did."

"Liam, you stormed out of the lawyer's office like a child when you found out," I said, slowly getting ahold of myself. The laughter had felt good, though. Some of the tension had bled from my frame. "Wow. It's been a while since I've laughed that hard. Thank you for that, truly."

"Glad to be of service," he ground out.

"You gonna tell me all those valid reasons?" I asked.

"Maybe another day," he answered evenly.

I snorted. "That's what I thought."

"Back to the subject at hand. You're leaving for a thing. Drop the kid off here, and we'll be just fine."

"I'm not just going to drop her off. You have to see her a couple times before you spend an entire weekend with her." I pointed to the binders. "You can read through those in the meantime; they'll help."

He tugged at one of the binders sitting in the middle of the island, his face going slack with shock when he opened the first one. "Absolutely bloody not."

"What?"

He gave me an incredulous look. "You've got a color-coded schedule in here. I'm surprised you don't time it out when she takes a piss."

"It's *helpful*. Believe me, I wish I would've had one at the beginning."

"I don't need one. We'll crack on just fine."

"Liam, I don't think you—"

He held up a hand. "I've done a lot of big transitions in my life, Valentine. Never had a pretty rainbow-colored binder for a single fucking one, and it all turned out just fine. Part of life is having to stumble through the shit when you can't see the outcome. You don't know how messy it'll get, and you don't always have a perfect plan."

Slowly, he closed the binder and pushed it back in my direction along with the others.

I narrowed my eyes. He narrowed his right back.

"You can take those back with you, thank you very much."

"No bullshit, right?" I asked.

He sighed.

"You want me to say what I'm thinking at any given time? Just so you can be aware of my emotional state?"

His face didn't so much as budge, but there was an anticipatory gleam in his eyes.

"You are impossible," I said slowly, making sure I enunciated every syllable. "And I look forward to the end of the weekend, when you admit that I'm right."

"I'd rather shove splints up my fingernails."

Instead of rising to the bait, I smiled. "I'll sharpen them before I get home."

He stood. "That it? I can move my stuff in now?"

I rubbed at my forehead. Was I getting another headache? "I guess. I'll call the lawyer and let him know about the house." I paused. "We still have a lot to figure out, Liam."

"Don't overthink it, Valentine." He took a few steps nearer, and if we'd been standing closer, I would've had to tilt my chin up to look him in the face. He was so tall. And big. And somehow those two things were the least intimidating aspects about him. "I'll stay here, help where I can. No need to bug the scary neighbor. It'll be fine."

"Fine? The last month, you've done everything in your power to avoid me, and now you think you can waltz in and take care of a two-and-a-half-year-old without any instruction?"

"I've got friends with kids. Little shits always love me."

Honestly, my jaw was about two inches off the floor.

"It's amazing because you *look* like the same Liam," I said, leaning back to study his face. "But you must be a clone or something." Then I tapped my chin. "That's not a logical answer either, because why would anyone want to have two of you walking around this earth unchecked?"

He sighed again. "We done here?"

"No."

Liam crossed his arms. The biceps bulged in a way that I did not appreciate. "What, then?"

What, then? I had a list of concerns the length of my arm.

First, and the one I couldn't say out loud, was: *How the hell are we supposed to coexist and coparent without killing each other?* I could hardly have a single conversation with him without becoming overtaken by vivid fantasies of inflicting some sort of violence on his big, grumpy person.

But I decided to start with the most obvious.

"What about the fall? I have to go back to work. And the regular season starts in August."

He gave me a look. "Right now, we're taking this one week at a time. We'll get it figured out."

"You really think it's that simple?" I asked him. Maybe . . . maybe he was a little bit off his rocker, and I just hadn't noticed yet.

"I'll watch her next weekend, and we'll talk again when you get back. It's just one pint-size little girl. How hard can it be?"

Chapter Nine

LIAM

I was fourteen the first time I lined up on a field to play American football. My mum had remarried by that point, and decent bloke that he was, Nigel suggested we find a league where I could learn how to play properly, if that's what I wanted.

And I did.

He didn't press as to why I wanted to play that sport; maybe my mum had told him not to ask.

They knew soccer—the real football where I was from—would never serve as a proper outlet for all that shit I kept bottled up all the time.

They didn't press me on that either. Trying to talk through any of the things I felt bubbling under the surface only served to make me angrier, because it was hard to find the right words for the things I felt. Mainly the things I didn't want to be feeling.

But on the field, I could let them go.

The first time I landed a clean tackle, on a mouthy little shit of a running back, I felt the most surreal sort of high.

He was fast. Faster than most of the guys on my team. But he wasn't faster than me. After chasing him down for thirty yards, I tackled him ten yards shy of the end zone and felt a rush of head-spinning euphoria that was completely foreign.

An addiction was born.

No matter how hard I had to work to keep playing the sport, that addiction never faded.

No one pushed me to play like my dad, reminded me where I came from, whom I came from.

There were no coaches asking me if I remembered the time my dad's team got promoted to the Premier League, asking me if he had taught me the things I knew, asking me if I had gotten my work ethic from the man who shared my face and build and speed.

They didn't ask me anything. I was just me.

It was freedom.

And across the pond, I found a family in locker rooms, along with the thing I was meant to do.

But never once had I imagined that the sport I loved, which brought me sanity and friends and a life, would have me staring down into the face of a little girl who was easily a thousand times more stubborn than I'd ever fucking thought possible.

"Come on," I coaxed. "Doesn't this look delicious?"

I swear on my ancestors' graves, she narrowed her eyes before giving me an emphatic no.

"It's macaroni and cheese, Mira. Every child in the known universe loves this orange bullshit."

"You make it wrong," she said.

My mouth fell open. "I did not."

She rolled her lips between her teeth and stared me down.

I scratched the side of my face and glanced over at the box. I'd gotten the *good* kind. The shells with the creamy shit. And maybe that was my error.

Like I could help it that Zoe got the processed powder crap.

I held the spoon out, contemplating airplane sounds and whether I'd need to create a song and fucking dance to get her to eat. She clamped her mouth shut and sat back in the chair.

Then she shook her head.

I sighed, pulling the spoon back and settling it in the bowl.

I crossed my arms over my chest and returned the staredown. "You need to eat something."

She shook her head. Emphatically. "No. Not hungry."

"It's been four hours since she dropped you off, and if you starve under my care, she will never, ever let me live it down." I pointed to the orange-coated noodles. "You have to try *something*."

With a weary hand, I scrubbed the bottom half of my face. I needed a shave. I needed some sleep. And I needed Mira to eat some bloody food.

Then she pointed at the counter. "I have a doughnut?"

"Of course you know what that box is," I muttered. "No doughnuts until you eat something real, little bit."

She pushed her lip out in a pout.

When I'd arrived that morning, Zoe was already at the house, bags of Mira's things neatly lined up in her sky-blue bedroom and a movie running on the large flat-screen TV in the family room.

The little girl in question hardly paid me any mind when I showed up.

Zoe watched me set bags of groceries on the counter and sling my duffel bag onto the floor. "Binders are right there, if you want them," she said.

Sure enough, tucked against the fridge were two of them. Mira's name was printed neatly on the spines. Slowly, I let my gaze wander from those fucking books back to the delicate features of Zoe's face. She was wearing makeup today. Her lashes looked longer and blacker than normal, and my stomach flipped weightlessly at how they deepened the color of her eyes.

Then she arched one of those eyebrows.

It was such a condescending arch too. Something meant to inflame.

That was what Zoe didn't understand about herself. What she'd never understood about how she dealt with me.

All she had to do—all she'd ever had to do—was simply be there.

Stand there.

Look at me.

Breathe.

That's all it took, and I was desperately, impossibly inflamed.

Nowhere to put the energy and nothing I could say to make her hate me less after a decade of contention between us.

I answered her slowly. "I'd rather pluck my eyeballs out than open those."

Contention was better than possibility, though, because the last thing I needed in my life—especially now—was for her to realize her absolute, impossible power over me, the kind she held tight in her fist and didn't even know about.

Zoe rolled her eyes and walked into the family room, where she whispered something to Mira.

The movie was put on pause, and Mira hopped up off the floor and pranced into the kitchen. She stopped when she saw me, and I tried my best to soften my face. I didn't crouch down, because I always hated it when adults made little kids hug them or high-five them or do stupid shit when they might be uncomfortable.

"Hey, Mira," I said. "You remember me?"

Carefully, she nodded. Then she took a few steps out from behind Zoe.

"You remember my name?"

Mira's hair was messy and wild, and she was still wearing cotton pajamas printed with little ducks in rain boots. She took another step and motioned me closer with her hand.

Zoe started chewing on her thumbnail, her nerves clear, as I bent my knees and put my hands on the tops of my thighs to lean closer.

Mira reached her hand up and pinched my nose. Hard.

I made a growling sound, deep in my chest, and she giggled.

"Uncle Liam," she said, then honked my nose again.

I tweaked one of her curls. "That's right."

From the moment Mira was born, Chris had insisted on the unofficial family moniker. No matter how much I'd argued it, she'd called me Uncle Liam since she was able to form the words. And of course Chris and Amie had popped out a precocious little shit of a child, so she'd been doing it for at least a year.

As I straightened back to my full height and Zoe let out a quiet sigh of relief, Mira stepped forward again and wrapped her arms around my leg.

It was like someone had punched a ragged hole right through my chest. All the skin and bone and muscles—designed to protect everything inside—they folded like wet paper. That's how it felt when those skinny little arms were wrapped around my leg.

Maybe a better man would've leaned down to pick her up.

Maybe a softer man who understood how all this worked.

But with Zoe's watchful golden eyes aimed straight at me, all I could manage was a soft pat on the top of Mira's head.

I had the creeping sensation that if I picked her up, if I gave her a proper hug, I'd fucking cry or something, and there was no way I was letting Miss Valentine get the satisfaction of seeing it.

The brick wall inside my chest was too high, too fortified after so many years, and already firmly back in place now that I shared space with her. It wouldn't come crumbling down again that easily.

Zoe crouched down for the hug I hadn't given, and she reminded Mira that I was going to take care of her and that Rosa was right across the street.

Like I'd call that woman for help. She terrified me.

"You coming back soon?" Mira asked. Her eyes were wide, and I had to look away.

Zoe nodded. "Very soon. I'll only be gone for two sleeps." She tapped Mira's nose. "You'll have so much fun with Uncle Liam, okay?" Then she leaned in for a dramatic whisper that I was meant to hear. "Make him watch *Moana* a lot; I think he'll love it."

I rolled my eyes but fought a smile when Mira giggled happily.

"I put the car seat in the garage," Zoe told me as she stood. "Do you want me to show you how to hook it in?"

"I can figure it out."

For a moment, she stared me down. "I highly doubt that, but okay. Rosa's number is on the fridge. She's around all weekend." She gave me a look. "Call her if you need help. Please."

I set my hands on my hips. "It's two days, Valentine. I can handle it."

I'd uttered those words before I knew.

Before I knew that saying no to a doughnut could cause weeping and wailing.

Before I knew that an entire day could pass in which she refused to eat any of the food I made for her.

Cold macaroni and cheese ended up being my meal for the afternoon, which I ate sitting on the deck and watching her blow bubbles. Doughnut crumbs still dotted her cheeks.

"You do it," she said, then shoved the bottle of bubbles at me. She'd spilled half the contents already, and the outside of the bottle was coated with a soapy film.

I took it from her hand and dipped the wand inside. Before waving it gently through the air, I paused to study the excitement on her face.

All day, I'd searched for some hint that she desperately missed her parents. And I couldn't see a shred of any such thing.

Yeah, she was as stubborn as a fucking mule, but she was happy. She bounced on the balls of her toes, her eyes gleaming while she waited for me to comply with her request.

A knot formed in my throat when I realized just how simple life was for her right now.

I pulled the wand through the air, and she chased the bubbles as she laughed.

No complications existed for her. All the things that had been thrown at Zoe and me over the last month and a half simply weren't there. Because she had all the things she needed, at least in her mind.

Someone to feed her. Someone to play with her. Someone to be there in the middle of the night.

Someone to make her feel safe.

That brick wall inside me quavered ominously, and I waited for a crack in the foundation, something unsettling and unsteady. But I took a deep breath, and it held.

Somehow.

After a few more minutes of bubbles, my phone vibrated on the table next to me.

Valentine: How's it going?

Me: She hasn't run away yet.

Valentine: Helpful. Did she eat lunch? She's picky. Which you'd know if you read the binder.

Me: She also hasn't starved. We're doing just fine, thank you very much.

Me: Busy playing bubbles. Can't talk.

Valentine: She should have a bath tonight. It's the first purple tab in the first binder.

Me: It's a bath, Valentine, not defusing a nuclear bomb.

Me: Go take care of your patient. Isn't that why you're there?

Valentine: I cannot tell you how much I hate that I can hear your voice in my head saying every single one of these things.

My lips curved unwittingly, and I was glad she couldn't see it. If I were a different man, I'd have sent her a different response. Something about how she imagined me when I wasn't there. But instead, I set my phone down.

It wasn't until after dinner—I wasn't proud of it, but once my scrambled eggs ended up on the floor with more tears, I let her raid the bags of groceries I'd brought—that I realized the temptation of those fucking binders.

Starting the bath was easy enough.

Turn on the water. Make sure it's not too hot. *Check.*

Pull some clean pajamas off the stack on top of her dresser. *Check.*

Find the baby shampoo and dump it under the running water. *Check.*

Mira was wildly unhelpful as I tried to wrangle her clothes off, which was my first hiccup.

"What in the bloody hell," I muttered when she contorted her body as I tried to pull the shirt over her head. "Hold still."

She set her jaw and gripped the edge of the tub when I tried to wrestle her hair free. "No bath. I need my ducky."

"What ducky?" I asked. Was I sweating? I wiped a hand over my forehead, and holy fuck, I was sweating from trying to get her undressed for a bath. "I don't know where your ducky is. Is he in your room?"

Mira ran across the hall, and I sank against the wall with a deep breath. "Fucking hell," I whispered.

"Where's Ducky?" she yelled.

I rolled over to my knees and sighed before standing up. "Hang on, hang on."

She was yanking clothes out of the bags that Zoe had packed.

"Whoa, okay," I said. "Easy does it. We'll find Ducky."

"Where's Ducky?" she repeated. Her voice had escalated. Tears were building.

"Can we find him after your bath? Your water will get cold soon."

She sucked in a breath. Her chin trembled.

"Oh shit," I muttered.

Then she tipped her head back and let out a massive, ear-shattering wail.

"Right, we'll find the duck now, then."

Except I couldn't.

While Mira sobbed—and truly heartbreaking sobs they were—I ransacked the bags in the bedroom. I tore off the blankets in her crib.

There was a yellow plush duck in the corner. I lifted it up. "This one?"

She cried harder. "No," she wailed. "Bath ducky. I need *bath ducky!*"

That's when I started noticing a theme.

Half her clothes had ducks on them.

On the bookshelf, there were easily a dozen books with *ducks* in their titles.

On her nightstand sat a small duck lamp.

Finally, the seriousness of this current plight hit me. We had ducks for every fucking occasion, and if I didn't find the bath duck, then I was bloody screwed.

I blew out a breath, pinching my eyes shut.

Fuck. I needed to go read that fucking binder.

"Hang on," I told her. "I'll be right back."

Not that Mira cared. She was too busy nursing a broken heart because I didn't know where the fucking bath duck was.

When I got downstairs to the kitchen, I set my hands on my hips and stared down the binders for a while.

I could practically hear Zoe's voice in my head.

I told you so.

My jaw clenched.

Mira's crying ratcheted up a decibel, and I imagined that at this point, all the neighbors could hear too. I'd be damned if scary Rosa sent Zoe a text telling her about the screams emanating from within these four walls.

I plucked the first binder up, my grim mood settling deeper inside my chest when I saw the alphabetized tabs.

Bath routine.

I flipped to it. The first fucking bullet point had me glaring at the page.

- Mira will not take a bath without her bath ducky. I always keep it underneath the sink in the bathroom, because if she sees it before bathtime, she'll try to hide it somewhere in her room so that she can sleep with it.

I slammed the binder shut with a weighty exhale and tossed it onto the counter, then bounded back up the stairs.

In the bathroom, I yanked open the cabinet door.

Salvation came in the form of a small rubber duck wearing a pink rain hat.

"Look what I found!" I yelled.

Her crying lessened, just for a moment, and when I walked across the hall, she sniffled piteously.

"You find it?" she asked, hiccuping around the words.

I held it out. "I found it."

Mira scrambled to her feet and ran across the room, stark naked and red-faced from crying, then plucked the toy from my hand and headed straight for the bathroom.

I exhaled heavily.

Thank fuck.

She played in the tub, and I got only a bit of water in her face when I tried to rinse the shampoo out.

Fifteen minutes later, she was dry and in clean pajamas, her bath duck safely returned to his hiding spot. I turned on *Moana* and caught myself fucking *humming* along when the titular character pushed her boat into the water for her adventure.

Thirty more minutes and I could put Mira to bed. Then I'd collapse face-first into the guest bed down the hall.

My phone vibrated.

When I flipped it over, my mouth dropped open.

Valentine: Thank you for the highlight of my day.

She'd attached a screenshot of a still frame from a small security camera that I hadn't noticed, but when I turned around, I saw it. Mounted on the wall and pointed into the kitchen. Which was how Zoe had a perfect view of me reading the binder before bathtime.

"Fucking hell," I mumbled under my breath.

Mira looked up at me, her eyes big and her hair a bit frizzy after her bath. "Fucking hell," she repeated. Then she honked my nose and giggled.

I laid my head back on the couch and closed my eyes.

Round one to Zoe Valentine.

◆ ◆ ◆

Mira climbed out of her crib before I'd moved from my spot on the guest bed. Quiet as a fucking ninja, that girl was, and I didn't even realize she'd come into the room until I slowly pulled myself to wakefulness and sensed someone staring down at me.

When I cracked my bleary eyes open, she was inches from my face, just fucking *staring* at me.

"Bloody hell, child," I said with a gasp, rolling to my back and settling a hand on my racing heart. "That is some freaky shit. Don't do that again, all right?"

She giggled, clambering up into the bed and flopping down on top of the blankets I'd shoved off before falling asleep.

I'd had not a single dream.

Chris hadn't shown up anywhere, not even with a *Hey, good job on bathtime, dick.*

I'd slept like a rock, hardly moving from the moment I sprawled myself across the mattress.

"I need coffee," I muttered.

She ignored that, turning onto her side with her hands tucked under her face on the pillow.

"I hold you?" Mira asked.

I sat up, wiping a hand over my face. "You hold me? I doubt you can manage it, kid. I'm a pretty big guy, if you haven't noticed."

But I ruffled the top of her hair, and she reached forward to honk my nose.

I growled.

She laughed.

And fuck if it didn't feel good to be able to make her do that.

"What about pancakes?" I asked. "Tell me you like pancakes, because if I don't get some real food in you before she comes home, I will never hear the end of it."

The suggestion was a hit. Mira jumped to her feet and started chanting the word.

I sighed. "I'll take that as a yes."

Except there was no pancake mix in the pantry. And I hadn't bought any.

When I went out to the garage and picked up the car seat, intent on driving us somewhere to find breakfast, I had a brief flash of Zoe's smug smile when I told her I'd be able to figure out how to get the car seat in.

Because I definitely could not figure out how to get the fucking car seat in.

"Shit," I grumbled.

Mira was jumping up and down the front steps while I worked in the driveway. "We get pancakes, Uncle Liam?"

She was still in her pajamas—this time, ducks holding umbrellas—because she refused to change her clothes, and that was not a battle I was fighting before fortification with food and coffee.

"Soon," I told her. "Just need to get this stupid thing in my car; otherwise, we can't go anywhere."

I pulled up an instructional video online and cursed through the entire thing.

"You need a fucking PhD to get this thing in," I mumbled.

I cut my hand trying to wrangle it. My forehead was beaded with sweat. Once I'd attached it to the metal hooks hidden underneath my seat—put in a place where no large person's hands could conceivably reach them—and pulled the straps hard enough, I knew without a doubt that I'd have to cut that damn seat out if we ever needed it moved.

My chest was heaving when I motioned for Mira. "Come on, duck. Time for breakfast."

At the endearment, her eyes damn near glowed with happiness.

"Duck, duck, duck," she chanted, hopping up into my car and settling herself into the seat. "I'm a little duck."

My lips curved into a reluctant smile. "Mira the Duck," I agreed.

We managed breakfast just fine, though I opted for the drive-through because the last thing I wanted to deal with was some intrepid Denver fan snapping our picture and making a big fucking thing about it online.

Chris's accident had been headline news for a solid week. There was no escaping the tragedy of it and how it made the fan base feel after seeing his face on the field for more than a decade.

He was a stalwart on the team. Same as me.

And as I drove back to his house, with his daughter happily munching on pancakes in my back seat, I knew that if the situation were reversed, he would've handled all this shit so much better than I had.

My bones still felt heavy with it all. Like someone had draped extra weights over my shoulders, looped them to my wrists, and hung them around my neck.

And instead of feeling remotely equipped to step into this new reality, I felt quite like someone had shoved me off a one-hundred-foot-high diving board into an angry, churning body of water. Just keeping my head up was a task; so was trying to suck in air while I navigated something new.

Not that kids were new to me. I had a big family back home. Cousins always running around. Because Mum had married Nigel when I was just starting seventh grade, I was tiptoeing into my teenage years by the time she had a few more kids.

I knew how to change a nappy. Knew how to properly warm up a bottle.

But not once had I ever felt comfortable doing any of it.

I loved them just fine. Got along with the new family. Despite that, whenever I visited, I counted down the days until I could leave. I hated walking around that house, walking around a neighborhood where people recognized me, looking, as I did, exactly like my dad—all my pent-up anger coursing under my skin.

Every once in a while, a British tabloid would snap a picture of me out and about in London, and soon enough, Mum would see a small article with a quippy headline about my career in Denver. Inevitably, there'd be a few lines in the piece talking about how I'd never gone to any of my dad's games after my parents divorced. Conjecture and assumptions abounded as to why, but there was always a comment about how I wasn't playing the game he loved.

No. I was playing the game *I* loved. And he could fuck off if it bothered him.

So, yeah, going home always came with a bucketload of tangled feelings that I strove to avoid. It was easier to let my family visit me. Kept things clean. Neat. Simple.

My mum never held that against me. Not any of it. The lack of visits. The articles. That my eyes, my jaw, the dark shade of my hair— they were all from him. But I always felt, just a little bit, that it must be hard to have his face staring back at her.

It was hard to shake the gloom of my thoughts when we got home from breakfast, and I worried that the dark turn in my head had some- how seeped into Mira.

Because the first thing she did when I unhooked her from her car seat was run up the stairs and stand in the open doorway of Chris and Amie's bedroom.

It took me a moment to find her because she'd hardly looked at that room the entire time I was there.

"Duck?" I asked. "Where'd you go?"

Her voice came from the top of the stairs. "Mommy and Daddy here?" she asked.

My stomach bottomed out, landing somewhere by my feet, and I was fairly sure that it had yanked my heart out of place on its way down.

Had Zoe put this one in the binder? Some neatly colored tab that would tell me what I was supposed to say to her when she asked this question?

I scratched the side of my face while I walked up the stairs. "No, little duck," I said gently. "They're not here."

She stared into the room. "They still gone?"

"Yeah." My voice sounded like I'd shredded it with knives. Rusty, broken knives.

Most days, I couldn't figure out what I believed about God or death or the afterlife. What this whole bloody existence in the world even meant.

I went to church on Christmas and Easter, and I was smart enough not to pray before games, because I knew whoever *was* up there didn't give a shit whether we won.

Nevertheless, I couldn't help but feel like meeting Chris, standing there with his kid, was the act of some invisible hand of destiny. That someone had orchestrated the pieces on the chessboard, positioning us exactly where we needed to be. That Zoe moving in next door to them was meant to be. A single other decision made by either of us and who knows what might have happened to Mira?

Maybe that was a divine hand moving us all into place. Maybe it was all fucking chance. I might never know.

But I sure as hell wouldn't be having a theological talk with this little girl until I checked with Valentine.

"Come on, duck." I held out my hand. "Let's go do some bubbles, yeah?"

It was too late, though. Her mood, it seemed, was already ruined by thoughts of her parents.

For the rest of the day, we battled.

She didn't want to eat anything I made for her, except some horrible sugary cereal, which I allowed because I was too fucking tired to worry about it.

She didn't want to play outside, knocking over the bubbles and then crying because we couldn't get them back in the bottle.

She wouldn't nap, and if there was one thing I could not do, it was stand there while a little kid cried their eyes out, stuck in their bed because I'd put them there.

We watched *Moana* two more times, and I'd probably be singing the songs in my sleep before long, but it made her happy, so I didn't care.

By bedtime, I saw the meltdown ramping up in her big eyes.

I was braced for it.

She fought me through putting on clean pajamas. Fought me through brushing her teeth.

Even handing her the stuffed duck in her crib didn't help. She ignored it, tears flowing steadily, her face growing hot and red as she lay there and cried.

"I want Mommy and Daddy," she sobbed.

"I wish they were here too," I told her. I scrubbed a hand over my face, unsure of what to do. She wasn't reaching for me; she simply lay there, her tiny chest heaving with body-racking sobs. "You have no idea how much I wish that, little bit."

She hiccuped through her tears. "Mommy hold you," she said urgently. Mira turned to the duck in her crib and finally clutched it to her chest. "Mommy hold you."

I didn't know what that meant. Whatever it was cleaved my chest in fucking two, because I couldn't do anything about it. I braced my hands on the side of the crib and hung my head down toward my chest, completely out of my fucking depth.

It didn't seem possible that this one room could contain everything she was holding in her tiny body. If I had looked up and seen the walls splitting at the seams, I wouldn't have been surprised. That's how my own flesh and bones felt, absorbing all the sadness swelling between me and Mira.

If I pressed down, it would all come spilling out, like liquid from a sponge that had been sitting in water for too long.

"Mommy hold you," she sobbed again. Her eyes pinched shut, and big, fat tears rolled down her reddened cheeks.

My ribs creaked as I sucked in a breath, my skin getting cold and clammy the longer I stood there—helpless and useless and wrecked down to my core.

"I don't know what that means, duck," I whispered brokenly.

Her arms were wrapped so tightly around the stuffed animal that they shook. My hands, still gripping the frame of the crib, eased off the wood, and I shifted toward the wall so that I could lean some of my weight there.

She was so small, and it was bloody unfair that she had to deal with this when she didn't even know what life had been like before.

Before.

My fist unclenched as I lowered it over her head. The wisps of her curls were soft against my palm as I gently curled it around her skull.

She took a big, shaky breath, her eyes slowly opening in my direction. Her arms still clutched the duck. I slid my hand to the line of her forehead and eased it over her hair again.

"I miss them too," I told her quietly. I ran my hand over her little locks once more, and slowly, her crying subsided as she stared up at me. "They were my best friends, yeah? It's so fucking hard to figure out how to live your life when they're both just . . . gone."

My voice cracked, and Mira hiccuped again, another giant tear spilling over the splotchy skin on her cheek.

Then she inhaled again, and her eyes never left mine.

Bloody hell, I'd have to talk my way through this, wouldn't I? There'd be no shoving it down or ignoring that it was there, rumbling under the surface.

Not if I really wanted to take care of her the way Chris had wanted me to.

"Your mum was always so nice to me," I said. I kept my voice low and soothing, my hand still making slow strokes over the top of her silky curls. "The first time I met her, she asked if I was always such an asshole to people. And when I said yes, she laughed and laughed. She had such a good smile, duck." I swallowed around the growing tightness in my throat. "You'll have her smile someday, you know? You've got her eyes too." My eyes burned dangerously as I stared down at Mira. "Breaks my heart when I think about how much you look like her."

Mira sniffled, briefly rubbing her face against the duck, but her tears dwindled as I talked.

"God, I don't know what I'm doing," I whispered, my eyes squeezed shut as I dredged up anything I could say to soothe her. I had a decade's worth of memories of Chris and Amie, moments that numbered into the thousands, all good and all worthy of Mira knowing. How was I supposed to distill an entire friendship into one conversation that would calm her down?

She sniffled again, and I pried my eyes open. Overthinking this wouldn't help, so I just tugged on the first thread in my mind.

"I wasn't going to dance at their wedding," I said in a low voice. "It was a fun party too; that was another thing your parents knew how to do. They always made people comfortable, you know? And I'd almost made it the entire night when your mum came right up to me at my table with some of the guys from the team." I exhaled a short laugh with a shake of my head. "She held her hand out and said if I didn't dance with her, it would be bad luck for their marriage. She was so bloody stubborn, and I loved that about her. Because she kept your dad in his place, never let him get away with anything."

She kept listening. Her tears stopped.

"It was a slow dance," I told Mira. "I actually know how to dance; Mum made me take lessons when I was twelve. Hated it. But the look on your mum's face when I actually knew what I was doing was worth every bloody lesson. She smiled so big, duck. I'll remember that forever." I pinched my eyes shut again, details pelting me like darts. Like arrows and bullets. "Then she told me about their pretty neighbor that just moved in. Thought I should meet her."

I had to pause then. For a brief moment, it hurt too much to think about how differently my life could have played out if Amie had gotten her way. If Zoe had been single.

If they were still here to be part of our lives.

But it hadn't happened that way.

"She thanked me," I said. "Your mum kissed me on the cheek and told me she loved me, even if I couldn't say it back, and she thanked me for dancing with her on her wedding day. Don't know why I didn't say it that day," I said in a tortured whisper. "You never know when you'll regret those little moments, duck. I told her that she looked beautiful and that Chris didn't deserve her, which made her laugh, but I didn't fucking tell her I loved her too. Maybe I did later and just don't remember."

I scrubbed at my cheek when a single stray tear escaped.

"All right, then," I managed with a rasp. "Might have to stop talking about your mum. If anyone's gonna make me cry, it'll be her. Your dad, though, he was such a shit, and the closest thing I'd ever had to a brother, yeah?"

I told her about playing with Chris. What it was like to have him as a teammate.

Her arms relaxed around the duck, and she kept her eyes on me while her breaths steadied, her blinks lengthening, slowing.

"You'll hear more about him from everyone as you grow up," I told her. "You'll see them talk about him on the telly. You'll see clips and videos of all the things he did, how good he was on the end of that line." My chest hollowed, raw and ragged. But I forced the words out, because she deserved to hear them, and Chris deserved to have them said about him. "They'll tell you all the ways you remind them of your dad, especially if you play any sort of sport, and God, Mira, you can be so proud of that. If you have even a little bit of that man in you, you'll be such a good fucking human."

My throat closed up, and I had to stop because my voice cracked again, a trembling deep in my gut that I didn't dare allow. When I risked a glance at Mira, I saw that her eyelids were fluttering shut.

I breathed out quietly, easing my hand off her hair.

For a moment, her eyes opened, but when she saw me there, they slowly closed again.

Her breathing evened out. Her eyes stayed closed.

Moving slower than I thought possible, I straightened and wiped a hand over my exhausted face. My bones felt ready to collapse, the weariness seeping through every inch of my body.

I was this tired after two days.

Two bloody days.

Zoe had done this alone the entire time—and it made me feel like absolute, utter shit.

It wasn't like the realization of it made me any more comfortable with the idea of parenting. But I couldn't ignore the reality of it either.

The next day, when I heard Zoe's car pulling into the driveway, I breathed out slowly. Part relief, part anticipation, and part fucking stress because now it was real.

"Zoe!" Mira cried, racing for the door.

Her hair was a mess, the kitchen was a bleedin' disaster, toys were scattered throughout the house, and I didn't care.

Zoe walked in right as Mira reached the door, and the way her face transformed when she saw the little girl . . .

I'd see that smile in my sleep, no fucking doubt about it.

I'd see it stamped behind my eyes when I closed them.

I'd feel it carved into my chest.

That smile was love, and the thought of anyone being on the receiving end of that smile was too much to consider.

"I missed you so much," Zoe cried, peppering kisses all over Mira's face. She swept the little girl up into her arms, both of them laughing.

Mira held her so tightly, and I realized that much of her meltdown the night before had probably been about Zoe being gone. The person who had kept her anchored since the accident was suddenly absent.

Whether Mira knew it or not, people in her life leaving would likely always trigger something cataclysmic in her head.

Zoe locked eyes with me, her smile gentling. "How did it go?"

I sighed. "Go ahead and say it."

The edges of her smile lifted. "Say what?" she teased.

"Just fucking say it, Valentine."

"Oh, that I was right and it brought me an unholy amount of joy to see you read that binder?"

"Yeah, that."

She laughed, dropping another kiss on Mira's head. Then her attention shifted to the kitchen, her eyes widening at the mess there. "Oh my."

"Don't you dare judge me," I told her, my finger jabbed into the air.

Zoe set Mira down, and she ran off to play with her toys. "I'd never," she said gravely.

I rolled my eyes. "No bullshit," I started. "Yeah?"

Zoe nodded. "No bullshit. How *did* it go?"

I told her about Mira standing by Chris and Amie's bedroom door, how hard it had been to get her to sleep, and Zoe's eyes welled with tears.

"Probably because I left," she said quietly.

I crossed my arms over my chest. "We can't put our lives on hold forever, though. We can't always be by her."

"I know," she said, sighing.

"She kept saying something last night; I didn't know what she meant. She kept saying, 'Mommy hold you,' over and over."

Zoe held my eyes for a moment before answering. What I saw reflected back at me was nothing less than heartbreak.

"That's what she says when she wants you to do those things. Or someone to do those things. So if she says, 'I kiss you,' it means she wants a kiss good night. 'I hold you' means she wants a hug."

"Well, fucking hell." I rubbed at my chest. "Like someone ripped my guts out."

She gave me a tiny smile. Only one side of her lips curved up. "It's in the binder."

My eyes snagged on hers. "'Course it is."

It was quiet for a moment, and in that quiet, words filled my head, rolled off my tongue before I could consider the ramifications. "If you don't mind leaving those binders," I said, "I promise not to burn 'em when I'm done reading."

Zoe's face filled with something I didn't want to define. Couldn't bring myself to read into it too deeply.

"You're really gonna help?" she said quietly.

"Yeah."

It wasn't wise to tell her that it was as much about her as it was about Mira. That I couldn't leave either of them alone in this situation anymore. It wasn't wise to admit just how far she'd gotten under my skin.

That she had *always* been under my skin.

That when I didn't see her, I could pretend she wasn't there. But now it was like bloody hooks had been dug into my skin, and I felt myself being tugged in her direction every time she walked into the room.

"I'll stay here," I told her. "We'll make a schedule, yeah?"

And much like she had the night I met her, standing at this exact island in Chris and Amie's kitchen, Zoe held out her hand.

"We do this together," she said. "I still want to slap the shit out of you most days, and I don't think that impulse will go away anytime soon. But we do this together," she repeated. "Deal?"

I fought a laugh, fought a massive swell of lust, adoration, and frustration. All the things I felt in spades whenever she was in the room with me. The things I'd ignored for years.

Would continue to ignore.

But this time, when I took her hand, there was no ring on her finger. No husband. No boyfriend.

Just me and her, and the little duck linking us together.

"We do this together," I promised.

I took a deep breath, fought like hell to shove my fear aside, and slid my palm over hers. This time, with her cool skin against mine, I had to worry—just a little bit—that the damage done in this scenario would come from both of us. The difference was that Zoe had no fucking clue what she did to me. What she was capable of doing.

And if it were left up to me, she never would.

Chapter Ten

ZOE

Living next door to Liam was easy. For about a week. Mainly because I hardly ever had to talk to him.

He watched Mira three times. Once so that I could do an online meeting with a client. Once so I could run errands without interrupting naptime. And once because she basically demanded to go hang out with him.

"You *want* to?" I asked her one day.

Mira nodded emphatically. "Bye, Zoe. I go see him."

And she marched through the connecting gate, juice box in hand, to join him on the back deck, where he was assembling a new grill. While I watched curiously, she clambered up onto a chair, kicking her legs happily as he glanced over his shoulder to verify that I knew she was there.

He arched an eyebrow.

If he were anyone else, someone I was friends with, I might have responded with a confused shrug. But because he was Liam, I arched an eyebrow right back.

Liam set his jaw, then turned back to his assemblage, his mouth moving as he said something to Mira. She giggled.

"Huh," I said under my breath.

◆ ◆ ◆

"I'm bringing the girls here for our next book club," Rosa said. "Martha's heart may not be able to take it, but it's worth the risk."

I refused to ask.

Refused.

But because I wasn't rude, I made a polite humming sound.

Then I stopped, because damn it, that sounded like *his* humming sound, and now I couldn't help but think about all the times he used it instead of answering.

Was he actually trying to be polite in those moments?

"Damn it," I muttered under my breath.

Rosa ignored me. "You need to join us some night. It'll do you some good."

"I know, I know." I gestured toward the house, the stacks of folders atop my laptop, the toys littering the family room, the dinner mess covering the island. "I've been a little busy."

"Did you read the last one I told you about?" she asked. "The one about the pool boy? Goodness, it was spicy."

A laugh escaped under my breath. "I didn't get to it, no. My reading time has been nonexistent. It was hard enough to get through tax season."

"The curse of people who deal with the numbers," she said, going up on tiptoe.

Her attention never wavered, and I damn well knew why she wanted her book club friends over here. I gritted my teeth and kept my focus on the pizza dough in front of me, thank you very much.

"Are you sure you don't want to watch this?"

Her ass was perched in front of the slider overlooking my backyard and, consequently, the pool in Chris and Amie's backyard.

When Denver had decided to usher in May with a hot spell, Liam took it upon himself to open up Chris and Amie's pool.

"Positive," I told her. "I see enough of Liam now to last me the rest of *eternity*." I said the last word with a particularly vicious slap of the pizza dough onto the island. "I don't need to gawk while he's doing perfectly normal things."

Rosa glanced over at the dough, one eyebrow arched. "Easy, dear. The dough hasn't earned your vitriol."

With a sigh, I plopped the ball back into its bowl and laid a towel over top so it could rest. "I know."

"And I don't care how much you see him. His arms," she mused. "They should be illegal."

They *should*. My face felt suspiciously warm when the agreement registered in my brain, which was why I gave her an annoyed look. She couldn't even appreciate it because she'd already turned back to the slider, going up on tiptoe to watch whatever his cranky ass was doing.

My vitriol, she'd said.

In the last few days, as one week turned the corner into two, I wasn't even sure what word I could use to encapsulate what I felt toward Liam.

Rosa now came over just to hang out, because I didn't need her babysitting help as much. To hang out . . . and shamelessly stare at Liam, by the looks of it.

I pushed the bowl of pizza dough to the center of the island. "Don't you have something better to do?" I asked her.

"In a minute I will, I'm sure." She angled her head. "Besides, now that I'm in my dating phase again, allow me to harmlessly gaze upon someone who is a perfect specimen of what I'd be looking for."

I snorted. "He is way too young for you, and your dating phase is a train wreck, Rosa."

She sighed, moving away from the slider. "Because they're all idiots. The last guy—who seemed nice enough when we met for coffee—asked if I'd consider getting implants. On our second date."

My nose wrinkled.

Rosa nodded. "He was a plastic surgeon."

"Ah." I took a sip of my water, enjoying the quiet of the house while Mira took her afternoon nap. Because I knew as soon as she woke, she'd start making her demands.

"I go see him," she'd say on her way down the stairs, tucking her stuffed duck under her arm and marching toward the slider.

Liam was now a daily fixture instead of an as-needed presence, and I was desperately trying to get used to that.

"The thing I don't understand is why kids like him so much," I told Rosa. "Mira is *obsessed* with Liam, and it makes no sense. He's so rude all the time. I've never seen him pick her up. But she always wants to be over there."

"A problem you can't solve with a simple equation," Rosa said absently.

My eyebrows rose in concession. "I suppose not. Maybe that's why I'm constantly trying to figure it—him—out. I can't handle it when the rows and columns don't add up."

Rosa snagged a piece of cubed watermelon from the bowl in front of her and nibbled thoughtfully. "You don't think it's because he's a big, strong guy like her dad? Now that he's next door, it's a pretty convenient substitute." She held my gaze. "You know I'm not saying that to be thoughtless."

"I know," I assured her. "And, no, I don't think that's it. A couple of the guys from the team have stopped by with their wives, bringing us food, checking up on us, and even though she knows them, she's never acted the way she does with Liam."

Because I couldn't help myself, I wandered just a bit closer to the slider. He was crouched down, making sure the hose from the vacuum thingy wasn't getting tangled while it cleaned the bottom of the pool.

All week, I'd caught glimpses of him working on the pool. The yard. The landscaping. Trimming tree branches and pulling weeds. Mowing the grass and spreading new mulch in the flower beds.

When he wasn't at the facilities, Liam was constantly doing something.

I wasn't sure I'd ever seen him relax.

Most mornings, I'd just be finishing my coffee when he returned to the house after a run, his shirt soaked in sweat and his chest heaving.

Not that I'd noticed.

But I couldn't deny the warmth that bubbled under my chest when I saw how well he was taking care of the house. How he was making it look like a home again.

"Talk to him much this week?" Rosa asked.

"Not really. Just in passing when Mira goes over, and when she does, it's always about her."

"I still can't believe you're passing her back and forth between the houses like this. Wouldn't it be easier to just be under one roof?"

Oh, sure. *So* much easier.

Living next door to Liam was hard enough.

"If that man were my roommate, I'd end up in jail."

Rosa laughed.

"I'm serious," I told her. "He's the most aggravating person I've ever met in my life. I'm *nice*, Rosa. I'm nice to everyone. But the second I'm in the same room as him, it's like I'm a different person."

Rosa hummed thoughtfully but didn't say anything.

Her silence made me very twitchy.

"He still holds himself back from Mira," I continued. "I can see it plain as day."

"It's been less than two weeks since he started helping," she pointed out. "Give him a little time."

"I know. That's also why she's not sleeping over there unless I'm actually gone." I tugged at the ponytail holder keeping my hair back. "I think she likes sleeping there, but . . ." My voice trailed off for a moment. "If she wakes up with a nightmare or something, I can just about imagine how he'd react. He'd pat her on the head and tell her to go the fuck back to sleep or something."

Rosa laughed. "He can't be that bad."

"He sure can. The day she was born, he patted her on the head and said, 'There, there, you can stop now.'"

Her laughter increased, and it was enough to have me cracking a smile. If nothing else, at least Liam was consistent.

The man in question stood up, and the motion caught my eye.

My head angled to the side when he stretched his arms high. The hem of his black shirt rode up, and I caught a glimpse of his hard stomach and a thin line of dark hair that disappeared into the waistband of his shorts. His gaze snapped over to mine, and I immediately backed away from the slider, my heart thumping just a little bit harder.

Exactly what I didn't need—that jerk catching me ogling.

Rosa smothered her smile, and I glared. "Not funny."

She waved it away. "A little funny. Or it's inevitable, at least. Two attractive, single people *thrust* into a situation where they can't escape each other."

"I do not appreciate your emphasis on the thrusting. There's no thrusting happening anywhere in this situation, believe me." I peeked at the dough with as much nonchalance as I could muster. "Zero thrusting since my divorce, actually."

Rosa whistled. "Long time, sweet cheeks."

I shrugged. "I guess."

"And you've never missed it?" Rosa looked highly skeptical.

"Put that eyebrow down," I told her. "It's so judgy."

She laughed.

Somehow, I managed a swallow as I untangled the knot of my thoughts.

"My whole life, I've wanted the fairy tale, right? My mom always teased me about being the math girl who loved her love stories, but they're similar to me. Math is predictable; it has rules and structure and known outcomes, as long as you plug everything in correctly. And while I hate using the word *predictable* to describe the books I love to read—it sounds too inherently negative—there is comfort in knowing that these two people are perfectly matched in their flaws and that they'll cherish and respect and fight for each other and come out the other side with a happily-ever-after."

"There is," Rosa agreed.

"I miss feeling like that's possible for me," I said quietly. "That someone will sweep me off my feet because he can't help himself. Because I'm just exactly what he is looking for."

Rosa was quiet for a few moments, studying my face before she spoke. "Why doesn't it feel possible?"

"Less possible," I amended. "So much harder now, because Mira's my priority."

Rosa hummed.

"And maybe I've changed too much in the last ten years. Maybe I don't even know what I want anymore."

"Definitely not a grumpy Brit," she said lightly.

"Definitely not. I don't care what his arms look like."

She hummed anew.

"Stop it," I told her. "He can hardly stand being in the same room as me."

Rosa arched that eyebrow again.

Naturally, it made me nervous enough that I kept babbling. "Besides, Liam has been single for as long as I've known him. And I've been divorced from Charles for *well* over two years now. Almost three."

I used to keep track of the days, because every single one by myself felt like freedom. But now I simply enjoyed living my life, because I didn't have a pretentious douchebag living under the same roof.

Every single day that passed meant healing. Discovering the parts of myself that I'd lost or ignored during that marriage because it was easier to try to keep the peace.

But that's the insidious thing about "keeping the peace." It sounds like such a simple phrase, with such good intentions, but it hides the slow erosion that eats away at your soul when you do it for too long.

And, sure, now I had a rude, grumpy one living next door, but as much as I couldn't explain it, none of the things Liam had ever said to me had actually left a wound.

There was no peace when that man was around, and there never had been.

Definitely no erosion of the soul, because half the time when we were in the same room, he pissed me off so much that I felt like my eyeballs could shoot fire.

If I dared give that feeling a word, which I wouldn't, it was almost . . . *exhilarating*.

But I *didn't* label the feeling, because it didn't make sense, and I hated things that didn't make sense.

For a while after I left Charles, a part of me wondered if Liam would treat me differently. If he'd be nicer. If our bickering would take a dissimilar tone.

It never did.

And that, to my mind, was my answer. We'd carry on through infinity in the same way we always had—with eye-rolling, last names being tossed around like grenades, and his annoying little humming noise that made me want to inflict bodily damage.

That being said, I still had perfectly functioning eyesight. There was no escaping how the pieces of him unfortunately came together in one really attractive package.

Unfortunate because the moment he opened his stupid mouth, he ruined it.

"Your point?" Rosa asked.

"My point is that this situation doesn't change anything between us. It simply changes the amount we see each other. Liam has never once shown any interest in me, and I like my men . . . nicer."

"No, you don't."

I made an affronted sound. "Yes, I do."

"Charles wasn't all that nice. The only reason Chris and Amie were so kind to him was because they loved you and they thought you saw something in him they hadn't yet."

There was no arguing that point because I already knew it to be true. By the time I met Chris and Amie, I was already a package deal with Charles. Amie didn't tell me what she really thought about him until the first few years of our marriage had passed and she could see the unhappiness written across my face as if tattooed there.

"He was nice at first," I corrected quietly. "He was charming and funny and gregarious. And so handsome. He'd walk the halls of that hospital in his three-piece suits when he'd come for board meetings, and everyone wanted to be noticed by him."

Rosa's eyes were sad.

I toyed with the edge of the towel. "I was the quiet girl in accounting, Rosa. It's not like I minded, but I was never the woman who attracted the guys like him. Not in high school or college. And it didn't break my heart or anything. I didn't like myself less because of it. Dating the sweet, quiet men suited me just fine." I shook my head. "I don't know why I'm talking about Charles now."

"Our past dictates how we move through our future, honey," she said.

Didn't I know it?

The sigh that escaped my lips was heavy, laden with all the complications that currently dictated my future.

"I still like nice guys, though," I told her. "No matter what Charles turned out to be."

"Liam's getting a *little* bit nicer," Rosa added.

I held my thumb and forefinger apart by a scant inch. "Microscopic."

"I should go," Rosa said. "I have another date tonight."

"Send me his profile, in case you go missing."

She rolled her eyes. "You watch too much *Dateline*, young lady."

"Maybe," I conceded. "But I've also never been kidnapped, so . . ."

Rosa wrapped me in a quick hug. "He won't kidnap me. We're meeting at Union Station for drinks, so there will be a million people around."

As she tucked her cell phone into her pocket, I couldn't help but marvel.

"What?" she asked.

"I don't know if I'd have the energy to date if I were you. I'm in my early thirties, and I'm too exhausted to consider it."

She tapped the edge of my nose. "You *were* considering it, though, before Mira. The last one was nice."

I sighed. He was.

Tyler was sweet and quiet. I'd known him for years at work. Every time my computer needed fixing or some piece of tech equipment copped an attitude, he was the one who came to the rescue. Which he did with a friendly smile and kind eyes.

I didn't blame him for not wanting to pursue our relationship in the wake of the accident. Hell, it was my life, and sometimes *I* wanted to hit the pause button on all this change too.

"Maybe he was too nice," she added quietly. Then she winked and left.

I laid my head down on my folded arms and sighed. After a few moments, the telltale sounds of Mira climbing from her crib filtered downstairs.

Then I heard the soft thump of her feet on the steps.

"I go see him, Zoe!" she declared.

Her hair was a matted mess, and the duck was getting dragged across the floor.

I gathered her up into my arms for a hug, and she laid her head on my shoulder while we snuggled. But after a quick moment, she wiggled to get down.

"Want me to walk you?" I asked.

"No, I do it."

And she was off.

I stood at the slider while Mira skipped over the pathway and into Chris and Amie's backyard. With his cell phone pressed to his ear, Liam was standing by their own sliding door, and he glanced up when she yanked it open.

He gave me a slight nod.

The proverbial passing of the torch.

Or child, as it were.

Mira would be back for dinner. She always was. I stepped away from the door, out of Liam's line of vision, and ignored that it was easier to breathe when I couldn't see him.

◆ ◆ ◆

Three days later, neck-deep in end-of-the-quarter bookwork, I took a quick glance at my phone screen.

Nothing.

I rubbed my tired eyes, which were bone dry from staring at my computer screen for the last couple of hours. My neck was tight and achy, and my attempt to roll out any of the tension was met with stubborn resistance by my rock-hard muscles.

From where I sat at the kitchen table, I couldn't see into the backyard next door, but Mira had been over there for a few hours.

I blew out a slow breath and stood, stretching my arms over my head with a groan.

There was no sign of either of them by the pool or patio. I started picking at my thumbnail without even realizing I was doing it.

What did they *do* over there every afternoon?

With a frustrated huff, I picked up my phone and tapped out a text.

Me: How's it going? I'm done with my work if you want to send her back.

Liam: We're watching SportsCenter and drinking beer. I might show her how to properly light a cigar next.

Me: I sincerely hope you can hear me rolling my eyes from here.

Liam: Oddly enough, I can.

Liam: Fine. She found weird magnet block things in the playroom, and we've been building a fucking epic castle.

Then he attached a picture, and my heart went all warm and gooey.

Mira had her tongue tucked between her front teeth, her face the picture of concentration as she set a bright-red tile on top of a tower.

Playing with blocks on a beautiful summer afternoon.

The man didn't deserve a gold medal for doing something so simple, but every ounce of his being had rejected the idea of being involved with Mira. And despite that hefty reserve, he was taking care of her well, from what I could see.

I smiled and told him to let me know if I needed to come get her, then set my phone down to go take a shower while the house was quiet.

I'd just stepped out of the steaming bathroom with my hair wrapped in a towel and a moisturizing mask coating my face when the doorbell app on my phone chimed.

"Shit," I whispered, swiping over to see who it was.

When the picture came up, I burst into laughter.

Rosa stood front and center, holding a giant bottle of wine. Behind her stood two other silver-haired women—one with a cane and the other with a plate of food in her hand.

Looked like the book club ladies were ready for their first glimpse of Liam after all.

I pressed the button. "Door's unlocked, but I just got out of the shower, so I'll be down in a couple minutes."

"Take your time. Martha wants to watch the neighbor for a bit," Rosa said.

With a shake of my head, I discarded the mask into the trash and massaged in the remaining serum. I squeezed the excess moisture out of my hair and added some curling lotion, then tugged on my favorite joggers and a soft T-shirt over my simple bralette. The pants hung low on my hips, and the crop of the shirt left a stretch of my stomach bare.

When I got downstairs and turned the corner into the kitchen, I exhaled a quiet laugh.

All three women were staring out the slider.

"I thought you were kidding," I told her.

Rosa turned with a sly grin on her face. "About this? Never." She motioned to her friends. "Martha, Phyllis, this is Zoe."

Martha came forward, enveloping me in a tight squeeze. She smelled like roses, and her birdlike frame was shockingly strong. "Honey, we've heard so much about you."

I smiled. "Likewise."

Phyllis winked. "You've been reading half these books with us, according to Rosa. You might as well get the pleasure of our company too."

Warmth settled sweetly into my bones, even though being around them made me miss my mom. "I'm glad you came over," I told them. "I wasn't prepared to host, though. I don't have much food to offer, and there are toys everywhere."

Martha waved it off. "Don't you fret. Phyllis is a slob, so we're used to it."

"I am not," Phyllis argued.

Rosa smiled at her friends. "Come on, girls, let's pour some wine and sit out on her deck. If we're lucky, he'll show up right when we get to the part where the hero uses handcuffs on her for the first time."

Two hours later, I knew unequivocally that I was never skipping book club again.

"Phyllis," I gasped, "I'm pretty sure that's illegal in most countries."

She shrugged. "Never stopped us. My husband was an active man," she said meaningfully. "God rest his soul."

Martha cackled into her wineglass and flipped her Kindle case open. "That was a good one, ladies. I feel bad for whoever has to pick our next read."

Rosa raised her hand. "That would be me. But don't worry, I've got a great choice. No handcuffs or pool boys, but you'll love it."

"Probably good," Martha said. "My grandson was over the other day, and he asked what I was reading."

I tugged a blanket up over my legs and laughed. "Did you lie?"

"Hell no," she said. "I'm not ashamed of what I'm reading, but that doesn't mean he needs an early education either, you know what I mean?"

Liam's slider next door opened up, and an expectant hush fell over the group.

When his tall, muscular body appeared on the back patio, Martha sighed happily.

Somehow, I managed to stifle the eye roll. "He's not that good-looking," I mumbled.

Phyllis snorted. "You're so full of shit it's a miracle your eyes aren't brown."

Okay, fine, as he strode toward my side of the yard, the hard line of his jaw and his chiseled features caught the fading light in a fairly pleasant way.

And his shirt stretched across his chest rather nicely.

He was just so manly that it was almost unfair. There was a nice amount of dark hair on his arms, which meant he'd likely have a smattering of it over his broad chest.

My throat went tight because the image cemented itself very quickly in my thrust-free brain.

Martha coughed pointedly, and I realized I was staring.

At the sound, Liam's head snapped up, and he froze in between our yards. "Oh bloody hell," he muttered. "There's so many of you."

Phyllis sat back in her seat. "You must be Liam."

He exhaled heavily, eyes lingering on mine while I tried not to laugh. "I'm not admitting to shit because you lot look like trouble."

The laugh burst free; there was no stopping it.

His jaw clenched, and he took a deep breath, like he was bracing for something.

"What is it?" I asked.

"She fell asleep on the floor of her bedroom up there."

"Ah."

Rosa gave me a questioning look. "Should we . . . ?"

"Yeah, I need to get her into bed anyway."

The trio stood, complaining of various aches and pains as they did.

"At least your bunion isn't as big as mine," Martha said.

Liam pinched the bridge of his nose.

Phyllis peered over the rim of her glasses in his direction. "Be nice to our friend, young man. You might be a football player, but I could shove this cane where the sun don't shine without blinking."

He dropped his hand, gaping at her when she gave him a knowing look.

"My God," he breathed.

I exhaled a laugh. "Nice to know someone's still looking out for me," I said.

It was meant to be a breezy statement, but it fell with the weight of a stone into my stomach.

Liam's gaze tracked briefly down to the waistband of my pants, returning heavily to my face when I passed, and I wished I could take back what I'd said. What I'd worn. Just . . . everything.

We walked in silence into the house, and having his big, looming presence behind me as we went up the stairs was more disconcerting than I would've liked.

The cropped shirt and low-hanging joggers made me feel a bit . . . exposed.

When I cleared the landing of the stairs, I allowed myself a brief glimpse into Chris and Amie's empty bedroom across the hall.

"You're sleeping downstairs?" I asked him.

He hummed.

"I'll take that as a yes, but feel free to use a full sentence next time," I said.

Mira was sprawled out on the floor, using her duck as a pillow, and a gentle snoring sound came from her button nose.

I had a fleeting thought that she'd done this on purpose, just to see if she could get away with sleeping in the house.

I glanced at Liam. His back was against the wall, his hands tucked into his jogger pockets.

"Why didn't you carry her over?" I asked.

He glanced down at the floor. "Wasn't sure what you'd want to do."

It felt like a cop-out. A flimsy one too. But I decided not to press.

Mira was warm and sleepy and sweet when I gently pulled her into my arms, even though my muscles quivered from picking up her full deadweight.

I kissed her forehead as she snuggled into me. "Let's get you to bed, okay?"

"I not sleepy," she mumbled.

Everything inside me trembled under the weight of how much I loved her, and as I glanced outside the room to where Liam watched us with guarded eyes, I tried to remember what Rosa had said.

He was trying.

And for now, it was enough.

◆　◆　◆

"I stay here."

Behind me, I could practically feel Liam's long-suffering sigh.

I crouched low. "Mira, honey, I know it was nice taking your nap here today while I got some work done, but you sleep at my house, remember?"

The storm brewed ominously in her eyes, and when she set her jaw, crossed her arms over her body, and plopped down onto the floor in front of the crib, I knew I'd have to bodily remove her before she'd concede.

"It's my fault," Liam said. "I'm too bloody likable."

If he'd *ever* made a comment I was bound to ignore, it was that one. "Come on, Mirabelle, let's go back to my place. We'll have a picnic dinner in the family room."

"No picnic. I stay here."

I held her gaze for a few moments longer, then sighed.

Instead of getting into an epic battle of wills with an almost three-year-old, I stood up and walked out of the room, then down the steps. Liam murmured something to Mira that I couldn't under-stand, and then he followed behind me.

When he entered the kitchen, I was sitting at the island with my hands speared through my hair. "This is new," I said.

He grunted.

Then . . . nothing.

Another season of change was near. I could feel it. Right before the bucket filled and those millions of drops of water spilled over the edge.

The problem was, I didn't know how to logic my way through this problem. Didn't know the formula to use to make it line up at the end. There were too many variables, too many unknowns.

"I don't know how to navigate this," I said quietly. The words hurt coming out, just a little, because I couldn't help but brace for him to weaponize them against me.

But in true Liam style, he didn't say a damn word. Lifting my head, I pinned him with a long look. "Nothing? No commentary? You're usually brimming with helpful suggestions about how I'm doing this wrong."

"Nothing for me to say, Valentine. She's obsessed with me and wants to be here more. I told you that kids have shit taste sometimes."

He leaned up against the counter, and I took a moment to study him. There was a lightning-quick sort of tension in his eyes, there one moment and gone the next.

"What?" he barked.

"I'm trying to figure you out," I admitted. "It's not working."

He snorted. "Nothing to figure out. I'm an open book."

That had me laughing. Hard. And by the darkening of his face, he didn't appreciate it.

"Sorry," I said after my laughter had subsided. "You are anything but, Liam Davies. Though it's been a decade since we met, I can honestly say that I don't know you any better now than I did that first day."

He didn't like that either and darted his eyes away from mine. "She can stay," he finally said.

My eyebrows arched.

"If you don't feel like fighting her." He shifted uncomfortably. "I don't mind."

"Doesn't it set a bad precedent, though? She can't just demand to stay here all the time."

"Fuck if I know," he said.

I rubbed my face and sighed.

"No page in the binder for this one?" he asked.

Dropping my hands, I narrowed my eyes in his direction.

His lips quirked up like he was fighting a smile.

"Fine," I said. "We'll let her stay tonight, but just remember whose idea this was."

Chapter Eleven

Liam

Mira sat on the couch and stared up at me with those big eyes.

"You listening?" I asked her.

She nodded. "I listening."

"All right." I set my hands on my hips. "Here's the deal. You don't get to choose sleepovers all the time, yeah? You still need to stay with Zoe, because she's better at this shit than I am."

Mira blinked. "I stay here."

"Tonight, yeah. Tomorrow, you go back to Zoe's."

"I stay here," she said again. "Zoe stay here too."

The reaction in my gut was immediate and visceral.

Absolutely fucking not, I thought. I would rather have strung myself up by my toes than have shared a house with a woman who had no idea she was stuck under my skin like a fucking tick.

But a sexy tick.

With big eyes and wild hair and a perfect smile.

"No. Zoe has her own house. And that's where you're gonna be sleeping tomorrow night."

Then, as I'd swear it in a court of law, that little girl made a decision in her devious little brain that I'd rue the day I ever crossed her about this.

When her eyes sharpened and her jaw notched up, it almost fucking took my breath away how much she looked like her dad at that moment.

"Duck," I said in a warning tone, "we're not arguing about this right now. We're having a good night, aren't we? You ate an entire fucking meal, and that's a first. Let's not muck it up with a temper tantrum when you're already getting your way. If we have problems tonight, she'll probably never let you stay here again, and I'm kinda getting used to your afternoon visits. We won't tell her that, because I've got a reputation to uphold, but I think I'd be bored out of my mind if you stopped coming over. I don't mind watching you when I know she's right next door. Don't tell her that either, because she'd gloat forever. So if you argue with me now, we risk all that. Okay?"

I'd never been around a ton of kids, so I had no real points of comparison, but I didn't know how Mira could speak so well and seemingly understand so much at her age. Maybe she was a fucking prodigy or something. But bloody hell, I'd swear on a stack of Bibles that my logic made sense to her.

She'd been good all evening. Almost *too* good.

No fussing or throwing fits about anything. She ate nearly her entire dinner—it helped that I'd started buying all the shit I knew she'd eat, just to keep it in the house. Like chicken nuggets in the shapes of fucking dinosaurs and letters. If I thought too hard about how they got chicken into those shapes, I'd probably never let her eat them.

"I'll even turn on that movie *again*, as long as we get through this night in peace so that Valentine doesn't think I'm completely mucking this up, okay?"

Mira eyed the TV screen, then me again, clearly considering her options.

"We watch *Moana* again?" she verified.

I sighed. "Yeah, but I'll probably regret it, because yesterday at the field, I almost sang 'You're Welcome' to someone who said thank you, and it made me want to take a drill to my temple."

Mira dragged her stuffed duck from the couch cushion to her lap, where she wrapped her arms around it and buried her face into the faded yellow, fuzzy covering.

"Zoe bought you that duck," I told her as I took my seat on the couch and cued up the movie.

Mira nodded, rubbing her nose against the duck's bill. It was a little matted and clearly well loved after being lugged everywhere. "My birthday present," she said.

"Yeah," I agreed, "your first birthday present. I remember her bringing it to the hospital."

The duck had seemed so big at the time, dwarfing the impossibly tiny bundle in that white blanket with the blue-and-pink stripes.

"Mommy and Daddy in the hospital too?"

"They were there that day too, yeah," I told her.

As I watched her face, I found myself holding my breath. The last time Chris and Amie had come up, the whole evening had turned to utter shit. But Mira simply snuggled back into the couch, turning her legs to the side so that she could press her feet tight against my thigh while we watched.

"Why do you do that?" I asked her. "The foot thing. You're always pushing your feet against me while we watch something."

Instead of answering, she clutched the duck closer to her chest and glued her eyes to the screen, her little feet pressing against my legs.

I sighed, pulling my book from the end table by the couch. My phone was next to it, and I noticed the screen lighting up.

Valentine: What's she doing? Is she okay?

Me: We're watching a movie. She's fine, relax.

Valentine: Do you realize that telling a woman to relax when she's worried about something has literally never achieved the desired results?

Me: Valentine, I'd never dream of you listening to me anyway, so it was an empty directive.

Valentine: At least you're aware.

I set my phone down with a beleaguered sigh.

There were a million reasons I'd gone so long on my own. It wasn't a lack of options—being a football player alone made it disgustingly easy, if that had been the path I wanted to take.

It wasn't even a lack of attraction. I'd met women who were beautiful, funny, and smart. I'd met women who piqued my interest.

But once you'd learned how to cage your instincts, it was almost impossible to unleash them at the right time.

My whole life, I'd known that starting a family wasn't for me. I'd never, ever risk repeating the cycle I'd been born into. The one my mum had gotten us out of. The wall I'd built around those particular wants and desires was thick concrete. My own Hoover Dam, holding back torrents of emotion.

So, yeah, I said stupid shit to Zoe, like telling her to relax when I damn well knew she wouldn't relax.

With that thought in my head, I dozed off while the movie played in the background and Mira's tiny feet arched into my leg from time to time.

When it was over, she stayed curled up on the couch, her eyes drowsy.

I studied her face. "You feel okay, duck?"

"I just tired," she said.

My brows furrowed. She never admitted she was tired, even if she *was* tired. "Let's go get ready for bed then, yeah?"

Mira clutched her duck in one hand and dragged it up the stairs behind her.

She didn't put up a single fuss when I brushed her teeth, which was my second hint that something wasn't quite right. She perched quietly on the bathroom counter and opened wide when I wielded her sparkly pink toothbrush.

"You sure you're all right?" I asked.

Mira nodded, then held her arms out so that I could help her get down from the counter. Gently, I lifted her off the edge and settled her feet on the floor. Mira walked quietly back into her room, gathering the necessary stuffed animals and tossing them into her crib.

I set her inside, and she gave me a big-eyed look that made me want to tear my ribs out.

"I kiss you," she said.

My heart turned over, remembering what Zoe had told me. I leaned down, smoothing the hair off her face, and pressed a featherlight kiss onto her forehead.

Her incredibly warm forehead.

"You normally feel this warm, duck?" I asked her.

But Mira immediately lay down, settling into the corner of the crib that she liked best and pulling her duck in toward her face.

I pressed the back of my hand to her forehead again, but my hands were so calloused that I probably could have held them over a fire and hardly noticed the heat.

My stomach tightened uncomfortably.

I walked out of Mira's room and started searching through a hallway closet, but I couldn't find a thermometer.

With a deep breath, I pushed open the door to Chris and Amie's room. It was the only room in the house that I left alone. I still felt a bit like I was intruding into someone's private space, despite the fact that I'd been living in their house for the last couple of weeks.

I didn't study the large framed photos on the wall and kept my gaze straight ahead, directed toward their massive bathroom suite.

The soaking tub in the corner was big enough that I could fit comfortably inside, and that was saying something because I never fit into bathtubs. The shower—with glass walls and beautiful tiles—was about as big as my current bed.

And along the back wall, next to the toilet, was another door. I opened it up and saw a bin labeled "Mira—Medicine." I pulled it out, passing my hands over bottles of liquid ibuprofen and boxes of Band-Aids. Tucked in the back was a wand that looked sort of like a speed gun that a cop might use.

I held it up and shrugged.

When I peeked back in on Mira, I saw that she had fallen fast asleep in the short time I'd been gone from the room. My chest felt heavy, like someone had parked a linebacker right over my sternum and I couldn't move the fucker no matter what I did.

Zoe was right next door, I reminded myself as I aimed the thermometer gun at Mira's forehead and pressed the blue button.

It emitted a small beep, and the screen flashed red.

"Shit," I whispered.

One-oh-two point five.

That was bad, right? I'd had a fever the year before, hardly above one hundred, and I'd thought I was dying for about twenty-four hours.

I swiped a hand over my mouth and straightened.

Mira bolted up in bed, her eyes blank.

I settled a hand on her back. "What's wrong, duck?" I whispered.

She didn't see me, though. She started spewing nonsensical words and glancing around the room. Her hands started patting the duck.

Bloody fucking hell, what was I supposed to do with a feverish sleep-talking child?

I gently patted her back and made a small shushing noise. "Back to sleep now," I whispered. "Come on."

She blinked a few times, still not seeing me, then fell back onto the bed and snuggled up against her duck.

I tried very hard not to sprint down the stairs, deciding to bypass my phone completely. If Zoe was asleep, she wouldn't be for long.

I pushed open the gate connecting our yards and strode quickly to her back slider, then knocked on the glass.

"It's me," I called. "Come on, Zoe, I need those fucking binders or something."

A light flipped on in her family room, and she pulled a blanket tight around her shoulders as she unlocked the door. "What is it?"

"She's got a fever." I was out of breath. How was I out of breath from just crossing one backyard? "A bad one."

Zoe nodded. "Okay, let me pull some pants on, and I'll be right over."

My eyes darted unwillingly down the bare length of her legs—and locked there.

Underneath the blanket, Zoe was wearing a long T-shirt, and that was it.

"Right," I managed. Then my gaze snapped back to her face. "I'll be in her room."

I jogged back to the house and took the stairs two at a time, then paced Mira's room with my arms crossed until I heard Zoe coming up the steps.

My heart was racing.

She came into the room, and I moved out of the way. Zoe leaned over the crib and gently pushed Mira's hair out of her face, making a small humming noise as she pressed the backs of her fingers to Mira's forehead. "She's a bit warm, yeah."

"A bit," I barked out. "That fucking little thing was flashing red at me when I scanned her. Red lights are never a good thing, Zoe."

She gave me a tiny smile.

Why the fuck was she smiling? This was an emergency, for fuck's sake.

When she exhaled a laugh, I realized a bit too late that I'd said it out loud.

With a small shake of her head, Zoe picked up the thermometer and scanned Mira's forehead again.

One-oh-one point nine.

I punched a finger in the air. "That thing is full of shit; it was higher for me."

"How much higher?" Zoe asked.

"One-oh-two point five." I tucked my arms tight against my chest again. "Shouldn't we take her in or something? There's an emergency room not far from here. I can go put that fucking car seat back in if you want me to drive, because I refuse to drive that shit little car you've got."

Zoe stared at me for a few moments, and there was this soft fucking look in her big golden eyes.

"Why the bloody fuck are you looking at me like that?" I said. Yelled. Whatever.

Mira stirred a little, and Zoe rubbed her back for a moment before she motioned me out into the hallway.

Before coming over, she'd tugged on some black joggers, but her feet were still bare. Her toenails were painted a muted pink. It was so much easier to stare at her feet than to meet her gaze, because I did not like what I saw there.

And because it felt like my insides were about to combust.

"Liam, kids get fevers. She'll be fine, I promise."

I lifted my head, pinning her with a glare. "You can't promise that. I told you how high it was."

She smiled again, seeming secretive and sweet and so fucking irritating. I wanted to punch a wall.

"And she probably doesn't feel great, but letting her sleep is the best thing we can do. If she wakes up, we can make sure she drinks water, and we'll take her temp again, but one-oh-two isn't anything we need to worry about. A couple more degrees—"

"A *couple* more degrees? You have lost the plot, Valentine." She was mad. Absolutely nutters. And here I had thought she was the responsible one.

But she was completely unfazed. "A couple more degrees, and we want to make sure medicine brings that fever down, but we don't need to bring her in. Her body is doing its job."

My jaw was clenched tight while I measured the truth of what she was telling me. When I spoke again, my voice sounded like it had been scraped bare by rusty razor blades. "How are you so sure?"

"I worked at a hospital for over a decade, Liam."

"In *accounting*," I said. "It's not like you were interviewing the bloody doctors."

She narrowed her eyes. "Fine. My best friend had a kid, and I was always over here, and I remember her talking about this any time Mira got sick. Is that better?"

I conceded that with a grunt.

"I'll take that as a yes."

I grunted again. "Fine. But I'm taking her temp every hour."

Why were her eyes gleaming like that? And why was she studying my face that way?

"You're worried about her," she added gently.

Denial swiftly pushed to the tip of my tongue, but I couldn't force the words out.

"It's kinda sweet," she continued.

"It's not fucking sweet, Valentine. I've just never . . . I'm never around sick kids, and I hate feeling out of control, and I don't know what I'm supposed to do."

It was dark in the hallway, and we were standing close.

She smelled good. Like mint and chocolate.

Then she set her hand on my arm, as if comforting me. "She'll be okay, I promise."

Was my skin sizzling where she'd touched it? Did it feel to her like I was burning up from the inside? Because I fucking was.

I took a step back, and her expression immediately shifted.

There was no other choice to be made, though. I was too wildly out of control of the snarling beast locked tight behind the walls. He was already rattling his cage and pressing at the seams because the little girl I didn't want was sick and there was fuck all I could do about it.

No. Touching Zoe right now was the worst possible thing I could do.

Without another word, I walked into Chris and Amie's room and pulled one of the decorative pillows from the mound on their bed, then grabbed the blanket folded over the large chair in the corner. Zoe was back in Mira's room when I returned. With one hand, she gently stroked the little girl's cheek. In her other was the thermometer.

"Any change?" I asked.

"No. Same."

Same was good.

I tossed the pillow and blanket onto the floor next to Mira's crib, studiously avoiding Zoe's shocked facial expression.

"What are you . . . ?" Her voice trailed off.

"What does it look like I'm doing?" I said. "Someone's gotta be able to hear her if she needs something. I'm not gonna make you sleep on the floor."

Zoe covered her mouth with one hand, her eyes fixed unwaveringly on the makeshift bed.

I felt naked. Twitchy. Like I was under a spotlight, exposing every fucking vulnerability I had in one fell swoop.

Naturally, that made me take a swipe at her, because I was a bloody idiot.

"Don't beg to join me, Valentine. I'm not in the mood for cuddling."

Except she didn't roll her eyes. Didn't get annoyed or snipe back. She just kept those eyes locked dead center on mine.

"You trying to pry into my brain? I can guarantee you won't like what you find there."

Why wasn't she rising to the bait? It would be so much easier if she did. If she fought back, if she let those sparks fly between us like she always did, I could keep a level head.

Nothing about me was feeling level.

And maybe, just maybe, I could pull her into that unsteadiness with me. Because I was a selfish bastard. The thought was enough to make me pull my eyes away from hers. To cool the rising swell inside me.

Zoe exhaled slowly, like she knew what internal battle I was fighting. How could she, though? "How was she before you realized she had a fever?"

"Quiet," I answered. "That should've been my first clue that she felt poorly. She admitted she was tired."

Zoe's lips curled into an amused smile.

"She kept saying she wanted to stay here," I told her.

The smile fell, and she pinched the bridge of her nose. "I was afraid of that."

We were tiptoeing around something big. And right now we didn't have time to tiptoe around anything. "No bullshit," I said.

Zoe dropped her hands and stared at me. "No bullshit."

"Maybe she *should* be able to stay here." The words came out quietly, a little raw around the edges. "Maybe that's best for her. It was her home."

Zoe opened her mouth but didn't speak at first. Behind her eyes, thoughts raced; I could practically see them. She'd be assembling binders in that brain of hers, figuring out the millions of things that went into what I'd just said.

"I'm assuming you don't intend to become the primary caregiver," she said carefully.

"Fuck no."

She exhaled a quiet laugh. "Didn't think so."

Why couldn't I say the words? They were just a few letters strung together.

You could stay here too.

That's all. That's all I'd have to say.

But they stayed lodged somewhere deep inside my gut. Out of self-preservation, most likely. I was losing every battle when it came to these two girls. The little one and the very grown one.

And I knew that if I were faced with Zoe and her eyes every fucking day, it was only a matter of time before I'd never get over her.

Not for the rest of my life.

Hell, I was halfway there the day we met, and each time I'd shared a room with her—had to watch her with that idiot who never deserved her—it got worse.

"I could stay," she said quietly.

My eyes snapped to hers and held.

There would've been no shock on my end if an actual bolt of electricity had arced through the air between us. I half expected to see one. Bright and white and powerfully hot.

"If you're open to some company," she continued. "I'd still spend some time at my place during the day. I know we'd have a lot to figure out, and we *have* to try and be nice to each other."

"And when you say that, what you mean is . . ." My voice trailed off. I bloody well knew what she meant.

"I mean that *you* have to be nicer to *me*." She swallowed, looking so uncharacteristically nervous that it was hard to keep hold of her gaze like that. "I know you don't like me, Liam. You've always made that clear. But I won't have Mira grow up watching us act the way we used to. I'll mind what I say when you piss me off, but you have to promise the same thing."

Right.

That was why I'd done it. Why I'd always snapped and snarled when she came too close. Zoe believed exactly what I'd always wanted her to believe.

She didn't know what she was asking.

The slight pause before I answered had her cheeks flushing the slightest bit of pink.

"I can be nice." I said it like someone had yanked the words out with a hook, and her eyes sparked with the tiniest hint of amusement. Glad she found this so fucking funny.

"I'll sleep on the couch tonight. Are you really gonna take her temp every hour?" Zoe asked.

I nodded. "I won't sleep much anyway."

She nodded. "Wake me up if it crosses one-oh-three, okay? We'll give her some medicine."

There. A plan.

I could handle it as long as we had a plan.

Zoe gave Mira one last look, and then her eyes landed on mine. "It's okay to be worried about her. At least I know you have a heart now."

With that parting shot, she quietly left the room, her sweet scent trailing behind her. I took a greedy inhale and wondered what she'd been eating before she came over. If I'd taste it on her tongue.

Be nicer, she'd demanded. That's probably not what she had in mind when she said it. But then again, I'd allowed myself, over the years, fleeting moments in which I imagined kissing Zoe. Imagined punching her husband for the fact that he got to do so. When the bloody ring came off her finger, I imagined her naked, her thighs tight around my head. Imagined the sounds she'd make when they were. Imagined waking up buried under all that hair, with her fit fucking body draped over mine.

Niceness didn't factor into any single one of these reveries.

And now she'd be under the same roof. Day after day after day.

"Bloody hell, what did I just agree to?" I whispered.

With a sigh, I stretched out on the floor, punching the pillow under my head and settling in for a sleepless night.

Chapter Twelve

Zoe

My body was trained to wake up early, even before Mira had moved in with me. But I knew from experience that Liam wasn't usually far behind.

When he didn't wake me up in the middle of the night, internal alarm bells rang, alerting me to being the first one awake among the three of us. The couch had been surprisingly comfortable, but my back was still sore when I stood and stretched.

I quietly made my way up the steps, then peeked around the corner of Mira's room.

And my heart stopped.

Liam wasn't on his floor bed anymore, because Mira had taken his place. She was sprawled out underneath the blanket, her hair a tangled mess and her chest moving up and down evenly. He was sound asleep, his back against the wall and Mira's stuffed frog shoved against his shoulder as a makeshift pillow.

And he was holding her hand.

My aforementioned heart, which had stopped, turned a slow, sweet roll behind my ribs.

He'd kill me for doing it, but I pulled out my phone, crouched down to get a better angle, and snapped a picture.

Then I sent it to Rosa.

My phone buzzed almost immediately.

Rosa: My Lord. That is criminally adorable. Doesn't that make you want to get pregnant with his babies??

I smiled. There was no helping it.

Me: Logical guess.

Me: I think I'm ready to admit that he's not completely without a soul, as previously thought. The last twelve hours have been . . . educational.

Rosa: Do tell . . .

But I wasn't able to respond, because Mira started stirring, turning onto her side. I tucked my phone away and slowly rubbed her back. Then I touched the backs of my fingers to her forehead.

The weight of Liam's stare was tangible, but I kept my focus on Mira. She smiled sleepily.

"I have a sleepover with Liam," she said, her voice heavy with sleep.

"I see that." I sat on the floor, crossing my legs underneath me and opening my arms. She clambered onto my lap and snuggled into my embrace. I pressed a kiss to the top of her head.

Finally, I brought my gaze up.

With his hand free of hers, Liam had crossed his arms, and I did my very best not to study how the black cotton shirt stretched over his chest.

His expression wasn't blank, but it was brimming with reserve.

"You look tired," I told him.

"That your way of telling me I look like shit?" he asked, voice a slow drawl. I'd never heard him speak after just waking, and at the scraping roughness of it, like a cat's tongue over my skin, I fought a shiver up my spine.

Instead of answering, I kissed Mira's forehead.

"How'd she end up down here?" I asked.

"She woke up around three and saw me down here. Said she wanted to sleep by me, and I couldn't fucking say no." He arched his back and winced. "I'm too old to sleep like this."

I hummed, hiding my smile in Mira's hair. She had this big, surly man wrapped entirely around her little finger, and he would rather die than admit it. He'd fight it the entire way, and I wondered what would happen if I pointed it out.

My mom used to tell us all the time, *Look for the ways people show their love; don't just wait for the words. Not everyone can say them easily. But they almost always prove it with their actions.*

Should've been my first clue with Charles, because he had all the words. In the beginning, he told me all the time how beautiful I was. How much he loved me. How good we were together.

In hindsight, it would have been so easy to berate my past self for how easily I'd fallen for those words. And in the end, they were fairly empty. Because his actions indicated something else entirely.

"How're you feeling, duck?" Liam asked.

"I okay," she said, still nuzzling into my chest.

He looked at me. "Should we take it again?"

"We can," I told him. "But I think the fever broke."

"You cannot fucking know that just by kissing her forehead."

At his dry tone, I smiled. "No, but she's sweaty, which probably means it broke during the night."

He eyed me carefully, then grabbed the thermometer. He scanned Mira's forehead, and when he rolled his eyes, I laughed quietly.

"Don't be so smug," he said. "It's rude."

"Should we go make some breakfast?" I asked Mira.

She hopped out of my lap. "Can we have doughnuts?"

"Maybe later," I told her. "How about some eggs this morning?"

"I don't like eggs," she said.

"Sure you do. Remember when I put the cheese on them a couple days ago? You ate every bite."

She thought about that, then nodded. "Extra cheese."

"You got it." I motioned for her to come closer so I could open the back of her pajama pants and check if her overnight pull-up was dry.

"Nice work, Mirabelle." I pointed across the hall. "Pee first, and then we'll go downstairs."

Instead of lingering with the knowledge that Liam might be feeling a bit emotionally naked after Mira's short-lived fever, I hopped up and left the room.

It took him a couple of minutes to come down, but as he started down the stairs, he yelled over his shoulder: "I see you ignoring that soap, you little heathen."

"Good Lord," I muttered. "We're gonna have to explain this to her therapist someday. If I can ever find someone without a six-month wait-list, that is." I cracked a couple of eggs into a bowl and started whisking. "Well, it all started when Uncle Liam said the f-word seventy-four times a day and called me a little heathen . . ."

He gave me a look. "What, no coffee yet?"

"I am not moving in here to wait on you hand and foot, Liam Davies." I pointed to the machine. "You are perfectly capable of making your own."

"Calm down," he said. "You were the first one up. First one up always makes the coffee." Then he sighed. "But isn't that a nice mental image? You walking around with a little apron on . . . making anything I'd like."

Shockingly, my answering glare did not incinerate him on the spot. He did, however, whistle a happy little tune as he started filling the coffeepot with water.

When Mira came downstairs, he was saved from any possible retort I might have had. And I had plenty of options burning the tip of my tongue.

He knew it too, the ass. Because he walked past me and *winked.*

The egg in my hand cracked because I was gripping it so hard. Bits of shell and egg white went all over.

And then he laughed.

I'd never heard him laugh like that before. The sound was so deep and rich that I almost forgot I wanted to shove the egg straight into his face.

"What are you laughing at?" I asked. "You're the one who's gonna be picking eggshells out of your breakfast for the next hour."

"No eggs for me, Valentine." He patted his perfectly flat stomach. "Not hungry yet."

Mira took her spot at the island, and I quickly peeled a banana and set half on her plate before eating the other half myself.

"You want some?" Liam asked me as he started measuring the grounds.

"Please. I usually only have one cup in the morning, but I think I'll need two today."

He grunted.

While I made the eggs for Mira and myself, Liam went to the guest room to take a quick shower. He came back into the kitchen as I was taking my seat at the island, his hair almost black because it was still wet.

When he walked behind me, the scent of clean male had me chewing a bit more slowly. Good Lord, what soap did he use? Dirty Sex in a Bottle?

That's about what he smelled like. Clean, fresh, a little spicy. I blew out a harsh breath and ignored it while he fixed his coffee.

"Black?" he asked.

When I looked over, he was pulling a second mug from the cupboard. It took me a moment to swallow around my shock, but I nodded.

He set the mug down in front of me, and I gave him a small smile.

Liam wouldn't make eye contact.

Mira finished her eggs and pushed the plate away.

"Good job," I told her. "Why don't you go read some of your books, okay?"

She nodded, hopping off the stool and running toward her play-room down the hall.

Silence filled the kitchen.

"So," I said slowly, "is this our new morning routine?"

He took a long sip of his coffee, finally letting his green eyes settle on me. When he lowered the mug, he let out a heavy, measured sigh. "Don't know."

"Maybe we need some sort of schedule. Who's responsible for what meals. Who's gonna buy what groceries." I made a vague gesture with my hands. "Division of labor and all that."

"Do not make another bloody binder."

I gave him a look. "They're helpful. Structure is our friend right now, and you can't deny that. This is a unique situation, and it's not like I can go ask my friends how they do it at their houses."

He conceded that with a slight raise of his eyebrows.

"I can understand why Mira wants to stay here." I set my coffee down. "If anything, I'm surprised it took her this long to ask. But I'm not willing to say we're moving in here permanently just yet. Maybe we take this a month at a time."

For a moment, I allowed myself one quick glance at my house and felt a pang underneath my ribs. It must have shown on my face.

"I bet you can get her back there after a while," he said. "This might just be a phase."

"*Or* she'll always want to be here because it's where her parents lived. Because it's her home. I can't begrudge her that." Looking at Liam's face, I tried to puzzle out what I saw there and, as usual, came up blank. "You really didn't mind leaving your house?"

He shook his head. "Just a house. Didn't feel too much of anything about it, really. Wasn't big and flashy."

"And you don't have a place in London?" I asked. Was it shameless prying? Absolutely.

Liam gave a slight nod. "Not mine, though. Bought it for my mum and her family."

"*Her* family?" I asked. "Aren't they yours too?"

He rolled his neck, which popped audibly when he tilted to the right. "She remarried when I was a teenager. They had a couple more kids."

"How old were—"

Liam held up his hand. "Zoe, I know you cannot physically stop yourself from being nosy right now, but I believe we've reached our daily quota for personal questions."

"It's not even seven a.m.," I told him.

His eyebrows arched slowly. "Exactly."

I took a slow sip of coffee, my mind buzzing from the interaction. Bantering with Liam Davies perked me up faster than any caffeinated beverage in the world.

What an inconvenient realization.

"How many do I get every day?"

Liam set his mug down, his face inscrutable. "How many what?"

"Personal questions."

His eyes traced my face. "You are not serious," he said slowly.

"As a heart attack. We're about to *cohabitate*. We're raising a child together. You can't expect me not to be curious."

It took him an annoyingly long time to answer. He just stood there, staring at me like I was the world's most complicated puzzle. No one had ever looked at me like that.

The moment he came to a decision, I saw it in his eyes. "You get one on weekdays, two on weekends."

I couldn't help it. I burst out laughing.

Except . . . he didn't so much as crack a smile. He was serious.

My laughter faded. "Holy shit, you're not kidding," I whispered.

Liam sighed. "Let's keep focused, yeah?"

I sank back on my stool and studied his shuttered facial expression. My mom would have a field day with him. "Have you ever seen a therapist?" I asked.

He barked out a harsh laugh. "Absolutely fucking not. And no shrink would have me either."

"My mom is a therapist."

"*That* explains a lot."

"I bet she'd see you. She takes online clients."

"Not in a million years, Valentine."

With a sigh, I stood and picked up the empty plates. While I rinsed them off in the sink, I tried very, very hard not to inhale Liam's sex-soap smell, because he was standing close by.

"You moving your shit in or what?" he asked.

I put the plates in the dishwasher and shrugged as I closed the door. "Some of it. Not everything, though. I'll keep most of my clothes and stuff over there. Just bring a couple of days' worth at a time. I'll probably still work in my office if you're around."

He eyed me carefully. "You taking their room?" he asked quietly.

My stomach filled with sloshing ice, the cold seeping up into my lungs, and I breathed through it. Mainly because I didn't have a choice. The other option was to dive headfirst into a pint of ice cream, and that didn't feel like a healthy coping mechanism. "I think so. I might change out the comforter and some artwork, make it look a little bit more like me."

"Your ex's head mounted on the wall?" he asked lightly.

"I don't keep those trophies out for public consumption, but that's really sweet of you to ask."

Liam licked at his bottom lip, and my cheeks went a little warm.

There was no reason for him to make anything of mine warm, which just went to show how long it had been for me. Tyler, sweet though he was, had never progressed to the bedroom-activity phase of our relationship. He'd wanted to take things slow, and I hadn't really hit a point with him where he made me want to tear my clothes off.

Which meant that Charles was, unfortunately, my last experience with sex.

And his idea of sex had been early-evening missionary so that he could stare at himself in the mirror over the dresser, as the lighting and the angle made his body look better than it actually was. After about seven minutes (give or take), he'd leave the room, and I'd always have to roll over, tug open the top drawer of my nightstand, and finish myself off with a little help.

It was the *only* reason I was having this reaction to Liam. The only thing that made logical sense, at least.

Because now I was thinking about sex with Liam, and absolutely nothing good would come from that.

"What about *your* trophies?" I asked, head tilted to the side. "Do I have to worry about intrepid football fans sneaking out in the middle of the night? Finding them in the kitchen in the morning, wondering when the coffee's going to be made?"

He took a careful step closer, and I backed into the counter. His eyes searched my face.

"What do you think?" he murmured. "You think I'd parade women around here?"

I swallowed. Quite desperately, I wanted to answer him with something clever or snappy, to keep this little dance going, but I couldn't find the words. They were frozen somewhere under my sternum, and the air was thick with unnamed tension.

I damn well knew that Liam didn't sleep around. Chris and Amie had talked about it enough—how he was never in relationships.

Quite inexplicably, they'd felt like that was a shame. Personally, I could understand why the groupies didn't go after him, considering he was a raging dick and all.

But raging dick or not, he looked like a man who'd never leave a woman needing to roll over and finish anything by herself. With the arms and the eyes and the accent and the voice . . .

No. There'd be no help needed. My throat went bone dry as I stared up at him.

Finally, I shook my head.

He nodded slowly. "You'd be right, then."

Liam stepped back, and I let out a slow, uneven breath. "I'm gonna go shower at my place and bring back some stuff."

He was staring down at the floor when I stepped out of the kitchen. My heart jangled in my chest. I registered its uneven beats and racing thumps.

This would not do. Not on day one. I opened the slider and paused. "No bullshit?"

Liam's eyes locked onto mine.

"I'm really nervous to live under the same roof as you, Liam. Most of the time, I'm completely convinced that you hate me." My voice cracked on the word *hate*, and I cursed this little moment of honesty. "I think we're liable to kill each other if we don't figure out the right way to do this," I continued.

His jaw clenched.

"I don't . . ." I paused. "I don't want to mess this up."

When he didn't answer, I ducked my head and started out of the house.

"I don't either," he suddenly said, quiet and demanding. I stopped, my hand still on the door, my head swiveling slowly to stare. The thick line of his throat moved on a swallow. "And I don't hate you," he added in an urgent tone. "I never have."

My hand dropped to my side, and I turned to face him. "Never?" I repeated incredulously. "You've *never* hated me?"

Then Liam's face took on an entirely different cast. He could hardly meet my eyes. His jaw was tight, and he shifted on his feet.

He was nervous.

I was tempted to take another picture, because this needed to be recorded for posterity.

"I'd love a few more words than this," I prodded gently. "Because for a decade I have operated under the assumption that you can't stand being in the same room as me. You could hardly look at me for years."

Liam's eyes closed, and his chest expanded on a massive inhale. The kind you took when you were mentally prepping for something big.

"At the beginning, I couldn't," he ground out. "But not . . . not because of that."

My brow furrowed.

"I didn't hate you," he said again, his voice low and fierce, and absolutely nothing about that fierceness was computing in my brain.

"You certainly didn't like me." I crossed my arms over my chest. "Which was fine. I didn't expect—"

"I *did* like you," he interrupted hotly. "That was the problem, yeah?"

His eyes weren't closed anymore. They were wide open, blazing with intensity—and locked straight on mine.

Something invisible cinched itself tightly around my ribs and squeezed.

"When I met you . . ." Liam continued, voice halting as he chose his words. "I got over it. It was . . . just a little thing, and I don't want you to think I'm still . . ." He stopped, then blew out a hard breath. "But I liked you, Zoe."

My breath was coming in short, shocked little puffs. My mouth hung open, and my cheeks were hot. "You . . ."

I couldn't even say it, let alone wrap my brain around what he was telling me.

"Fuck," he muttered, swiping a hand over his face. "I'm bollocks-ing this up. I shouldn't even be . . ."

Weren't we a pair? He was stumbling over his words, and I couldn't find a single friggin' one.

"You liked me? *Liked me* liked me?"

He gave me an exasperated look, but holy shit, there was a spark of warmth buried in his eyes, and it was just enough to snap me back into the moment.

"Liam, I . . ."

"Men get crushes too," he barked. And, oh my, his cheekbones flushed pink. My heart couldn't take it. "Don't make a big bloody thing about it. It was a long time ago, and once that twat walked in for dinner and you set down your book and I saw the ring, I got *over* it, all right?"

I'd forgotten so many details of that night. The only one that remained seared in my memory was the way he'd locked eyes with me and wished me luck with husband number two.

It was so audacious, so rude, and—worst of all—so incredibly accurate.

"I was reading at the island while Chris and Amie were grilling on the deck," I said quietly.

"Harry Potter," he added. "I think it was the third book."

Slowly, I nodded.

His eyes traced over my hair, which was undoubtedly a mess, as it always was in the mornings. "It was curly that night, and I thought"— he stopped, swallowing again—"I thought you were Hermione come to life for a minute. Older, though."

Was my jaw on the floor?

Tucked behind my chest, my heart hammered wildly, and I had the vague worry that he could hear it. "Have a crush on Hermione, did you?" I asked lightly, an attempt to break the tension building and building and building.

"Of course." He looked at me like I was nuts. "Who didn't?"

"You've read Harry Potter." It wasn't a question. Just . . . making sure I wasn't hallucinating the entire exchange.

He shifted on his feet again. "My youngest half sister loves those books. She was always reading one of 'em when I visited in the summers."

I rolled my lips between my teeth and studied him. He looked like Liam. Sounded like him. What had I said to Rosa in my text earlier?

An enlightening twelve hours, indeed.

As it turned out, he was desperately endearing when being teased. *Maybe too endearing,* something in the back of my head whispered, but I steadfastly ignored that.

"You're a Hufflepuff, aren't you?" I asked. "It makes so much sense."

Liam reared his head back. "I am not."

I arched an eyebrow.

"I'm a fucking Slytherin," he snapped. "Have you met me?"

I hummed.

He jabbed a finger in the air. "See? Everyone makes judgy little noises when I say that. Slytherins are massively misunderstood." He tucked his arms over his chest again, his chin notched in the air. "You can't tell me Draco didn't get dealt a shit hand. He was no bad guy in the end, and no matter what you say, I'll never change my mind."

The battle against my growing smile was lost, and I couldn't stop it fast enough.

Liam rolled his eyes, exhaling a harsh puff of air. From anyone else, I'd have thought it was one step away from a laugh. But with him? I hardly knew anymore.

In his halting voice and choppy words, with the blush of embarrassment high on his cheeks, he'd admitted something to me that he'd probably never intended to reveal.

And if we'd never decided to share this space, he probably never would have.

I was starting to realize that maybe I'd never really known Liam Davies at all. It was the sort of knowledge that could rock the foundations if I wasn't careful, sloshing water over the edges at an alarming rate.

Tidal waves had less impact than this conversation, and something sweet expanded in my lungs as I felt the implications crash over me.

"So you had a crush on me," I said quietly.

He couldn't meet my eyes. "Don't make a big thing about it."

Slowly, I nodded. "So that night, you were like . . . the boy on the playground who pulls the girl's hair because he doesn't know how to use his words."

Liam's face was implacable, but he managed a tight nod.

"A healthy life choice," I said, voice even and dry and only mildly sarcastic.

He gave me a look. "I didn't say my reaction was healthy, I just . . . hated him that first night, and even more as the years went by and you looked so . . ." His voice trailed off. "Never mind. It's not important; it was a long time ago."

It felt important to me. Really important.

Everything about the last few years of my life had left me feeling just a little bit battered. My divorce and my breakup and the fact that I was burned out from a career I loved.

That I'd changed, been hurt, and wasn't exactly sure what moving forward looked like.

All of it added up to a version of myself that I hardly recognized. Someone tired and weary from all those shifts and changes.

Not less, though. None of those things made me a lesser version of Zoe Valentine.

But it was still nice to hear that in the midst of some of those things, someone had *seen* me.

But I wouldn't ask, wouldn't push. The fact that he'd admitted this much was a big deal. A decade of keeping himself locked down wouldn't change overnight, and I knew that too.

It was enough right now that I knew. That he'd trusted me enough to share it.

"Thank you for telling me," I said.

He heard the sincerity in my voice, because he held my gaze for a long moment before jerking his chin in a short nod. "Welcome," he answered, voice tight and uncomfortable.

Oh yeah. My mom would have a field day with him.

My hand rested on the slider again, my finger tapping against the frame. "So . . . two questions a day on the weekends, huh?"

"Fucking hell," he muttered. "I wasn't being literal, Valentine."

With a laugh, I left the house, pulling the slider door shut behind me. Immediately, I tugged my phone out of my pocket.

"Rosa," I said when she picked up. "You are never gonna believe this."

Chapter Thirteen

ZOE

"And then what did he say?"

Martha crowded in on the couch next to Phyllis, the former elbowing the latter when she wouldn't move quickly enough.

"I know Rosa already told you this story."

Phyllis elbowed Martha right back. "I missed this part. I didn't have my hearing aid in when she called."

"I told you not to take those out," Martha yelled.

Phyllis glared. "It's in *now*. You don't have to yell, for gosh sake."

Rosa shook her head from her perch in the armchair. "Martha never listens to my stories anyway."

Martha sniffed. "I'd rather hear Zoe tell it, because then I can watch her facial expressions and figure out what we need to do about this little development."

The little development, as they were calling it, was Liam's bombshell from the day before. As soon as I'd gotten off the phone with Rosa, she'd in turn called the girls.

A few years ago, I would've sat around with a group of my coworkers, or Amie. And now . . . I had these three.

Taking care of Mira took so much of my mental energy that I could hardly stop to process what it meant to my life most days. It was hard enough to find good, trustworthy friends in your thirties and beyond, but even more so when you could hardly keep your head above water.

I liked Rosa's friends. They were funny and sweet and had no inhibitions. It was refreshing to be around women who weren't trying to impress anyone and had a lifetime of insight to share.

Maybe it wouldn't make sense to a lot of people that I'd inserted myself into a group of Golden Girls, but I found myself liking this new friend circle an awful lot.

Liam was training and would be gone for a few hours, so Rosa had declared an emergency meeting. Their shiny cars pulled into the driveway less than five minutes after he left.

With Mira fast asleep upstairs and a bowl of ice cream for each of them, they were a rapt audience. When I got to the part where Liam said he thought I was Hermione come to life, Phyllis sank back into the couch with a happy sigh.

"This is good, Zoe. *Damn it*, this is some good stuff."

I laughed. "He said he got over it years ago. He was just . . . being honest."

Rosa snorted. "Okay."

"You don't believe him?" I asked.

Martha swallowed a heaping spoonful of ice cream. "I believe him. He'd never tell you if he still had a crush on you."

Rosa arched an eyebrow. "Or that's what he'd want you to think."

Phyllis's spoon scraped the side of her bowl when she scooped up her last bite of mint chocolate chip. "He didn't put that much forethought into it. He wanted her to know he doesn't hate her, and I think that's admirable."

Martha tapped her chin thoughtfully. "What if you thank him by hopping into the shower with him?"

"No," the rest of us said in unison.

She held up her hands. "All right, all right. Calm down. She said the shower gel made her crazy. It's a unique way she can break the ice." Then she tilted her chin down, peering at me over her glasses. "Besides, one day you wake up and you can't maneuver shower sex anymore, and you never know when that day is. The tiles are unforgiving on your joints, and unless you've got all those really ugly hand bars installed, you'll never be able to withstand the position."

I blinked. "This isn't helpful," I whispered.

She laughed, patting me on the shoulder.

"Having sex with Liam, even if he were amenable, is the worst possible thing she could do," Phyllis interjected. "If they make it about something as trivial as attraction, they're doomed before they get started."

My eyes dropped to the bowl in my lap. Everyone fell quiet.

"It was hard for me to view Liam differently when it was just about Mira," I said slowly. It wasn't just about Mira anymore. And maybe it hadn't been for a while. Nothing about this was black and white, neatly confined to boxes that made sense. Absently, I rubbed at my forehead as those boxes melted into each other, as black and white mixed into varying shades of gray. "He's not . . . he's not this horrible, cold person that I always assumed him to be."

The women surrounding me listened. They were really good at that. Probably because they'd had decades of experience with building good friendships. Talking is fine, but sometimes the thing you need most from the people in your life is for them not to talk. Not to push. Not to pry.

The best thing a real friend can do for you is give you a safe space to speak your truth.

"I'm glad he told me," I continued. "Maybe he could've approached it differently, but it's good that I know."

His words tumbled unbidden through my head again, even though I'd already replayed them a hundred times. That first night was crystal clear now, the memory dragged up to the forefront of my mind.

For so long, I'd remembered only his parting shot, felt the wound of it like it was fresh, like the impact of it still stung my skin.

When I pushed beyond it, dredged up those first few moments, there *was* something very different about the Liam who'd walked into the kitchen when I was nose-deep in a book.

He wasn't flirty, and he wasn't forward.

He was kind, though. He shook my hand, and we made small talk. Pleasant, easy questions. I think I even made him smile. Just a little.

But his eyes . . .

I swallowed past a lump in my throat.

I remembered his eyes when they'd looked at me. When they'd locked on mine. There was one moment where my stomach had swooped weightlessly, and then guilt had followed in the very next breath. And when I'd set my book down, his gaze had moved straight to my ring, shuttering immediately.

His expression had only closed further when Charles arrived, straight from the office and high off closing a big settlement for the hospital. He'd kissed me on the top of my head and asked if I was being rude again, ignoring the people around me for the people in my books.

That was when Liam's eyes had flattened and he'd walked out of the room.

"Where'd you go?" Rosa asked gently.

I blinked a few times. "The past."

She hummed thoughtfully.

"Sometimes it's simple to change your perspective of your past," I said. "The way we view our own choices and our culpability in how things played out. I don't think this is one of those simple ones. It feels complicated."

"What are you going to do now that you know?" Martha asked.

I ate the last bite of my ice cream, set my bowl down on the coffee table, and slowly looked at each of their faces.

"Now I try to get to know Liam Davies." I smiled. "One question at a time."

Phyllis's face lit up, and she reached for her phone, peering over her glasses as she typed slowly with her thumbs. "I googled this the other day."

Rosa hid her smile.

Martha rolled her eyes. "Googled what?"

"What questions to ask your crush," Phyllis said. "I had that date with the retired doctor and didn't want to screw it up."

I blew out a slow breath through puffed cheeks.

"Liam's not her crush," Martha said.

He wasn't. I was just . . . obsessing over the way he smelled and the way he freaked out over Mira's fever and the fact that he'd thought I was a literary heroine come to life when he'd had a crush on me.

Curious is what I was.

He was a problem to be solved.

A story that I wanted to unpack.

I'd never been able to resist a great story, and I had a feeling that Liam had one, if he'd let me see a little bit beyond what he was already showing.

"Oh, this is a good one," Phyllis said. "What would you do if I called you in the middle of the night?"

With a groan, I covered my face with my hands.

Rosa laughed delightedly. "She doesn't have to call him," she said slyly. "He's just a quick trip down the stairs."

A sound escaped my lips. A whimper, maybe.

Martha snickered.

"Wait," Phyllis added, "this one is better. Have you ever had a crush on a teacher?"

"That reminds me," Martha said, "that we should add a teacher-student book to our list."

Rosa pulled out her notepad. "Got it."

I sat up, hands raised. "Thank you, truly, but I think I've got it handled."

"I'll email you the list," Phyllis said.

"She doesn't need the list," Martha yelled.

Phyllis gave her a look. "I can hear you just fine, Martha. Stop yelling."

My phone dinged with an email notification. I smiled at Phyllis. "Thank you, but I don't think I'll use this."

"Just in case, deary." She winked.

"We're going grocery shopping tonight when he's back from training. I need to look at this like a fresh start, I think. He's not the guy I thought he was. Right now, that's all I know."

"Don't fall in love with him," Phyllis warned. "Or be so concerned with finding out the hidden parts of him that you ignore the red flags."

Martha and Rosa traded a look.

Like me, Phyllis was divorced. Like me, she'd been hurt. Sometimes those hurts meant just a little bit less trust. In others.

Or, worse, in ourselves.

Drops in the bucket that we couldn't pull back.

I settled my hand over hers. "I'm not going to fall in love with him. But I'm not going to ignore the way he's trying either. If I write him off based on his past, then I can't expect anyone to give me a second chance when I might deserve one."

◆ ◆ ◆

"That's all you're getting?" I asked. My nose wrinkled when I looked at the additions to his cart.

Healthy, gross bread.

Enough eggs for a family of six.

Chicken.

Veggies.

And then more veggies.

Mira sat in my cart, kicking her legs, and when she tried to lean forward to grab a box of cookies, Liam pulled it from her hands and set it back on the shelf without dropping his gaze from mine.

"What's wrong with that?" he asked.

"Nothing," I answered carefully. "I just noticed that it seems to be all you eat."

He patted his flat stomach. "Gotta fuel right heading into the season." Then he peered into my cart, eyebrows lifting at the three cartons of mint chocolate chip ice cream.

"Don't judge my ice cream consumption, okay? It's my single vice, and I will not apologize for it."

Liam's lips twitched, an almost smile, and I found myself holding my breath.

"You only have one? I'm jealous."

I pushed my cart past him. "Why? What are yours?"

"That your question for the day?"

My lips twisted in frustration. "No."

In a weaker moment, I'd opened the link that Phyllis sent me, shaking my head at some of the questions.

"What if we trade off who makes dinner?" I asked. "Or are we making separate meals? Because I need more variation than that."

"You gonna cook for me, Valentine?" Liam leaned past me to grab a bag of apples, his arm brushing mine. Our eyes met and held as he pulled back.

"I will if it means I don't have to eat chicken and veggies every single night."

"You'll eat late during the season if you wait for me," he said.

Risking a quick glance in his direction, I noted that his eyes were steadfastly fixed on the display of bananas. Regular season was still about three months away, training camp just around the corner.

The assumption there was that we'd still be living together.

I didn't correct him.

"True," I added quietly. "You have Tuesdays off, right?"

He nodded. "I'll be in for a bit, though. No one really gets any days off during the regular season. Fridays I'm done early."

These were things I knew from living next to Chris and Amie for so long. I always had extra time with Amie when Chris was in the thick of his busyness. Once Mira was born, it was tough for her in a different way.

"I can save you leftovers," I said. His gaze cut over to mine. "For when you get home late."

Liam didn't answer right away. His jaw tightened, and he finally conceded a nod. "That'd be nice."

This was *so weird*. I'd been dropped into an alternate reality where we spoke nicely to each other. We had polite conversation. He wasn't dropping f-bombs every other word.

Oh gawd, we were, like . . . friends now?

I gave him a quick once-over out of the corner of my eye. Chris was the only man I'd ever considered to be my friend, and he came with a wife, so this was a situation where I was wholly out of my element.

None of my friends had ever looked like Liam. Or had ever had crushes on me.

"You like to cook?" he asked.

I shrugged. "I don't love it, but I'm good at it. Charles always liked a big home-cooked meal waiting for him when he walked in the door."

Liam's brow furrowed. "You worked full-time too, yeah?"

"I did." And then some. During tax season and the end of each quarter, I'd fall asleep on the couch with a stack of papers on my chest.

"Why couldn't he make the dinners?" Liam asked.

"An excellent question," I said lightly. "I stopped with the fuss of a fancy meal after a few years. I was too tired."

"Did he help?"

I smiled. "Depends on your definition. If by helping, you mean make passive-aggressive comments about the lack of effort I was putting into our marriage, then yes, he was incredibly helpful."

Liam's mouth opened like he was going to ask something else, but then he closed it.

"Just ask," I said, nudging him lightly with my shoulder. "I'm not the one with the limit."

He set some bananas in his cart, face bent in thought.

Mira tapped my arm. "Can I have a snack?"

I tweaked her nose. "What else?"

"Please," she said dutifully.

"Go ahead," I told her. Immediately, she dug into the front pocket of my purse and found an applesauce pouch and a small bag of Goldfish.

Liam eyed her carefully. "Am I supposed to carry food everywhere now?" he asked.

"Pretty much. Better get a manbag."

"What the fuck is that?"

I exhaled a laugh. "Probably not your thing."

"Probably not."

He glanced over at me as we walked toward the checkout. When we'd pass someone, he'd garner an occasional look of recognition, but so far, no one had approached him. He was wearing a dark cap, the brim tugged low, but it was impossible to hide the sheer breadth of his frame.

With the way it sat on his head, there were moments when I looked at him and could see only the hard line of his jaw and his firm, unsmiling mouth. His eyes were hidden, and I couldn't decide if that was good or bad.

It was his eyes that softened him, I'd realized. Guarded as they were, they gave away when he was letting his walls down, even the tiniest bit.

The question popped into my mind immediately.

"Do you hate the fame that comes with playing?"

Liam stopped, that green, green gaze fully visible now as he pivoted to face me. "That your question?" His voice was a low, bone-shivering rumble.

Somewhat breathless from asking it, I nodded slowly.

He licked at his bottom lip and glanced across the store. "It's a yes-or-no question, Valentine. You sure you don't want to rephrase?"

My mouth curled in a smile. "How do you feel about the fame of playing?"

We started walking again, the aisles wide enough that we could stay side by side. He was so much taller than me, but he matched the length of my strides so that I didn't have to hurry.

The skin of his arm was warm, and even when we didn't touch, I could feel that warmth coming off him like an aura.

"It's complicated." He inhaled, and his arm touched my shoulder. I didn't move away. His eyes flicked down to mine before he continued. "I don't mind when people come up to me, ask for a picture or whatever. Most are nice."

"But?"

Again, the corners of his lips hooked up incrementally. So close.

"But," he added, "I never want to disappoint a fan if I'm not some smiling, outgoing guy. I'm just . . . me. And that won't always be enough for people looking to meet someone they idolize, whether they should or not."

This new side of Liam, which I was just now uncovering, left a warm, aching sensation crawling up through my throat.

He was far more self-aware than I gave him credit for. That much was undoubtedly true.

And like I had conjured their existence by asking the question, a little boy and his sister approached carefully, their mom standing back about fifteen feet with an encouraging smile on her face.

Liam and I stopped, and he gentled his face. Just a bit.

The boy opened his mouth but couldn't speak. His sister, a bit taller than him, nudged him in the back. They were both wearing Denver shirts.

His freckled cheeks flushed pink the longer they stood there, and his eyes darted down to the ground.

"What's your name?" Liam asked.

The boy's eyes darted up. "N-Nathan Maxwell."

Liam held out his hand. "Nice to meet you, Nathan. What about you?" he asked the sister.

"I'm Daisy. He was too nervous to come say hi by himself."

Nathan gave his sister a wide-eyed, incredulous stare. "No, I wasn't," he hissed.

Liam glanced between them with a wry grin. "You like football, Nathan?"

He nodded frantically. "Denver is my favorite team. I wanna play there someday."

"Gonna have to work really hard if you want to do that," Liam said.

"I know; I will," Nathan said. His eyes held the fervent light of unfettered hero worship.

"You ever been to a game?"

Nathan and Daisy traded a look. "No. Mom said the tickets are too expensive for her. But I'm gonna ask for my birthday again. I ask every year," he said quietly.

Liam swallowed, slowly pulling his phone out of his back pocket. He crouched down so that he was closer to eye level with Nathan.

"Tell you what," he said gently. "If you give me your mum's email, I can send you and your sister passes to come to training camp one day. How does that sound?"

"Sweet! Mom, he needs your email," Nathan yelled over his shoulder.

I stifled a laugh.

Mira munched on her Goldfish and waved at Daisy.

Daisy smiled, studying both Mira and me openly.

"Thank you so much," the mom told Liam, her eyes shining with grateful tears. Her ring finger was empty, and the bags around her eyes told me just a bit about how tired she was. "This will be the highlight of his year."

Liam finished tapping something out on his phone. "Just sent it over to the office. They'll have it under your name." The three posed for a picture, and Liam leaned over to speak to Nathan. "You make a nice sign for camp, all right? I'll make sure you meet some of the guys."

His chin trembled. "I'll make the best sign *ever*."

"Good." Liam nodded. "See you in a few weeks, yeah?"

Even though Liam had started walking away, I paused for a moment, watching as Nathan crumpled into his mom's embrace and lost his battle to tears, completely overwhelmed by what he'd just experienced.

My cheeks were wet when I joined Liam again, and he studied my face.

"You're crying?"

I exhaled a watery laugh. "I can't help it. You made that kid's life."

I could tell that Liam was uncomfortable with the praise, because he adjusted his shoulders and sighed heavily. "Just sent an email, is all."

"Okay."

At my patronizing tone, he gave me another look. "Don't make a big thing of it, Valentine. And I'm still not hugging you if you keep crying."

I rolled my lips together, a weak attempt to hide my burgeoning smile. "I'd never expect you to."

One question at a time, I thought.

A few more like that and I could only imagine what I'd uncover. Or how dangerous these new sides of Liam could be.

Chapter Fourteen

LIAM

Let it be known that I had the patience of a fucking saint.

Either that or I was the worst kind of simpering fool for this woman. I could've ignored the questions. But I didn't.

"Would you rather speak any language in the world or have the ability to communicate with animals?"

"Honestly, Valentine."

"What? It's a hard question."

I took a moment to think. I sighed. "Animals. Because then I could bribe spiders to stay away from me for the rest of my fucking life, and I'd never have to see them again."

She smiled, and it made my chest go all soft. "Hates spiders. Noted."

That was a good one, and I barely stopped myself from asking her how she'd answer, but somehow I managed.

The next day, it was like she wasn't even trying.

"Favorite place to shop?"

"The grocery store."

She sighed dramatically. "That doesn't count."

"Does to me."

Zoe set her chin in her hand and stared, finally rolling her eyes when I didn't change my answer. "The bookstore," she said. "The one in Lone Tree. They have the best romance section."

I grunted as I flipped through the mail, but I found myself wanting to tuck each little nugget away for safekeeping. Things I hadn't known about her before.

I liked it when she answered on her own.

She'd set aside the envelopes with my name on them, and I paused when I found a heavy one addressed to me but stamped with the logo from Chris's alma mater. He'd gone to the University of Michigan, and I'd come from their bitter rival, Ohio State, so I took a moment to growl at the sight of the blocky *M* in the return address. Zoe angled her head when I ripped at the back. "What's that?"

"An envelope."

She sighed heavily, and it brought me an unholy amount of joy. "What's *in* the envelope?" she clarified.

Skimming the invitation, I didn't answer right away, and she tried to edge around me to look. I moved the letter so she couldn't see it. She narrowed her eyes in a glare, and I fought the urge to smile.

"They're doing something for Chris and Amie," I said as I continued reading. "First home game of the season. They'd like us to come with Mira."

She nodded. "Do you think we should go?"

"I hate that fucking stadium," I told her. "But yeah. I might call Burke, see how the house is coming along. He was probably invited too."

"Why do you hate it so much?"

"You want a list?" I laughed, short and dry and devoid of humor. "It's ugly, and it's too big, and there's way too much blue and fucking yellow."

"Ahh." Her eyes were wide and serious. "It sounds . . . awful."

"Don't you make fun of me; you have no idea what it's like to play in that place."

It was the first place where I'd played against Chris, and we'd split during our years in college. He won two, I won two—something we'd never let each other forget in all our years playing pro ball together in Denver.

Zoe chewed on her bottom lip as she studied me, her eyes gleaming.

"What?" I snapped.

Her grin blossomed slowly. "Nothing."

"Yeah right, fucking nothing," I muttered, brushing past her and out of the kitchen to the sound of her laughter. She'd somehow managed to get a few extra questions in, and I decided to blame that on Michigan too. Bloody Wolverines.

Thankfully, she'd dropped it by the next day.

"What movie have you watched more than any other?"

"Are you joking?" I asked her.

"No."

"What's yours?"

She stared past my shoulder for a moment as she thought. "*Back to the Future.*"

"Really?" I asked. "That's your favorite movie?"

"I didn't say favorite," she pointed out. "I said what movie have you seen the most. I always watch it when it's on TV, and it's on a lot."

I conceded that one with a grunt. Then I pointed at Mira. "What do you think?"

Zoe's face bent slightly in confusion.

I sighed. "Duck, what's your favorite movie?"

Mira was pushing her food around her plate, and her head snapped up. "*Moana*! We watch it?"

Zoe laughed, and even though I rolled my eyes, the mood in the kitchen was light and happy while we finished our dinner.

"If you could have only one meal for the rest of your life, what would it be?"

I cocked my head to the side as I grilled chicken for dinner the following night. Mira was drawing with sidewalk chalk on the concrete, and Zoe was sitting in one of the lounge chairs with her Kindle in hand.

"Do I get sick of this meal?" I asked.

"No. And it never makes you gain weight either."

"Not chicken and veggies, I can tell you that."

She laughed, and I tucked the sound away in my brain. Something to think about later. Something to pull out when I wanted to make my heart feel warm and happy.

What was my big accomplishment for the day? I'd made Zoe Valentine laugh.

Simpering.

Fool.

Zoe set her Kindle down. "That's not your answer, is it? Because that's cheating."

"Not my answer," I told her. "Just thinking."

"Mine is pizza," she said. "And mint chocolate chip ice cream for dessert."

Zoe would inevitably spend all day thinking about her one question and hit me with it sometime around dinner.

"You and that ice cream," I mused.

She arched an eyebrow. "It's the perfect flavor."

Yeah, and every night when she opened the freezer to dig her spoon into the container, making those fucking noises after a few bites, I had the startling realization that I'd probably always get hard when I smelled mint and chocolate.

Not ideal.

"If it's not chicken and veggies . . ." Zoe prompted.

Right. My daily question. I closed my eyes and conjured up the first thing I'd ask my mum to make if I were back home. "My mum's bacon butty."

"What's that?"

I glanced at Zoe. She'd turned in the chair, her legs tucked up to the side. Even though it was perfect out, sunny and in the midseventies, she had that fucking Wolves sweatshirt covering her to midthigh, her thumbs poked through holes in the sleeves.

I'd come to realize she did that to all her favorite shirts, and fuck if that didn't delight me.

A few curls had escaped her ponytail, and they framed her face— open and attentive and curious.

When I didn't answer, she widened her eyes meaningfully.

"You know, your one question somehow turns into quite a few. *That's* cheating."

Zoe grinned, a dimple popping up in her cheek.

I had to turn away because I was not liable for my actions when that dimple appeared. Bloody hell, it made my stomach tremble dangerously.

For a moment, I focused on the chicken, flipping a few of the pieces and then transferring some others to the top rack to finish.

"A butty is just a sandwich," I told her. "My mum fries up bacon— ours is much larger than anything you use here. She puts salted butter on the bread. If tomatoes are in season, she'll add a fresh slice from the ones in her garden. Sometimes it's got brown sauce." My voice went a little quieter the longer I talked, the longer I thought about sitting at her banged-up kitchen table, eating one of those fucking sandwiches. It had been years. "It's nothing fancy, and you can find it in a thousand pubs across Britain. But hers are the best."

Zoe was silent after I stopped talking, and when I risked another look in her direction, she'd lifted her Kindle again, but her smile was soft and happy.

Slowly and quietly, I exhaled all the air from my lungs.

Some days, the questions were easy.

My biggest pet peeve? People.

That one made her laugh. I liked it when that happened.

Favorite candy? M&M's.

She'd said I needed to get out more.

Some questions called for a bit more of a filter, something I often struggled with.

When you were little, what did you want to be when you grew up?

I couldn't say the real answer—*anything but like my dad*—out loud.

It had taken me a few minutes to answer this one. Somehow, she realized that the question was harder for me than most and didn't push.

"Don't remember a lot from when I was little," I told her. What a bloody cop-out.

"I wanted to be a ballerina," she said. "Alas, I wasn't born with the long legs or the talent for dancing."

Of course that made me look at her fucking legs. I tugged my eyes away before she noticed. Her legs looked just fine to me.

"Didn't most little British boys and girls want to be footballers when they grew up?" she asked. "You know, *your* football. Believe me, I know better than to call it soccer."

I grunted. "Most did, yeah."

"You didn't?"

I shook my head. "No. Loved watching it. But I never wanted to play." Why did my voice sound like that? Like answering this question was slicing up my insides.

Wisely, she dropped it.

That first week, time passed in a strange sort of way. We were getting along better but would often go long stretches without even seeing much of each other throughout the day. Every now and again—usually when we had dinner together or afterward—I caught her staring at me. When I did, she never yanked her eyes away. Never acted embarrassed. Sometimes her cheeks flushed pink, but fuck if she wasn't so much braver than me.

She'd smile when I caught her. A tiny smile. Nothing more than the gentlest curve of her sweet lips, because in her view, she wasn't doing anything wrong.

What must that be like?

When I stared at Zoe, I felt like a thief. Like I was stealing some little piece of her that didn't belong to me, a piece that I'd hoard, that I'd hide away so no one could take it from me. I'd guard it like a big, snarling dragon who'd just gotten his golden egg.

And fuck if those little stolen glances didn't have devastating consequences. It had been easier when she hated me, I realized. Because then I didn't wonder.

I didn't hope.

Hope was the most dangerous of emotions, something I didn't have much experience with off the field. And even on the field, I didn't *hope* we'd win a game. Didn't hope we'd win a championship.

In that space, I'd simply work harder. Push my teammates to work harder too. Hope implied a lack of control. If you desperately wanted to reach the place, you likely couldn't do much steering to get there.

Hope is the only thing stronger than fear, my mum used to say.

No matter what I did, I couldn't tear those words out of my head. And one afternoon, as I drove home from the facilities, I did something I hadn't done in far too long.

I picked up my phone and punched a button.

"Bloody hell, is that really you?"

I smiled. "Morning, Mum."

"Nice to see you're alive, son."

"I texted you yesterday."

She snorted. "What was that text again? Three entire words?"

I sighed, battling the sticky coat of shame that told me I was, in fact, a shit son.

She reminded me what I'd written: *Maybe next year.*

"We'd all love to see you, Liam. It's been two years since you've been home, and I've half a mind to hop on a plane without telling you so I can come see your little girl." She paused. "You still haven't sent me another picture, by the way."

169

"I sent you two a couple weeks ago because you wouldn't stop pestering me about it," I said. "And she's not my little girl. I'm just . . . helping."

"She didn't even have her eyes open, Liam. They were blurry, and you could hardly see half her face." She clucked her tongue. "You're rubbish at taking photos, and you know it."

"Believe me, spend an afternoon with her and tell me how easy it is to get her to sit still."

Mum went quiet, and fuck if that didn't make me nervous.

"I'd love to meet her. See you with her," she added. Then she emitted a soft laugh. "You with a little girl, Liam. I can't tell you what my heart does thinking about it."

As she said this, I pulled onto the street that led to the house. Words crawled up my throat, and it was almost impossible to ignore them. Before the accident, Chris had been the one who'd get them, who'd listen without judgment to all the thoughts churning through my head.

"She scares the absolute bloody hell out of me, Mum."

"Oh, Liam." She sighed. "Talk to me, darling."

Everything about my life was in a surreal state of limbo, and I didn't know how to change it. Things felt . . . normal. They were anything but.

"I didn't want kids," I ground out. "Didn't want a family. I was fine on my own, and I had no intention of changing that."

"I know, son."

Bloody, bloody fuck, it sounded like she was battling tears. Something about my mum crying had black clouds filling my head. Always had. I needed someone to bleach the memory clean from my head, because the sound of her sadness was the thing that always haunted me the most.

"But you're not him. You're *not him*, Liam. You're so good and loving, and it is an absolute tragedy that you won't let yourself love someone."

It did no good to argue with her. I'd given that up long ago.

But I knew.

Every time I looked in the mirror, I saw his eyes. His jaw. His height and his strength.

By now, though, I was likely taller and stronger. In my mind, he was a giant, capable of so much destruction. But as I'd grown, that mental image of him didn't shrink down.

He simply got bigger and bigger until I couldn't wave him away, because I'd spent so many years running from the idea of what he was. Running from all the ways I was constantly told that I was just like him.

No one knew what it meant when they said it, of course. Not what it meant to me.

No part of me could be carved out to rid myself of his memory. I'd have done it if there were a way. And no matter what my mum said, the reason I'd left in the first place was because I'd never been able to understand how she could look at me and see anything *other* than him.

I'd left because I couldn't handle being stacked up against him my entire life.

With a slow turn of the steering wheel, I pulled my car into the driveway and waited quietly while the garage door opened.

"You ignoring me, son?"

I grunted. "I know better than that."

"You're ignoring me." She sniffled. "You know what my biggest regret is, Liam?"

"Marrying him."

Mum exhaled a short laugh. "No, you twat, because then I wouldn't have you. I wish I'd left the first time. I wish you never remembered anything about him at all, but it's hard to be brave when you're scared witless, isn't it?"

I shifted the car into park and leaned my head back against the seat, pinching my eyes closed. "Yeah," I answered in a gruff voice. "Yeah, it is."

"You were the reason I was brave, Liam. Just you." She sighed. "There's no magic to taking a first step, son. You let yourself be scared for a bit. And then when that feeling ebbs—and it will—that's when you move forward."

With a hand covering my eyes, I opened them again, staring sightlessly at the creases in my fingers.

"How's the friend?" she asked.

I dropped my hand. "Zoe."

"Zoe." Her voice was soft and questioning, and I cursed myself up and down for feeling like I needed to bring her name into this moment. As if Mira weren't enough for me to deal with right now.

"She's fine."

At my curt tone, Mum laughed under her breath. "You being nice?"

"Nice enough."

"That means no," she said. "What does Zoe do for work?"

"She used to be an accountant at a hospital. Was for years. But she's been . . . working from home for the last couple years. Does some bookkeeping for small businesses."

"Nice to have that flexibility when you're a new mum," she said. "It's the hardest transition in the world. Figuring out who you are and not getting lost in that new person you're in charge of."

My brow furrowed. Was Zoe getting lost in Mira?

I murmured in agreement, my mind snagging on how differently Zoe and I were reacting to this. She dived in headfirst, no questions asked, filling every role that Mira needed her to fill.

If Zoe was scared by any of this, she sure as hell wasn't letting it show.

"I'm home now, Mum. It's my night to make dinner, so I should head inside."

"And what are we serving?"

I smiled a little. "She told me I'm banned from making chicken and veggies more than twice a week, so I'm having to expand my horizons a bit."

"And?"

"Fish and veggies. Grilling some salmon."

She laughed. "I did you no favors, did I? I always preferred to do it myself rather than have anyone mucking up the kitchen when I was trying to cook."

"You did just fine, Mum," I told her. My throat felt tight because it had been too long since I'd talked to her.

"I miss you, son."

I closed my eyes. "You too."

"Can I come visit during the season? I haven't seen you play in person in a couple years. I miss it. And I want to meet these girls of yours."

Absently, I rubbed at my chest, because the denial was quick and sharp on the tip of my tongue.

They weren't mine. Not by a landslide.

"I'll send you the schedule."

She went quiet for a moment. "I love you, Liam. The first love of my life, you are."

"Don't tell Nigel."

Mum laughed. "Oh, he knows. And don't deflect when someone says something nice to you, all right?"

I sighed heavily, because there was no hiding any of my shit from her. "All right."

She disconnected the call, and after a few moments in my car, I felt steady enough to go inside. The kitchen was silent. Papers and crayons and books were strewn all over the island.

I tugged at one of the drawings. Mira must've asked for ducks, as Zoe had a sheet with about fifteen little yellow ducks in various shapes and sizes. On the paper next to it were giant yellow blobs slashed through with orange scribbles.

"So close," I said quietly.

Movement from the backyard caught my attention.

Zoe stood next to the pool, bending over to try and coax Mira onto the top step with her. When Mira shook her head vehemently, Zoe straightened, and my throat instantly went dry.

There was nothing overtly sexy about her suit; the clean lines of the pale-pink one-piece were cut high on her thighs and low on her chest. The ripe curves of her breasts were high and sweet. Maybe not much more than a handful, but fucking hell, my mouth watered at the sight.

Around her shoulders, all those golden curls tossed about in the breeze.

She smiled sweetly at Mira and adjusted the delicate straps of the suit. Everything she did was sweet to me, even in the moments when she'd spit fire over how mad I'd made her.

Wasn't that the crux of my problems? I could hardly see any of this clearly because I was tied up in a million knots over this woman.

And as much as Mira scared the shit out of me, the things I felt for Zoe were just as terrifying.

Scary in an entirely different way. The kind of scary that shredded my insides because I couldn't make sense of where to put that feeling anymore.

It couldn't be ignored, not with her in my face every single day.

Mira already loved me, already looked to me for comfort and kindness and encouragement. I still wasn't sure how well I could give her any of these things.

But she didn't have the power over me that Zoe did. The power to inflict massive damage with a single word.

Zoe glanced into the house, doing a slight double take when she caught me staring.

I didn't look away. Didn't drop my gaze. But I didn't soften the moment with a smile either.

That was something *she* did. A gift that she was willing to give.

And maybe it was easier for Zoe to offer it because she had a heart bigger than the ocean. She'd had it broken before, and she still stepped right up to the plate when people like Chris and Amie demanded a sacrifice of such magnitude that it was hard to comprehend sometimes.

We weren't playing house. This wasn't a game. And, still, she and I were just trying to get through each passing day without making a monumental fuckup of the task we'd been handed.

"Question of the day," I said to myself. "What the bloody fuck are you gonna do with these two?"

I wished I knew the answer to that one. And I hoped she never asked.

Chapter Fifteen

ZOE

Most days, I didn't know what to make of Liam.

Especially on the days when he clearly kept his distance from both me and Mira.

The bulk of the emotional labor involving her was my responsibility. When she tripped and scraped her knee on the concrete around the pool, she ran to me. I was the one to clean her up and dry her tears.

One particular night, a couple of weeks after I'd moved in, she woke inconsolable from a fierce nightmare.

Because I'd gone to bed before Liam, he must have still been awake, and the sound of him pounding up the stairs woke me just as much as her cries. But once in the room, as I pulled Mira into my arms and settled on the chair in the corner, smoothing my hand over her sweat-soaked back while she cried for her mom, he stood with his back against the doorframe, his face stoic.

He was watchful.

Clearly worried.

And noticeably distant.

Around the house and in the yard, I hardly had to lift a finger. When I cooked dinner, the dishes were washed and put away within an hour of us finishing.

The yard was immaculate, the pool always clean and sparkling, even though it mostly went unused beyond trying to bribe Mira into getting in. We were usually unsuccessful, but we still tried.

In the more mundane moments, when emotions didn't run so high, Liam was much more present.

The nights when I was bent over my laptop, eyes blurry from staring at numbers, he stepped in to do bathtime, and down the stairs I'd hear the low rumble of his voice as he talked her through the evening routine.

"Don't you try to steal that bath duck, young lady," he said sternly. "No, don't give me those eyes—they won't help you one little bit." A pause. "Thank you. Now go get your jams on, yeah?"

Because he couldn't see me, I grinned. No matter how rough he seemed to be with Mira, she adored him. It was the only reason his demeanor didn't bother me.

And some days, he was the most dangerous version of himself.

Playful Liam.

With Mira in bed early because of a nap-free day, I brought my Kindle closer to my face, my heart racing as I tapped to the next page.

The hero leaned in, cupping her face, his thumbs brushing her cheeks. Her breath came in short, choppy bursts, her chest heaving and her lips begging to be kissed.

"Be sure," he whispered.

Just after he said it, she grabbed him and surged up, their lips—

"What the bloody hell are you reading?"

I jumped, my Kindle clattering out of my hands and onto the kitchen counter.

Right into the puddle of melted ice cream that had been dripping off my forgotten spoon.

My eyes narrowed in a glare. "Thanks."

Liam picked up my Kindle by its corner, whistling at the mess of ice cream coating the case. "Look at that. It's *everywhere.*"

The page I'd been reading was still on the screen, and I leaned forward, trying to snatch the device out of his grip. Liam tugged it higher, turning it toward him.

I reached for it again, but Liam was too fast.

I went up on tiptoe, grabbing at his arm, which was as hard as a steel beam. Even when I tugged with all my strength, his arm didn't budge. "This is gross abuse of your height, Davies."

"This is what you're reading every day, is it?" Liam peered at the screen. "*His hands, big and rough and demanding, coasted over her . . .*"

Liam must have skimmed a few lines, because he stopped reading, brows raised. Then he handed my Kindle back, the slightest flush on his cheeks.

I clutched it to my chest. "Thank you."

He gave a slight nod, then proceeded to tear off a few squares of paper towel, which he dampened under the water and handed to me.

As I cleaned off my case and the mess on the counter, I laughed under my breath. "You know it's good when I waste my ice cream." Digging my spoon into the bowl, I took a huge bite.

His eyes were heavy on me while I did. "That's what Rosa and her little gang read at their book clubs?"

I nodded. "They told me the first time I came that if I wanted depressing literature, I should go elsewhere. Strictly the happily-ever-afters for that group. According to Martha, it's because reality is sad enough and they need to get their rocks off where they can."

Liam arched one eyebrow, the firm line of his mouth gentling slightly. "Makes sense."

When my Kindle case was clean, I balled up the paper towel squares, tossing them in his direction when he motioned for them.

The garbage container was tucked away inside a built-in drawer next to the sink, and as Liam tugged it open, my eyes snagged on the flex of muscles in his forearms.

Strength was such a weird concept if you thought too hard about it. Underneath flimsy skin, so easily bruised and torn and cut, he held an incredible amount of power. He could manhandle a man three times my size. Run down a receiver and knock him off his feet.

It was all too easy to imagine what he could do with someone my size.

"And you like it?" he asked.

My gaze shot up to his. "Like what?"

Liam gave me a strange look, and I wondered if my cheeks were bright red, because they *felt* bright red. "The books," he said slowly.

"Oh. Yeah, they're great." I took another quick bite of ice cream, sucking the spoon clean. Liam's attention stayed locked on my mouth as I did. "I, uh, didn't read much romance until college. I was always more of a fantasy-slash-magical-powers-slash-riding-dragons kind of girl."

He made a quiet noise in the back of his throat. "Let me guess—men in the books make men in reality look like a bunch of wankers."

I laughed. "You have to admit, it doesn't take much, considering some of our choices out there. With blinders on and stars in my eyes, I married a man who was more in love with his own reflection than anything else." I shook my head. "The men in these books aren't perfect, and I think that's what makes the stories even better. Imperfect people still have to find a way to overcome their issues if they want to be happy. It's as simple and as difficult as that. Reading their stories is the best way to have hope for our own, I guess."

If I hadn't been watching his face while I answered, I might have missed it. A flicker in his gaze, a shift in his frame.

"And you have that." The thick line of his throat moved on a swallow, and my eyes tracked every single movement. "That hope."

It wasn't a question. Just a low, scraping statement that I felt in the pit of my belly.

"Sometimes," I admitted quietly. "Not always. When I look at the time I wasted with Charles, it's hard for me not to feel like I missed out on something . . . my own fairy-tale ending, I guess."

Liam didn't say anything, but his eyes studied my face with an intensity that I couldn't name.

"Fairy tale," he repeated. Liam took his time with those two words, tasting them a bit.

It was unfortunate how delicious they sounded to me in that voice of his. But there was an edge of cynicism to it that had my stomach swirling.

Did I really want to talk to him about this? We'd hardly settled into a comfortable existence, let alone gotten to a point where I was willing to talk about my relationship insecurities.

So I did what any self-respecting woman would do if an inconveniently hot guy started asking her about what hope she had for future relationships . . .

I deflected like my life depended on it.

"What about you?" I asked. "Haven't you ever been tempted to marry?"

His eyes were steady on mine. "That two questions or one?"

"You know it's only one."

Liam grunted in concession. "No. Never been tempted."

"Because you don't like people," I said seriously.

His lips twitched. "Part of it."

I would get a full smile out of Liam Davies if it was the last thing I did on this earth.

My mouth opened, then closed.

"Oh bloody hell," he muttered, "she's lost for words. That's never good."

"It's the weekend, so I get two questions," I reminded him.

After releasing a beleaguered sigh that had me rolling my eyes, he made a go-ahead gesture with his hand.

I chose my words carefully. "I know it can't be from a lack of opportunity. You're a professional athlete."

"Takes a *bit* more than that to end up married."

"It does," I conceded. "And you're not exactly ugly," I added lightly.

His eyes burned into mine, but he didn't so much as blink.

"So why haven't you?" My throat was bone-in-the-desert dry, and I swallowed against it. "I've never even known you to date. Men or women."

Liam licked his bottom lip.

My stomach flipped, weightless and quick, when he did that.

For a moment, I didn't think he'd answer. I thought he'd just sit there and stare and make me want to pry his head open with a can opener so I could physically extract his thoughts.

But when he did, his gaze was unflinching, and I felt it in my bones. "There's people in this world like you, Goldilocks. The ones who have stars in their eyes, make decisions based on what they've always wanted. You want Prince Charming to sweep you off your feet, so you can ride off into the sunset together."

My heart was hammering. Why did all of this feel so loaded?

"That's quite the oversimplification, but I'll allow it for the purposes of polite conversation."

He continued as if I hadn't spoken at all. "I've made decisions based on what I *don't* want. What I've never wanted."

Something about this conversation had me imagining that I was walking a tightrope. The slightest tremble or a single misstep and everything would get all wobbly. We'd found an equilibrium, even if it was tentative and new and untested.

But I couldn't stop myself from wanting to test the limits.

Curiosity was often painted as a bad thing, given that it killed the cat and all.

Maybe my own tendency to want to know things, to understand things, would kick-start something I couldn't undo. The impetus for derailing all the forward progress we'd made.

Still . . . there was no pause button on all those questions I wanted answers to. Couldn't stop myself from wondering why I suddenly wanted to know more and more and more about this man.

I just didn't know what would happen when I pushed past the limit of what he was willing to give.

But with his cryptic words hanging between us—*what I've never wanted*—I knew what I'd choose.

"A family," I said quietly.

He hummed. "Got it in one."

"That's why you panicked so badly at the lawyer's office."

Liam gave no indication as to whether I was right or wrong, but I knew the truth.

"Why, though?" I couldn't wrap my head around it. Despite all his protestations, he was *good* at this. *That's* why I wanted to know more. Learn more. Figure him out on a deeper level.

Nothing he said aligned with the way he acted.

Liam inhaled slowly, his eyes dropping to my mouth for one prolonged moment. "That's three questions, love."

At the endearment, my heart ached. I knew he didn't mean it, not like that, but even so, there was a tangible reaction deep under my ribs.

I'd never had a green thumb, but I could imagine what it was like to pry open a small pocket of lush, dark soil, to plant a seed when you had great hopes for what might blossom later.

Something to tend and take care of.

That one little word—*love*—was Liam pressing the hope of something lush and beautiful into a neglected place I didn't realize I'd been holding on to.

For now, though, I ignored whatever might grow from that seed.

I had to. It was far too complicated to give it anything more than simple recognition.

My chin rose an inch. "No, that's two. You never really answered me."

He stepped toward me until I had to tilt my face up to look him square in the eye. My heart careened wildly at the closeness. "You're right," he said quietly. "I didn't."

And then he brushed past me.

"Good night, Valentine. Enjoy your book."

The air left my lungs in a hard punch, and my eyelids fluttered shut.

"Oh boy," I whispered. "This is not good."

Chapter Sixteen

LIAM

Structure is our friend, she'd said when she moved in.

And bloody fucking hell did she mean it. Zoe Valentine had a schedule, and she didn't deviate from it.

Mira knew it too, dutifully trotting off to mealtime and naptime and bedtime whenever Zoe made her secret little comments that I wasn't privy to. Those two had a whole private language that they'd developed.

And fuck if I'd ever admit it to her, but I shamelessly eavesdropped, because she had to deal with far fewer temper tantrums from Mira than I did.

I stood in the kitchen, drinking some Gatorade after my workout and watching Mira happily munch away on the exact same macaroni and cheese that she'd initially rebuffed. The same bowl that had made her cry because it tasted "too yucky."

"Admit it," I said to Zoe. "You slipped her a twenty, didn't you?"

She brushed past me in the kitchen. She smelled like lime and vanilla today. "No. I find the hundred-dollar bill is more effective," she said. "Also, you know, not swearing at her all the time."

"Funny." But I felt the furrow in my brow. "I don't swear *at her*," I argued. "I just . . . swear a lot."

Zoe laughed, a light, happy sound of genuine amusement.

"What?" I barked. "I don't."

She shook her head, but unlike at the beginning of all this, it was now paired with a different look in her eye. It wasn't an I-hate-you-and-actively-wish-violence-on-you shake of the head.

There was warmth there. A fondness that I didn't dare dissect.

"You have to admit, you swear more than most human beings."

I crossed my arms. "You got data to back that up? I bet it's on a spreadsheet somewhere, isn't it?"

Zoe's eyes narrowed. "Do you ever stop and ask yourself why you feel the need to curse so much?"

"No, and I'll tell you why. First, I'm British. We come out of the *womb* saying, 'Bloody hell.'" I started ticking off points on my fingers. "Plus, I read an article once that said there's a positive psychological effect when someone swears. Pain is lessened. Frustration cools. Stress is reduced." I set a hand on my chest, speaking in the most condescending voice possible. "I do this for my mental health, Valentine."

She crossed her arms too, hitching her hip against the counter and pinning me with a look.

I'd started categorizing them, a sick little obsession.

I could tell when she was confused, trying to study my face for some clue that I'd never give her.

I could tell when she was annoyed, likely plotting violence in her head. I loved those looks, if I was being honest.

I could tell when she was feeling feisty, the moments when our banter rode that knife-edge of flirting or something more. We stayed away from that, or tried our very best to, at least.

That line was dangerous, something we'd edged up against only a few times. The first time was when she asked me if I'd be parading groupies through the house, and the second was when she wanted to know why I'd never married.

In both of those moments, I almost asked her if she was jealous. But I didn't think I could handle her laughing at me. Not about that.

And I could tell on her face when the annoyance slipped into something more thoughtful.

That look scared me.

Sometimes, she and Mira went over to her house for a while, just for a change of scenery and to give me some quiet. Usually in the afternoons so Zoe could get some work done while Mira took her nap at the other house.

It was a boundary, apparently. Some therapy shit her mom had suggested. Keep Mira comfortable in Zoe's house; make sure that the main house isn't the only place where she feels safe and secure.

And as much as I hated admitting it, our roommate/coparent situation wasn't going horribly. I had thought it would. I had thought we'd argue all the time, because Zoe was incapable of backing down.

I loved it. And it was fucking terrible.

Somehow, the forced nature of our situation had bred a fairly peaceful first few weeks of coexistence.

Peaceful if you counted the absolute agony I was going through by being in a confined space with her.

Luckily for me, that agony was something I could live with. I could work it out every single time I was at the gym, let my want of her come out through burning muscles and sweat-soaked skin.

It wasn't like I thought of her every time I was at the facilities, but there was an extra buzz of energy that I couldn't quite shake, something that pushed me harder than usual. And my teammates noticed.

Our quarterback walked past me as I pushed through one last rep on the bench, whistling under his breath. "You trying to prove something, Davies?"

I racked the weights, my chest heaving and my muscles shaking. He handed me a sweat towel, and I took it with a nod. "Never."

He raised his eyebrows. "All right, then."

"You don't believe me?"

Trey Wilkins was a great QB, a good leader, even if he was young. He'd been with Denver for four years, sitting on the bench for two until our previous starter ended up leaving for Green Bay. He was levelheaded under pressure, and when every single talking head said he'd be a one-and-done starter, he proved them all wrong.

We won thirteen games his first season under center, and he ran the offense with a steady hand and a knack for reading defenses.

More importantly, after Chris died, he stepped up when it counted. When I was busy breaking chairs in that conference room, he was the first one up and out of his seat, pulling me in for a hug.

It wasn't one that I wanted. But, in hindsight, it was more than needed.

Anyone who could look the cold, hard rage of grief in the eyes without backing down, without backing away, was fearless.

After he was done with me, he spoke to any player who needed a listening ear. And it seemed like he was now deciding that I was the one who needed a listening ear.

"What?" I asked. Barked it. Yelled. Whatever.

He was undeterred and simply smiled down at me.

"How's it going with Chris's little girl?" he asked. When he took a seat on one of the benches next to mine, I pinned him with a hard stare. "What? Can't I make conversation?"

"This is workout time, not therapy."

He just laughed.

"It's not fucking funny, Wilkins."

Trey shrugged, yanking a hair tie off his wrist so he could pull back his shoulder-length braids. "You still didn't answer the question. That's a big transition."

I grunted.

"You realize I'm just doing the thing you always do to people on this team, right?"

This time, I full-on glared. "Yeah, but I'm old, and everyone knows not to bother me."

"Except me, apparently."

"You know, I used to admire you for your cool head, and now I think you should take it elsewhere."

"Going that good at home?"

He wasn't going anywhere. That much was obvious. I could push back. I could get up and walk away. But there were just enough young players watching us from the corners of their eyes that I stayed right where I was.

"It's . . . fine," I admitted. "We moved into Chris and Amie's house because Mira wanted to stay there. Can't blame her."

Sympathy filled his dark eyes, and I didn't want to see it. "How's it going with the friend? My wife asked me about her the other day. She asked if Zoe wanted to go out with some of the girls."

How was it going with the friend? That wasn't a question I could answer honestly.

She looked fucking adorable in the mornings when she hadn't brushed her hair yet.

She frowned when she was on her laptop, leaning close to the screen if something didn't make sense. When I asked her if she needed reading glasses, she flipped me off.

And she favored solid-colored pajama sets. Black and white and light blue and lilac.

When she wore the lilac, I couldn't look straight at her because it made something in my chest hurt.

At least a few days a week, she wore a Washington Wolves shirt, an eyebrow arched when I frowned, like she was daring me to comment. I'd already snagged her three shirts from the Denver pro shop but hadn't gotten up the balls to give them to her.

When she laughed, I wanted to snog her senseless, and I had imagined all sorts of scenarios involving the kitchen island.

So, no, I couldn't answer him honestly.

His eyes sharpened at my long pause.

"We get along well enough," I growled. I jabbed a finger into the air. "Don't."

"What?"

"Don't read anything into that, you great big tall prick."

Trey laughed, holding up his hands in concession.

But somehow I kept talking. "It's just . . ."

"What?"

Fucking hell, I could hardly say the words. "I may have fucked something up when she moved in."

Trey studied my face for a moment. "Are you asking for my advice?"

The entire weight room went silent. I swore under my breath.

Rookies stared at the ground but angled in our direction. Newer players bounced their gazes from their weights to us and then back again. A few of the veterans started edging closer.

I rolled my eyes. "Fuck's sake," I muttered under my breath.

"What'd you do?" Trey asked.

Simply as a defensive gesture, I scrubbed my hands over my face. Didn't work, though, because I could still feel them staring.

"I told her . . ." I paused, dropping my hands and blowing out a harsh breath. "I told her that when we first met, I . . . I sort of—" I stopped, glancing around the rest of the room, where every single player was shamelessly listening. But the lingering unease I'd been feeling around Zoe pushed me into speaking again. "I told her that when we first met, I liked her. Had a thing for her."

There were a few whistles. "Idiot," someone whispered under their breath.

Trey covered his mouth with his hand, his eyes dancing in amusement.

I glared mightily in his direction. "See, you're laughing at me, you asshole, and I'll never ask for your advice again."

Christiansen, one of our receivers, came closer, settling a hand on Trey's shoulder. "Why'd you tell her?"

"She thought I'd always hated her," I answered. "And doing what we're doing . . . it's hard enough without something like that hanging over the situation."

He nodded.

Another receiver, a young rookie whose name I could never remember, shook his head. "You gave her all the power, man. You never give them all the power. Now you're fucked because she knows how you feel."

"Felt," I barked. "How I felt. I was very clear that this was well in the past and that as soon as I realized she was engaged, it was over."

Trey's eyebrows rose. "*Is* it over?"

I gave him a look that promised any manner of violence if he persisted with that particular line of questioning.

Wisely, he stopped. He held his hands up again. "Got it."

When I continued, I kept my tone even, calm, peaceful—all the things that I absolutely did not feel. "Whether it's in the past or not is irrelevant. Zoe has never had those feelings for me, and I see no reason why that would change. The moment I told her, I wanted to take it back, because now she's all curious about me and asking a million fucking questions and trying to get to know me better. I can't help but think that if I'd just let us go on as we were, it would've been easier."

Christiansen nodded sagely. "You probably made her pretty anxious, shifting her entire perspective on your shared history. Now she won't have any choice but to wonder if the way you've acted is a defense mechanism against your own feelings."

I blinked.

The rookie hummed. "*And* he gave her all the power."

A few guys nodded, murmuring their assent.

I buried my head in my hands. "I am never coming to you lot for advice again. You are *rubbish* at it."

Trey laughed, laying a comforting hand on my shoulder. "You did what made sense to you in the moment, Liam. And if it's given the two of you a bit more peace in the situation, then I don't think you fucked it up. But I've always thought that being honest is the best choice in relationships."

I lifted my head. "Thanks . . . I think."

"Mira's three, right?" he asked.

I swiped the towel over my neck. "Not quite. In September."

Brian, one of the offensive linemen, stepped into the conversation. "You're planning the party already, right?"

"What party?" I asked.

His face got dead serious. "Bro, you need to throw her the most epic birthday party. Look at the shit year she's had. I'm talking princesses and bounce houses and those big-ass balloon arches and candy stations and shit."

Trey tilted his head. "What if she wants action heroes? Not all little girls want to be princesses. My daughter wants to be Hulk."

Brian rolled his eyes. "Fine. Hire Hulk, then."

Trey smothered a smile. "Or you could keep it simple. Not every kid wants a giant party."

Brian smacked the back of his head. "Yes, they fucking do. Don't you do huge parties for your kids?"

"No," Trey said. "Rochelle and I like family-only birthdays. Kids pick what dinner they want and what games they want to play."

Brian looked so offended on behalf of Trey's kids that I almost laughed. Might have if I weren't drowning in a cold wave of panic.

"How far in advance do you gotta book all that shit?" I asked him.

"Last week," Brian said. "I'm serious, man. We don't fuck around with kids' parties at our house. We hired all the Disney princesses for my daughter's fourth birthday. Even the mermaid, but you gotta make sure the kids can all swim, because you can't be putting a mermaid in the pool without knowing if they can swim. Can Mira swim?"

I was getting lightheaded. "I . . . don't think so. She refuses to go in the pool."

"I'll give you the name of our swimming instructor. My wife hates how hot she is, but she does a great job with the kids." He set a hand on my shoulder. "Now, do you need the other number? For the princesses?"

"What do you mean?"

His eyes widened. "Actors, man. They dress up as the characters; they're so realistic looking. I almost cried when Belle walked in. She was my first childhood crush."

My voice was rough and uneven when I spoke. "Do they have Moana?"

He nodded slowly. "Oh yeah."

"Fucking hell, I'll call today."

Trey glanced between us. "Shouldn't you check with the friend?"

I stood from the bench, restless energy making it impossible to sit still. "She'll be fine. I'll tell her after I book it."

He pinched the bridge of his nose.

Brian grinned. "Attaboy."

"I strongly advise against that, man," Trey said.

The door to the weight room opened, and as if we'd conjured her through the conversation, there was Zoe, holding Mira's hand.

You could've heard a pin drop on the floor when the guys realized it was her. More than a few eyes darted my way.

I wanted to murder all of them.

Mira glanced around the weight room until she spotted me. The guys greeted her with a mighty roar, and she giggled as she ran past them.

I crouched down, my hands hanging between my legs. "What are you doing here, duck?"

She smiled. "I tell Zoe I wanted to see you."

Well, fuck.

My heart was likely in a puddle of mush somewhere near the bottom of my feet.

Zoe approached behind her, nodding at the rest of the team—all of whom studied her with open curiosity—her cheeks flushed and her wild golden curls pulled back in a pretty braid.

I wanted to tug on whatever held all that hair back and let it loose. Dig my hands in to see how soft it was. Drown in it.

I was so beyond fucked.

"I hope it's okay," she said. "We were running some errands, and when we passed the building, she asked if we could stop."

I arched an eyebrow. "Security lets anyone in these days, eh?"

She hooked a thumb at Mira. "She's my golden ticket, apparently."

Some of the rookies behind Zoe were staring unabashedly at her ass. I straightened, leveling them with my fiercest glare. "Oy!" I yelled. Zoe jumped, slapping a hand to her chest, but I kept my narrowed gaze on the guys behind her. "Go find something else to do," I barked at them.

She blew out a slow breath, eyes wide in her face. "I guess I should feel comforted that you're like this with everyone else too."

Trey stood, holding out his hand to Zoe. "Trey Wilkins. Nice to meet you."

She took it with a smile. "You too. Chris and Amie always had such nice things to say about you."

Trey glanced at me. "Not Liam?"

"Liam doesn't have anything nice to say about anyone."

Trey laughed.

I rolled my eyes. "Brian," I said, "why don't you show Mira the stuff over there?"

His forehead creased in confusion. "What stuff?"

Zoe's eyes bounced between us.

"Make something up," I growled. "I need to tell her about the *thing.*"

"Ahh. Right." He crouched down. "Come on, Mira, we've got some cool ropes you can play with."

When she nodded, Brian hoisted her up in his massive arms and strode back to the weighted ropes.

Zoe watched them walk away with a soft smile on her face. "I think she misses coming here." Then her eyes lit up. "Oh, I got a call today. That pediatric therapist the lawyer recommended agreed to take on Mira. We can take her in a couple weeks."

I took a step closer. "We can talk about that later."

At the urgency in my voice, Zoe's eyebrows popped up. "What's wrong?"

"We fucked up."

"What are you talking about?"

"We didn't book shit for her birthday party."

Zoe's lips twitched. "Liam, we have *months* until her birthday."

I leaned in closer. "And I won't be the reason she doesn't have fucking Moana at her fucking birthday party. You wanted structure, yeah? Add it to your spreadsheet. I'm calling today."

So that I didn't have to hear Zoe laugh or see any fucking glimmer of happiness in her eyes, I started back toward the corner where Mira had gone.

I stopped, pivoting to face Zoe. "And she needs swimming lessons. I'll deal with it."

Zoe's mouth opened, but I turned before she could say anything. I'd pay for all this later, 100 percent, but I couldn't bring myself to calm the hell down.

Then I paused, glancing back at Valentine. "Want me to bring her home when I'm done? I've got about another hour yet."

Her face morphed with surprise. "You don't think she'll get in the way?"

I eyed the corner of the weight room, where Mira had five giant football players gathered around her, doing their best to look like fools in order to make her laugh.

"Nah. She'll be just fine."

Zoe snapped a picture of the display in front of us. Then she smiled at me. A real smile too.

My heart could hardly take it.

"Okay. I guess I'll see you at home, then?"

See you at home. Said like she hadn't sliced straight through my ribs.

I managed a nod and watched her go tell Mira that she could stay with me. Mira hugged her neck and then ran back into the group of players.

193

Zoe's eyes were locked on mine as she walked past, and I felt it through every inch of my body.

Structure, I thought again.

Structure was our friend.

And I'd need a structure forged from iron and steel to keep that woman out. But I could do it.

Maybe.

Chapter Seventeen

Zoe

"Where did you go?" I muttered under my breath. I scanned the printed statements on the table next to me, whispering numbers as my finger went down the column. With my leg tucked up against my chest, I could set my chin on my knee as I searched.

Or I would have been able to, if the walking peanut gallery kept his mouth shut.

"Your posture is awful."

I glanced into the kitchen. Liam wasn't even looking at me. His broad back was turned toward the sink as he finished filling his mug with coffee.

Slowly, I set my leg down. "It's not that bad."

"Doesn't your neck always hurt? You're constantly poking at it."

"It's not constant."

He turned slightly, one eyebrow raised.

Even as I denied it, I fought the urge to dig my thumbs into the sides of my neck, which really did always hurt.

"I have to look down at my computer for work, okay?"

"Don't you have those big fucking screens over in your fancy office?"

"Yes, but Mira is still sleeping, and you leave for training in an hour."

He made a grunting noise.

Over the last few weeks of living with Liam, I'd learned that this was his way of agreeing with me without actually saying the words.

"Doesn't *your* neck hurt? You tackle people for a living."

His face was even, his eyes tracking over my face as he settled his hips against the edge of the counter. "Nope."

"Not even a little?"

"Not even a little. We've got a masseuse who beats the shit out of us on the regular. And training staff whose sole existence cycles around making sure our bodies don't hurt so that we can do our jobs."

I snorted. "Must be nice."

"What's stopping you from going to get one?" he asked. "They've got all those fancy fucking spas around here. Make you listen to gong sounds and weird chime music. And the techs all whisper when they talk."

I fought a smile. "Yes, they do have those."

"Why don't you go to one?"

Slowly, I set the stack of papers down. "Is this really bothering you, or do you just suck at making morning conversation?"

And I'll be damned, Liam's cheeks turned the rosiest shade of pink when he paused to take a sip of his coffee.

I sat back in my chair and studied him openly. We'd found a strange rhythm in our days. It wasn't bad; we never outright argued about anything, but there was a simmering sort of tension behind every single interaction we had.

I'd been operating under the assumption that Liam didn't notice it, because he was prickly with everyone. But *I* felt it. It was like the air vibrated, just a little bit, every time we found ourselves without the natural buffer of Mira. And every time that vibration hit my skin, I couldn't help but wonder if I was imagining it.

I hadn't lived with a man since Charles, and things had been so bad those final few months that any existing tension was the byproduct of me wanting to smack the shit out of my then husband anytime he opened his mouth.

As much as I'd threatened or imagined violence against Liam, my feelings toward him were never rooted in that same place. Liam niggled under my skin, an itch that I couldn't quite scratch, and now he was everywhere.

A constant, unyielding source of irritation that I couldn't quell.

Maybe *irritation* wasn't quite the right word.

Provocation came the closest.

Yup. That was it. Liam provoked me more than any man I'd met in my entire life.

We talked the most in the mornings. Especially on the rare days when Mira slept in past six thirty. He'd already gone for his run, and now he was drinking his coffee, his sex-soap smell wafting around him, while I was taking advantage of the quiet morning by getting a bit of work done.

Or had been until Grumpy Pants decided to critique my posture.

"It *is* likely that I'm bollocks at polite conversation," he said slowly, eyeing my face as he answered. "But I can't help noticing that you don't . . . go anywhere."

See? Provoking. The man must've had a weird argument kink.

I crossed my arms. "I go places. Mira and I ran errands yesterday; we saw *you* at the facilities."

"Yeah, but don't women need to do, like, self-care shit?"

"Self-care shit," I repeated slowly.

"You know what I mean, and don't pretend like you don't. Massages and facials and I don't fucking know—going for a walk or hanging out with friends. You have friends, right?"

A hot prickle of defensiveness clawed its way up my throat, and I fought very hard to push it down. "Of course I have friends." Who I never saw. Hardly talked to.

"Who?" he asked.

"Well, I had friends I worked with at the hospital. But they're busy; they work full-time and have families of their own. And I have Rosa—she's my friend. And Martha and Phyllis."

"Why'd you quit at the hospital? Didn't you love it?"

I blew out a slow breath. "I did. It is possible to love your job and still need a break from it. After the divorce, it just felt too hard to try to find a new job at a different hospital. I couldn't stay where I'd been and not run into Charles all the time—he was still the hospital's legal counsel. And with the settlement, I could afford to reduce my hours. I wanted something flexible in case I decided to travel or volunteer somewhere." I sighed, waving my hand around the room. "And then . . . all this. I can't imagine going back full-time right now. Not until Mira is in school."

"Let me get this straight. You were burned out, so you quit your job, and now you go even fewer places in order to fix that?"

"I've been a touch busy raising my friends' child, if you hadn't noticed," I said, desperately trying to keep the edge from my tone.

There was the tightrope again, only this time it wasn't a wobble that I worried about. We hadn't fought in weeks, and I wasn't looking to break that streak. Something like that could snap the rope in two.

"I have," he said in a rough voice. "But you're not doing it alone, if you hadn't noticed."

I snapped my laptop shut and pinned him with a searching look. "Obviously I know you're helping, but you're heading into training camp shortly. Then the season starts. It's not like I can run off and spend half my day trying to relax when you're traveling to away games and practicing every day."

He nodded slowly. "You're right. Once the season starts, you'll have the lion's share of the work."

We'd stuck so firmly to our one-month-at-a-time motto that we'd never tiptoed into these conversations about the future.

What would the fall look like? As much as I missed my house, and I did, it was strange to imagine us moving back after just a few weeks in this new setup.

Already, this felt like home too.

"I'm prepared to carry my weight during the season," I told him. "Why bring this up now?"

He ran a hand over his stubbled jaw, and the sound it made, the scratch of his facial hair against his skin, had me fighting a shiver. "You should get out of the house."

My chin notched up an inch. "What if I like being at home? It's not like you're Mr. Social."

"I spend all fucking day with my friends," he said. "I had break-fast yesterday with the defensive line and our coach. Today, I'm having lunch with Trey and his QB coach so we can discuss a few things. Who do you see besides me and the kid?"

I swallowed.

No one. That was the answer. I'd hardly even seen Rosa the last few weeks because I didn't need her babysitting services and didn't have the energy for her book club once the evenings hit.

The truth of it had me answering just a touch defensively. "Well, my best friend died in a car accident, and the guy I was dating at the time decided he didn't want an instafamily, so my calendar has been a little light. Sorry I'm not a social butterfly, but I haven't really been in the mood for it the last couple months."

The moment I said it, I wanted to suck the words right back in. But that was the thing about words and how we say them to people. No matter how much we want to, we can't undo them.

"That wasn't fair," I said immediately. "I shouldn't have said it."

Liam's features were so immovable that it was easy to imagine an artist somewhere carving his profile into marble. He'd look harsh and unforgiving etched into stone. Like a warrior or a king.

And it was beyond comprehension to me that he was aiming that look in my direction because I didn't get massages or go see my friends.

It was also beyond comprehension that I found myself feeling grateful for it. That he hadn't backed down simply because I'd swiped at him unfairly.

"People say a lot of unfair shit when they're hurt, yeah?"

I nodded.

"I might have done that a time or two," he added quietly.

My eyebrows arched of their own volition.

He frowned. "Fine. I've done that a lot." At his admission, I desperately tried to swallow down the lump in my throat. It was big. But he wasn't done. "I've done that a lot to you."

I sighed, rubbing at my forehead. "I know I don't get out much. I just . . . get really tired when I think about trying."

Liam's jaw clenched. "You need to get out of this house, Valentine. Go have some fun."

Fun. My definition had changed the last few months. I wasn't even sure I knew how to define it anymore.

If I was being honest, there had been a slow shift over the last few years. Amie had always been the one who pulled me out of my ruts, and if she were here, she'd smack me upside the head and tell me the man was right.

Finally, I nodded. "I think Rosa and her book club friends are going out tonight. I can probably join them."

If possible, his already serious face flattened even further. "You are joking."

"What?"

"I tell you to go out and have some fun, and you're joining the local group of octogenarians while they talk about their Amish romances."

"Please, you should see the books Rosa brings home." I blew out a puff of air. "So much dirtier than what I read."

He arched an eyebrow. "You taking notes, Valentine?"

"Like I'd tell you."

Liam's eyes held mine for a moment, and then he looked away. "I'll take care of it."

"Take care of what?"

He set his mug down and crossed his arms over his chest. Whenever he did that, it did horrible things to the muscles in his arms. Biceps weren't supposed to flex that way. It wasn't natural.

"Finish your work. If planning it makes you tired, then I'll get it figured out." Mira called his name from her bedroom, and he jerked his chin. "Coming, duck," he called out.

With my jaw hanging open, I watched him stride from the kitchen and bound up the stairs.

Less than five minutes later, he sent me a text.

Liam: Be ready at 5:30. That's when you're getting picked up.

At the early hour, my head tilted in confusion. Liam Davies had planned a girls' night for me?

"What the actual hell," I whispered.

Liam

It was good that I'd hardly seen Zoe the rest of the day, because I wanted to take back everything I'd said to her.

Who wanted to go out? Not me.

Who was I to judge her lack of a social life? No one.

I'd rather have had my balls chopped off with a rusty blade than have been forced to go clubbing, and I'd sent her out with a group of the team wives, knowing they'd be taking her someplace fancy and fucking loud.

By the time I got back from the facilities, she was on the phone in her bedroom, and after we danced politely through the postnap transfer, she disappeared back to her own house to get ready for the night.

The long dark car with tinted windows picked her up at her own front door, and I tried to swallow my disappointment that I hadn't gotten to see her ready for a night out. Hadn't quite managed it, unfortunately.

Thankfully, I had a very effective built-in distraction in the form of one very bossy almost three-year-old.

"I can't read it again, Mira. I swear, I'll lose it."

She shoved the book at my chest. "One more time." Then she opened it and pressed it by my face. "Please," she begged.

"For fuck's sake," I mouthed, quiet enough that she couldn't hear me. I gently lowered the book, and the sight of her big, pleading eyes was like a blade straight into my fucking chest.

I growled under my breath, and she bounced a little on the couch, like she could taste the victory already.

"One more time," I bit out. "And then I'm done."

Mira nodded dutifully, plopping herself forward so she could see the book.

"Brown bear, brown bear, what do you see?" I said by rote. Immediately, she joined in on reading the pages.

When we got to the bloody duck, she showed just as much excitement as she had the first hundred times. But if I tried to let her read it by herself? No bloody way did she let me get away with that.

I tried skipping a page, and she shook her head vehemently. "No, no, you missed it." Her little hands, surprisingly strong, flipped back to the correct page.

We ended up reading it four more times.

"We go outside?" she asked, tugging my arm to the slider.

"It's hot, duck. We could swim. You gotta start practicing."

"No swimming. I don't like it." Her face scrunched up with a fore-head-creasing frown, and she crossed her arms over her chest. Fucking hell, she looked like me.

"Swim lessons start tomorrow, kid. We gotta be safe, all right?"

Mira got that look in her eyes; a tantrum had begun brewing in that brain of hers.

"Zoe wants you to swim too," I said. "I'll be right out there with you."

The mention of Zoe wasn't wise, though, because Mira immediately ran to the front door, slapped her hands onto the window overlooking the street, and pressed her nose to the glass. "Where'd Zoe go?"

"She went out with some friends, duck. Remember? She'll be back when you're asleep."

For a few more minutes, she stared. "Zoe come home?"

Her voice was quieter, and something horrible and cold bloomed in my stomach. "Yeah, she's coming home. I promise."

Mira's tiny frame expanded on a deep breath, her eyes never wavering from where she watched the silent street. "I hold Zoe?"

I swiped a hand over my face, gentling my voice when I answered. "Soon, little love. She'll be home soon."

Eventually, I was able to distract her while we put together a puzzle, even though it was missing a piece, which bugged the living fuck out of me.

I glanced at the time. Zoe had been gone for a couple of hours, and I couldn't help but wonder if she was having fun. Even though I wasn't close with Trey's wife, he'd given me her number when I'd asked if they'd invite Zoe to their night out.

Me: How's she doing?

Rochelle Wilkins: She's sweet. I can see why you like her.

Me: WHO THE FUCK SAID THAT? No, I don't.

Rochelle Wilkins: . . . right. Never mind.

Me: Tell your husband to quit gossiping when he's at home.

Me: And tell him he doesn't know what the hell he's talking about.

Rochelle Wilkins: I'll do my best. Back to Zoe, though . . .

Rochelle Wilkins: She needed to get out of the house. You did the right thing.

I fucking hated the immediate warmth that spread through my chest. Taking care of Zoe wasn't my responsibility. But bloody hell if I could convince that useless organ trapped under my ribs of this.

When she looked tired, I fought the urge to cup her face and trace the dark circles under her eyes. When she looked stressed, my fingers twitched from wanting to press all that tension out of her muscles. See if her skin was as smooth and soft as I'd imagined.

If I did that, I'd damn us both.

There was no universe in which I could touch her without consequences. The kind that shook the walls and cracked all the foundations that held our world intact. That's what would happen if I kept letting this thing for her slide out unchecked.

Instead of replying to Rochelle, I tucked my phone away.

It buzzed almost immediately.

Zoe: Are you checking up on me?

Me: No.

Zoe: Liar. Now everyone is asking about you, and how unfair is that? I can't even escape you at girls' night.

Me: What are they asking? I can guarantee none of those women think anything good if they believe what their husbands say.

Zoe: I'm not telling you shit, Davies. The stuff they're saying would inflate your ego too much.

Zoe: Ignore that. I shouldn't text and drink. I'll see you when I get home, unless you're asleep, which would probably be safer for me because I never drink and I can't have you holding any of this over my head.

I found myself fighting a grin. And at the thought of their husbands, I switched over to a different message thread and punched out a text with brutal taps of my thumbs.

Me: What the bloody fuck did you tell your wife about Zoe?

Trey: Nothing that wasn't true, my friend.

Me: Oh please, be cryptic, I so enjoy it.

Trey: If I tell you the way your eyes changed when you saw her, you'd call me a fucking asshole and go about your night. But if she hasn't noticed it yet, it won't be long before she does.

Trey: I think she'd be good for you, if you're wondering.

Me: I'm not. Fuck off.

Trey: I love you too.

Me: I'm knocking your ass to the ground in practice. No holding back.

Trey: Good. You just keep proving me right, and there's nothing I enjoy more than that.

When I set my phone down again, Mira ran up to the couch.

She poked at my cheek. "You smiling?"

"No."

It made no sense that my gruff response didn't deter her in the slightest. But she smiled, giggling at whatever she saw on my face.

I wasn't like Chris.

Zoe wasn't like Amie.

We were both just muddling through each day, trying to do our best in a shit situation that neither of us had asked for. Most of the time, I could hardly make sense of this place where the three of us had ended up. And I was an adult; I had more than three decades of life under my belt.

Mira was so little. Her entire world revolved around what she could see and touch and experience. And right now that was me and Zoe.

"Sometimes I wonder what you think about when you look at us, duck," I said quietly.

She'd never tried to call us Mum and Dad, and I was thankful for that. It was already hard enough to be in my position, trying desperately to be something that I'd never wanted to be. Even though I'd made peace with it, there was still this gaping hole that would never quite heal. A wound that would never be erased, because this strange family unit had been cobbled together from something unnatural.

One who wanted it more than anything.

One who didn't.

And one who had no choice in the matter.

Someday, Zoe would find someone. She was too beautiful and too fucking perfect not to. Where would that leave me? Leave Mira?

Mira sensed the shift in my mood, perceptive little shit that she was.

Tentatively, she climbed onto my lap, something she didn't usually do. I kept my hands on the couch. Zoe was the cuddler, and we all knew it. But Mira settled her slight weight onto me and studied my face.

In turn, I studied hers.

She was tired. I knew the signs now.

"What is it?" I asked her. "And, no, I'm not reading that book again, so don't even think about asking with that little face you make. It won't work."

Mira blinked, and I got the oddest sensation that she was looking into my fucking soul or something.

After another moment, she finally asked, "I hold you?"

Something tight and hard lodged itself in my lungs. It was big and wildly uncomfortable. My breath came faster, and my pulse thundered in my ears.

This entire time, I'd held myself back from Mira, and not once had Zoe called me out on it, even though she had every right. But could I say no to her now?

I couldn't. I'd never forgive myself if I did.

Somehow, I managed a jerky nod, and in the next heartbeat, she snuggled herself onto my chest, settling her head just under my chin.

Despite her request to hold me, Mira tucked her hands underneath her own body. Carefully, I settled my arms around her, holding her as tight as I dared.

The weight of her against my chest shouldn't have felt so warm, so sweet and heavy. But it was. It was all those things.

My heart was racing, and I wondered if she could feel it against her face. If she wondered why this made me so fucking nervous. Why this gutted me so thoroughly.

My nose was hot and uncomfortable, my eyes dry and full of sand or something. It felt like someone had punched a block of dirt down my throat, and I couldn't swallow past it no matter how hard I tried.

And I *tried*.

It was anchored right there, in my eyes and nose and throat and heart. Things I didn't want to name, grief that I'd shoved down, and all my fears were wrapped up in one tiny package, hell-bent on choking the shit out of me.

If I dared move, I might be tempted to break something, just to see if it would release some of this tension.

But I wouldn't, I realized. Not for the world.

It was inevitable, I suppose, that this tiny little girl would be the thing to knock over the first brick, to shove through all the mortar and bindings keeping the bricks in place.

All along, I'd been so terrified of Zoe because she'd been in the back of my head for bloody *years*. But I'd been afraid of Mira too.

That was probably why I'd resisted moments like this. I couldn't breathe, not with the sweetness trying to push through my lungs. I felt like Mira was suffocating me with all that pure, innocent love.

Whatever I felt for Zoe was complicated. It was hemmed in by all the history between us. But this, with Mira, wasn't. Not really. Not once I'd set aside all the bullshit fears clouding my head. They were still there. They were always there. But right now, in this singular moment, I could ignore them.

She'd taken a bath after dinner, and when I pressed a featherlight kiss onto the top of her hair, I tried to imagine a world in which that soft smell wouldn't remind me of her.

You didn't think too much about the responsibility of raising a child until they were there in your arms. There was no committee telling you what to do. No coach screaming in your ear about how you could improve. No binder or training manual that could guarantee you'd one day be able to send this person out into the world as a self-sufficient, non-asshole human being.

There were so many of those—the assholes. It was highly likely that I was one of them, a product of my own upbringing and history. And I refused to let Mira become a victim of that.

She'd be a good person, because she was born from good people and had at least one other good person with a hand in raising her.

All I could do was not make things worse and do what I did best.

Fucking destroy anyone who got in the way of Mira having the best life in the entire world.

Her breathing was even and slow, and I gently rubbed circles on her back to see if she stirred. I tilted my head and sighed.

Eyes closed.

Mira had been sound asleep during the middle of my emotional epiphany.

"Fucking hell," I whispered. "You're killing me, kid."

But I kissed the top of her hair again, then settled my head back against the couch. My eyes closed after a few minutes and stayed shut until my back protested the position.

Slowly, I shifted Mira in my arms until we were stretched out on the couch, a pillow wedged under my head and the soft weight of her body tucked against my chest.

Just a few more minutes, I thought to myself.

It was hours later when I woke, the house dark around us, the two of us covered with a big fuzzy blanket.

I grabbed my phone to check the time, and Mira stirred slightly.

It was after midnight, and there was an unread text on my phone.

Zoe: Thank you for making me go out.

Zoe: And I promise that your secret cinnamon roll side is safe with me.

She had attached a picture, a dimly lit snap of Mira wrapped firmly in my arms. My face looked calm in sleep, but when I saw the way I held her, my chest went tight and my ribs hot, a strange, undefinable ache growing underneath them.

I didn't know how to do any of this, didn't know where to put all the feelings growing out of this situation. How to pretend like I didn't want the things I wanted.

Maybe that's what I needed to make peace with now.

I could no longer pretend that I didn't want those things. I just didn't know how I was supposed to have them either. Not without ruining everything.

Chapter Eighteen

ZOE

Rolling over the next morning, I was pleasantly surprised that I wasn't immediately greeted by a pounding head and a dry mouth. What I *was* greeted by was a rambunctious Mira crawling up into bed with me.

"Good morning," I whispered, opening my arms as she pushed herself under the blankets.

"You slept for so long," she said.

I kissed the top of her head. "I know. I went to bed later than I usually do."

She pulled back from my embrace and gently tugged at the hairs around my face. "You see some friends?"

I smiled. "Yup. They were very nice," I told her. "We laughed and talked and had a girls' night."

"I'm a girl," she proclaimed. "I come too."

"Maybe when you're older." I tapped the tip of her nose with my finger. "Did you have a good sleepover on the couch?"

Mira nodded, then leaned in close and dropped her voice to a whisper. "I hold Liam," she told me.

My heart squeezed, warmth seeping into my veins. "Did you?"

She nodded again, her fingers gently twirling a lock of my hair.

If I had seen a parade of naked men walking through the house, I would've been less shocked than by what I saw on that couch when I sneaked quietly through the front door.

I would've been less turned on too.

Why was it so stupid attractive that he was slowly letting her in? It had been easier when Liam fit into a tidy little box. When my definition of him was clear and crisp and left no room for negotiation.

But everything felt just a little muddier today. A bit more unclear.

From the outside, it didn't look like much had changed. He had taken charge when I didn't realize I needed a push, and he had given this precious little person a bit more space in the heart he kept hidden. But my entire perspective was altered. Again.

It was almost like someone had dialed in the focus on a camera. The details, hidden before by all the other things blurring my view, had become more precise.

"Did you have breakfast yet?" I asked Mira. A glance at the clock on the bedside table had my eyes widening a bit. I hadn't slept past eight in months.

She nodded. "Liam made me cereal."

I smiled. "What kind did you have today?"

"Toasty Crunch," she said.

I leaned in to blow a raspberry on her neck, and she giggled. "Yum," I told her. "Maybe I'll have that too."

Mira returned the gesture, attempting her own version, and I ended up with far more spit on my skin and much louder laughter. When I tickled her enough that she pulled back, I realized we weren't alone anymore.

Liam was standing in the doorway, one broad shoulder braced against the frame and his arms crossed over his chest.

His face was inscrutable, and something about his eyes had my cheeks going warm. I thought about what Rochelle had said the night before.

Liam is a tough nut to crack because he never wants anyone to see what's on the inside. You'll know what that man feels when he does his damnedest to hide it from you.

"Morning." I sat up, slowly extricating myself from Mira's octopus arms. With hair everywhere, no bra on, and probably rocking some really great smudged mascara, I could only imagine how I looked to him.

And he was looking.

"Sorry if she woke you," he said, voice a low rumble. "She sneaked upstairs when I had my back turned." His green eyes followed the movement of my hands when I attempted to wrangle my hair into submission.

"It's fine. I need to get up anyway."

"Have fun?" he asked.

I nodded easily. "Thank you for arranging it."

Instead of a "You're welcome" or a peppering of questions, Liam grunted.

A small laugh escaped my lips.

"What?" he asked.

With him, it would have been so much easier to say it was nothing. In the past, that's what I would have done. It's what I did with Charles for years—brush aside what I was thinking because it was easier. Because it kept the peace, and we were both too busy and stretched too thin to add arguments into the mix.

With Liam, I didn't want to do what I always did. So I took a deep breath and let my gaze linger on his.

No bullshit.

"I was wishing you came with a translation guide."

At my admission, his face gave nothing away. Only the tiniest tic of his jawline and a slight inhale through his nose.

"What's the fun in that?" he asked, then backed out of the doorway to head downstairs.

I flopped back into bed, a sigh escaping my lips and a few errant butterflies fluttering in my chest.

"No sleeping, Zoe," Mira said, bouncing on the mattress. "Time to get up."

I turned toward her. "Swim lessons today, right? Are you excited?"

"No."

With a laugh, I rolled out of bed and tossed the blanket back over her head. "It'll be fun, I promise."

But three hours later, I wanted to take back every word I'd said.

"What the hell?" I whispered.

On the other end of the phone, my mom whispered back: "I can't see what we're mad about."

I'd called her to make sure I knew what to expect at Mira's first appointment with the counselor, but I quickly got derailed when the backyard swim lesson turned into a never-before-tapped nightmare.

"Hang on. I'll switch it around so you can see." I flipped the camera so that it was aimed into the backyard. "The swim teacher is here," I said. "Liam told me he'd handle the whole thing, so I'm trying to give him his space."

My mom's forehead wrinkled as she tried to see what I was showing her. When I panned the camera to the left, her jaw fell open. "Holy shit. Look at her ass."

Yeah, I was looking. I couldn't help it.

It was a work of art.

"I bet she does a *lot* of squats."

I rolled my eyes. "Thanks, Mom."

"What? She's hot."

Indeed, she was. The swim teacher, in the most basic terms, was a ten. Maybe an eleven.

Long, flowing brown locks that shone under the sun. Flawless golden skin over impressively toned muscles. Her legs were long, and underneath her simple black one-piece was some tasteful cleavage that had even me tilting my head to the side to study her proportions.

She slid into the pool like a mermaid, coiling all that hair onto the top of her head with a neat flick of her wrist. And when Liam said something, she tipped her head back and laughed, revealing perfectly straight, white teeth.

"Oh, sure, he's so fucking funny," I muttered.

He was sitting on the edge of the pool, his legs in the water and a dark shirt covering his chest. Mira was clinging to his arm, refusing to get in.

I chewed on my bottom lip, fighting the urge to go out there to help.

"What are you thinking so hard about, my girl?" Mom asked.

I flipped the camera around. "Nothing."

She eyed me. "Lying helps no one, Zoe."

"I bet she wakes up with her hair like that. Not a single strand out of place."

Mom smiled. "Yours looks . . . nice too."

"I went out last night, and I haven't showered yet."

"I can tell."

The instructor moved toward Liam and Mira, leaning in and speaking softly until Mira begrudgingly let go of Liam's arm, then reached her hands out to the teacher.

She had a name, of course. And that was beautiful too.

Lizette De Luna.

Like angels and moonbeams and glitter all rolled up into one neat little package. With really great hair and an ass you could bounce a quarter off of.

"What's the face?" Mom said.

I dredged up the words because there was no point in lying. "I feel like I'm in high school again. Watching the pretty girl get the attention from the popular athlete."

My mom hummed. "I didn't know that bothered you so much."

"It didn't," I said truthfully. "But I was still aware of it. Knowing something is true doesn't always mean you're mad about it, you know?

I was the quiet girl who was more focused on my homework than the boys. So they didn't really notice me."

Mira said something to Liam before she conceded her edge of the pool, and he listened before giving a short nod.

Into Lizette's arms Mira went, but she clung to the woman's neck.

Lizette backed into the pool, clearly trying to soothe a very nervous Mira. And, I swear, I would've watched them like a hawk, but Liam reached a hand behind his neck and tugged his T-shirt off.

I almost dropped my phone into the sink.

His back was all rippling muscles, his ink-covered arms and shoulders carved with a friggin' chisel. His shoulders were wide and strong, his waist trim, and when he hopped down into the water and turned toward Mira, I caught my first glimpse of his chest and stomach.

The smattering of dark hair over his pecs and the thin line that led down the stacks of ab muscles had my heart fluttering unevenly deep inside my chest.

My mom cleared her throat, and I blinked a few times. "What did you say?" I asked, only slightly out of breath.

"Nothing." Her eyes were knowing and the smile clear in her voice.

I covered my face. "Shut up."

Despite my embarrassment, I couldn't unglue myself from the window. Lizette was instructing Mira to kick, helping aim her body toward Liam, who waited with a patient almost smile and outstretched hands.

My mistake was moving slightly to the side, because the movement caught Liam's attention. His eyes snapped to mine, and I couldn't move out of sight quickly enough.

He arched an eyebrow, his lips curving up on one side when I narrowed my eyes.

Begrudgingly, I walked out of the kitchen and flopped onto the couch. "This is not me, Mom. I don't get jealous of other women. Especially not for something as superficial as their looks."

She hummed knowingly again. "No, but you've also never been in this kind of situation before."

"No shit." I rubbed my forehead. "Until last night, I didn't realize how I'd slipped into a tired-mom rut until I was out with some other moms. All I was thinking about was surviving the day-to-day."

"Taking care of yourself is vital when you've got a little human depending on you." She had her counselor face on.

"I know. It's just . . . easy to forget. I feel guilty."

She made a sound of understanding. "Guilt is just a feeling, honey. It's not a bad feeling that we have to avoid. It means you care about Mira. But just don't get so stuck in it that you can't move forward."

I nodded. "Feelings aren't facts," I said, something I'd heard from her for years.

She smiled. "I'm glad he did that for you," she said.

I dropped my hand and stared for a second. "I am too, but . . . it's confusing. I've always known certain things to be true about Liam, and now . . ." My voice trailed off.

"Now they're not true?"

"That's the thing. He's still kind of a dick. But he's not. Or he pretends like he's a dick, but he's actually a very thoughtful person." I groaned. "That's what I don't know."

"From what you've told me, he's got very high walls up. He's probably never had to let them down before."

I sighed. "The highest walls. I've heard him say over and over that he never wanted a family, that it's not for him. But I have no idea why he says that or, even worse, why he genuinely believes it."

Silence bloomed between my mom and me as she studied my face. I had her eyes, and it was unnerving to see them pinned on me with such precision.

"You like him. That's why this is triggering you."

There was no accusation in her voice, but it wasn't really a question either. Just a statement of fact.

This time it was harder to slip into the no-bullshit mode. My mom could always read my face, which was a double-edged sword. She was also a therapist, so I couldn't talk my way around something she knew to be true.

"I don't want to like him, if that helps." Maybe I sounded a little petulant about it.

She smiled. Then she left me space to continue.

"And I don't know that I trust what I feel about him."

"That's an interesting distinction. Tell me more about that."

"Are you shrinking me right now?" I asked.

"Yes."

I laughed. But the smile faded quickly. Next to me on the couch was the blanket that I'd used to cover Liam and Mira when they slept the night before.

"Rosa and her friends have this book club," I told her. "And they read all these spicy books. She always tells me about them because, until recently, I never joined in. Every once in a while, I pick one up because I like to read a little bit before I fall asleep."

My mom smiled. "I can't tell you how many times I found you with a book on your pillow when you were little."

I loved that she didn't ask where I was going with this story.

"I read one last month where the hero and heroine get snowed into a cabin together. He's this tattooed bad boy, you know? Absolutely not her type. But they're stuck in this place, and she has no choice but to see him for who he really is." I swallowed. "And of course they have great sex with simultaneous orgasms—which I still highly doubt happens in real life. But they never would have if they hadn't been trapped there. The forced proximity makes it impossible for her to write him off anymore. Even if the real world is waiting to mess everything up once they walk out the door."

Understanding filled my mom's face.

Cynicism was new for me, the product of a messy divorce and a fizzled relationship that hadn't been able to survive those equally messy real-world things.

I didn't want to be cynical. I wanted to feel hope and excitement and butterflies. I wanted all the things that came with them.

But I couldn't. Not yet.

Or I couldn't fully trust it when the flutterings of hope appeared.

Absently, I rubbed at my breastbone. "But how do you know it's real? Outside this house, Liam and I could hardly stand each other. I've known him for over a decade, and not once have I felt a spark like this."

"Not one?" she asked gently.

A burst of sound came from the pool—Lizette's angelic laughter—and I pinched my eyes shut. "Okay, some little ones. But I was practically married when I met him. And afterward . . . I was so focused on how much he aggravated me that I never let myself stop and think what was behind it."

Mom had a soft smile on her face while she listened. "First," she started, "simultaneous release is not a myth—"

"Stop," I interrupted. "I swear, if you say anything about your sex life with Dad, I'll chop my ears off."

She laughed. "And second, there's nothing wrong with being cautious about Liam. A guarded person usually has a reason for being that way, and they can hurt people whether they mean to or not, simply because they're so used to protecting their own heart."

"I sense a *but* coming," I told her.

"But just because you two are in this situation with Mira doesn't mean that real, beautiful feelings can't blossom from such an unexpected place. Don't let the unlikely nature of it keep you from the possibility of the kind of love and family you've always wanted."

There was an ache I'd had for so long that it was almost impossible to find the words to name it. Like I was missing a vital piece of myself, but I wasn't sure where to find it.

Even with everything I'd experienced, it was elusive. Frustratingly out of reach.

My whole life, I'd wanted love and family, to be surrounded by that unconditionally safe feeling. My parents had it, and even before I knew what I wanted to be when I grew up, I knew I wanted that.

Thankfully, my parents had raised me to believe that I was enough on my own, and I'd never doubted that. Charles hadn't chipped away at my self-esteem; he'd simply made me mourn the time I'd wasted with someone who wasn't right for me.

"*Unlikely* is right," I said. I stood and wandered over to the slider. "*Impossible* seems more accurate."

When I saw Mira push off the step, her eyes covered in bright-pink goggles, her head straining to stay above water as she kicked toward Liam, I couldn't help but laugh.

She was smiling so big that she kept swallowing water.

Liam, with his big arms outstretched, snatched her up and tossed her into the air. She shrieked with delight.

"Something changed last night," I said.

"What do you think that is?" my mom asked.

I watched them for a few more moments. "I don't know, exactly. But he's different with her."

And maybe with me too, if I was willing to admit that out loud. I didn't, though. Because when Liam pressed a quick, impulsive kiss to the top of Mira's head, I couldn't help the soaring, elated feeling from taking wing under my ribs.

The sheer weightlessness of it was savage and relentless.

Terrifying in its intensity.

And I wasn't sure there was anything I could do to stop it.

Chapter Nineteen

Liam

Something was fucking bugging me, and I couldn't push the thought out of my mind. Not after the swim lesson, and not after I went to the facilities for a particularly brutal session with our conditioning coach.

It wasn't anything Zoe had done or said. There wasn't a specific action I could point to.

Maybe it had happened when I set up the girls' night for her—shouldering responsibility for her well-being and something that didn't involve Mira.

Maybe it had happened when Mira decimated the last of my reserves and I slept on that fucking couch all night, just so I wouldn't have to move her.

I'd hardly noticed the slow crumbling until it was all too late.

Not long after my mum married Nigel, we went on holiday in Wales, the first time I'd ever been to the beach. For hours, I slid wet sand into a massive pile, cupping my hands and patting it down into place, crafting a structure that seemed, to my mind, indestructible.

It wasn't one wave that knocked it over. Nothing that came in from the offing to bring all my progress down. It was gradual. Little laps of water at the base until the top started to slide out of place and the whole thing went sideways.

I still wasn't sure if Zoe was the water or if the passing of our days had simply slowly destroyed something that I'd built over time.

Whatever it was, my mind couldn't stop spinning around the question that I'd never really gotten an answer to.

Whatever it was . . . I felt off-balance. Exposed.

"You okay?"

I glanced over at Richards, dipping my chin in a brief nod. "Fine."

My brusque reply didn't deter him, and I had to give him credit for that. Kid might've had a rocky start to his time here, especially with me, but he'd mellowed the last couple of months.

No tabloids. No strip joints. Just keeping his head down and working his ass off as we rounded the corner to training camp.

One of the veteran linemen gave Richards a friendly shove. "Don't let him off that easy. We all know when he's in a normal pissy mood and when he's extra crispy."

I rolled my eyes. "I'm not extra crispy, you twat."

"You did almost rip Coach's head off during the tackling drill."

"You also set the Denver record for most curse words dropped in a thirty-second span when Richards knocked you over that one time."

Richards grinned, holding his hand up for a fist bump, which I ignored. But he *had* planted his feet well and managed to knock me over, so I smacked him in the stomach instead.

"All of that usually adds up to an extra-bad mood for Liam Davies," Richards continued. "I know the variations well enough by now."

"Yeah? Tell me what this means." I flipped him off and increased the length of my stride as we neared the locker room.

"Come on, Liam," he said. "It's never healthy to keep all that shit bottled up. My mom used to let me scream into a pillow whenever I got mad."

He meant it to be funny, but I was too worked up and had too much energy still pulsing unchecked through my veins with nowhere to go. I gave him a look, and his smile faded.

To his credit, he squared his shoulders and didn't drop my gaze. "Just trying to say that we're here for you, if there's anything you want to talk about."

I held his stare for a few seconds longer. "There's not."

I kept my shower quick and cold, and when I finished rinsing off, I whipped a towel around my waist and marched back into the room.

"I'll tell you what my fucking problem is," I barked. They all turned toward me, not a lick of surprise on any of their asshole faces. "It's going fine at home, yeah? We're getting along, and I'd probably die for that little girl, and it feels like this weird little family unit that I don't under-stand, and Zoe is . . ." My chest heaved, and I was unable to follow the threads of that thought. She felt like *home*. One that I didn't deserve. I didn't deserve either of them. "We've got to take Mira to some fucking shrink tomorrow to talk, but what the bloody hell am I supposed to say? I still can't fucking tell you why my best friend chose me for this and didn't explain it to me. Didn't ask if I wanted all this responsibility." I could hardly breathe because the words were coming out so fast and furious. "He *never* asked. And it pisses me off."

Trey looked around the room, then settled his steady fucking eyes on me. "Would you have said yes if he did?"

"Fuck no."

"That's probably why he didn't ask," Trey answered smoothly.

"Well, isn't that fucking logical," I snapped. "But he still didn't explain it. I can't . . . I can't wrap my head around any of it. Why it feels different now and why it seems easier, because it shouldn't. I'm not good at any of this."

Blood churned hot in my veins, and my heart was thudding in my ears, a rapid-fire drum that I couldn't slow. My fist clenched, and I felt that urge.

Pick something up and throw it.

Smash a chair against a wall, just to have an outlet.

Trey saw it in my eyes too, because he didn't look away. The asshole hardly blinked.

"Would it matter if he'd explained it? If he'd written a big heartfelt letter telling you all the reasons why you'd be perfect for her?" Trey's eyes burned, and I wanted to look away, but I didn't. "Would you have believed him?"

The denial stuck deep in my throat. I'd need a fucking crowbar to pry it loose, and it would likely make me bleed if I managed to get it out. Rip at an artery, something vital that I wouldn't be able to fix.

No.

I wouldn't have believed him. No matter what he would've said.

Trey nodded slowly, and I knew the answer was clear in my eyes.

Richards glanced between us. "Y'all talk about some deep shit in this locker room," he said quietly. "My last team, all we talked about was football and women."

A few guys laughed, and I managed to exhale some of my tension.

"What about the stuff in his locker?" Richards added.

My head snapped in his direction. "What do you mean?"

"Did you ever look through that stuff? You know, after you had that last temper tantrum where you shoved everything into a box and pretended like you were ready to move on."

Someone whistled.

I took a step closer to Richards, chin lifted defiantly. "Pretended?" I asked, voice dangerous and low.

And that little fucker, he shrugged. "Just calling it for what it is. You're clearly not over anything. That's why you were asking for advice about the friend and why you're asking this now. You keep all that shit locked down until there's nowhere for it to go."

His words haunted me the entire drive home, as did the telling silence coming from my teammates.

Probably because he was right.

I drove aimlessly, in no rush to get home, because I knew that I'd have to open that stupid box only to come up empty-handed. Only to wind up frustrated yet again.

The sun was starting to set when I finally pulled into the garage, and I took a moment with my head resting back against the seat before I went into the house.

I wondered when the thought of Zoe and Mira in there waiting for me would feel normal. When the sight of them together wouldn't gut me the way it had that morning. The two of them cuddled in bed, her hair a bloody nightmare, so beautiful that my heart locked tight in my chest.

I didn't want to feel anything like that when I saw her. Saw them together. I didn't want to shoulder this overwhelming burden that would never go away.

Because somehow they both felt like mine.

Mine to take care of.

To protect.

And that also meant they were mine to hurt. Mine to ruin with all the shit that ran through my head.

My phone was heavy in my hand, and I stared at the screen, gripped with the sudden urge to call my mum. I'd been independent of my family for so long that it wasn't an impulse I dealt with often.

Ruthlessly, I pushed that down because I knew what she'd say.

She'd never really understood why I was so firm in my resolve to stay alone, chalking it up to a child's fears that would ease as I got older. Except they hadn't.

That's the thing about our fears. They don't magically disappear unless you're willing to face them, and this was the one thing in my life that I'd never been able to look squarely in the eye.

The house was quiet when I entered, and I had to wrestle past guilt over likely missing Mira's bedtime. There were sounds coming from upstairs, and I decided not to interrupt, especially if Zoe was winding her down. Imagining Zoe's annoyed expression if I got Mira ramped up right before bed took a corkscrew to my heart.

How was it possible to crave something so simple?

That's how I should've known I was arse over tit for that woman. I wanted her ire. Her irritation. The fire she seemed to spit at *me* alone. It was a heat I'd never felt from anyone else, and with slow, steady tending—moments and days and months and years—an addiction to it had been born.

I found myself heading down the hallway and past the playroom, then slowly pushing open the door to the office. The room was dark, the walls covered with family snapshots in black frames next to candid shots of Chris's career.

A masochistic part of me wanted to stand there in the dark and study them. Let the pain of the moment slice me open. Analyze my friend's face from the pieces of his past.

But I didn't.

The box sat on the corner of the desk, and I took a deep breath before ripping off the tape.

There was stupid shit from his locker: mouth guards and eye black and a sleeveless shirt left behind from his last day at the facilities.

My fist grasped on to that shirt so tightly that my fingers shook, and with slow, methodical breaths, I was finally able to set it down.

I'd underestimated the anger I still held inside over the senseless way they'd died, something carefully locked away where I refused to poke at it.

And I still refused. In that moment, I knew better. It snarled dangerously, like if I came too close, it would take off a limb.

After only a couple of minutes, I thought maybe I was on a fool's errand. That a fruitless search for some piece of clarity would leave me frustrated, leave things worse than they were before.

I made it to the bottom of the box and found nothing.

My chest felt cold and empty, and my hands twitched restlessly. I tugged open the drawer closest to me, then riffled through pens and paper clips and loose cords.

I'd left this room alone since the day I moved in, and I couldn't quite figure out why. Maybe because it was the place that most felt like his.

I pulled open another drawer and exhaled a short laugh when I saw a bottle of whiskey, the black-and-gold label of an expensive brand. Chris rarely drank, much like me. But when we did . . . this was what we shared.

Turning the bottle in my hands, I studied the way the light from the hallway came through the rich amber liquid.

Down the hallway, I could hear Zoe moving through the kitchen. A drawer opening, soft music emanating from the little speaker she kept in the corner underneath the cabinets. If I concentrated hard enough, I could probably make out the sound of her humming along.

Longing hit me like a lightning bolt, clean through from head to toe. That particular feeling—the craving for something I didn't have—was a strange beast, something I wasn't sure I'd ever master.

I couldn't mold it like a muscle, hone it with a machine or certain exercises, the way I'd done with my body, with my ability to play the game.

I couldn't discipline it into submission, because it operated on its own whims. And I was a bloody idiot for not considering how it would rule my days once I was sharing space with her.

What a fool I was.

Slowly, I uncapped the bottle, allowing the smell to hit me first. Letting the glass touch my lips, I tipped it back until the smoky warmth hit my tongue in a smooth burst.

I swallowed, keeping my eyes closed while it settled warmly into my belly.

I opened one more drawer and shifted things aside, but there was no envelope with my name on it. No scribbled handwriting, no magical explanation that would allow me to lay down all my questions.

"Fucking Chris," I whispered into the dark room. Made these big plans for his friends but hadn't seen fit to bring us into them beforehand.

Months earlier, I'd talked to Burke—the friend from college who'd gotten their wreck of a house in Michigan. He'd struggled with the why of all this just as badly as I had.

What had I said to Burke when we spoke? They were directing our lives from the bloody grave. That's what it felt like. Chris and Amie were privy to some big universal plan, something I couldn't see. And I wanted to know what that vision looked like to them.

After another drink, I dug through a small plastic container holding a few keys. Each was marked with a number that didn't give away any information about what it went to.

Then I refilled the box, tossing all his useless shit back inside until nothing was left but the picture of the three of them. I carefully set it against the wall next to a small black picture frame holding a shot of the day Mira was born.

Amie, propped up in the hospital bed, was holding Mira, and Zoe was crouched next to her, holding that bloody duck, smiling that big, happy smile—the one that always twisted my lungs a bit tighter.

I shouldn't have, but I took another swig of whiskey, allowing the pleasant burn that pooled in my stomach to loosen my muscles, soften all the hard-edged thoughts in my brain.

With the bottle in hand, I left the office, closing the door behind me with a quiet click.

Zoe was still in the kitchen, her hand rubbing at her neck, her hair slowly falling out of whatever useless configuration she'd tried in order to contain the mess.

It hadn't worked. And I desperately wanted to push my fingers through those golden strands, anchor my hands somewhere within her curls and memorize the way they felt.

Her eyes met mine, and my head reared back at what I saw there.

"Why do you look like you want to rip my head off right now?" I asked.

She swallowed. "You didn't come home at your normal time," she said. After a pause, her chin rose a notch. "I was worried." Then she eyed the bottle dangling from my hand. "Maybe I still should be."

I approached the island and set the bottle down. "Nah. Found it in Chris's desk and had a couple sips for old times' sake." I arched an eyebrow. "Want one?"

Zoe studied me for a second, exhaling an incredulous laugh. "You want to drink with me?"

Among other things.

Maybe pour it down her chest and see what it tasted like off her nipples.

My hands curled into fists. Thoughts like those were kept locked in the same place as the worst of my anger. Only when I wanted to punish myself did I let them see the light of day.

I didn't answer her question, merely held her gaze to see what she'd do next.

"How many have you had?" she asked quietly.

"Enough to know that I probably shouldn't drink with you," I answered. Too easily. "I never do it, so it always loosens my tongue a bit when I have a couple shots. I'm not pissed, though. Don't worry."

"I don't really like whiskey," she admitted. She came closer, pulling the bottle toward her as she took a seat on one of the stools where she could still face me. "I don't think I ever saw Chris drink this."

"He didn't much. We'd break it out every once in a while, have a couple shots and talk about all the bullshit in life we couldn't figure out."

She smiled, and fuck—it was so soft and sweet. If she were a drug, I'd take every little smile like that, crush it and snort it to see if all those pieces of her somehow made me feel better once they hit my bloodstream and made it sing.

"You trying to figure something out tonight?" she asked.

"Maybe."

Zoe held my gaze, looking away only when the tension stretched so tight that I worried something might break. Something might shatter into a million pieces, and I'd never be able to pick them up, never be able to set them back to rights.

She uncapped the bottle, wrinkling her nose when she smelled the whiskey. Before she touched it to her lips, she paused. "Do I get a chaser?"

"Fuck no. I didn't." I hitched my chin in a dare. "Woman up, Valentine. Show me what you've got."

Her eyebrow arched. "One drink."

I studied the graceful line of her neck when she took a pull from the bottle, and I tried not to think about the fact that she'd put her lips in the same place I'd put mine.

When she swallowed, I fought a laugh at the wrinkled expression on her face.

But I did smile. I couldn't help it.

She coughed. "Holy shit, that's terrible."

I grunted, motioning for the bottle. "Speak for yourself. That's some damn good whiskey." I wasn't drunk. Wasn't even really buzzed. But there was a pleasant, fuzzy warmth coating my thoughts, loosening my muscles.

"What were you looking for in there?" she asked. Then she shuddered, still feeling the bite of the drink.

"Clarity," I answered.

Her eyes were big in her face, her cheeks a sweet shade of pink. "Did you find it?"

I sighed, then shook my head slowly.

Zoe nodded, bringing her hand up to rub at her neck, the same spot she was always fussing with.

"Now what?" I asked gruffly.

"I was reading while Mira watched a movie." She blushed. "Rosa gave me a new book, and whenever I stare down at my Kindle too long, my neck starts hurting again."

"I told you that you need a massage or some shit."

She stretched her neck, wincing when she pulled it too far. "I know." Then she snapped her head up. "Don't make an appointment for me; I can handle it."

I notched my fingers to my temple in a mock salute. "Noted."

Zoe grinned, pushing her middle and pointer fingers into the curve of her shoulder again.

Because I couldn't fucking help it, I watched.

I always watched what she did. Had for years. And for some reason, that night, with my inhibitions lowered just the right amount, watching wasn't enough. "You're doing it wrong."

At the gruff sound of my voice, her fingers stilled. Her eyes searched mine.

I jerked my chin at all her bloody hair. "Pull that out of the way. I'll show you."

Don't.

Don't.

Don't fucking do it.

The voice was so loud in my head. Fucker was screaming at me, because every part of me knew that it was a horrible idea to touch her, even just this tiny bit.

And like the idiot I was . . . I ignored it.

Chapter Twenty

LIAM

I took another swig of whiskey while she wrapped a tie around her hair, bunching it up onto the top of her head. I could watch her play with that hair all fucking day.

Slowly, I walked behind Zoe, swallowing hard at the delicate bumps of her spine.

Did she like to be kissed there?

Her shoulders were tense, and I could understand why. I was too, my whole body strung tight like a bowstring.

The shirt she was wearing was pale blue, with thin, delicate straps stretching over the golden skin of her shoulders. Tiny wisps of hair curled against the nape of her neck, and the impact of them damn near had me swaying on my feet. I wanted to bury my nose there and pull in the sweet scent of her.

This was a sick test of my control and a testament to how badly I couldn't leash my own thoughts. And I'd likely regret it.

But I didn't now.

Her breath was choppy as she sat in front of me, her head bowed in supplication, like she was about to pray. What she didn't realize was that I was too.

For control.

For restraint.

For a moment like this that I didn't deserve, not even the littlest bit.

My hands looked big and clumsy when I lifted them, settling my palms over the curve of her shoulders. Her skin was warm and smooth, and she exhaled in a hard puff at the touch of my hands.

There was no choice but to close my eyes at the feel of it. Of just touching her.

But instead of a racing heart and jangled nerves, something very close to peace settled along my skin.

It wasn't hard to find the cord of tension with my thumbs, and when I pushed against it, trying to draw the tightness along the line of her back, she made a low moaning sound that plucked at all the little hairs on the back of my neck.

"Yeah?" I asked.

"Oh my Lord," she groaned. "Yes, there."

Her head dropped lower, and I smiled faintly.

"When your muscles are locked up like this, you can't just leave them to keep getting worse. A knot under your skin like that—you have to find a place to push all the tension away." My voice stayed quiet and low. "You have to move it along; otherwise, it'll build and build, causing a whole host of other problems."

The layered meaning of my words wasn't lost on me, and what a dumbass I was for thinking it'd be lost on *her*. She tilted her head as she listened, humming in understanding.

I used the heel of my hand to push against her muscles, and she hissed softly.

"Relax your shoulders," I murmured. "Don't keep tensing."

"Easy for you to say. You're not the one feeling what I'm feeling."

I smiled again, thankful she couldn't see. But I moved back to my thumbs all the same, gentling the pressure just a touch.

Zoe's entire body melted, and I dug my thumbs harder into the knot. "What kinds of books is she sending you that cause this? I don't even have knots this big, and I'm getting knocked around for a living."

She made a small laughing sound. "Dirty ones. This one is, at least."

My eyebrows popped up, hands stilling in an instant. "How dirty?"

"Don't judge."

"I'm not," I said easily.

I continued working on the knot, drawing my thumbs along the muscles, then pushed the heel of my hand along the full length of her shoulder blade. She shivered, and I closed my eyes.

"Too much?" I asked, and fucking hell, my voice sounded like I'd been chewing glass.

Yes. It was too fucking much, and I was the idiot who'd put us here.

"No," she whispered. I brought my thumbs along the base of her neck and pushed up to the base of her skull. Those little curls tickled my fingers, and I fought the urge to keep pushing, to bury them in her hair, to tug her face back and taste her skin with my tongue. "It's nothing," she added.

"No bullshit, remember?"

What a stupid thing to say.

We should absolutely bullshit our way through this if we wanted to come out unscathed.

But I was a weak man who sorely needed to get laid, because the sight of her neck was causing a life-threatening loss of blood flow to my head. It was all going straight between my legs, where I was so bloody hard it was a miracle I could still stand up straight.

But instead of taking back the prompt for honesty, I let it dangle in the air.

One more second and I might have succeeded in my last grasp for sanity. But then she answered, and when she did . . . I was so bloody fucked.

"I haven't been touched like this in a really long time," she whispered. "Years, really. It feels . . ."

My jaw clenched tight because I desperately wanted to know what she was going to say next.

"Incredible," she whispered.

It was entirely possible that I'd lost the ability to breathe. I definitely couldn't swallow. My heart might've stopped cold in my chest.

"Which is silly, if you think about it," she continued. "Because I get hugs from Mira. And Rosa. But something like this . . ." Her voice trailed off, and I fought the urge to tighten my hands on her skin until she finished. Thankfully, I didn't have to. "I'm not sure Charles ever rubbed my neck the entire time we were married."

"Yeah, well, Charles was a prick."

I hated thinking about him. So I told her that too.

Zoe laughed. "Indeed. You pegged him right off the bat."

I grunted.

She laughed again. "You'd have every right to gloat, you know. I was fully expecting you to."

I slowly sucked in a breath through my nose. "It's not a fun thing to gloat about, really. I fucking hated seeing you marry a twat like that." My voice deepened, rough with emotion. "The longer you stayed with him, the worse it got."

The words hit the room like a bomb, silence descending in an immediate vacuum. My hands slowed as I frantically tried to think of something, anything, to say.

But there was nothing there.

Stupid fucking whiskey. Fucking Chris stowing his fucking alcohol in a spot where anyone could find it in a moment of weakness.

My chest was tight, my pulse racing wildly. Fuck, I'd probably stroke out if I didn't find a way to salvage this. The peace was gone, obliterated at the turn that our conversation had taken.

"No bullshit?" she asked in a whisper.

I pinched my eyes shut, my hands slowing even more, the tips of my fingers tracing those delicate little knots of bone under her impossibly soft skin.

Now the words came easily. Because of fucking course they did.

"I wanted to tear him apart that first night," I said, voice dark and full of violent promises. "He didn't deserve to breathe the same air as you, let alone take you home, take you to bed, have you for his own."

Careful, that screaming voice in my head cautioned. *Careful now.*

I was treading on glass-thin ice, hairline cracks spreading out as far as the eye could see.

Zoe took a massive breath, her entire frame expanding. "Do you know what I hated?" she said.

I didn't answer.

I was too fucking busy. My thumbs absently trailed up the length of her neck until those hairs hit my skin again. I wound one around my finger, testing the softness of it.

Fuck the alcohol—I was getting drunk on touching her. My head swam dangerously, my pulse feral and far too fast for anyone to sustain.

"I hated that I always wondered why it bothered you so much," she admitted. "Because I thought about it. All the time."

My hands trembled. It was a good thing I couldn't see her face. If she pinned those golden-green eyes on me, gave even the slightest hint that she was feeling anything on the magnitude that I was, I'd lose myself completely.

But my traitorous fingers were already lost. I traced the shell of her ear, and she shivered again. She tilted her head, granting more access, nothing I deserved.

I was looming over her now, her back only a scant inch away from my chest.

My head bowed, and the scent of her hair was too tempting to ignore. I buried my nose in the crown of her head and filled my lungs with the sweetness I found there.

The moment after I did, as I slowly pulled away and wondered how I'd blame the whiskey for *sniffing her hair*, Zoe turned, tilting her head up, and the full impact of her eyes sent an electrifying jolt through my chest that I wasn't prepared for.

Her pupils were blown wide. Her cheeks flushed a rosy pink, and her lips opened in a gentle O.

For a few heartbeats, I could hardly register what I was seeing in her face because I'd wanted it for so long.

It was desire—reciprocal and clear—and the realization dealt a staggering blow. The desperate way I'd craved her for so long clawed at my reserve.

I wasn't strong enough to deny myself.

Not anymore.

I didn't know who moved next. She surged up onto her feet, I swooped down, and our mouths clashed in a fierce kiss.

At the touch of her lips, bone-melting relief had me groaning into her mouth.

But we weren't close enough. I couldn't get my body close enough. Never close enough.

With one hand, I knocked the stool out of her way and wrapped my arm around her waist as it fell onto the ground in a loud clatter.

Her lips were so sweet and delicious. Her skin was soft and firm, and I wanted to absorb her into my entire being.

There was no hesitation, not a single heartbeat in which we didn't take exactly what we wanted from the other.

And we took.

We took and took and took.

With tongues and teeth, sucked-in breaths, and hands furiously grappling against skin.

Zoe clutched my head in her hands, opening that sweet, sweet mouth when I licked at the seam of her lips.

The dirty sweep of my tongue over hers had her body melting into mine. The power of this kiss almost knocked my knees out from under me, because it was nothing I'd prepared for.

The universe split open, bursting at the seams with something new and vivid, revealed just by the way she kissed me.

In my wildest dreams, I'd never imagined it would be this good. And I'd imagined a lot.

My fingers dug into her hair, all that glorious golden hair, and I tilted her head to the side, deepening the way I could take her kiss.

Take her mouth. Take her sounds and her breath.

I'd take all of it, just in this one moment that I had it.

Her arms wound around my neck, her back arching as I slid my hands up and down, touching as much of her as I could. Up the supple line of her back, down until I could fill my hands with the curves of her backside. I bent at the knees to get a better angle, my hips pressing my hardness against her belly, and she let out the sweetest mewling sound.

I wrenched my mouth away, keeping my forehead tight to hers. "Fuck, I could live off that sound, Valentine. Give me more."

Then I sucked up the line of her jaw, tugging at the velvety-soft lobe of her ear with my teeth while she gasped for breath. Her cool, clever hands tracked down my chest, pushing at the hem of my shirt until she could find purchase on my overheated skin underneath the flimsy cotton that separated us.

Desire mangled all rational thought. There was nothing there to gentle the way we touched each other.

Because those touches felt like my salvation.

I'd wanted them for so long and had found no peace in her presence for all those years. Having this one moment with her now felt like being granted a brief reprieve from a decade of purgatory. One of my own making, something I'd never really tried to escape.

And it was worth it now to have the taste of her on my tongue and the glory of her body in my hands.

I pushed a hand up her waist, past her ribs, until I brushed a thumb against the side of her breast. The warm weight of it had my mouth watering.

She tugged my mouth back to hers, whimpering when our tongues twined, when our lips pushed and pulled with heat and fervor and something messy and wild.

Zoe nipped at my bottom lip with her teeth, and my whole body shook. My hands tightened, my grip on her turning greedy and fierce, straddling a line that felt whisper thin.

We were pressed against the island, our bodies wound tight against each other, hands seeking and touching and memorizing, expressing something frantic that I didn't want to name because if I thought about it too hard, I'd stop.

And I didn't want to stop.

Zoe moaned into my mouth when I filled my hand with her breast over the cotton of her shirt.

No bra.

Only a thin layer of fabric between us, and it wasn't enough to hide the hard point of her nipple. My thumb traced it. Over and over and over until it was her turn to shake.

Zoe tugged her hands away from where they traced the muscles of my stomach, then slowly curled her fingers over the front of my shorts, where I was in the most pain.

A tortured growl emerged from the deepest pits of my chest as I rocked my hips into her touch. There was no hesitation from this woman, and she'd be the death of me someday. Of that, I was sure.

And if I wasn't careful, her hand around me would end everything in an embarrassingly premature fashion, simply by nature of how fucking badly I wanted her. How long I'd fantasized about this, in the dark of my room, under the heat of my shower.

It was always her, even when I tried to think about something, someone, *anyone* else.

Always Zoe.

It *would* always be Zoe too. There was no escaping it, even if I wanted to. I wasn't sure I did anymore.

I'd suffer the want of her for the rest of my life without complaint.

She whimpered when I tore her hand off me, nipping at my bottom lip in retaliation, and I grinned. Against the impossibly soft skin at her wrist, I placed a sucking kiss, my eyes locked on hers.

Her chest heaved as she watched me, and the bottomless pools of her gaze had my head spinning.

Did she know how helpless I was? How quickly I'd fall to my knees to worship her?

She couldn't possibly.

Zoe pulled her arm out of my grasp and cupped the side of my face, cradling the line of my jaw as she tugged me down.

With a groan, I took her mouth again.

Through endless sucking kisses, through tangled tongues and nipping teeth and abused lips, I gripped her hips in my hands and boosted her up onto the island. Zoe split her thighs around my hips, bracing her legs around my ass to tug me closer.

The added height allowed me to cup her face in my hands, weave my hands through her hair, and study the sweetness of her face. She grinned.

"You look a right mess," I whispered against that smile.

Zoe exhaled shakily, tracing her thumb along my bottom lip. And her eyes . . . they were on fire. "Why don't you mess me up some more, then?" She kissed my lower lip, and my eyelids fluttered shut at the gentle touch. What a sweet undoing of my sanity this was. "Please, Liam."

My bones rattled from the force of that whispered request.

I gripped her chin and took her mouth with another savage kiss.

Zoe softened, her pliant body melting into mine.

The animal impulse to tear at her shirt, to bare her body before me, was almost impossible to ignore. I wanted to suck and taste and bite. Leave marks where she'd see them for days.

I wanted to spread her out on the island and hold her hips down with my hands while her thighs shook on either side of my head. Gorge my fill on her sweetness, kiss her with her taste on my lips. Get drunk on nothing but Zoe.

I wanted to unleash years of bottled longing in between her legs, where we'd both shake and sweat and scream when it was over.

When it was over . . .

What would it be like when it was over?

The thought was like a bucket of ice dumped right over my head.

When torn clothes and sticky, messy skin morphed into a face of regret. *Her* face.

I tried to imagine that, even as my mouth was fused with hers.

I'd rather wrench my heart out of my chest and deal with the gaping hole left behind.

Slowly, I gentled the kiss, unable to stop as quickly as I likely should have. "Zoe," I whispered against her lips.

She paused, her eyes locked on mine when she registered my tone. "No," she begged. "Please don't stop." She rubbed her nose against mine, sucking my bottom lip in between hers. This was a pleading kiss, an unnameable request that I'd never be able to fulfill.

Because eventually, I'd let her down.

Eventually, we'd be left standing in the smoldering ashes of what remained, and there was no possibility of that happening in a way that didn't leave Mira in the middle.

"We can't, love," I whispered. The endearment came out thoughtlessly.

Her eyes fluttered shut.

"We can't," I repeated. "There's too much at stake."

Slowly, her hands slid over my chest, and I fought the urge to lean into her.

Slowly, she lowered her feet to the floor, and I studied her unashamedly, her hair mussed from my hands, her lips pink and puffy from the kisses, and her eyes . . .

I couldn't look away, even though I should have.

Her eyes were disappointed.

I'd done that.

It was why the things I felt for her were better kept leashed and caged and locked away. Why my self-induced purgatory was where I deserved to live.

"I'm sorry," I told her. "I shouldn't have done that."

"Don't," she whispered fiercely. "Don't you dare."

Finally, I nodded. No apologies, then. I hadn't meant it anyway. I wasn't sorry.

I might be tomorrow. But with her taste still lingering on my lips, I couldn't find any regret.

"Go to bed, Zoe," I told her. "We've got that appointment in the morning, and we both need sleep."

Her eyes narrowed, thoughtful and sharp. "We're not done with . . . whatever just happened here. We *will* talk about it eventually."

I slicked my tongue over my teeth. "Not tonight, though."

When she glanced at the whiskey bottle, I saw the moment she conceded. "Not tonight," she agreed quietly.

I swiped a hand over my mouth, slowly bending to pick up the stool that I'd swept aside. Once it was upright, I pushed it back into place.

Zoe stared, her gaze unflinching and unguarded. She wanted more. And I couldn't possibly think about what that meant.

"Good night," I told her.

She swallowed, silently watching me leave the room, and I wondered how many more times she'd watch me walk away before it got to be too much.

Chapter Twenty-One

Zoe

When I couldn't sleep, I had a terrible habit of staring at the ceiling and pondering really deep existential questions.

About mistakes and regret. These two things had plagued me for months after I kicked Charles out of the house.

About finding your purpose. I'd spent a solid year on this one when I decided to take a sabbatical from working full-time because I knew I needed the break.

Loss and love and heaven and God.

Whether there were predetermined plans for our lives that we couldn't see, or whether it was all truly left to chance. I was still wrestling with those.

And tonight I thought about first kisses.

I thought about what it meant when those kisses were the best first kisses I'd ever had in my life. Nothing I'd experienced came close.

It had to mean something, right?

I'd doze for a while, my eyes heavy with the tug of sleep, only to jolt awake when I remembered how Liam's thumbs had played my nipples like instruments until I made sounds so perfectly aligned with the heat building between us that I couldn't hear over the rush of my thundering pulse.

When I thought about his firm lips and the hot, demanding slide of his tongue, my breath would come faster, and my heart raced in my chest.

For hours, I tossed and turned, kicked at the sheets covering my legs, and smashed my overheated face into the pillow when I couldn't pry the thoughts of him from my head.

My pulse was stretched thin across my entire body; I could feel it everywhere.

Feel *him* everywhere.

As the night wore on, interminably slow, I picked apart every millisecond of what had happened.

The gnawing worry that had plagued me all evening when he hadn't shown up at his normal hour. The bone-melting relief when I realized he was home. The whiskey bottle in his hands. The look on his face because I knew something was wrong.

And the way my body had reacted when he laid his hands on my skin. The way my heart took a slow, tortured turn in my chest when he curled his body over my back and pressed his nose into my hair.

Honestly, it was a miracle I hadn't shoved him down on the island and ripped his shirt clean in half. I wanted to. I wanted to finish what we'd started, and I couldn't deny—no matter how much I should have—that I would have finished it if he hadn't stopped us.

There would have been sex.

Kitchen sex.

Messy, hard, glorious kitchen sex with Liam.

Complicated, glorious kitchen sex with Liam.

I laid a trembling hand on my face and tried to will myself to sleep, but it was a lost cause.

The worst part of all these Technicolor flashbacks was the line of questions that came after them.

Why hadn't *I* thought about all the reasons we should've stopped?

And, even worse, if Liam hadn't stopped us, what would have happened afterward?

The nature of our situation made any future relationship that much harder. It didn't matter if that relationship was between me and Liam or with someone new. For either of us.

To call it murky was an understatement, and I still couldn't parcel out whether my attraction to him was real or simply a byproduct of the situation.

We were both single. Forced to be together every day. Seeing sides of each other that we hadn't before. The prospective changes were inevitable.

And terrifying.

Then there was the added awareness that he'd been attracted to me once upon a time. Maybe he still was. Would I have been tempted to kiss him if I hadn't known that? Did his admission plant a seed of possibility that I never would have considered on my own?

It was foolish to deny that I'd been lonely. Having heartbreak in your past didn't automatically turn you into someone who hated love.

I *wanted* to be in love. Butterflies and first dates and first kisses and all that came with it.

I wanted someone to love me in the same way. Where the sight of me set millions of wings aflutter in the pit of their belly and tangled their tongue when they tried to speak.

No, I didn't hate love. Maybe I just didn't fully trust myself yet. And for good reason. What I'd been through allowed for some hesitation where I might not have had any in the past.

Why, then, hadn't I hesitated last night?

This was the worst of the questions that plagued me in the darkest parts of the night. There were no clear answers. There was no right or wrong. No black and white about any of this.

We just had to figure out the best way to move forward. And I knew before the sun came up which version of Liam would greet me in the morning.

We'd be back to the man behind the iron wall.

"Bloody hell, what did we do?" I whispered. Then I sighed heavily and turned to the side, pinching my eyes closed, determined to get at least a few hours of rest before I had to face him.

◆ ◆ ◆

Most of the time, being right came with an undeniable sense of satisfaction.

But when Brick Wall Liam was back in full force that morning, satisfaction was the last thing on my mind. I wasn't annoyed either. His eyes were so wary, so guarded as we danced around each other at breakfast and as I got Mira ready for the day, that I couldn't be upset.

Mine probably held a similar gleam.

Don't hurt me, mine said.

Don't break what we've built. It was plain as day in his.

The two thoughts crashed head-to-head, and from our past history, I knew exactly what kind of stubborn determination we were capable of.

I didn't want to break what we'd built either, but I was willing to tiptoe into a new reality if he'd join me there.

The drive to the therapist's office was quiet. Even Mira seemed to sense our contemplative moods, because she sat silently in her seat, watching the scenery pass.

Being seated next to him while he drove, with one big hand resting atop the wheel and the other casually draped over the console, made my entire being dizzy.

It was so easy to imagine an alternate reality where he'd look over at me and smile. Maybe settle one of those big hands on my thigh as he ferried us where we needed to go.

A wave of longing hit me in the chest, right in the center of my breastbone, and I had to close my eyes against the force of it.

"You all right?" Liam asked.

The quiet rumble of his voice inexplicably brought the burn of tears to my eyes. Somehow, without looking at me, he'd noticed. He'd *seen*.

What a stupid, simple thing to bring tears to my eyes.

But it wasn't stupid. It wasn't stupid that it meant so much to be seen.

I managed a small nod. When I opened my eyes, his hand was tight around the wheel, and the muscles in his jaw twitched ominously.

"We here yet?" Mira asked from the back seat.

"Almost, Mirabelle." As Liam pulled his SUV into an open spot across the street, I pointed to a short brick building with a simple sign on the lawn. The white door was flanked by large black planters over-flowing with red and white flowers. "It's right here."

"Looks like a house," Liam said.

I nodded. "Used to be one. Makes the kids more comfortable than a sterile office."

He hummed, distrust still clearly stamped over his features.

"Thank you for agreeing to this," I said quietly. "I know you don't believe in therapy."

Liam's eyes found mine, and what I saw there left me breathless again. How could someone say so much with a single look?

He wanted me.

He didn't *want* to want me.

And he didn't know what the hell to do with me. That was clear as day.

Mira started unhooking her straps, and Liam pulled his gaze from mine, arching an eyebrow at the little girl in the back seat. "When did you learn to do that?" he muttered under his breath.

She simply giggled, pulling her arms out once she was free. "You coming inside, Liam?"

Oh. The way he looked at her, loaded with affection and reluctant love. My heart would never, ever survive it.

He nodded. "I won't let you do it alone, duck. Zoe and I will be right there with you, yeah?"

She clambered across the console until she straddled it like a seat. "And I go meet a new friend?"

I picked up her bag and smiled. "Yup. Her name is Miss Carol. She's got a bunch of fun toys for you to play with."

Zoe bounced excitedly. "Okay. We go inside now?"

Liam and I locked eyes again.

He swallowed roughly. "Is it weird that I'm more terrified to walk into that building than I am to face down a linebacker?"

I exhaled a laugh. "No. I think it's pretty normal."

Liam narrowed his eyes. "If she makes me cry, I'll never forgive you."

Quite desperately, I wanted to cup his face with my hand, lean forward, and kiss him. A normal kiss, with no desperation or frantic edge. The kind you'd take for granted if you'd done it a million times.

When his gaze flickered down to my lips, I wondered if he'd read that in my face as clearly as I seemed to have read his.

"I don't think today will be too intense," I told him. "She's just getting to know us."

"Promise?" he asked.

I held out my hand. "If I'm wrong, I'll do your stinky football laundry for two weeks."

Liam's lips twitched. Then he slid his palm against mine, and when his long fingers curled around, I exhaled shakily.

When I pulled my hand away, I fought the urge to tuck my fingers up against my chest because of the way my skin buzzed. I wanted to bottle the feeling, drink from it on a day when I felt tired and lonely down to my bones.

Liam blinked a few times.

Less than ten minutes later, I knew I never should have made that bet.

Chapter Twenty-Two

LIAM

"Why don't you tell me about your family of origin, Liam?"

I exhaled slowly, somehow managing to keep a growl from emerging along with it. "Do I have to?"

Carol, fucking sadist that she was, merely gave me a calm, steady, patient smile. "I can't force you to tell the truth, no. But it will help. Both of you bring history and baggage and trauma into this situation. It's not just about Mira; it's equally about you and Zoe. How the two of you communicate, how you manage inevitable disagreements. Those are all swayed by what you've been through."

My options were slim.

I could bolt through the door. And there was a window behind Carol's head. If I shoved her out of the way and used a lamp to break the window, I might be able to squeeze through before they dragged me back to that bloody couch.

To my right, Zoe sat with her legs crossed and her hands clasped in her lap. Slowly, I turned my head to pin her with a look. She gave me an apologetic smile.

I narrowed my eyes.

Carol tilted her head. "You seem upset by this change of direction. Would you like to talk about that?"

"Not particularly," I drawled. "I thought this session was for Mira."

"And it is. My colleague is with her in the main living area; I believe they're playing with blocks right now."

I pinched the bridge of my nose, speaking softly enough that only Zoe could hear me. "Can't we play fucking blocks at home for free?"

Zoe cleared her throat.

Right. I dropped my hand and sucked in a large, fortifying breath.

My whole body felt squeezed tight with tension, like these two women had set me in a man-shaped vise and were cranking the handle over and over and over until I had no choice but to spill my fucking guts onto the floor.

Carol smiled. "She's a bit younger than we normally start with our kids. Usually, we wait until they turn three before initiating any form of play therapy, but given the circumstances of losing her parents, I think it's wise that we establish a bond with her as she grows older."

A lift of my eyebrows was all the concession I could manage.

She tilted her head. "A distrust of therapy is incredibly common, Liam. Where did that start for you?"

I leaned back on the couch, my shoulder brushing Zoe's, and I settled my hands over my stomach so I could study Carol. She was friendly enough. Short gray hair and a grandmotherly manner that probably instilled a sense of comfort in all the little kiddies she saw every day.

Probably knitted the purple sweater she was wearing, even though it was easily seventy-five degrees outside. And the pearls around her neck looked real.

Next to me, Zoe inhaled slowly. She smelled like something fresh and clean and sweet. I couldn't name it. The entire drive over, I'd tried to place what that smell was and couldn't.

I imagined I'd have a better chance if I tucked my nose underneath that soft spot just below her jaw, where her scent was the most potent.

Those thoughts wouldn't help shit, which was likely why we had both wandered into the kitchen with dark circles under our eyes. No sleep for either of us, as we'd been thinking about what had happened.

Thinking about what *hadn't* quite happened.

Carol smiled patiently, completely undeterred by the silence that followed her question.

Of course we'd found the most stubborn therapist west of the Mississippi. She'd wait me out—I could see it in those shrewd eyes of hers.

"My mum had me sit down with a shrink when I was maybe ten?" I said. "Complete wanker, he was. Had a little notebook that he wrote in when I refused to answer his stupid questions about what I was feeling and why my mum had sent me there. I went twice. Never said a single word to him, and in front of me, he told my mum that I'd do well with intensive psychiatric help someday." I shrugged. "When I told her I didn't like him, she cried the whole way home and never made me go back."

Carol's eyes got sad. "I'm sorry that was your experience. I don't blame you for not trusting people in our profession. But it says a lot that you're willing to let Mira have a different experience. Do you feel like you'd trust people more if you'd been able to talk about your parents' divorce at a young age?"

I trusted people just fine.

It was myself I had less faith in.

"I never told you my parents were divorced," I answered evenly.

My voice was the only even, calm thing about me. Inside, everything burned. The flames were too high, threatening to flow over dangerously.

It was far too tender of a place to poke when I was already walking on the edge of my sanity after the kissing.

Our entire situation felt precarious. And that was just me and Zoe. If this woman tried to rope my past into the conversation, I was likely to detonate in a messy burst.

A scar that was best left alone. An itch I couldn't scratch because it was buried so deep beneath the surface.

The moment someone tugged at my past, a sticky discomfort spread over every inch of my body, and there was nothing I could do to make it go away.

So I ignored it. Until I couldn't.

"You're right, you didn't," Carol said. "I made an assumption when you only mentioned your mother, but I shouldn't have done that." She held up her hands. "Let's change the subject for now. We can schedule separate sessions to discuss upbringings if that makes you both feel more comfortable."

Zoe nodded, glancing sideways. "That's fine with me." She looked tentative. Her eyes were filled with hesitancy. Apology.

It made me want to claw my skin off.

This was the woman who'd met me fearlessly the entire time. For years, she had. Chased me down in the parking lot to give me a piece of her mind. Swung a *bat* at my head. Granted, she didn't know it was me at the time, but even if she had, I couldn't help but think she still would've done it.

A couple of kisses and she wasn't sure how to handle me.

I stood before I knew what I was doing. "Gonna go check on Mira," I said tersely. Neither woman said a word as I strode from the room.

What I found stopped me short.

They weren't playing blocks anymore. They'd moved to a big farmhouse-style table in the area just off the kitchen. The surface was covered with papers, crayons, and colored pencils.

The young woman next to Mira had her head bent over her own paper while Mira scribbled messily on a giant piece of yellow construction paper. She'd hardly noticed that I'd entered the room, so I walked quietly.

The therapist sitting with her lifted her head and smiled encouragingly as I approached. "Want to color with us?" she asked.

I didn't answer her, though. My eyes were trained on Mira's paper. At first, I could hardly make sense of the shapes and pieces. Jagged lines of brown and yellow and red and blue and black.

The proportions were completely off. It would never win any art awards, not in any universe. And there was no doubt in my mind that I'd see that picture when I closed my eyes for the rest of my fucking life.

The longer I stared, the more I wondered if anyone else in the room had heard the break of my bones as my chest cracked wide open.

It was us.

My hand, a wobbly line, was on Mira's. My hair was a giant black blob, and in the area of my face, she'd given me a straight line for a mouth. Zoe—clearly identifiable because of the wild hair and the big, red, crooked smile—was on the other side of Mira.

In between the larger figures flanking her, Mira was only clear because of the brown hair. Instead of her body, she'd attempted to draw a heart over her chest.

I crouched next to her, settling my hand on her back. She was so little. Sometimes that was easy to forget because of how bloody big her personality was.

"What do you have here, duck?" I asked quietly.

Mira stopped, beaming up at me with a smile so big that I felt it in my fucking soul. "I drawing a family."

My vision blurred. Why couldn't I fucking see anything? I blinked rapidly, trying to clear that shit away. "It's really good," I told her. Fucking hell, my voice was all wobbly and shit.

I covered my mouth with one hand and stood on weak legs.

The therapist at the table watched me carefully.

I hardly noticed, because it felt an awful lot like all the carefully constructed blocks of my world were coming down in a spectacular crash, and there was nothing I could do to stop it. What was left in the aftermath was a cloud of dust and me standing like an idiot in that room, with wet cheeks and a painfully tight chest.

My breaths came faster and faster, and I shoved a hand through my hair as I stared back at the door leading to the office I'd just exited. My fingers tingled ominously.

"If you need a minute, my office is empty," the woman at the table said in a gentle voice.

I didn't need a minute. An hour wouldn't help.

I needed this out. I needed to slice out the poison because it felt like it was choking me, and I couldn't handle the bitter taste in my mouth anymore.

I wanted the sweetness I'd gotten glimpses of before.

Mint and chocolate and whatever else she'd given me.

After taking only a few steps, I shoved open the door to Carol's office.

Zoe glanced up in surprise. Her eyes sharpened when she saw my face, mouth falling open.

"I don't like talking about my old man," I said.

I wasn't yelling. I didn't bark it out. Every shred of control I was capable of summoning funneled straight into that one thing.

Carol sat back in her chair and watched wordlessly, but I kept my eyes on Zoe.

"The only thing I remember about him is how he sounded when he yelled, which he did a lot. When he called my mum names and kicked a chair into her path to trip her when she walked past. And what he looked like when he punched her in front of me for the first time." My hand curled into a fist—it was huge when I looked down at it. "Full on, no holding back, and I was sitting five feet away. I'll never forget what it sounded like when his fist hit her face."

Zoe sucked in a sharp breath, her eyes filling immediately.

"After he hit her, I screamed at him to stop," I rasped, "and he turned right toward me, so fucking pissed off that I'd tell him what to do. That fist never disappeared, and my mum jumped right in between us. Told him that if he was still mad, he should take it out on her."

My entire frame trembled, and I forced the words out. They were bitter and vile. "He didn't. Probably just smart enough to know people would notice if she turned up completely black and blue. He went to the pub instead—where they always fucking idolized him, treated him like he walked on bloody water. She packed us a bag each, took all the cash she'd been hiding in her sock drawer, and we walked out of the house. Never went back. Never saw him face-to-face again."

Silent tears tracked down Zoe's cheeks, every single one of them carving up my heart.

With a closed fist, I tapped my chest. "But I see him every time I look in the fucking mirror because I look exactly like him. My whole life, I've been reminded how much I'm like him, and when you hear that enough at seven and eight and nine and ten years old, you start believing it. Even worse when you're older. I promised myself I'd never put myself in a position where I could hurt someone like he hurt her." I was choking on the words, so they came out tight and urgent and fierce. "I did everything I could to not end up like him. Found a way to channel all this anger I have rooted deep inside me. It's ugly, and I hate it. I won't do it to you, Zoe. Or her." My voice cracked. "It scares me fucking witless to think I might. I'd never forgive myself."

Zoe had a hand over her mouth now because she was crying openly.

I dashed my palm over my cheeks. "I don't like talking about him," I said brokenly.

She inhaled raggedly. "Why are you talking about him now?"

"For her," I managed. But that wasn't true. Or not entirely. So I held Zoe's gaze and thought of all the ways she'd shown me how to be brave. "And for you."

Her chin trembled.

Carol cleared her throat, a delicate sound that echoed like a gunshot. I blinked.

"Thank you for sharing that, Liam," she said.

I nodded, but even if she paid me a million dollars, I wouldn't make eye contact with that woman while I had tears in my eyes. I already felt like I'd been stripped naked in the middle of the fucking room.

"It takes a lot of strength to break the cycles of abuse," Carol added. "I give you and your mother all the credit in the world for doing that."

"I didn't do shit," I said. "She's the strong one."

Neither woman argued with me, and I was thankful for that. But I was too busy staring down at the floor to know whether they wanted to.

"Can we be done for today?" I asked in a raw voice that I hardly recognized.

"I think that's a good idea," Carol answered. "I hope you'll come back, Liam. My door will always be open to you. Both of you."

Zoe stood, and as much as I didn't want to look at her, I found my attention shifting to her face.

Her eyes were slightly red from the tears, and she was smiling softly at Carol.

When her gaze moved to mine, my legs threatened to buckle. I knew that if they did, I'd end up on my knees in front of her, my head pressed against her stomach and my arms around her.

No one in the world had ever looked at me like that.

The understanding in her face was more than I could handle, especially with the sharp buzz of vulnerability still hanging thick in the air.

But there was so much more buried there, things I couldn't name and didn't dare try to define. All the things I'd insulated myself from, if I was being honest.

Zoe would be able to gut me with the simplest of actions because I'd all but rolled over at her feet.

"Ready to go?" she asked.

No.

Yes.

I didn't know anymore, but I nodded all the same.

The only thing I knew for sure was that there was no going back from this. And based on the look in her eyes as we loaded Mira into the car and started on our way home, the conversation that waited for us was about to get a whole lot bigger.

Chapter Twenty-Three

Zoe

The rest of the day seemed to conspire against us.

Not that any sort of meaningful conversation could happen with Mira running around in the same room. I had a client call me shortly after we returned home from the therapist's office, prompting me to dig out my laptop so we could discuss how to categorize some of his spending.

Liam stayed with Mira in the playroom so I could have some quiet.

By the time I was finished, he'd received a call from his quarterback, Trey, about some last-minute drills. Training camp was just around the corner, he said by way of explanation. That meant extra eyes on them.

He changed into practice gear. His shirt bore a small Denver logo on the chest, and he wore a black hat turned backward on his head.

"Probably won't be home until after dinner," he said quietly.

As Mira hugged his legs, I smiled. "I'll save you a plate."

The line of Liam's throat revealed a heavy swallow when he ruffled her hair. "I'll be back soon, duck. Maybe you could practice your big-girl kicks in the pool with Zoe?"

But she buried her face into his thighs and shook her head vehemently.

I exhaled a soft laugh.

His gaze locked onto my mouth, then slowly lifted higher. "I'll see you later, then."

As I nodded, I tried to keep the heartbreak from my eyes, but it seemed like an impossible task. The last thing Liam would want was my pity.

I didn't pity him. But I couldn't help my natural reaction to imagining him as that young boy either.

"No wonder," I murmured as I watched him get into his car, slam the door with a mighty heave, and rest his head back against the seat for a moment.

It all made so much sense now that I had the last piece of the puzzle snapped into place. His absolute terror at the beginning. His reticence toward getting close to either of us.

Liam would have done anything to make sure history didn't repeat itself. He'd even built an unscalable wall that no one could attempt to climb.

I kept thinking about it in the hours he was gone. Kept thinking about what I might've said if we'd been alone in that moment.

I'd simply need to add it to my list of questions that might never be answered. It was something I might ponder in the middle of the night. My curiosity rode a knife's edge, but I knew he'd only sate that curiosity if he felt safe enough to talk through it. More than anything, I wanted to wrap him in my arms and tell him a thousand times—a million times—that I trusted him. That we felt safe with him.

But I wasn't sure that would be enough.

All day, I replayed his face, his words, the tense way he'd held his body as he delivered them. Something he'd said niggled at the back of my head, and I pulled out my laptop, then carefully typed "Liam Davies father" into a search engine.

Numerous articles popped up immediately, along with pictures of an older man who looked so much like Liam that I exhaled in a sharp gust. I scrolled, picking up on a few key details that locked everything into place.

His dad was an athlete too. There were older pictures, older articles talking about wins and losses and promotions and relegations related to a British football team. He wasn't quite as large as Liam, but the fierce look on his face was stunningly similar to that of the man I'd known for a decade.

I covered my mouth as I read, trying to imagine a young boy making peace with something of this magnitude. A man revered by so many because of his talents on the field was a complete nightmare at home. Coaches would esteem someone like Liam simply because of that connection, never knowing what it did to his young brain to be constantly held up in comparison.

My eyes lingered on an article about Liam during his college days. There was a mention of his famous footballer father, the writer making it very clear where he got his strength and speed and determination, and I had to rub at my sternum to quell the growing ache.

Slowly, I closed my laptop and pushed it away with a sigh.

Mira and I stayed busy. We went for a walk through the neighborhood, and while she took her postlunch nap, I ignored the fact that I had work to do and decided instead on some self-care in the form of a small nap of my own and a sinfully long shower afterward.

We ordered pizza for dinner because the entire day felt so heavy with anticipation that it was hard for me to focus on anything.

I hadn't touched my phone in hours, and as we finished eating, I stared at where it lay face down on the counter. I didn't flip it over until Mira was done and I'd cleared our dishes. My eyes quickly scanned the messages waiting for me.

One from my mom.

Mom: How did the session go this morning? I'm off tomorrow if you want to call.

The temptation to call her and process all of this was strong. My entire life, I'd done that. I'd learned that having someone to listen to what lay between the lines was crucial.

But there was a stronger impulse gnawing away at that one.

I found myself wanting to protect what Liam had told me. It wasn't fodder for anyone's consumption. Not even hers. For now, I ignored her text.

There was one from Rosa.

Rosa: Martha picked an alien romance for next month. Not sure how I feel about tentacles, but I'm nothing if not open minded. You in?

I smiled and told her I'd let her know.

The third had my brow furrowing a little.

Tyler: I found something of yours when I was cleaning out a closet. Let me know if you're home later. I can drop it off.

I didn't have the mental bandwidth to touch *that* one, so I sighed and swiped out of the message.

The last one was from Rochelle.

Rochelle: Let me know if you want to join us for training camp! It's one of my favorite parts of the year. You and Mira should be there.

I tapped out my reply carefully.

Me: I'll talk to Liam. He hasn't mentioned anything about it yet.

Rochelle: Trust me, he'll want you there.

I pinched my eyes shut and fought the churning sense of unrest in my gut. It wouldn't have shocked me if Liam wanted to hide for the next month after what he'd admitted this morning. He could hardly look at me before he sped out the door for training.

There was no other choice but to compartmentalize all of it. Tuck it away in a safe place, locked tight, even if I was the one not allowed to poke at it.

Understanding often came at a heavy price. And you didn't always know what that price was until you were forced to pay it. It didn't really matter if you were talking about understanding a person or a situation.

Understanding grief came saddled with the loss. You couldn't extricate one from the other.

Understanding what it was like to become a parent came with an irrevocable shift in your entire world. No one could adequately prepare you before it happened, no matter how hard they tried.

Understanding the fears that made up someone's foundation came only when they were at their most vulnerable. The hardest part came next. Once you knew . . . you had to decide if you could handle those fears or if they were too much for you.

Liam knew mine, but it wasn't a fair comparison. The groundwork of my fears didn't hold nearly the same consequences as his did. I didn't have to face them every time I looked in a mirror.

Mira begged to watch her movie while I cleaned up the kitchen, so I turned it on in the playroom before wiping down the counters, then sliding the leftover pizza slices onto plates and setting them in the fridge for Liam.

Not that he'd eat them. Based on the state of his abs, the man hadn't touched pizza in a decade.

I set my hand on my fluttering belly because I did not need to think about the muscles anywhere on his body. Those were a distraction.

But, then again, everything I'd done in his absence was a distraction. There were no decisions to be made when it was just me doing the thinking. All I could do was wait until we could talk.

Talk without the help of whiskey or a therapist or kissing with wandering hands.

The sound of the door opening had me blowing out a slow breath.

Liam looked tired when he tossed his bag down onto the kitchen floor. He was in different clothes than when he'd left, his hair still dark and damp from a shower. "Where's the little bit?"

I nodded toward the playroom. "Watching her movie."

One side of his lips hooked up. "How many times you think she's seen it?"

"A hundred at this point, if not more."

Liam rubbed the back of his neck, wincing as he pressed against the muscles there. "*I've* watched it at least that many times. She's got to be rounding closer to five hundred."

"Your neck okay?" I asked.

He grunted. "Didn't take the time for them to work on me after we practiced."

I leaned up against the counter and watched him fill a glass with water. "I'd offer to help, but . . ." My voice trailed off. "I have a feeling I know what you'll say."

Liam gave me a wry look. "Probably not the best idea, yeah?"

I sucked in a quick breath and prayed for some courage. "I liked what happened last night when you helped me."

At my answer, Liam's eyes burned into mine. He didn't drink his water, and he didn't move from where he stood.

"Did you?" he asked, voice low and intensely charged.

Slowly, I nodded. As I did, I took a few steps closer to him, and he watched warily.

"I think you did too," I told him. "You just don't know what to do with it."

He exhaled a soft puff of air. It was an incredulous sound. "Jumping right into this, are you?"

"I don't know any other way to do it, Liam." I raised my shoulders in a slight shrug. "We certainly can't pretend it didn't happen. I can't, at least." My gaze stayed locked on his. "Can you?"

There was a moment of quiet, and judging by the look on his face, he was trying to decide how to reply.

Without a single word, his eyes on mine, he let the silence stretch.

I opened my mouth to say something, and my phone dinged with an unfamiliar tone.

Blowing out an exasperated breath, I snatched it off the counter and let out a surprised "Oh."

"What is it?"

There was a nerve-laden brick lodged in my throat, and I attempted to swallow past it. "My doorbell," I said quietly. As I stared at the app, Tyler's clearly nervous face came into view.

I couldn't help it—I started laughing. Settling a hand over my face, I tried desperately to get myself under control, but it felt like some giant cosmic joke.

At the actual moment when Liam and I had started making some headway, one of those reminders from my past decided to physically show up at my door.

Liam didn't ask who it was; he simply watched me.

I let out a deep, slow breath and pressed the button on the app so I could talk to the person on the other side. "Hey, Tyler," I said.

Liam's gaze sharpened, his throat working a visible swallow, his chin notching higher. A slightly defensive gesture.

Tyler leaned in toward the camera. "Hey. I'm sorry to drop by unannounced, but I found your sweatshirt. The one with the holes in the sleeves that you loved. Figured you'd want it back."

Liam's eyes—bright with curiosity and something much deeper—refused to drop from mine. Every inch of my skin burned from the heat in his look.

"Thank you," I said quietly. "I'm not there at the moment—"

"Go over there," Liam interjected.

My hand released the button. "What?"

"Go talk to the man." There was no malice in his tone. No nasty, jealous tinge in his eyes. If anything, Liam looked calmer than I'd ever seen him. "You said you never got closure, yeah?"

I nodded.

"So go fucking get it." There was a charged urgency in his tone that had my pulse racing.

Why? I almost asked.

"Go," he repeated before I could.

I blinked down at the floor a few times, and with a slight shake of my head, I pressed the button again. "I'll be over in a minute, Tyler. Hang on."

In the pixelated shot from the camera, he exhaled in visible relief.

Guilt tore at my insides. Maybe he really did just want to drop off a sweatshirt, but if Tyler was relieved for any other reason, he was about to be disappointed.

Staring down at the floor was easier, because if I looked Liam in the eyes again, I might not go. I wasn't going to ask if this was some weird man test, because he wasn't the type to play games. And if he was, I'd probably feel less inclined to have his tongue in my mouth and his hands in my pants. I'd feel zero desire to hand him my heart.

Mira came hurtling down the hallway, running full speed at Liam. "You home!" she yelled.

He swung her up in his arms, his face softening. "Got you something."

She wiggled excitedly. "I get a present?"

He hummed, tucking a hand into the side pocket of his gym bag. "It's a special one. You can only use it one place."

Mira started tugging on his arm. "Where is it?"

With a soft chuckle, he pulled his hand from the bag. Mira's eyes widened, and I couldn't help my smile.

It was a rubber duck painted with the British flag.

I vacillated wildly between wanting to hug him, wanting to kiss him, and wanting to tear his clothes off. Maybe all three in rapid succession.

Mira's eyes sparkled. "It's blue," she whispered. "It's so pretty."

"You know what ducks do when it's really bloody hot out?"

"What?"

Liam leaned in. "They go swimming. That's your pool duck, and if you want to play with it, you gotta get in. Go put your suit on."

He blew a raspberry on her neck, eliciting giggles as he set her down.

"Zoe swimmin' too?" she asked.

Liam glanced over at me.

"I have to go next door. I'll be back soon."

She zoomed off to her room to change, and I exhaled a wondering laugh. "A pool duck," I said quietly. "Genius."

He grunted. "Should've thought of it sooner." His eyes met mine. "Don't you have to go?"

Slowly, I nodded.

Liam didn't say anything else as I left. Neither did I.

The cord of tension between us had steadily grown and grown, thickened dramatically by the kiss and jerked tight after this morning in Carol's office. It felt impossible that this cord had enough slack for me to go next door and do whatever it was he was encouraging me to do.

I didn't walk through the back of the house, deciding instead to cross the front yard.

Tyler was sitting on the step, his smile friendly as I approached. "Good to see you," he said.

"You too." I studied him as he straightened. He was so nice. Always had been. His blue eyes were friendly, his manner polite and sweet.

"You staying there?" he asked, tilting his head toward the house next door.

I nodded. "I have been for a while. Mira is more comfortable there," I said. "And it's easier with both of us under one roof."

"Makes sense." He blew out a slow breath, studying the navy-blue sweatshirt in his hand before carefully handing it back.

The letters on the back of the sweatshirt were the only visible part, and my heart wrenched with a painful thump when I brushed my thumb over them.

A lot of things made sense now, had been made clearer by the passage of time. Circumstances that I had no control over. And some that I did. Changes that had happened so slowly I'd hardly noticed them.

Thoughts tumbled around in my head. But this wasn't the person I wanted to talk through them with.

That person was next door, in the pool with a plastic duck that he'd bought to make it easier for our little girl to learn how to swim.

"Thank you, Tyler," I said quietly. I smiled up into his face. "You have no idea how much I needed this."

Chapter Twenty-Four

LIAM

"Zoe coming swimming?"

"Soon, duck." My voice was harsher than I intended, but honestly, how bloody long did it take to go next door and listen to some tall string bean say he was sorry for dumping you and then come back? Seventeen fucking minutes she'd been gone, and I was about to lose my mind watching the clock on the back of the house. "She'll be back soon."

Closure.

What an idiot I was. She'd been standing there staring up at me with those fucking eyes and telling me she liked it when I kissed her, and I'd sent her straight back toward an ex.

The fact that I'd stayed single so long was *completely* unsurprising. I didn't know how to act when the thing I wanted was right there in front of me.

Mira pushed the duck under the water, making a quiet quacking sound when it resurfaced.

I nudged her shoulder. "Come down a couple steps. Let's practice your floating."

Mira ignored me, because she was perfectly happy up on that top step, thank you very much.

Leaning in, I whispered in her ear: "Don't you think the pool duck wants to come into the water more?"

"No." She splashed it under the surface again. "He likes the step."

"Does he?" I asked dryly.

Mira nodded, her eyes glued right on that Union Jack duck. "He's scared of the water."

I sank down until just my chin hovered over the water, my gaze steady on hers. "Ducks are good swimmers, though."

She nodded.

"But he's still scared?"

She nodded again, a bit more fervently this time.

Fucking hell, I was so twisted up by this little bit of a girl. And when I took another quick glance at the clock—eighteen minutes—I knew she wasn't the only one tying my insides into knots.

I held out my hand. "Can I see him?"

Mira gave me a shy look, then carefully set the duck in my hand.

"It's okay that he is," I said. "Everyone's afraid of something, little duck."

Pretending to give an emotional pep talk to a tiny plastic toy was a new experience, and I was endlessly thankful that no one was there to witness it. If a single member of our team got wind of this, I'd never live it down.

"You afraid too?" she asked.

"All the time." I held the duck up closer to my face, pretended to study its expression. "When I was little, I was afraid of the dark. Afraid to be home alone."

My fears as an adult were a bit much to lay on her, so I decided to keep those quiet.

"But I still had to figure out a way to sleep in the dark," I told her. "Still had to stay home alone when my mum was at work. And it wasn't so scary after the first few times, once I knew I could do it. Maybe Mr. Duck needs to see he can do it, and then he won't be so afraid anymore."

Why were those words so easy to say when the advice was meant for someone else?

I couldn't take my own bloody advice, that much was clear.

As I stared at Mira, I couldn't deny that my fear was only part of what held me back. I'd just never been able to put words to the rest of it until I was faced with these two, faced with the absolute certainty of how they'd wrecked my world.

And if I ever broke this little girl's heart like mine had been broken, I'd never be able to live with myself. As for Zoe . . . I had a feeling that her heart was already just as fucked as mine.

With another glance at the clock, I nudged Mira's leg under the water. "Maybe we can try again tomorrow? It's bedtime for little ducks."

Despite the new toy, I didn't have to tell her twice.

With the clock's hands ticking ominously and me doing my very best to ignore them, I got Mira ready for bed in record time. It was one of those rare nights—no begging for more books, no wrestling match during pajama time.

I kissed the top of her head as she settled into her favorite corner, the beat-up duck snug and secure under her arm.

"G'night," I whispered. "Feel free to sleep in very late tomorrow."

She smiled against the duck. Little shit would likely be awake with the sunrise because I'd asked.

With my chest aching and my head racing with possibilities, I knew I couldn't sit still until she got back home.

Thirty-three minutes.

It took everything in me not to walk around the front of the houses to see if his stupid car was still there. What good would that do me?

None.

Even if he was still there, it meant nothing.

He was probably begging. Who wouldn't beg if they'd had her and let her go?

Fuck. I'd done nothing but kiss her, and I was ready to tear bare-handed into all my reservations because the thought of not having her was impossible.

Of *course* he was begging.

Maybe he was a crier. Or maybe he was emotionally grounded and wanted to talk through every fucking thought he'd had since the moment they broke up.

I bet Carol would *love* him.

"Pull yourself together," I ground out.

The spiral of my thoughts was quick and, quite frankly, a little embarrassing.

Before I could overthink anything else, I hopped into the pool, sinking under the water. Everything was muffled and quiet, a stillness that I needed.

I broke the surface, tipping my head back to stare at the sky.

Thirty-five minutes.

I'd never known time to move this slowly. Not even during a game, with time-outs and bullshit commercial breaks and God knew what else.

Movement from the corner of my eye had my thoughts trailing off.

When the sight of her registered, it was a good thing I wasn't mid-sentence, because she completely decimated my ability to speak.

Zoe had her hair pulled up, piled high on her head, a few rogue waves around her face.

She was wearing a Denver sweatshirt.

Only a Denver sweatshirt. Her legs were completely bare. And her eyes glowed.

"What are you . . . ?" I swallowed. "Where'd you get that?"

My question came out sounding angry and rough. But we both knew I wasn't.

She merely smiled.

I was just trying to *breathe*. I hadn't seen that particular shirt in years, though there was one shoved in the back of my closet. They'd printed them up only once.

She glanced down at the shirt and smiled. "Amie bought it for me as a joke one Christmas. She thought it was hilarious."

Slowly, Zoe turned, and the sight of my name on her back, the flex of the muscles in her legs, had my skin tightening, my chest blazing with heat.

When she was facing me again, there was an impish grin on her face. "But then I just kept wearing it. It was soft. Warm. Fit me perfectly." She held her hands up, thumbs poking through holes in the sides of the sleeves, that same thing she did to all the shirts she loved. "I've never found another one that I liked as much. When I lost it, I was inexplicably sad," she said.

Why did it feel like she wasn't really talking about that sweatshirt?

Why did my chest feel like it was caving in?

Zoe made her way to the edge of the pool, toward the middle, where I stood. She sat, easing her legs into the water with a satisfied hiss.

There was a flash of red underneath the hem of the sweatshirt, and my heart settled into a more natural rhythm, knowing she wasn't stark-ass naked under there.

I watched her carefully and slid closer to where she sat but stayed just out of reach. "How'd your visit with what's-his-name go?"

"Fine. We didn't talk long." She smiled. "He apologized for how things ended. Asked if I wanted to meet him for coffee sometime."

"What'd you say?" Fuck, I sounded like such an asshole. Like I had any right to ask.

"I said that there was no need. I'd already forgiven him"—she paused, eyeing me meaningfully—"and I was too hung up on someone else to have coffee with anyone."

My ribs squeezed tight, and my heart thundered painfully. "Did he cry?"

Zoe's lips twitched. "No. I wouldn't tell you if he did, though."

My eyebrows arched. "What were you doing for the rest of the time?"

"Watching the clock, were you?"

I gave her a droll look, and she laughed under her breath. Zoe shook her head slightly, studying my face like she was still desperately trying to figure me out.

Join the fucking club. I'd been attempting that one for more than thirty years and was still coming up empty handed.

With absolutely no regard for my sanity, Zoe gracefully pulled the sweatshirt up and over her head.

"Fucking hell," I muttered.

Her bikini was red. Small. Tiny straps holding it over her body.

There was so much skin. So many curves.

Freckles dotted her shoulders and chest. And the tiniest little diamond winked in her belly button. She grinned a Cheshire-cat grin as she gently kicked her legs back and forth in the water.

"We weren't done talking when he showed up," she said.

Why did she keep looking at me like that? Like we were already naked. Like I was already inside her. My hands curled into helpless fists at my side. "We weren't. But I don't know if it's wise we continue it here."

"Why not?"

"Look at you," I growled. "It's not fair."

Maybe there was something magnetic woven into that bloody suit, because quite helplessly, I drifted closer to the edge where she sat. When I got close enough to touch her, I braced my hands on either side of her hips, her legs shifting to accommodate my upper body. Her calf brushed the side of my hip, and my jaw locked tight.

"It's very fair. You've always had me off-balance," she said. "From the day we met."

My head reared back. "I have not."

She laughed. "You have. I never knew what to make of you. That's why Amie got me that shirt." Zoe tucked her chin down toward her chest and exhaled a soft laughing sound. "I think she knew," she added quietly. "I think they both did."

"Knew what?" I asked, voice raw and heart in agony.

When Zoe raised her head, the sheer naked longing I saw in her eyes had my pulse racing. She didn't answer, though.

My hands drifted helplessly toward her legs, but all I allowed myself was a brush of my thumbs along the outside of her thighs.

Zoe exhaled slowly, a slight shiver racking her body. "I was looking through some old stuff," she whispered. "Tyler wasn't even there for ten minutes. I just . . . I needed to know if I'd been missing signs this entire time." There was no need for me to ask the question. "I think maybe I didn't want to see them," she admitted.

"Why?"

Zoe took a deep breath, the sweet curves of her breasts rising and falling behind that measly scrap of fabric. That breath, as it turned out, was for fortification, because she gently lifted her hips off the concrete and slid into the water.

The air was thick, and hardly an inch separated her body from mine because I kept my hands braced on the edge, effectively caging her in to the side of the pool.

She wasn't the only one caged. My want of her kept me locked in place. This hidden way I'd loved her for so long kept me frozen, staunchly refusing to miss another opportunity to touch her.

"It's hard to admit when you've wasted years of your life on someone who didn't deserve them," she said quietly. Slowly, she raised a hand and traced the bottom edge of my lip with the pad of her finger. "It's even worse when you realize the person you want to be with has been in front of you the entire time."

My entire fucking soul sighed in relief to hear her say it, no matter how complicated it might be. How many of those complications still waited for us. Gently, I rolled my forehead against hers. She settled her hands over my chest.

"I found pictures from that night," she continued. "The night we met. And then some from a year or two later. More after that." Zoe licked her lips. "In almost all of them, you were looking at me. For *years*."

I couldn't help but close my eyes as the massive fucking wave of feelings swamped me. It was amazing how weak my body felt the longer I listened to her talk. *She* made me weak. Always had. I'd just lost my ability to hide it anymore.

"I think you didn't tell me the full truth, Liam."

Opening my eyes again, I found hers locked straight onto mine.

There was no need for me to ask, because I damn well knew what she was talking about.

"I *couldn't*," I managed in a gruff voice. "Imagine knowing that, with all the shit we were dealing with."

"I know."

"It was too much that you actually thought I *hated* you." My hands, unable to stay off her for a second longer, inching slowly up the sides of her arms. "I still don't know how to do any of this, love. I've spent my entire life making sure it never happened."

There it was.

The thing we hadn't discussed yet, and I fought the urgent swirl of nerves in my stomach, the desire to claw back behind my walls.

Drops of water clung to Zoe's chest and shoulders, and her hands gently coasted over my chest and shoulders. "That's the other thing I was thinking about," she admitted quietly.

In the silence that followed, I fought the urge to crush her body to mine, because this tiny sliver of space between us felt like the Grand bloody Canyon, given what we were talking about.

"We both have things that we're afraid of, Liam." Her eyes were clear and wide and candid, and I felt the directness of her gaze straight into my fucking chest. "The worst thing that my divorce did is that I trusted myself just a little bit less, and no matter how you feel about me, that doesn't disappear. You can't remove my fears any more than I can erase yours."

How I wanted her to, though. I wanted her to obliterate them from existence. Destroy the deep, dark pull of those thoughts, the ones that had held so much power over me for so long.

"That's what so many of us get wrong about relationships," she continued. "At the end of the day, battling those fears will always be our own responsibility, our own choice. You cannot fix mine, and I can't fix yours. All we can do is hold on to each other, Liam. Fight those battles side by side."

Fuck, how simple she made it sound.

"And if it all goes wrong?" I asked. "What about her?"

Zoe sighed. "We'll always make decisions based on what's best for Mira. But I can't pretend anymore. Can you?" She'd said it before she left the house, and I hadn't been able to say the words. I glanced beyond her to the house, but she took my face in her hands so that I couldn't look away. "Can you?" she asked again.

My eyes closed for a moment, and no matter how much it fucking terrified me, I ripped the words from my throat so I couldn't take them back. "You know I can't."

She exhaled in obvious relief.

"Here I thought you'd want to dissect what I said this morning. Pin me to a board under some giant fucking spotlight so you can figure out all the bullshit in my head." Wariness was heavy in my tone, dripping off every word.

She didn't smile. She didn't laugh.

Because she saw straight fucking through me when I said it.

Panic was icy cold, prickling ominously up my spine, because if that was the direction in which she took this . . . if she asked me to slice that part of myself open, I'd probably fucking do it.

"We don't ever have to talk about it again if you don't want to," she promised me. "I will *never* ask that of you."

"Simple as that?" I asked in a rough, disbelieving voice.

Zoe shook her head slowly. "There's nothing simple about it, Liam. I hate that you've carried this for so long, but I understand why you did. And the only thing I can tell you," she whispered, coming closer until her nose brushed lightly against mine, "is that I trust you, and I know I'm safe with you. I believe that enough for the two of us, until you believe it too."

Her thumbs traced gentle lines over my cheekbones as she pulled back to look into my face, and that gentleness was my undoing.

I didn't stand a chance against it.

Maybe that's why I'd always poked at her, stoked the flames of contention and irritation, knowing that I was the only one who brought it out of her.

If she'd treated me like *this* for all those years, it would've been a million times harder to watch her live a life without me.

Slowly, I plucked her hand off my cheek, turning the palm toward my mouth. Her fingers curled helplessly as I pressed a fervent kiss on her soft skin.

"I don't know what to do with all the things you make me feel, Zoe," I whispered. "Every time I look at you, it's like someone is ripping out my fucking heart. When you smile, I can't bloody breathe."

I'd never be a poet. Even the clunky way I tried to tell her I was in love with her came from my chest like someone had pried it out with a crowbar.

And she simply smiled.

Maybe after all the uncertainty, all the hesitation, this was the part I needed to make peace with. Whatever I was, whatever I had inside me, it was exactly enough for her.

Rough edges and all.

"I do have one question for you," I said quietly, slipping my hands up the line of her back, tracing my fingers over the impossibly thin strings holding up her suit. "I think it's my turn after all."

"If the question has anything to do with permission to untie my top, then the answer is yes."

"That's not it," I said, my lips brushing against her temple.

"That's . . . sad."

My mouth curved into a smile. "Is this how it would happen in your books?" I ghosted kisses over her forehead. Brushed my fingers along the curve of her waist. "Something like this to get the fairy-tale ending?"

"Sometimes," she said shakily. Her hands tracked over my stomach, sliding around my back. "But in a lot of them, we'd have fought. Yelled about the things we couldn't say earlier. Someone would've stormed out. Probably you," she teased.

"I don't want to fight with you, Valentine. I'm done fighting." I nipped at the shell of her ear. Her breasts were pressed tight against my chest, and my palms skated over the curves of her ass. "I think this suits us better, yeah?"

She moaned in assent. "In some of them, when you'd come back, and we had our big realizations, you would've torn my suit off, and we'd be having highly improbable pool sex by now."

A chuckle escaped from low in my chest. "Why *improbable?*"

She hissed when I mouthed the line of her jaw. "I-I don't know. It always seemed . . . highly illogical that all the chemicals make for a pleasurable"—her voice hitched higher when I wrenched her thigh up against my side and pressed her tight to the side of the pool—"p-pleasurable experience."

I pulled my face back to study her. Zoe's cheeks were flushed pink, and so was her chest. Her nipples were hard points behind the fiery red of her suit.

My hands itched to do exactly that. Give her all the pleasure I was capable of. Tug off those tiny scraps covering her body, and sink inside her.

She wrapped her other leg around my waist, hooking her ankles behind my back, and I pressed my forehead against hers with a hiss of pain.

"Not like this," I whispered against the edge of her lips. "Whenever I thought about you—and fucking hell, I had a lot of thoughts—we were in a bed. A big fucking bed, and we had all night to use it."

"We have beds," she said, rolling her hips in a sinuous motion that had me seeing stars. "My bed is *huge* and empty."

I clamped a hand over her hip, hard.

"You better stop, love." I dragged my teeth down the line of her shoulder, and she whimpered. "It's been too long for me, and we are doing this the right way."

Her eyes were dazed, her pupils blown wide. "What's that? Because this feels very, *very* right."

"I'm taking you on a proper date," I said simply. "I'm picking you up from your house tomorrow night. We're going out someplace quiet and romantic, and I'll ask you all the questions I still want answers to." I kissed the tip of her nose. "I'll even let you ask more than two."

Zoe's face softened, and she slid her hand over my cheek again. "That sounds nice."

I hummed. "Good."

When I started to pull back, she tightened her legs, her brow furrowing. "You're still gonna kiss me, though, right?"

My lips curved into a devilish grin. "Not tonight."

"What?" Oh, her eyes were on fire. "You just told me that when I smile, you *can't bloody breathe*," she said, mimicking my accent. "And I don't even get a kiss?"

"Won't kill you to wait, Valentine. Imagine how *I've* felt all these years."

With firm hands, I unhooked her legs and slid backward into the water, hard as a fucking rock and my chest lighter than it had ever been.

Zoe immediately started following, and I held up a hand. "You can't change my mind."

She stopped, setting her hands on her hips, mouth hanging open. "You're serious."

"Trust me, it pains me more than you can imagine."

Her eyebrow quirked as I started up the steps, still facing her. "Yeah, I can tell. I'd be more than happy to help you relieve that pain."

I wagged a finger in the air. "I'm courting you the proper way, and that's that."

Zoe stayed in the pool, staring at me incredulously, hands still propped on her hips.

Snatching a towel from the chair, I rubbed it over my chest and swim trunks, wincing only once when I brushed a bit too hard against my very angry hard-on.

She snorted. "Serves you right."

"I'm sure it does, love."

Her eyes took on an evil gleam.

"What's that face?" I asked.

Her fingers trailed up over the edge of her bathing suit until she was fiddling with the strap around the back of her neck.

"Zoe," I said in warning, "don't you dare."

She plucked at the knot behind her neck, and the suit loosened. My breath caught in my throat when she sank slightly below the water, then tugged her top off and tossed it up onto the concrete, where it landed with a wet slap by my feet.

Through the distorted filter of the pool, I saw just enough—the ripe curves and the pink of her nipples—that my mouth watered.

"You are a menace," I whispered.

Zoe laughed. "You could come back in and show me just how much."

Without a word, I leaned down and snagged her bikini top, tossing it back into the pool.

"Sweet dreams, darling," I told her. "I'll be locking my door tonight so you don't think about sneaking in."

She crossed her arms and stood up, water streaming down her glorious chest, and holy fucking hell, she was a vision. "As if I'd give you that satisfaction now."

I grinned, notching my fingers against my temple. "See you in the morning."

With a whistle, I walked back into the house.

Behind me, she let out an ear-blistering curse. She might have wanted to kill me now, but her reaction was exactly what I'd been aiming for.

Zoe was right that I couldn't erase her fears. But maybe I could help a little.

I was still smiling when I closed myself into the guest room and turned the lock.

Chapter Twenty-Five

Liam

Despite the way my brain was buzzing when I crawled into bed, I slept like a rock. But when I woke, the sun hadn't even begun to rise, and the sky was still dark. There were messages on my phone when I turned it over to check the time, and I laughed quietly. She'd sent them after midnight, which meant she'd been lying awake long after she'd gone to bed.

Zoe: I can't believe you made me go to bed alone. Is this where I'd call you a twat? I'm still learning British slang.

Zoe: We could've CUDDLED. It's not like I only want to use you for sex, though I'm excited about that too.

Zoe: Is that a first-date activity? It wouldn't normally be for me. But we've basically had months of foreplay, and I think all normal date boundaries should be reevaluated under these types of circumstances.

With a smile, I typed out a quick reply.

Me: Patience, love.

As I stared at the ceiling, I laid a hand over my chest and registered the heated glow seeping through there. This was such a new, foreign landscape to me in every regard. The flirting, the anticipation, that aching warmth only she seemed to leave in her wake. With a deep breath, I rolled out of bed and scrubbed my hands over my face. The day already seemed both eternally long and not long enough, because I wasn't quite sure how I was supposed to be ready for this. For her.

And maybe that was the point. I'd never really be ready. Never really feel like this was something I could do. But for her, I would try.

I hopped into the shower, leaning my frame up against the tile, hot water pouring down over my body while I wrapped my hand around myself and imagined a completely different ending to our conversation in the pool last night. Imagined the ending she'd wanted.

Slick, wet skin.

Panting moans in my ear.

Her legs tight around my waist.

We'd have left the pool and stumbled inside, found the nearest flat surface.

The images came faster and harder then, as I imagined Zoe in every position that I wanted to try. But the thing that took me over the edge, the very thing that I wanted most, was her under me, atop a big, soft bed with plenty of room and the lights on so I could see every bloody detail.

I groaned her name after less than ten minutes, hanging my head under the blistering water as my chest heaved.

I'd need to take four showers before this date if I expected to keep my hands off her. When I emerged from the steamy bathroom and wrapped a towel around my waist, I felt more clearheaded.

More than that, I was excited about where the day might lead. It was fucking terrifying.

The house felt different when I walked through the dark kitchen to put on the coffee. Hovering on the edge of such a massive change, it felt more like a home than any I'd had since I moved to the States. Slowly, so slowly I'd hardly noticed, it had become ours. When had that happened?

Zoe wouldn't be up until Mira woke, which was probably for the best. I wanted her to think about the possibilities all day, just like I would be.

I scooped enough grounds for her to have two cups of coffee and added the water.

While I waited for the pot to fill, I looked through a pile of mail and plucked out a few pieces with my name on them. When I set them back down, they brushed against the little blue duck with the British flag.

I picked up the plastic toy and stared at it, thinking about my conversation with Mira the night before. All three of us, to varying degrees, had fears we were working to overcome. On paper, Zoe's might have seemed like the smallest, but I still wanted her to trust in what she was feeling for me. What I was feeling for her.

Making her wait until tonight wasn't a test; it was proof.

Of all the things that scared me, the possibility that what we felt for each other wasn't real was not one of them.

Mira's fears might have been those of a child, but in her head, they loomed so large that it was almost impossible for her to see a way past them. Once she did, though, she'd be fine.

And what of mine?

Zoe had made it sound so simple. But it was still years of conditioning, something I'd embedded into my very outlook on life, etching it deep into my subconscious. The fear of mine had been the single line I'd never strayed from, no matter what choices I'd made. Until her, of course. Both of them.

When the coffee was ready, I poured myself a travel mug and tucked my keys into my pocket before packing a gym bag. I was out the door for a workout at the facilities before either Zoe or Mira woke, and that was likely for the best.

The weight room was quiet too, only one other guy from the special teams there that early, and we did our conditioning with headphones on, focused on our own shit. By the time I finished, I was ready for my second shower of the day, but I kept thinking about that bloody duck.

About Mira and how she deserved to have both of us face our fears the way we were asking her to face her own.

About Zoe and how badly I wanted to get this right more than anything I'd ever done. I'd only ever loved her, even if I'd refused to put a name on it for years.

I'd refused to do a lot of things, and I didn't want to drag that habit forward.

Conditioning was something I knew and knew well. Keeping my body in shape was part of my job, a responsibility that I'd taken on when I signed my contract. And if I expected to keep earning that trust Zoe had given me, then I needed to break old, ingrained habits just as much as I had to create new ones.

That's how I found myself leaving the facilities still in need of a shower, driving toward a small house that wasn't a house and then striding up the front steps about thirty minutes before it was supposed to open.

Through the windows, I saw warm yellow light, and I tapped my fingers nervously against my thigh before I pushed open the door. The big farm-style dining table was empty, and fuck, I almost turned and bolted out of the house before someone saw me.

I didn't, though.

And I wouldn't.

I strode into Carol's office, and her head snapped up in surprise, her eyes wide as she studied me over the rim of her glasses.

"Liam," she said, "I wasn't expecting you so soon."

My throat was tight and uncomfortable, denial and excuses crawling up like a reflex. I could say it was about Mira. She'd never know the difference. Instead, I squeezed my eyes shut, sat on that stupid fucking couch, and with my elbows perched on my thighs, I held my clasped hands between my opened legs.

"You said your door was always open, yeah?"

She was wearing the pearls again and had on a different sweater than the day before. Carefully, she pulled her glasses off and set them down on the surface of her desk. "I did." Then she smiled. "I do have an appointment in about an hour, though."

My teeth ground tight, and my jaw clenched firmly. It took every shred of discipline to relax my muscles as I stared her down.

When I didn't speak right away, her lips curled in a faint smile. "How did it go with Zoe last night? You shared a very big thing in here yesterday. That must have triggered some conversation."

So we'd take it like that. She'd coax me through this, like I was a fucking child. And I didn't quite feel like acting like one anymore.

I swallowed thickly, holding her gaze. "I was trying to help Mira swim last night," I said. "She's afraid of the water. I told her that I used to be afraid of all sorts of things when I was her age, but once I faced them, I realized they weren't so bad."

Carol sat back in her chair and studied me curiously. "That's good advice."

"I'm a bloody hypocrite, aren't I?"

Her face stayed even. "Why do you say that?"

My hands tightened, and I inhaled slowly. "As long as I can remember, I've been afraid of turning into him. That somehow being related to him, that watching the way he treated her—it was in my blood. Something I couldn't escape."

"That's a very common reaction for kids who experienced what you did growing up."

"It's stupid, though, right? I'm a grown fucking man, and I'm still afraid of the same thing that I was when I was a child."

Carol's eyes were soft and understanding. "Liam, that's part of the human experience. Almost everyone I've ever met navigates relationships based on fears and wants and desires that have roots in their upbringing. Some people realize it. Some don't. You're not stupid for your worries, but you have to challenge those thoughts when they spring up."

"How?"

She smiled at my terse reply. "When's the last time you lost your temper on a friend or family member?"

I swallowed again. "I don't. Only when one of my teammates fucks up. Assholes always deserve it, though."

"Ever hit anyone?"

"No." Then I paused. "Thought about it a couple times during a game, but I'm not stupid."

She was unflinching in how she stared me down. "Ever verbally abused a partner?"

My head reared back. "No."

Then she nodded like she'd proved some great big fucking point. "That's how you challenge your fears, Liam. With a lifetime of actions. You remind yourself that *every* time you had the chance to be like him, you chose a different path."

Hope crept stealthily up my throat, past the immediate denials that this was too simple.

"You don't believe me," she said.

I held her gaze. "Zoe said something similar. And you both make it sound so bloody easy, and it's not."

"I didn't say it was easy," she said. "But it's fairly straightforward, and there's a difference. When we tell ourselves a story long enough, we begin to believe it, no matter what anyone else says. And you've believed yours thoroughly because you grew up in the shadow of the person you hated most." Then she leaned forward, her eyes burning with sincerity. "You're here, Liam. You stepped up to help Zoe and Mira, and you could have walked away. That's challenging your fears, even if you weren't aware that you were doing it. You may have to do it every single day, but the fact that you're worried about it shows more awareness than most people ever have."

"Don't give me a fucking medal," I muttered.

"I won't. But I'm going to give credit where credit is due. You should as well."

I raised my hands, scrubbing them over my face. "Fuck. Do I have to come and vomit my feelings all the time now?"

She laughed softly. "Only if you feel like it helps. What brought you in here today specifically?"

I dropped my hands and sat back against the couch. "I'm taking Zoe on a date tonight," I told her, waiting for a judgmental look and a sharp reprimand.

Her eyes merely sharpened with interest. "Are you? Is that a new development?"

"Been in love with her for a bloody decade, so no, it's not new for me."

This time, her smile was fleeting but pleased. "And you're excited about this?"

"Yeah." I shifted on the couch. "And that's scary too."

"And what worries you about tonight, specifically?"

"You want a fucking list?" I drawled.

Her lips twitched, but she didn't smile again. "Let's just start with the first thing you can think of."

I pushed my hands down the tops of my thighs and sighed. "It feels intense already. Big." I tapped a hand to my chest. "Right here, anchored under my ribs, just too bloody big to be real."

"Intense in a good way?"

Slowly, I nodded. "Yeah. Like I'd marry her in a week or something stupid if she wanted me to."

Carol laughed. "How about you just take tonight for what it is? Enjoy your time with her. If it feels intense and big for you, it probably does for her too. She'll be clear about what she wants because she cares about you, Liam. It's obvious."

That hope bled through my throat, down my shoulders, and into my chest again. And for the first time, I wasn't scared of it.

I nodded. "Thank you," I told her sincerely.

"You're welcome." She glanced at the clock on the wall. "Unfortunately, I do have to get some work done before my appointment, but please email me if you want to sit down again. I'll always make time for you and Zoe if you need my help."

It was just one appointment.

One date.

But it felt like so much more.

By the time I got home, my steps were light, my heart practically dancing a fucking jig with anticipation. I was smiling when I walked into the kitchen.

Zoe was at the island feeding Mira a late breakfast, and she did a double take when she saw the look on my face. I wanted to lean in and kiss her, but I didn't.

"Hi," she said softly, her eyes glowing.

I brushed my hand along her lower back, holding her gaze as I stepped away. "Sleep well, Valentine?"

Her eyebrow arched. "Not particularly."

I dropped a kiss on Mira's messy curls and then grinned when I saw the flush in Zoe's cheeks. As I stripped my shirt off, I locked eyes with her across the island. "You probably won't tonight either."

She huffed an incredulous laugh, and I tossed the sweaty shirt in her direction.

"Gonna go take a shower, and yes, my door will be locked for that too."

"I don't like this new side of you," she yelled as I left the room.

"Yeah, you do, Valentine. Yeah, you do."

Chapter Twenty-Six

ZOE

"You're sure it's not too much?"

Rosa leaned back, her discerning eye studying my finished look, from the top of my perfectly tousled sex-hair curls to the tips of my toes.

"Not at all." Her lips curled in satisfaction. "The plaid skirt is a very particular sort of torture, but I approve."

I tugged on the hem. "It's short."

Martha tapped her walking cane on the floor. "That's the point, sweet pea. Make him wonder what you've got underneath it."

"I don't even know where he's taking me," I said. Leaning in toward the mirror, I adjusted the deep V neckline of the fitted green tank. My splurge on a new bra was worth every penny because it pushed everything up, giving my usually modest cleavage a spectacular boost. "I could be terribly overdressed."

"Did you shave . . . everywhere?" Phyllis asked.

When they laughed, my cheeks flushed hot. "Yes, Phyllis. All unwanted hairs are gone."

She winked.

With a shake of my head, I did one last swipe of mascara.

"How was it with him today at the house?" Rosa asked.

"Torture," I said. "He was so . . . flirty. But, like, *Liam* flirty."

"What does that mean?"

Slowly, I closed the tube of mascara and set it back in my makeup bag.

Once Liam had returned home from his workout and errands, his flirtations were like nothing I'd ever experienced before. Hours of achingly slow anticipation. With very little touching, the man had me ready to crawl out of my skin if he didn't do something soon.

"He'd look at me from across the room, and . . ." My voice trailed off, and I waved a hand in front of my face when it overheated. "Have you ever made eye contact with someone and you just *know* they're thinking about sex?"

Martha nodded. "The widower across the street looks at me that way."

Rosa rolled her eyes. "He looks at everyone like that."

Phyllis blinked. "He does? I thought it was just me."

"It's not," Rosa said.

I laughed. "So you get it."

"Yes," they all answered.

I turned and sat on the bathroom counter. "Or he'd walk behind me and brush his fingers along my back when he passed. He never said or did anything outright sexual, but I have never been this worked up before. I'm afraid I'll get in the car and climb straight into his lap."

"Do it," Martha whispered. "He's got a big car. The frame on that baby could handle a lot."

With a laugh, I covered my face. "Okay, I appreciate you helping me get ready, but he'll need you over there for Mira."

"No, he's bringing Mira to my house tonight," Rosa said.

My eyebrows shot up my forehead. "Really?"

She grinned. "My suggestion. That way, if you're done early, the house is still empty. I'll bring her home right before her bedtime."

With a fluttering stomach, I processed the ramifications of that one. Liam was taking me out for a late-afternoon date, given they didn't have practice. Even if we had a three-hour meal, we'd have a couple of hours at the house without Mira.

"I owe you," I told her.

She eyed the length of my legs underneath the skirt. "I think *he* owes me too."

"Good underwear, right?" Martha whispered.

When I blushed bright red, they laughed in delight.

The house was quiet after they left, and I took a few moments to enjoy the way all of this felt. *Butterflies* wasn't even the right word to describe the feeling of waiting for him. I'd always thought of butterflies as fragile little things, wisps of feeling when they brushed their wings against your skin.

This was a great big whoosh of air, a swirling sort of effervescence that floated through my veins as I closed my eyes at the thought of him.

I wasn't sure I'd ever had it this bad, even before I was married.

Maybe because this date held an omen of the kind of future I'd always wanted. There was weight to it. Not because he was perfect. If anything, he wore his imperfections with pride, and I liked him even better for it.

The sound of a car pulling into the driveway had me checking my reflection one last time.

The woman who looked back at me was hardly recognizable.

I'd gone heavier on my eye makeup and spent a bit more time crafting my normally wild hair into something a bit more intentional.

But I'd kept my lips bare because that man *was* kissing me tonight. Preferably in the first ten minutes.

Liam's broad frame filled the glass of my front door, and I blew out a low breath.

Smoothing my hands over my hips one last time, I slowly opened the door.

If I lasted ten minutes without attacking him, it would be a fucking miracle.

He looked *good*.

He wore a blue dress shirt, the sleeves rolled up his forearms and molded around his biceps. In one of his big hands, he clasped a small bouquet of lilacs, a bold splash of purples and deep pinks and bright-green stems.

"Bloody fucking hell," he murmured under his breath, his eyes locked on my skirt. "Look at you."

I sank against the doorframe, my legs suddenly a little weak. "Where did you find lilacs in July?"

He blinked away from my legs, snagging briefly on my cleavage and then landing on my face. "Uhh . . ."

I laughed. "I'll put them in water before we go." I held out my hand, and he handed them over. The fragrance was sweet and strong, something I'd always equated with spring. "How did you know I liked these?"

He'd recovered himself. Sort of. "Didn't, actually."

Liam followed me into the kitchen while I went up on tiptoe to pull a vase down from above the fridge. The moment I set it down, he crowded behind me, bracing his hands on the counter and burying his nose in my hair.

"Holy shit," I whispered, sinking back against him. He was hard. Already. One of his hands swept the hair away from my neck, and he mouthed the skin he found there. His other hand spread over my waist, his thumb brushing the bottom of my breasts, his pinkie toying with the waistband of my skirt. "Please tell me we can just have our date here," I said breathlessly.

I tried to turn in his arms, but he held me fast. "Can't." He spoke into my skin. "Fucking want to, but we can't."

"Why not?" I arched my back, shamelessly pressing my hips into him, and he hissed at the movement. He rocked into me once, twice.

"I have plans, love." He kissed the back of my neck and took one last deep inhale of my skin. "But my plans didn't account for this skirt. You're going to be the death of me, I just know it."

He moved away, and I practically pitched forward. With shaking hands, I tried to catch my breath as I filled the vase with water. The flowers were so simple and sweet, nothing adorning them except their bright-green leaves and a black velvet ribbon.

"Why lilacs?" I asked once we were in the car.

Liam glanced at me, a slight curve to his mouth that was so endearing I had to press my thighs together. He noticed, the slight curve turning into an unrepentant smirk. He moved one big hand from the console to my thigh, sliding his calloused palm along the skin he found there. His pinkie danced along the inside of my thigh, and I sank my head back against the seat, fighting the urge to grip his wrist and just shove his hand between my legs.

"I asked for something fairly specific at the florist's shop," he said.

It took every shred of focus to pay attention to what he was saying. "What did you ask for?"

Liam eased the car to a stop at a red light. Then he pinned me in place with those searing green eyes. "Told her I had a date with the first woman I fell in love with. Only woman I'd ever felt that way about. And I wanted her to feel special while we have this fresh start."

In the next heartbeat, I unhooked my seat belt and surged forward, sealing my mouth over his. And oh, the sound he made! It was like it had been yanked from deep inside his chest, and it had my toes curling into my heels. Liam anchored his hand in my hair and held me firmly in place as he slid his tongue into my waiting mouth.

Then he tilted his head to deepen the kiss, and I tried to scramble up onto my knees to bring myself even closer. My hands clutched his face as I kissed him with desperation.

The sound of a horn honking behind us had me breaking away with a laugh.

Liam blew out a hard breath, adjusting the front of his dark jeans while I pulled my seat belt back into place.

He lifted a hand in a wave when the driver honked again, longer this time.

"Cool your fucking jets," he muttered. "If you had any idea . . ."

The kiss had unlocked some of the unbearable pressure building in my chest. It was decadent, allowing that feeling to sweep over me. There was no more fighting this, and there was something so unbelievably freeing about that.

"Where are we going?" I asked, shifting the hem of my skirt after it had ridden up a bit too high for comfort.

Liam held his hand out, and with a smile, I let my fingers settle in between his. He pulled my hand up to his mouth for a kiss, then let our joined hands rest on the rock-hard muscle of his thigh.

"Be there soon," he promised. "Which is for the best because I won't survive another red light with you in that fucking skirt."

With a grin, I toyed with the hem. "Like it?"

"I know what you're trying to do," he said evenly, his eyes fixed straight ahead as he drove.

I hummed.

"Won't work."

My answering laugh was light and happy. Everything inside me bubbled up with a dangerous level of hope. "We'll see."

Some part of me needed to touch him more, so I started with slow sweeps of my thumb against the work-roughened skin on the side of his hand.

"Your text last night got me thinking," he said. "Are you a cuddler at night?"

I glanced in his direction. "With you, I will be. Preferably soon." The man's body was built for it, and I'd cuddle the absolute *hell* out of him the moment he actually let me get him into a bed.

He exhaled a soft laugh. "Not normally, though?"

My shoulders lifted slightly in a small shrug. "It's been a while since I've had the opportunity." And because I knew he'd never ask, I added, "Tyler and I never got to the cuddling-at-night phase."

Liam made that thoughtful little humming noise that made my thighs clench. It was halfway between a grunt and a growl, and quite desperately, I wanted to hear him make it in my ear while I had my thighs wrapped tight around his sides.

The car turned into a large parking lot, and immediately, my mouth split into a smile.

"Pretty sure they just closed," I said.

"Did they?" His tone was so smug, so certain.

My mouth fell open. "You didn't."

Liam put the SUV in park, his wrist hanging over the steering wheel as he turned in the seat to face me. "I did," he said softly. His eyes traced my face, and I felt so beautiful, so seen and understood.

I let out a slow breath, unhooking my seat belt with a bit more finesse than the last time. It took some slight maneuvering to angle in my seat without flashing my black lace underthings, but I managed it, easing my hand to cup his stubbled jaw.

"You're taking me on a date to a bookstore that you kept open just for us?"

He didn't answer, simply kept those eyes straight on mine.

My lungs strained to push out enough oxygen because everything was coiled so tightly underneath my skin. Each vital organ struggled to keep up with the things he was pulling out of me. I'd never felt so much at once, and it was all *good*.

The kiss I gave him was light as a feather, just a whisper of my lips over his.

He brushed his nose against mine, returning that peck with the same sort of soft promise.

"Ready to go in?" he asked.

I nodded, keeping my face close to his as my eyelids fluttered shut.

"You smell good, Valentine," he whispered.

I ghosted another kiss over his waiting mouth. "I smell even better when I'm naked."

His booming laugh echoed inside the car.

Happiness, when it had no place to escape to, could swell against the boundaries of your skin, as if a single ounce more would make you burst. That's how I felt as we exited the car and he held out his hand for me while we walked through the parking lot.

Even a single second more of this kind of sustained lighthearted hopefulness didn't seem feasible.

But holy shit, I was willing to risk it.

A smiling staff member opened the door for us when we approached the big brick building.

"Thank you," I told her.

She blushed after a quick glance at Liam. "You're welcome. We're thrilled to have you both here. Take your time, and let us know if there's anything we can do to help." She locked the door behind us. "The store is yours."

I gave him a wry look because he must have paid them a fortune.

We wandered through the stacks, each of us with a basket in hand, while he asked me perfect first-date questions. I steered us toward the romance section.

"Cats or dogs?" he asked.

"Dogs." I glanced over my shoulder. "You?"

"I like both actually."

My face must've shown my surprise.

He shrugged. "I want one of those asshole-looking cats that hates everyone except us."

"So . . . you want the feline version of you?"

He gave me a dry look, and I laughed.

"Movie that always makes you cry?"

"Ooh." I picked up a book and studied the cover before setting it into the basket I was holding. "*Old Yeller.*"

"Fuck that movie," he said. "You've watched it more than once? What is wrong with you?"

I sighed. "Sometimes you just feel like crying, Liam. It's good to get it out."

"Whatever you say, Valentine." He nudged me with his shoulder. "Don't ask me to watch it with you, though. I'd rather gouge my eyes out."

"Noted."

"*Old Yeller*," he muttered. "Fucking awful."

I hid my grin while I checked out a couple more books.

In the next aisle over, I found a few that Rosa loved and tossed them into my basket for her. He laughed when my pile of books started nearing Mira's height. I quirked an eyebrow. "What are you laughing about? You're the one who's gonna carry these."

After carefully setting down his basket, Liam walked toward me, a predatory gleam in his eye, and I backed up against the bookshelf. My basket fell with a thump.

He braced one hand on the shelf next to my head and caged me in, taking a quick glance down the aisle to make sure no one was within view.

His other hand brushed along the outside of my thigh, flirting with the edge of my skirt. My breath came in shallow pants when his nose traced along my cheekbone.

"Buy every fucking book you want, love." He kissed the edge of my lips, and when I turned my mouth toward his, he pulled back, his eyes nearly black with how much he wanted me. "Buy the whole bloody store and you won't hear a word of complaint from me."

My hands curled helplessly into the fabric of his shirt while I tried to tug him closer. "Don't tempt me."

"You mean like you're tempting me with this?" His fingers dipped underneath the skirt and traced the edge of my black lace underwear. Then he snapped the elastic against my skin, and my head fell back with a helpless moan. "What color is it? I want to imagine it while I watch you walk in front of me."

"B-black," I whispered.

He buried his head into the curve of my neck and inhaled audibly. "Black lace," he murmured. The pad of his finger slid between the elastic and my skin, and my mouth fell open. "I bet you've got a naughty library fantasy, don't you, my little bookworm?"

If I didn't before, I did *now*.

Hard bookshelf edges, his hands digging into my hips, and the impossible task of staying quiet while he worked me into a frenzy.

Yes.

Yes, I had that fantasy and wanted to act on it immediately.

My hand gripped his wrist, and I tried to slide his hand from the outside of my thigh to the ache throbbing between my legs.

But he held firm, clucking his tongue as he slid his nose along the line of my jaw. "Not yet, love."

"You are a sadist," I whimpered. "Pretty sure courting behavior doesn't track when you have your hand up my skirt on our first date."

His chuckle was dark and low, and a shiver racked my spine.

Liam lifted his head. He pulled his hand out from underneath my skirt and coasted his palm up the side of my waist, not stopping until the weight of my breast was fully in his palm. "This black lace too?"

My gaze held his. "Yes."

"You get dressed today and think about me?" he asked.

I nodded. "Thought about you taking them off too."

I didn't know who this sex goddess was, but I liked her a whole frickin' lot.

Not once in my life had I wanted dirty-talking first-date behavior where we might get caught, and experiencing it now—with him—was the best kind of excellent.

His jaw clenched, and his palm coasted up my chest until his fingers lightly gripped the back of my neck, his thumb pressing under my jaw so that my mouth tilted up toward his.

"My turn for a question," I said in a hushed tone. My fingers curled around his belt buckle, and my knuckles brushed the heated skin of his stomach. The muscles there twitched. "If I'd been single when you met me, would you have asked me out?"

In reality, it was a pointless question. But I still wanted to know.

"Not at first," he admitted. His gaze was intense, filled with hunger and heat. "Likely would have pined for you like a bloody idiot all the same. Would've fought it tooth and nail even if you'd never had a ring on your finger." I nodded, dropping my eyes to stare at his mouth. "You know that's not about you, yeah?"

Again, I nodded. "I know. Maybe I wasn't wasting my time all those years. We both needed it. Needed to know for sure."

He hummed, his eyes tracing my face.

"Eventually," he said, "we would've ended up right here. No matter how we got there."

Have you ever had a smile that starts from your heart? I felt it deep in my chest, warm and soft and sweet, before my lips even thought about moving. "You're not scared anymore?"

His slightly crooked smile was self-deprecating, his eyes adoring. "Fucking terrified. But I know what it's like to kiss you now." He leaned in, whispering against my lips, and my eyelids fluttered shut. "So as long as you keep doing that, I won't let it stop me anymore."

I pushed up onto the balls of my feet, slanting my mouth over his while he wrapped me tightly in his arms.

The kiss was fierce and passionate, a bright flash of heat, over almost as quickly as it began, and we panted against each other's lips when he pulled away.

"I can do that," I promised.

Liam set his chin on the top of my head, holding me tight as his chest expanded on a deep, relieved exhale.

With my face tucked against the steady hammering of his heart, I suddenly wanted to cry as the poignancy of the moment stretched into something beautiful and heavy and wonderful. And I wanted other things too.

I wanted to read on the couch with him while it rained outside.

I wanted to wake him up in the morning and hear how his voice sounded when it was rough with sleep.

I wanted to go for a walk through our neighborhood, holding his hand while Mira rode her bike in front of us.

I wanted to be at every game, watching him do the thing he loved.

I wanted a *life* with him, and not just because we'd found ourselves in one that we didn't choose.

Because he was protective and thoughtful. Because of the big heart that he'd so effectively kept hidden all these years. Because he was willing to sacrifice any shred of happiness if there was even the slightest possibility that he might hurt someone he cared about.

I wanted it because I was in love with him.

"I can feel you thinking," he murmured.

My arms tightened around his back before I lifted my head to look him in the face. "Will you take me home?" I whispered.

His face softened. "Already?"

I nodded.

"I had big plans at the ice cream shop next door for dinner," he said, leaning in for a sweet kiss. This one lingered, a soft, luxurious slide of his tongue over mine, and a contented groan blossomed from deep inside his throat. When I pulled back, I felt dazed.

"Did you say ice cream for dinner?"

He nodded.

That had me pausing.

At the conflicted look on my face, Liam laughed, sliding a hand up and down my back, like he couldn't stop touching me. I knew the feeling.

"We have ice cream in the freezer," I told him. "I might even share my mint chocolate chip, since you're buying me all these books."

He hummed, leaning down for one more kiss.

"Why else do you think I bought them for you?" he said against my lips. "I'm going to eat that ice cream off your body, love, and then I'll wash you off when I'm done."

I grabbed his hand, snatched my basket off the ground, and marched toward the register with the sound of his laughter echoing through the empty store.

Chapter Twenty-Seven

LIAM

The books stayed in my car.

She turned, her back braced against the door leading into the house, and I caged her there, slotting my mouth over hers. Her hands were greedy, sliding over my chest and stomach and shoulders. Her tongue, slick and hot, licked delicately at mine.

My whole body shook, and I worried for the thousandth time that I'd be too much for her.

Too turned on.

Too intense.

Grip her too tightly, put my hands on her body too hard, kiss her too deeply because I couldn't fucking believe that she was mine.

I palmed her ass underneath that skirt and boosted her up, her legs immediately locking around my waist. When she sucked my tongue, a groan wrenched from my chest, and goose bumps tugged along my arms and back and neck.

"No sex against the door." I spoke into her mouth. "I get you in a bed, Valentine."

"Here is fine," she begged, practically climbing my body. "Any hard surface is great."

But I shoved at the doorknob, and when the door gave, I swept it open, kicking it shut behind us with a room-shaking slam.

Depositing her on the island, I dived back into the kiss, sliding my hands over every inch of her that I could touch.

Her back arched, the heat of her core pressed tight against my stomach, and I yanked at her top where it was tucked into the waist of that skirt.

Someday, I'd take her while she was wearing my favorite parts of this outfit. Just the skirt and her heels.

When the shirt cleared her head, all those glorious curls fell around her shoulders, and I pulled back to take her in.

"Perfect," I breathed. "You're so bloody perfect."

The lines of her tits in that bra had my mouth watering, and I ducked my head down, trailing my tongue along the lace edges.

She clutched my head to her chest and moaned my name.

There was an urgency that I couldn't fight—a debilitating crack of lust coursing through my body—no matter how badly I wanted to take this slow.

No matter how badly I wanted to luxuriate in every inch of her body.

We'd effectively lit the fire, and there was no putting it out now. Every time her fingers swept over my skin, I burned, and it was impossible to grasp how we didn't incinerate everything around us.

For months, for years, this thing building between us had been set to a low-level simmer, unnoticeable if you weren't looking for it.

And maybe that's how real desire was built and sustained—with careful tending and patience.

She squirmed on the island, and I shoved at her skirt until I caught my first glimpse of that flimsy black lace covering her backside.

My muscles screamed raw, wanting to rip it off her, but I sucked in a quick breath through gritted teeth, mouthing the lace that covered her breasts.

The room spun when I tugged her bra to the side and used the flat of my tongue against her tight skin.

She cried out, gripping my head while I licked and sucked across her chest.

I wanted to gorge on every inch of her. Inhale all that decadence and see if I could eat my fill of what I found underneath the gauzy protection of her clothes.

Zoe tugged at the back of her bra and ripped it off. I palmed her breasts, pushing them together so I could lick across the lush mounds.

The tips were hard as diamonds.

"You still hungry, love?" I asked. Then I kissed her gently there, blowing a soft stream of air over the wet skin that I'd left behind.

Zoe tugged my face up toward hers. Her eyes were on fire. "Ice cream can wait," she gasped, then kissed me. She sighed when I sucked on her lower lip. "Take me to bed," she begged against my mouth.

It took every shred of self-control for me not to rip open the zipper of my pants and take her just like that, with her skirt rucked up around her waist and her breasts shiny wet from my mouth.

I cupped her face in my hands, dragging my thumb over her plump lower lip. "You want me?" I asked, voice a hoarse whisper. "You're ready to take me, darling?"

She kissed me with a helpless moan. "I have never wanted anyone like this, Liam."

Somewhere deep in my chest, a rumbling roar of possession shot off like a racing pulse. I'd get high off those words of hers. An addiction that I'd never be free of.

With my hands under her ass, her mouth fixed firmly on mine, I carried her up the stairs, stopping only once, when she rolled her hips against my aching hard-on.

"No sex on the stairs," I said through gritted teeth.

She laughed in delight, and I wanted to live on that fucking sound for the rest of my life.

I'd do anything to hear it. Maybe I'd quit football, stop doing everything to devote my entire life to making her smile and making her laugh.

When we cleared the doorway, she started tearing at the buttons on my shirt, and it was halfway off when I dropped her in the middle of the king-size bed.

She bit down on her bottom lip as I tore the shirt off and tossed it to the floor.

Topless, hair wild, and her skirt wrinkled up around her waist, she was the most beautiful thing I'd ever seen.

And somehow—impossibly, inexplicably—she'd given me her heart.

The thought slowed my movements as I unbuckled my belt.

She lifted her hips and pushed the skirt down, kicking it off onto the floor.

When Zoe hooked her thumbs in the edge of the black lace left behind, I shook my head. "Leave that for me."

She exhaled shakily, sliding her hands up into her hair before she sat up on the bed.

What I didn't need was her hands on me when I was this close to the edge. But I closed my eyes and let her push down my pants and boxer briefs. Once I stepped out of them, she slid her hands up the front of my thighs.

At the first touch of her soft tongue against me, I wove my hands into her hair and tugged. She tilted her head up and stared at me.

"No?" she asked.

"Later," I managed.

I pushed her back with a hand in the center of her chest and prowled over her when she split her legs open.

Only a thin scrap of black lace separated us, and for a moment, I made slow rolling motions against her while we kissed deeply.

Filthy kisses too, where my tongue mimicked exactly how I wanted to feast off her, how I'd take her in slow, decadent waves. And she shuddered like I was too. Her hands carded through my hair, and she whimpered when I rolled my thumb over her chest again.

This was the version of Zoe I wanted, why I'd made us wait through an entire interminable day of torture.

She was riding that knife-edge of pleasure, and there was something borderline painful in how much we wanted each other.

Frantic need would ebb as we got used to being able to touch and kiss each other. But in its place, we'd have familiarity. And in order to get to the second, there was no choice but to stoke the flames of the first.

That need came from hours of doing nothing but imagining it. Despite the desperation in the way we touched, there'd been no rushing into this moment, so there was no chance that we'd second-guess it later. That there'd be even the slightest shred of regret.

I moved down her body, worshipping every freckle, every curve.

She rolled her body, lifting her hips when I tugged at the black lace covering those last bits of skin.

"One to take the edge off," I told her, placing sucking kisses against the insides of her thighs as they trembled on either side of my shoulders.

"What about you?" she said breathlessly.

I slid my hand between her legs, and she moaned, arching her back when I grinned at exactly how badly she wanted me.

"Darling," I said, tutting my tongue, "I showered twice today and thought about this." I kissed her hip bone. "And this."

Then I shifted down, held her legs open, and showed her exactly what I wanted for my dessert. The taste of her on my tongue was sinful, and I'd have died happily in that moment, knowing what she sounded like when she moaned my name, how she gripped my hair in her fists and rolled her hips against my mouth. "And this," I said, when I dived back in with a fierce, sucking kiss.

She broke on a helpless, sharp cry, her stomach trembling under my spread hand, and I'd remember it for the rest of my fucking life.

I pushed back up and covered her with the weight of my body, wiping my mouth with the back of my hand before I kissed her deeply.

Zoe was still gasping for breath when I took myself in hand and pushed in. Then pulled back.

In farther.

A painstaking retreat again, and my teeth clenched, because even with that, I was ready to shove forward with no finesse. Even if it hurt. Even if it was over that quick.

Forcing that methodical easing inside was the only thing I could focus on, allowing her a moment to adjust while her face briefly pinched with the next harder, deeper thrust.

Once more, and I curled my hips, gathered her tight against me, and let the sensation of her surrounding me settle into my bones, scream through my veins.

"Holy bloody hell, Zoe," I said. "Nothing, *nothing* feels this good, love."

She was perfect.

My eyes about rolled back in my head when she wiggled her hips to accommodate my next thrust.

Another . . . sharper, harder, and I swallowed her moan with my mouth.

Harder again.

I wanted all her noises. I wanted my hands tight in her curls, her legs shaking against my sides because of the things I could wring from her body.

I pulled back, rolling my forehead against hers. "I'm so fucking in love with you," I whispered. "It's always been you."

A tear streaked down her temple as she arched again, her eyes looking so deeply into mine that I had my first moment of wondering what she saw. It didn't seem possible she could feel anything like I was.

Didn't seem possible that she might love me in the way I loved her.

"I love you too," she said, her lips seeking mine as I snapped my hips forward.

There were no coherent words after that.

It was hands filled with flesh, sucking kisses with tongue and teeth, and sweat soaking my back as I drove my hips forward. The headboard hit the wall, and I braced my weight on my elbows, curling my hands around her shoulders to hold her firm while we both gasped words of love and want and sex.

My muscles screamed while I purged years of wanting her, glorying in the reality of what we were like together.

Our kisses were fierce and hard. There were gasping breaths when I tucked my head into the curve of her shoulder and told her I wanted to live like this for the rest of my life—inside her and over her and under her. That I wanted her in a million different ways, and I'd never, ever *not* want her.

I slicked my hand between us, and she tucked her leg up against my side, digging her teeth into the meat of my shoulder.

She sobbed through the first waves of her pleasure, a chorus of "Yes" and "It's so good" and my name that I'd hear for the rest of my life when I closed my eyes.

I felt the moment she toppled over the edge again. The tight grip of her flesh over mine had bursts of light zipping along my skin, and I shouted her name into the skin of her shoulder.

It was an exorcism. The release of something that had bubbled dangerously under the surface for so long.

My movements slowed, but I didn't stop, milking what was left of her release as she tilted her head back. Her exposed neck was too delectable to ignore, and I licked a long line up to her jaw, sucking at the salty skin there.

Zoe sighed happily, turning in my arms when I shifted to the side so that her legs were slung over top of mine. "Bloody hell," she whispered with her lips against mine.

I laughed. "Worth the wait?" I asked, brushing her curls out of her face. "And feel free to give details."

She grinned. "Yeah right. Your ego is big enough already after the last twenty-four hours."

I studied her face, memorizing everything that I saw there. This was blissed-out exhaustion, a complete mess because of hard kisses and greedy hands.

"You," I said quietly, "are a weapon of mass destruction, love."

"Yeah?"

I hummed, sliding my hand down the line of her waist and hip, then back up to curve my palm over her ribs. "Death by Zoe Valentine's—"

She cut me off with a hard kiss, then pulled back. "You're not going anywhere," she said. Her eyes were so full of love. "I forbid it."

Fuck, but she made my chest hurt when she looked at me like that. I wrapped her in my arms and sighed. "I'm not going anywhere."

We kissed again, our hands wandering over each other's skin.

She stopped after a few minutes and set her chin on my chest. "Do I still get my ice cream for dinner?"

I hummed, leaning up for another kiss. "As long as I get to try some too."

Her eyebrow arched. "I think you might have earned some," she said breezily. "At least one scoop."

"One? You got off twice, love. That should give me two scoops."

She sat up and stretched with a groan. "I suppose."

Zoe stood up off the bed, and I wedged a hand behind my head, enjoying the view of her walking naked as a jaybird through the room.

Didn't take long before another part of my body was noticing too.

She nodded at my lap. "After I eat," she said meaningfully.

With a growl, I got out of bed and tugged my boxer briefs on. She pulled my shirt over her head and closed the two middle buttons.

Just before she opened the door, I tugged on the back of the shirt and turned her in place, sliding my hands up underneath the shirt while I pressed her against the wall.

Zoe laughed into the kisses. "It's gonna take us a while to get anything done at this rate."

"What do you expect?" I asked. "Walking around in my shirt and thinking I'd keep my hands off you?"

Another happy sigh escaped her mouth while I snogged her senseless, and eventually, I managed to pull away before we fell straight back into bed.

We fed each other ice cream while she sat on the island and I stood between her legs. It took us longer than normal because I was obsessed with the taste of it on her tongue when we kissed, which we did between most bites.

We talked about training camp, and when I told her I'd already added her name to the list, she smirked.

"So you *did* want me there," she said. "You never asked."

"I would've." I scraped some stray chocolate off her lip and sucked my thumb into my mouth. "I always wanted you around, even if I never said so."

Her eyes fucking sparkled when I said shit like that, so I made a mental note to do it every single day for the rest of my bleedin' life.

She glanced at the time. "We have about an hour before Rosa brings her back." She took another bite. "What should we do?"

"Am I sleeping in your bed tonight, Goldilocks?" I asked. Leaning in closer, I let my lips hover over hers, humming contentedly when she pressed forward to snatch another kiss.

Zoe traced her thumb along my bottom lip. "Yeah."

I set my bowl down and wrapped her up in my arms. We sat there for a few minutes, and I didn't fight the feeling of warmth and contentment. Didn't guilt it away or tell myself that I didn't deserve it. Didn't question why we were here or what we'd had to lose in order to have this.

I simply closed my eyes and let the moment be what it was.

Fucking *heaven*.

I pulled back, sliding a hand over her cheek, cradling her jaw while we kissed again. Zoe was smiling when I rolled my forehead against hers.

"Let's go get our girl," I said. "Doesn't feel right here without her."

Zoe's smile widened. "I was hoping you'd say that."

When we were dressed, I waited for her by the front door. It was still bright outside, and that light felt harsh after the time we'd just spent indoors, wrapped up in each other.

She squinted into the sun, tilting her face up to its warmth. We made the walk across the street slowly, our fingers intertwined.

Rosa met us at the door with a knowing grin on her face. "Have fun?" she asked.

Zoe's face flushed a becoming shade of pink, and she turned her face into my shoulder. I wrapped an arm around her with a laugh.

Rosa's eyebrow arched. "I've never seen you smile before."

Before I could respond, Mira came tearing down the hallway toward us, messy curls flying, a smile so big on her face that my heart damn near burst from the sight of it.

"You're back!" she yelled. I swept her up in my arms and tossed her just high enough that she shrieked. When I settled her on my hip, Zoe leaned in to kiss her on the cheek.

"Did you have fun with Rosa?" she asked.

Mira nodded, then smiled at me. She honked my nose, and I growled. She wrapped her arms tight around my neck and squeezed.

"I missed you," she whispered loudly in my ear.

"Missed you too, duck."

Rosa cleared her throat, and I caught her swiping her thumb underneath her eye. When I narrowed my gaze, she waved me away. "Just got some dust in my eye. You three go enjoy your night, okay?"

"Thank you, Rosa," I told her.

She winked as Zoe leaned in for a hug. "Anytime," she told me.

"You want to walk?" I asked Mira.

She shook her head. "You carry me."

Zoe smiled. "Pushover," she whispered.

I held out my hand, and Zoe wound her fingers through mine as we walked back home.

"Now what should we do?" she asked.

The sun was warm on our backs as we approached the house. I paused, taking in the bricks and windows and doors, the place where our life had changed irrevocably.

I'd never believed in fairy tales and happily-ever-afters. But damned if it didn't feel a lot like those now.

I leaned down and placed a soft kiss on Zoe's lips.

"Now we live," I whispered.

Epilogue

Liam

Two months later

"That's it, we're fucked."

Zoe sighed, rolling her eyes as she put the last of the groceries away. "No, we're not."

She rolled her eyes at me all the time, so it hardly gave me pause. I held up the box of tea. Generic-brand tea. "This is a sin. My mum will take one look at this and immediately remove herself from the premises. You cannot buy cheap tea when my British mother is about to stay with us for two bloody weeks."

Zoe turned, her hands parked on her hips and a patient expression on her perfect face. "Liam," she said.

I tossed the box onto the counter with a grimace. "What?"

She walked closer, setting her hands on my chest. Immediately, I wanted to kiss her. I always wanted to kiss her, whether she was touching me or not, but the moment she made contact, some internal switch flipped on in my head, and I couldn't function until I tasted her lips. When I ducked down to do just that, she pressed her fingers over my mouth to stop me.

"Did you look in the pantry before having your little temper tantrum?"

"No," I said, the sound muffled behind her fingers.

Her lips hooked up in a smug fucking grin that meant only one thing.

I yanked her hand away from my mouth and ducked down to press a quick kiss to her lips. "Fine. Rub it in my face later." I deepened the kiss, slowly sucking on her bottom lip while my hand sneaked around to slide over her backside. "Much later."

She laughed against my lips, humming contentedly when my tongue teased hers.

Her kisses were my favorite thing in the entire world. The fact that I'd gone thirty years without knowing what they felt like was a bloody tragedy.

Zoe pulled away, swatting at my stomach when I tried to tug her back with my hand fisted tight in her shirt. "Look at the tea in the pantry. She'll have plenty of options. Now keep your hands to yourself, because we have to leave to pick up your mom in, like, ten minutes, and Mira's hair is still a disaster."

I eyed the explosion of curls falling around her shoulders. "Just Mira's?"

She narrowed her gaze, and I held my hands up while I backed away.

"Whose fault is that?" she asked dangerously.

"Yours, really. You walked through the room wearing that shirt, and you bloody well know I can't handle myself."

Even as she let out a beleaguered sigh, her cheeks flushed a pretty pink. Luckily for me, Mira had been napping, because even after two months—the greatest two months of my entire life—I couldn't see Zoe in the Denver sweatshirt that bore my name without turning into a raving, greedy beast.

Her hair had been in a neat braid, but I'd followed her straight into the kitchen and pressed her against the fridge for a fierce, brain-melting kiss as I shoved my hands up underneath that sweatshirt. At her pleading, I turned her around for a frantic ravaging against the kitchen island, where I gripped her hips and had to clench my teeth to keep from shouting when she arched her back. She almost had me blacking out because it felt so bloody good.

My girl liked it when I couldn't get enough of her, as it turned out.

And that suited me just fine.

Everything about our life suited me, really. We'd slid into the regular season with ease, Zoe and Mira becoming fixtures at the home games, usually joining Rochelle in her box. But tomorrow, with my mum, they'd be sitting in the stands.

I loved having Zoe there, watching me do my job. I loved having her wait for me afterward, and I loved scooping Mira into my arms as we left the stadium together. I loved crawling into bed with Zoe, even if my body was too beat up to do anything but hold her.

I knew I wouldn't be able to play forever, but not playing anymore wasn't sounding so bad either.

Zoe had taken to adding some of her artwork to the house and swapping out furniture for things that suited our taste. A month after our first date, she'd finally decided to place her home on the market. It made sense, and thankfully, the new neighbors were a kind, young family with a son just about Mira's age.

Even though we'd kept all the family pictures up, Chris and Amie's home felt like ours. And there was something very right about that.

Zoe was studying me as she nimbly fixed her braid, tying the end with a black band and a tiny smile on her face.

"What?" I asked, tugging her closer. Her eyes fluttered shut when I pressed a kiss to her forehead.

"Are you nervous to have your mom here?" She twined her arms around my waist and looked up into my face.

I shook my head. "Nothing to be nervous about. She'll probably like you better than she likes me."

Zoe laughed.

"And Mira," I drawled. "She's already spoiling her to bits, isn't she?"

"A little. The dollhouse with the family of ducks was a big hit, though."

I hummed.

Zoe's hands fisted around the material of my shirt. "Did you tell her about the letter we found?"

"Not yet." I kissed her forehead again, letting my mouth brush over her skin. "I don't know if I need to. I was really the only one who needed to see it, yeah?"

While cleaning out Chris's desk, Zoe had found the same small container of keys I'd found in one of the drawers. Just down the road at a storage facility, Chris and Amie had a small unit packed with sports memorabilia, some boxes of old Christmas decorations, and three boxes labeled "Chris Important Shit," written in his horrible penmanship. Why they'd moved the boxes there, we'd never really know. Maybe it was a mistake. Or maybe it was one of those cosmic chess plays, the final move revealed exactly when it made the most sense in all our lives.

Inside one of the boxes were two envelopes: one for me, one for Burke. I'd sent his off as soon as we found it.

In keeping with our friendship, the letter Chris had written to me was short, to the point, and free of bullshit.

> Liam,
> You're the best man I know. Don't fucking fight this,
> even if you want to. There's no other man I'd trust to
> raise her, and eventually, you'll trust that too. If you're
> still pissed at me after you read this, just come shove
> me a little harder at practice, and you'll get over it.
> Chris

With one hand, I cradled Zoe's jaw, tracing my thumb over the downy-soft skin of her cheek. "Are *you* nervous?" I asked.

She sucked in a breath. "A little," she admitted.

"You're perfect," I said in a raspy voice yanked straight from the center of my chest. "She'll just get to see it now. See why I love you so much."

Her face was so soft and open and sweet, and she pushed up on the balls of her feet for a lingering kiss. Immediately, I wrapped her in my arms and tilted my head, deepening the kiss as she sighed happily. When she broke away, she exhaled a laugh. "I really need to get that child ready, but now you're distracting *me*."

I was about to distract her more when Mira came running into the room. "Liam, we go get Nanny soon?"

I swept her up in my arms, glancing at the clock. "Bloody hell," I muttered. "Soon, duck. Zoe needs to fix your hair first."

She shook her head, the tangled curls whipping around. "It's so pretty."

I eyed it skeptically. "Uh-huh."

She laughed, honking my nose, then wriggled to get down. "Bloody hell, bloody hell," she yelled as she ran back to her playroom.

Zoe sighed, pinching the bridge of her nose. "It was only a matter of time," she whispered.

I scratched the back of my neck. "I'll, uh, work on that. Better warn Dr. Carol about that one."

At the look on my face, Zoe laughed, the bright, happy sound filling the room. I tugged her into my arms again and sighed.

"You laugh," I told her, "but me and the swearing child are your problems now."

Her eyes gleamed. "Yes, you are."

"You know I'm going to marry you someday, right?" I whispered against the shell of her ear. She tightened her arms, then tilted her head up for a soft, sweet kiss.

I'd started telling her that about a week after our first date. It couldn't be helped. We'd already planned so many aspects of our life together. She'd booked my mum's flights the day after our first date.

We'd scheduled a time to go visit Burke at the house in Michigan, to see the place Chris and Amie had loved so much.

We had decided to wait until the spring, mark the passage of a year without Chris and Amie with someone else whose life had been changed just as much as ours had.

Making those plans was easy too, because we knew with complete surety what the future held for the two of us.

"You better marry me," she said against my lips. "How else are you going to prove me right about picking better for husband number two?"

I growled, swatting her ass as she pulled away on a laugh.

With a playful arch to her eyebrow, she went off in search of our girl.

While I waited for her to return, I dug my hand into the pocket of my pants and pulled out the small box I'd taken to carrying, just in case the moment was right.

The diamond solitaire winked underneath the lights of the kitchen, and I snapped the box shut, tucking it back into place before she returned.

Maybe after the game tomorrow, I thought.

Maybe when it was just us in bed at the end of the day.

Maybe I'd take her out to dinner while my mum was here to babysit.

Maybe while we ate breakfast at the big kitchen island where I'd seen her for the first time.

It was easy to think about the future when all the possibilities felt good and fitting and perfect. I could ask her a hundred ways, and they all felt right, because she was the path I was supposed to take.

Zoe came back into the kitchen, Mira on her back and a smile on her face, and that warm glow sank deep into my chest again.

They were my path, and I couldn't wait for whatever came next.

ACKNOWLEDGMENTS

As always, my most heartfelt thanks go to my family, who keep me steady. Without their support and understanding, I wouldn't be able to keep doing this crazy job.

To Kathryn and Piper for being sounding boards and understanding my struggles with this book.

To Maria Gomez and Kelli Collins and the rest of the Montlake team for taking such good care of Liam and Zoe's story.

To Tina for keeping me sane and organized, and to my amazing readers, who've allowed me to make this lifelong dream a reality.

For we walk by faith, not by sight.

—2 Corinthians 5:7

ABOUT THE AUTHOR

Photo © 2018 Perrywinkle Photography

Karla Sorensen is the Amazon top 10 bestselling author of numerous series, including the Best Men, the Ward Sisters, the Washington Wolves, the Bachelors of the Ridge, and Three Little Words. When she's not devouring Dramione fanfic or avoiding the laundry, you can find her watching football (British and American) or HGTV or listening to Enneagram podcasts so she can psychoanalyze everyone in her life, in no particular order of importance. With a degree in advertising and public relations from Grand Valley State University, she made her living in senior health care prior to writing full-time, and never reads or writes anything without a happily ever after. Karla lives in Michigan with her husband, two boys, and a big shaggy rescue dog named Bear. For more information, visit www.karlasorensen.com.

CONNECT WITH KARLA ONLINE

Instagram

www.instagram.com/karla_sorensen

Facebook Reader Group

www.facebook.com/groups/thesorensensorority

Website

www.karlasorensen.com

Newsletter

www.karlasorensen.com/subscribe